Intentions

Muriel Bolger

W F HOWES LTD

This large print edition published in 2012 by
W F Howes Ltd
Unit 4, Rearsby Business Park, Gaddesby Lane,
Rearsby, Leicester LE7 4YH

1 3 5 7 9 10 8 6 4 2

First published in 2012
by Hachette Books Ireland

A CIP catalogue record for this book is available
from the British Library

ISBN 978 1 47121 339 7

Typeset by Palimpsest Book Production Limited,
Falkirk, Stirlingshire
Printed and bound in Great Britain
by MPG Books Ltd, Bodmin, Cornwall

For the Croissant Club
– Irene, Maeve, Davnet and Rosaleen –
and to many more leisurely breakfasts
in Budapest

PROLOGUE

1987

In a quiet suburb in Bombay, three-year-old Iswara ran in and out of the spray from the lawn sprinklers, an indulgence permitted only sometimes before breakfast by her *ayah*. She chased the arcs and shrieked with laugher when she managed to catch up with their random spurts. Her older sister Rekna, who was five, thought this was silly.

In the pillared front porch a manservant shook the doormat before starting to sweep up the garden debris that had blown in during the night. In another corner a gardener was picking flowers for the house. The metal gates swung open slowly to admit her grandfather's car. He waved to Iswara and she waved back. She'd had enough of this game. She ran to her *ayah* who wrapped her in a towel and brought her in through the back entrance to get her washed and ready to join the family for breakfast.

When Iswara and Rekna reappeared on the veranda, Iswara ran to her mother for a kiss. Daya tucked a stray tendril of glossy hair behind her daughter's ear as she escaped to give her father and grandfather a hug. 'She's a very bright child, just like her big sister, eh? She'll go far, I promise you. I am so very proud of both of you,' their grandfather said to the older girl as he patted her on the head. Rekna smiled back as Iswara scrambled onto a chair on his other side and the *kaamwali* started to serve them.

Grandpapa arrived every weekday morning to have breakfast with his son, Raj, and his family. This pattern had developed since he had lost his wife ten months earlier. It had seemed a logical thing to do as they both worked at the clinic he had founded some years earlier and he passed by his son's house on the way there.

The unconditional love of his little granddaughters set him up for the day and the visits also gave him the chance to discuss patients and life in general with his son. It also meant he arrived at work in a better frame of mind than he would have done had he eaten a solitary breakfast and sat in the back of his car with only his thoughts, as his driver got him to the hospital or to his rooms in time for another day.

Raj picked up the newspaper that lay beside his plate. He did this every morning. He always read *The Times of India*. Daya had long since stopped protesting about his reading at the breakfast table. It was one of the few battles Raj has chosen to win.

★   ★   ★

Almost 5,000 miles away in Ireland, ten-year-old Damien Doyle was bossing his sister, Rachel, around. She was younger and was often a pest, but she had her uses – like now.

They were spending the summer holidays at Brittas Bay, in County Wicklow, as they did every year. Their family had a mobile home there, and like those others who'd been going there for years, they still referred to them as caravans, but the newcomers to 'the field' talked about their 'mobile homes' as though they were great ancestral piles. Well, the long-termers conceded, they did have all the mod cons like showers and inside flushing loos, which eliminated the need to bury the contents of the Elson in a hole. The matter of whose turn it was to do this offending job prompted regular family rows. When the Doyles had upgraded, they'd still referred to their swanky new, L-shaped summer home as 'the van'.

Damien was in his element in Brittas, with its high sand dunes and meandering paths. In those dunes he was king of his universe. He could be anything he chose and he chose to be everything from a bionic warrior to Superman, an astronaut to a dirt-track rider. Today he was a bounty hunter and his sister was the tent pole – holding up the makeshift structure with a broken spade handle. A siege was underway in the rough terrain outside. Damien had just rescued a hostage, a neighbour's child called Irene, from the enemy. She was Rachel's friend and was still tied up. He set about undoing the knots with bravado.

He knew Rachel was happy to be included with the older children. Although they were only three years apart, at ten and seven that was almost a lifetime. He neglected to tell her the game was over but he knew she'd figure that out when the shouts and scuffles on the other side of the crumpled tarpaulin stopped, letting her know that she could let go of the handle and rest her arms. But all activity ceased abruptly when they heard the whistle: two short bleeps. This was the call their mother used to muster them for meals or when their cousins arrived from Dublin to visit. The whistle had been his idea. The van next to them used one long whistle and Irene's parents called her in with four short ones. All the parents had complied with his scheme. He'd even called a meeting to inform them and his mother had served coffee and scones while he handed out the instructions. It made sense, they agreed, instead of running all over the place looking for their children.

The game was abandoned, and as they'd already eaten, Damien headed the race back to see who had arrived.

In Ringsend in Dublin, the compact terraced house was unusually busy. There were aunts and uncles, neighbours and several people little Beatrice Cullen had never seen before, all crowded in.

When she caught their eyes, they seemed to be looking at her, pityingly. Several remarked on her white-blonde curly hair. 'Just like her daddy,' they said. 'She's a Cullen all right.' Of course she was a Cullen. Didn't they know that? Wasn't her name Beatrice Cullen? But she said nothing.

'And she's so young, the poor wee mite. How old are you now?'

'Five and a half,' she replied proudly.

'Ah the half is very important, isn't it?'

'Yes,' said Beatrice.

She had just come back from her neighbour's house. Mrs Murphy had taken her for the morning. Her house had smelled of warm baking and she'd been invited to help. The old neighbour had tied an oversized apron around Beatrice's waist and had allowed her help cut the tops off the fairy buns that were cooling on the kitchen table. She had never seen so many sandwiches or cakes in anyone's kitchen before. She had watched as Mrs Murphy deftly spread them with homemade raspberry jam. Then she had spooned whipped cream into the cakes, always the exact same amount, before showing her how to top them off with the pieces she had trimmed earlier.

'Now, Beatrice, you've learned how to make butterfly cakes. Your mum will be so pleased with you,' she had said, putting them carefully on to trays. 'I think you've earned one too, don't you, pet? We'll bring the rest around to your house.'

It hadn't quite registered what her dad dying

really meant. He'd been a shadowy figure at best and seemed to have been in hospital for a long time. Beatrice felt loved and cherished by her mother and liked it when there was just the two of them together. When her dad had come home from hospital at Easter she had really resented him being there because she couldn't make noise, have her friends from two doors down over to play, or jump on her mother's bed. And she had had to whisper all the time.

Now her mother was sad. She kept opening packets of tissues and putting them down, then not being able to find them again.

'Why did Daddy have to die?' Beatrice asked her Auntie Joan, who had replied, 'Holy God must have wanted another angel in heaven.'

She thought this over for a minute and then asked, 'Why couldn't he have just made another one?' That caused her aunt to go into a flurry, offering her cake and rushing off to make more tea for everyone.

Uncle Joe told her she had to be Mummy's special friend now. 'You have to take care of her, work hard at school and make her proud of her little girl. Give me your word now, won't you?' She promised she would and he gave her fifty pence, which she put in her moneybox when everyone had gone home. Her grandfather gave her a pound and told her she had to be brave and look after her mama now. She adored her granddad with a love that only exists between grandparents and grandchildren and would do anything for him, so she gave her word again and was determined to honour it.

Life hadn't been easy for Mary Cullen since her husband died, but she'd gone back to work and this helped her cope with her loneliness. However, she'd had to decide whether the nice pay cheque that went with her job as a PA in a food distribution company was worth the worry and guilt of having her only child minded in after-school care until whatever time she could escape, or whether it would be better all round if she took a more tedious position with less money but more suitable hours. She felt guilty about so much those days, but especially because her little girl's father was no longer around and her daughter never seemed to want to talk about him. Her father had been a rock for her and Beatrice. He was retired and a widower and was always happy when asked to babysit or collect Beatrice from school if Mary had to work late.

When she was ten, Beatrice's grandfather came over to have his dinner with her and her mother, sat in his winged chair and never got up again. Beatrice was inconsolable. Since her father had died, she'd had difficulty trusting people. Now she saw her mother go through grief again, and felt she had to hold things together for her, again. Her grandfather was always around and always a big part of her life. She couldn't imagine a world without him in it.

Shortly before this shock, Mary had met a man through work and he'd asked her out a few times. His name was Ray and she liked him, but when her father died, she didn't know whether she liked Ray because he was kind and understanding, which was just what she needed, or because she really cared for him.

Mary married Ray when Beatrice was twelve, but not without agonising for three years over what effect it might have on her child.

She told Ray, 'Beatrice never seems to miss her father and if she did she never showed it to me. Sometimes she comments on the framed photo of our wedding, but she's asked very few questions about how we met or about her dad and his life. It is as though she has shut him out of her memory or had never known him.'

'It's hard to tell with kids, you never really know what they are thinking.'

'I know that, but I've always felt a duty to keep him alive in her mind.'

'And that I can understand perfectly,' he said. 'You did a great job on her so far, and I'll be here from now on.'

When she had introduced Ray to her daughter, there had been none of the expected awkwardness, and there had been much relief all around when she'd whispered, 'I like him – he has kind eyes.'

'So do I,' laughed Mary. 'He has a kind heart too.'

Beatrice accepted Ray but only after she'd told

him, 'You needn't think you can be a replacement for Granddad, because you're not.'

'I'm only sorry I never met him, but from what your mum and you tell me about him, I'm sure I'd never measure up.'

'You wouldn't,' she agreed.

Mary, Ray and Beatrice soon became a close-knit unit. Beatrice was a curious child who sailed though school with little difficulty and made friends easily. She continued to shine at school and she headed the debating society and always loved a good argument. At college, she decided to specialise in developmental studies. It seemed inevitable that she would probably end up abroad somewhere when she qualified, working on some humanitarian project or other, and her mother was resigned to this when she headed off every summer to some far-flung corner of the world.

PART I

CHAPTER 1

2010

I t was a grey February day and Beatrice could see that the queue had already formed on the street outside the Department of Foreign Affairs offices on St Stephen's Green where she had been working for the past six years. It was always the same on Monday mornings.

It had been her mother who had spotted an advert in the daily paper for two vacancies in the visa/passport department and had urged her to apply. Having undertaken fieldwork for eighteen months after graduation, Beatrice was not sure that that was where her future lay, but to please her mother she had applied. She was surprised when she was offered the job and decided to give it a go. Once she'd settled in to regular office hours, she found she actually enjoyed what she was doing and quickly found herself working with real cases and real people, many naturalisation applicants, and had worked her way up to a supervisory position in the appeals area. The second position had been taken by Irene. They started work on the same day, novices in a bureaucratic world, both unsure. It was inevitable that they would become friends, and they did. They often socialised together, ate lunch, made each other coffee, shopped in Grafton Street and sat in St Stephen's Green together. They discussed their boyfriends or lack of, and followed each other's romances with interest, sympathy and encouragement.

'They must be frozen waiting out there,' Beatrice said to one of her colleagues as she sat down at her desk. 'I've just walked from the Dart station and my fingers and toes are numb.'

Her job was challenging, but over the years she'd worked there she soon got to recognise the scam artists from the genuine cases. However, they all agreed that things had became more and more frustrating when, despite the legislation and all the new best practices that had been introduced, marriages of convenience, having babies on Irish soil, bigamy and all sorts of other deceptions were used so successfully to obtain Irish citizenship or a stay of execution, while some applied for naturalisation. Those same laws often excluded needy and legitimate cases on technicalities. It was an imperfect system, one which she and her colleagues often talked about. It often dehumanised real people with real problems, but it was the best they had and they had to work with it. She had genuine compassion for those who were trying to begin again in a safe environment and she never minded working extra hours to reach satisfactory conclusions.

Then there were the cases that were genuine, but where desperation had clouded better judgement. She had been presented with forged documents, falsified references, bank statements and other paperwork, all carefully and expensively acquired, to try and ensure a safe passage through the whole bureaucratic maze. Such measures were never looked on favourably, and Beatrice knew that sometimes the families being deported had a much more valid reason for never returning to their homelands than many who had slipped though procedures without detection.

She made coffees in the tiny kitchenette and brought them through to their pod. She was just putting a cup down on the adjoining desk when Irene's phone rang. She heard Irene mutter a slow 'Well, good morning, Damien' as she rolled her eyes skywards, twisting a strand of hair around her fingers. Beatrice put her own cup down, ripped open two little tubes of sugar and poured them into Irene's coffee with a grin. She stirred them in with a wooden spatula. Damien's phone calls were always long, convoluted and most urgent. Irene rustled through some faxes on her desk. 'Yes, Damien, I have them here. Now what's the problem, this time?' she asked affably.

Beatrice knew that Irene was going out with Daragh, had been for a while now, but there seemed to be a real bond between her and this Damien guy. They'd known each other since they'd been kids and she was still friends with his sister, Rachel.

Damien was a Dean of Students at one of the medical faculties in the nearby university. He'd made the headlines when he was appointed – headhunted from HR in one of the IT multinationals – to become the youngest faculty member at barely thirty-three. He often rang for advice when an overseas student had got into trouble with the law, or became ill, or when a family needed to be sent for: his quickest route to finding solutions was to call Irene. Beatrice was used to hearing Irene's conversations with him range from intense to flirtatious, sympathetic to dismissive, but they were seldom brief. She sat down at her desk and clicked on her computer.

She'd only met Damien quite recently, when he strode in to the department. Irene had been in Morocco with Daragh. He had created a fuss in the foyer, and Beatrice had noticed his impatience. He was an imposing figure, tall, toned and casual, and his presence suggested that he usually got his way. He ignored the queue and demanded to see someone. Beatrice had kept walking but one of the ushers had followed her, asking what he should do, and Beatrice told him to tell Damien that he could have an appointment for the following week.

Damien had moved towards them and heard that exchange. 'This can't wait. It's a matter of extreme urgency. I demand to see somebody in authority.'

Beatrice had remained silent, giving him the once over before continuing upstairs to her office. The usher had tried to explain that every case they were dealing with was of the utmost importance and that, as there was a queue, it was only fair that he wait his turn like everybody else.

'I'll write to the minister about this.'

'As you wish, Sir, I'm just doing my job,' the usher had replied.

When Damien didn't leave, the usher had rung Beatrice and put Damien on the line. It was only when he'd given his name that she realised who he was. She'd explained that if there was a real emergency, a death, a murder or some such crisis, they could make an exception.

'This is an emergency. One of our final-year students needs a re-entry visa – urgently.'

'I can understand your concerns. Leave me your number and I'll get back to you,' she'd offered.

'Make sure you do – this afternoon,' Damien had said. 'There's a lot riding on this.'

Manners might get you a little further, she'd thought as she put the phone down. She'd called him later that day to tell him that she could see him the following day at eleven. His attitude had still been brusque and she'd formed an opinion of a short-tempered, self-important man with an attitude problem. Someone who thought he could just lift the phone and everyone would jump. However, Beatrice also knew a genuine case when she came across one, and, much as she was prepared to do battle with this arrogant man, she'd found herself nonplussed when she saw him again as he seemed quite different.

The following morning everything had gone wrong. She'd been running late and hadn't had time to buy her usual latte, and she hadn't brought anything for lunch. Paul had been doing her head in and she'd left him snoring away. She'd missed having Irene around.

When Damien had come in, his manner was not as abrupt as it had been on the phone. On closer inspection, she'd decided his dark-blond hair was overdue for a trim. He'd worn an open-necked cream shirt, a lived-in corduroy jacket and faded jeans. He'd been carrying a battered leather brief-case, and he'd plonked it down on her desk before retrieving some documents from it. And then he'd apologised.

'Thank you for fitting me in,' he'd said, disarming her. 'It's very good of you. I am sorry about yesterday. I'm inclined to be over-protective of my students. Unfortunately, Abdul, the man in question, is not with me. He had a bereavement and had to go home to Libya. Now with the unrest there, he's not able to process his exit papers and we are trying to sort things out at this end for him.'

Beatrice had been prepared to be brusque and put Damien in his place; instead she'd found herself offering him coffee before they began dealing with the matter.

'What effect will it have on his career if he can't get his visa renewed?'

He'd sat up ready to attack, but she'd forestalled

18

him, 'I only ask because I like to be the devil's advocate here. Let's look at the worst-case scenario and work back from that and see what, if any, possibilities are open to us.'

'I was dealing with Irene and she is aware of all these facts. When will she be back?' he'd asked.

Was he implying she was useless? she'd wondered. *Did he think she was incapable of handling this task?* She'd felt herself get angry again and had said, 'Not for two weeks.'

'Very well,' he'd said with a sigh. 'This is a human life we are talking about. This student is taking his finals in a few months. His family have made enormous sacrifices so that he could study medicine here and now he's been offered a postgraduate place in endocrinology, which is what he wants to specialise in, but if he doesn't take his interviews in the next few weeks he'll lose that place and the opportunity will go to someone else. Winning one of these placements is almost as rare as winning the Lotto. This guy is a grade A student. If he's forced to drop out now, in all probability he'll never get the chance to qualify or to practise medicine, never mind specialise, and all his years here will have been wasted.'

Beatrice was used to such requests, though they came in many guises and permutations. Some were bogus, and very cleverly presented, but in her experience most she had come across had been totally genuine. She had no reason to doubt the validity of this one.

'Let me have a look at the paperwork first and we'll proceed from there,' she'd said, as he produced photocopies of Abdul's passport, his Garda National Immigration Bureau certificate, which was now invalid because he had left the country, his student records, exam results and other relevant documents.

They'd spent a good deal of the morning trying to sort out the problems and by lunchtime they'd done all they could. Damien looked at his watch.

'Do you take a lunch break? I'm starving and I need sustenance. What about a quick bowl of soup and a sandwich?'

She'd declined. She'd been behind in her own work and this case really should not have fallen to her. She also admitted to herself that she was not prepared to spend time with another whimsical man. She had enough going on with her boyfriend.

'Well, maybe another time,' he'd said.' I'll look forward to hearing from you, and thanks again.'

'I'll do my best,' she'd promised. He'd stretched out his hand and shaken hers before leaving.

When he'd gone, Beatrice had remembered that she hadn't brought in any lunch. She knew she'd never survive the afternoon on more instant coffee, so she'd headed to a local pub for a quick bite to eat. As she'd squeezed through the crowd, balancing her food, she'd heard her name being called. Then she'd seen Damien indicating a space at a bar table in the corner, so she'd joined him.

'I normally bring my own lunch and eat at my

desk but my boyfriend and his mates cleaned me out over the weekend. I only remembered when my stomach started complaining. So it's got to be dubious catering soup today.'

'It's always dubious soup in here. I think they just toss a few different packets together in the pot and call it whatever they like, but I'm a sucker for their spiced beef and pickle sandwiches. Irene and I grab lunch together the odd time.'

Beatrice knew Damien and Irene had known each other since they were children, but spiced beef and pickles together? She'd have to ask Irene about that some time. Perhaps they'd been an item at some stage. They continued to make small talk and he never mentioned Abdul's case. She'd admired his restraint and respected him for that.

Back at her desk she'd spent the rest of the day trying to reach the relevant authorities in Tripoli, grateful that the time in Libya was only two hours ahead of Dublin. Cases were often really hampered by differences in time zones and it often meant working late, or very early, to synchronise calls. Despite modern technology and telecommunications, these were still an occupational downside.

It had been after seven when Beatrice had headed home, stopping at a convenience store to stock up on some quick food. She'd changed her mind when she'd realised that apart from a few slices of brown bread and the soup, she'd had nothing all day, so she'd bought steaks and some salad instead.

Paul had already been there when she got home,

and had been happily working his way through the bottle of wine she'd had in the fridge. He'd been sprawled out in front of the television giving his own commentary on a rerun of the first Irish match in the Six Nations Championship.

'Hi, babe. You're late. How was your day?' he'd asked, not getting up to greet her.

'Busy, tiring – and yours?

'Great. I just heard I'm getting the gig to go to Australia and New Zealand for the rugby test series in the summer. I'll be away for a few weeks.'

'And you call that work?' she'd laughed. Paul was a sports commentator with the outside broadcast unit for national television and radio. As such he ate, slept and even dreamed about sport in all its forms. He could get equally excited about the Cheltenham Gold Cup, the schoolboys' rugby, the Tour de France or the local under-11s match.

Beatrice was athletic in her own way, and she loved hockey and kept fit by running along the strand every day. But as she had been brought up in a house with just her mother, the most sports coverage they had ever indulged in was the total immersion of Wimbledon every year, accompanied by large bowls of strawberries and cream and little bottles of Prosecco. In secondary school, and after her mother had remarried, rugby became a passion. Her step-father, Ray, had played for a local rugby team when he was younger, so it had been difficult to escape the euphoria and the despair as their fortunes had fluctuated. He had taught Beatrice the intricacies of rucks, mauls, scrums and conversions, and she could now hold her own in any après match discussion.

Paul had said, 'I'll be able to look up some of my friends out there. We had such a blast during the Lions Tour in South Africa last year. Probably meet up with some of the guys we worked with too.'

Beatrice's sixth sense had tuned in – she'd heard a lot when he'd come back, too much even, about an Aussie commentator called Candy, but she refrained from asking about her. Instead she'd told him, 'I spent my day trying to get some poor medical student back into Ireland so he can sit his final exams. His father was injured in an accident and he did a mercy dash back home to be with him when he died. Now we don't want to let him back in and the Libyans don't want to let him out! It's a mad old world, isn't it? And there's you flitting off all over the place to watch matches and being paid for it too.'

'Yeah, great isn't it?' he'd laughed.

'Terrific.' Her sarcasm was lost on him as his eyes swivelled back to the plasma screen, which was not big enough by his calculations. He thought, and often told her, that she ought to buy a larger one and install it over the fireplace.

She hated big screens because you couldn't ignore them, no matter where you sat. When she'd got her flat, she'd furnished it with only her tastes in mind, minimalist with soft feminine shades and not too much clutter. The television had certainly not been on her priority list. Music was her passion and the first thing she always did when she came in was put on something classical that suited her mood. She'd got that from her mother who used to sit at the piano for hours, if she hadn't got Lyric on, playing everything from Scott Joplin to Haydn. She loved opera and together they'd been to Verona to see *La Bohème*. It never failed to lift Beatrice's spirits. She played the disc when she felt tired, when she was in a good mood and when she wanted to relax. Since she'd been with Paul that didn't happen so often, and it certainly happened less and less as he'd taken over her life in the sixteen months they'd known each other. He wasn't fond of classical music and hated opera.

Beatrice went through to the kitchen and turned on the pan. She chopped a few courgettes, onions and peppers and tossed them and the steaks in olive oil, before placing them between the hot plates on her healthy grill pan. She set the little table. Her flat was small enough – a starter one, her mother had said, when she'd generously helped her fund it – but Beatrice had felt it was big enough for her needs. However, it felt small when Paul stayed over, which he was doing with increasing frequency. It wasn't that she minded so much, it was more that he seemed to fill every inch of the flat and that made her feel in the way. She enjoyed his company, the sex was great, but lately she was beginning to feel – well – a little crowded and taken for granted.

When she had served up the food, she'd called him, but he had been fast asleep. She'd pushed his shoulder to rouse him and he'd grunted before his snoring took on a regular pattern of crescendo and lull. She'd felt herself getting annoyed. *How self-centred was he? Could he not have made something for her to eat when she came home for a change?* Maybe it was her fault, she always did it. She always made sure there was beer and wine in the fridge too. It had slowly dawned on her that he made no effort with their relationship. She'd taken the zapper, clicked off the television and sat down to eat in silence. She'd watched the juices from his meat congeal as they cooled on the plate and the vegetables become limp and unappealing.

When she'd met Paul, there had been an instant chemistry and, after a time, she'd wondered if he could become *the* significant other in her life. It had been after a match in a rugby pub, and he'd been surprised at her knowledge of the game. In the beginning, he'd brought her to all sorts of functions and she met many of his fellow broadcasters and journalists whom she'd seen on the television and read in the sports pages. It was a heady time, and gradually he'd begun to stay over more and more and she'd felt even closer to him, enjoying the cosy camaraderie of coupledom, being the centre of his world. Lately, though, she had noticed their outings had become fewer and fewer and he was less inclined to bring her along to events. He'd hinted several times about moving in with her, becoming more insistent that they take their relationship to the next stage, but something had made her hesitate. She hadn't been sure – she'd not known what was holding her back, but she knew she wasn't ready for that sort of commitment with Paul.

'The relationship is becoming somewhat pedestrian,' she'd told Irene before she and Daragh had headed off for her fix of winter sun in Agadir.

Irene had argued, 'But that's bound to happen.'

'I can't see Paul taking me away somewhere exotic, unless it involved some sporting fixture.'

'Why don't you drop a few hints? Bring home a few brochures and leave them lying around.'

'I don't think he'd take the hint, and even if he did, he'd probably want the lads to come along with him. They seem to be part of the package.'

'Well, Bea, you can't expect rainbows every day.'

'I suppose not.'

Beatrice had reflected how, recently, the only time Paul seemed to devote himself wholeheartedly to her was in the bedroom. She'd enjoyed those times too, but when she'd started to analyse the pattern that had been established, she'd begun to feel less and less fulfilled – and even a bit used if she were really truthful. Paul, it had seemed to her, now preferred a seat in front of the telly with a few cans or a bottle of wine, usually supplied by Beatrice. Then, his friends had started dropping in too. When this had happened for several weeks in a row, the novelty of their togetherness had started to pall – quickly. And that was the peculiar part, because although they were together, it never felt as though they were. With a shock, Beatrice had realised she felt lonely.

She had told her mother how she was feeling. Mary, who would normally hold her counsel on any of her daughter's boyfriends, had been quite emphatic with her reply. 'Maybe you and Paul are not right together. You don't have to settle for just anybody. In my experience, it's better to be happy with a good friend than unhappy with the wrong person just because there's chemistry between you.'

Beatrice had been surprised, and annoyed, at having to stand up for Paul. 'He's had a manic time at work lately, with lots of extra shifts.'

'When a man stops wanting to show off his woman, alarm bells should be ringing somewhere. You mightn't be able to hear them yet, but they'll get louder and louder. Too much work is not much of an excuse,' Mary had reasoned with her. 'If he's like that at this stage of your relationship, what would he be like if you were married?'

'Married? Who said anything about being married?'

Mary had changed the subject then, but the conversation had rankled Beatrice for a while afterwards.

Beatrice had thought about that conversation as she looked at Paul still sprawled on the sofa. She'd thought of Damien Doyle and his enthusiasm and passion for people, his commitment to others, and she'd realised that Paul Dargan was totally and utterly selfish. She'd wondered how she had never noticed this before. Suddenly she had been able to see that he was using her, playing on her good nature, her flat, her food and her favours.

After she'd cleared her dishes away and taken a bath, she'd closed her bedroom door and laid out her clothes for the morning before she'd gone to bed. She'd deal with Paul another time.

CHAPTER 2

Iswara dozed on and off during her flights back to India. She couldn't quite grasp that her studies were finally over and she was returning home for good, a fully-fledged doctor. She was dying to see her sister Rekna again and her nephews. She knew her mother would be in a frenzy of preparation, and hoped she'd given up on husband-seeking on her behalf. There had been some flirtations and romances along the way in Ireland, but she'd never seemed to find time for a real romance. Studying medicine had been a full-time occupation in itself.

However, she also knew that, as much as she was looking forward to being back in her home again, she would miss Dublin and all the friends she had made at medical college there. In one sense, she felt a huge relief that she was finished with the late-night study sessions, cramming and long nights on duty. But she had stores of other memories too – the camaraderie that had grown over the years, the parties, the sharing, the borrowing, the encouragement and the closeness she'd felt with her various flatmates along the way.

Across the aisle in the plane two of her fellow students, also both from India, were engrossed in the in-flight movies. She hadn't seen them since graduation the previous year, when she'd gone on her internship to Galway. Now one had secured a job in Mangalore and the other was going to a hospital in Dubai; they had vowed to keep in touch, and she knew they would. There were other fellow fledgling doctors farther back in the plane, all with destinies yet to unfold.

Iswara knew her proud parents were expecting her to join her father at his clinic. She also knew they would not be very happy when she told them her plans. She was about to throw a grenade into their normally ordered domestic life, shattering their hopes for her yet again.

She expected to have a real battle to get her own way, but she was determined she would, no matter how long it took.

Iswara's parents sat having breakfast. They expected their younger daughter back from Ireland that afternoon, and Daya Singhanid had thought this day would never come. Although they had expected their daughters to travel as all through their growing up, she and her husband Raj had had them tutored by English-speaking governesses so that they would have the perfect accents. Yet, seven years had been a very long time for her to be away from home.

Iswara had settled in Dublin in no time at all, and

she seemed to have made the most of the whole experience at medical college. Though she had been a timid, foreign fresher, her journey through the transition years of endless lectures, note taking, study, exams, tough professors, hospital rotations and demanding consultants had changed her, and she had finally emerged as a qualified doctor and a very confident, beautiful, urbane woman. Now, and not a minute too soon according to Daya, it was time for her to reintegrate into her own world, with her own people and her own culture.

'Anyone would think she'd been abducted by aliens the way you talk about her, Mama. She was only studying abroad,' her sister Rekna laughed.

When their father realised that he wasn't going to have a son to ensure the continuance of his name, he had adjusted his hopes and transferred them to his girls. And they hadn't disappointed him. He was very proud of Iswara even though his wife despaired of her because she wouldn't conform. She had spurned her parents' choices of carefully selected and meticulously vetted prospective husbands. It had been her mother's self-imposed mission in life to ensure that her girls married well and, after three failed attempts, she now deemed her youngest to be virtually unmarriageable at the age of twenty-six.

'Why couldn't she be more like her sister? A good and dutiful girl. They were both brought up the same,' her mother asked of no one in particular.

Rekna, who was two years older, had gone along very happily with her parents' choice of husband. She had qualified as a teacher, and married respectably and obediently. She had crowned it all by presenting them with three grandsons.

Raj and his father had been overjoyed when Iswara had opted to keep the tradition of medicine in the family. It was a great sadness to him that his father had died three years previously and had not lived long enough to see his granddaughter graduate. He died as he would have wished, and as he had lived – quietly, efficiently and with no bother to anyone. He had just completed an afternoon's surgery when he had had the stroke that took him in seconds.

Iswara had been devastated when she'd got the phone call to let her know. She had just been about to sit some fourth-year practical exams, but went to pieces. Her dean, Damien Doyle, was extremely supportive. He'd talked to her tutors and they'd allowed her some leeway and time to grieve before putting the pressure back on.

She'd always be grateful to her grandfather because he had been hugely instrumental in persuading her mother to let her study in Ireland. He had always been there. She had been able to tell him anything. He had been progressive for his time and had encouraged his son Raj to study abroad. Raj had gone to Dublin too, almost thirty-five years earlier, and had nothing but the fondest of memories of his time there, but sending his youngest daughter so far away did cause him some anxieties. It had been her grandfather who had persuaded her mother to visit her there, twice, to see for herself that she had 'not been sold into the slave trade and that she was eating properly'. Raj had loved being back on his old stomping ground, looking up old colleagues and mentors, but his wife hadn't shared his enthusiasm. She'd found Ireland strangely grey and austere and 'far too foreign' to feel comfortable there. As for the food, it had been 'bland, all of it, too bland', but she had admitted, somewhat grudgingly, that the people had been 'very hospitable'. They'd also laughed a lot, and this impressed her. So too did the fact that her daughter had been accepted easily and she'd seemed very happy. She'd had friends from among the other Indian students as well as from among the Irish ones. Raj had told his wife, 'They will always have a bond, no matter where they end up. You can't study for that number of years together and not feel part of something very special.' Although Raj was Hindu, he liked the Christian ethos. He also had had several respected colleagues over the years – surgeons, doctors and nurses – who had studied in Ireland.

'But what if she doesn't want to come back home at the end of it all?' Daya had said, worried. Raj had had no such doubts. He'd known she would return.

As they anticipated their daughter's homecoming, Daya fussed. 'When we get her home we will be able to change her mind, to better choose for her,' she said.

'Perhaps it's we who have to change, maybe we have to accept that she doesn't want an arranged marriage,' Raj argued. 'Many young people don't want that nowadays and, having spent so much time away from our culture, perhaps we should give in to her. It's a changing world.'

'But what of her dowry?' Daya replied. 'Your father's money is left to her on condition of her marriage to a suitable man. What if she's met a European? Do you think she has?'

'I don't think so, but if she has, wouldn't we be better off accepting it rather than fighting her?'

'But time is running out. No one will want an old bride,' her mother said sadly.

'She is not old. She's only twenty-six!'

'Yes, twenty-seven next birthday, but look,' she said, rummaging in a drawer, 'I cut this out of the paper yesterday.'

He sighed. His wife was always cutting snippets out of the papers – pieces to send to Iswara or to share with Rekna on bringing up a family, recipes for the cook, and items that endorsed her viewpoint on just about any topic. She usually waited until Raj was walking out the door to hand him the ones that she thought would interest him, so that he could read them in the car. Half the time, he never looked at them and he was always finding bits of crumpled paper in his suit pockets. Daya continued, 'It says here: "The latest figures from the Ministry of Health and Family Welfare reveal that the national average age of marriage for girls in India is now 20.6 years. It's up from 18.3 years in 2001."'

'See, I told you people are marrying later,' Raj tried to reassure his wife.

'Yes, but it also says fifty per cent of women in India were married before they were eighteen. It goes on to say down here somewhere. Yes, here it is: "In comparison, men got married at a median age of 23.4 years." She needs to hurry up if she's not to be passed by.'

'Iswara has her career and she is very beautiful. She will meet someone,' Raj insisted. 'Someone who is worthy of her.'

'But we found suitors who were worthy of her and she refused all of them. That's all I want for her – a good husband, a good home, a good position in the community and a family of her own,' Daya said despairingly. 'Like her sister.'

Raj nodded, 'I know that, dear.'

'What about Sanjay Ranjan at the clinic? He was recently widowed. He will surely be looking for a new wife to take care of his little girls.'

'My dear wife, I think we should stop match-making and let her make up her own mind.'

'That's all very well, but I think she is too headstrong for her own good.'

'And I wonder who it is she takes after?' he replied with a smile. 'I'm off to work.'

'Should I ask Sanjay to dinner some evening?

'Don't ask me – I'm not getting involved!'

Raj picked up his bag and went outside. His driver was waiting to take him to his consulting rooms. Later he would drive him to the airport to meet Iswara's flight.

Daya went into overdrive at home, making sure her daughter's favourite meal was prepared just as she liked it, that there were fresh flowers everywhere and cooled rose water in her bedroom. She was planning a party, a family reunion. Iswara hadn't seen many of them for so long. She hadn't been home for three years, not since her grandfather died. Rekna was coming with her husband and their little boys – the youngest was only one, so this was to be the first time Iswara would have seen him. Iswara's aunts, uncles and a slew of cousins had also been invited to help celebrate. After all, her mother had proclaimed, it wasn't many of their friends who could boast of having a doctor in their family, and a doctor daughter at that.

The first week home was a whirlwind. Iswara caught up with several of her school friends, went sari shopping with her sister and spent time with her nephews, who enjoyed being spoiled and having her around. Her mother organised numerous visits for Iswara, designed to make new friends and renew older ones. Her father did get involved, despite his determination not to. He set up an interview for his daughter at his clinic. There were two vacancies in paediatrics and nutrition, the areas he knew she favoured. Either would be perfect for her, he assured her, just the opportunity to get her on the ladder to a consultancy in the future.

'Of course, you'll be a junior for a period of probation, but after that there will be plenty of time and scope for you to specialise, if that's what you'd like.'

Her mother was delighted to hear this conversation, because working with her father would mean that her path would cross with Sanjay's, and who knew what might happen then? Perhaps she wouldn't have to get involved in the introductions at all. She let them talk, pretending to be interested in some magazine article, until Iswara confounded them both by refusing to even consider going for the interview.

'I don't want to work in a private hospital. I want to work with people whom I can help, and somewhere where what I do can make a difference to their lives.'

'You disrespect me, daughter,' Raj said with unaccustomed severity. 'My life has been spent working for those who needed me, and the fees I have received I have used wisely. I give to the poor, and I feed and employ several families who would have nothing if I did not earn what I do. Those fees, which you seem to scorn, also enabled me to educate my daughters and to give them opportunities in life, opportunities you seem to want to

37

throw back at me.' His slow, deliberate tone expressed his anger more than if he had shouted at her.

'Papa, I did not mean to be disrespectful. I just can't go to work in that environment. I mean you no discredit. I admire you, you know I do,' she sat beside him and put her hand on his arm, 'and I am grateful, really I am. I know how dedicated you are to your patients, and they trust you, but I need to follow my own heart and I know that means not working in a private hospital.'

'You seem to have it all worked out,' her mother said. 'So where exactly do you want to work? In some general practice where you'll sit dispensing prescriptions all day long?'

Her father put his hand up to stem his wife's angry tirade and to silence her from making matters worse.

'I have given it a lot of thought,' Iswara said. 'I want to work with the rag pickers.'

Her mother raised her hand to her face in shock and looked imploringly at her husband. 'Raj, try and talk some sense into that girl. Think of the disease, the germs, the unsanitary conditions. She can't work there. It would be insanity.'

'Your mother has a good point. Several of them, in fact.'

Daya let out a sob. 'Where did we go wrong with that one?'

'Let her have time to cool down and think about the consequences, Daya. She'll change her mind,

I assure you,' Raj said, as though Iswara was no longer present.

'I won't, Papa. I've already given this a lot of thought.' Iswara knew she was going to get nowhere with them this afternoon.

'It's preposterous. I will not permit it. Not while you are living under my roof.'

'Then, Mama, I will find somewhere else to live, because nothing is going to stop me. I know what I want to do with my life.' She got up, excused herself and left the room.

CHAPTER 3

Beatrice had had a rough day, even for a Monday. She'd been asked to look into the case of a couple who were planning their wedding. The prospective bride was from Lithuania, the groom from Nigeria. The paperwork seemed to be in order, but as neither had sufficient English to communicate with each other, or with Beatrice, it seemed unlikely they could have conducted a regular courtship. When Beatrice asked questions, the young girl, who was only eighteen, seemed frightened. She looked at the man for affirmation, before gathering some semblance of composure and answering. He was in his late thirties.

After a difficult hour, Beatrice decided to call for the interpreters and each was taken to a separate room for questioning. Only then did the man confess that he had bought his prospective bride on the internet. He needed European papers and had heard that marrying a bride for money was the easiest way to get them. He also confessed to being married already. He had a wife and three children back home in Enugu. His youngest had a heart defect and needed surgery or she would die before she reached adulthood. His intention had been to get his papers and send for his family, which would ensure that his little girl got the best medical attention and that they could all have a better life.

Beatrice hated cases like this. She could understand the frustrations and desperation that would drive someone to do what this man was doing. In truth, she admitted to herself, if she had a child in similar circumstances she'd be tempted to do the same thing. But legally she knew it was wrong and punishable. In humane terms, he was only following a natural instinct to protect his family, no matter what the consequences. There was no easy solution.

He had left Beatrice with no options; the rules stated clearly that he had broken the law, had made false declarations and had violated his visa terms. She had to involve the Garda National Immigration Bureau, even though, by doing that, she knew that he would be deported with immediate effect. It was her task to set that chain of events in motion. She apologised to the man and wished him well for his daughter. She also had to hand over the girl to the police for questioning to investigate who was behind her trafficking. Once she had done that, and with a blinding headache, Beatrice went home.

She spotted Paul's car in the car park. She hadn't expected to see him this evening and had been looking forward to a quiet night in on her own. Increasingly, he was taking over her life and her space, and she wasn't comfortable with it. She didn't want him in her life every minute of every day. She needed to have her independence – emotional and physical. She'd been clear with him about this from the start of their relationship, and they'd been going out for several months before she'd let him stay over. However, once they'd had their first anniversary, things had changed and now he stayed over with increasing frequency.

They'd been at a rugby match together the previous Saturday and had gone out on the town that night. Sunday morning they'd played tag rugby and in the afternoon had watched another match, this time on her telly, with two of Paul's friends and a slab of beer. She'd only had one, but couldn't escape the noise and the bodies draped across the sofa and chairs. They hadn't known when to go home, and she'd ended up going to bed at eleven. She'd left Paul sleeping that morning but had expected him to have gone by now, leaving the apartment in a mess, as he usually did.

She was greeted, not with a smile and a cheery hello, or by someone who would understand how she was feeling, but by a raised hand appearing over the back of the sofa and by the noisy volume of a boxing match – the roars from its adrenaline-charged supporters filling the room. There was a pungent smell of stale beer and pizza. That was when she snapped. She reached over to the coffee table, took the zapper and pressed the power button.

'Hey, babe, I was watching that,' Paul said rousing himself into a sitting position. 'It's gone into round seven – they never thought the Argentinian had it in him, but he looks as though he could win.'

'Paul, we need to talk.'

'Babe, don't be mad. It's my day off and I'll be working for the next six days – straight.'

'Well, it's not mine. I've just had a very stressful day and it would have been nice to come back to a tidy flat, at least one where the remnants of you and your friends' late-night suppers had been put into the bin.' She walked over to the window and flung it open. 'I think maybe you should go back to your own place and have a shower and get yourself ready for your busy week.'

'I was thinking about that. Maybe it's time I gave up my flat and moved in here permanently. It would save a lot of hassle.'

Beatrice stood staring at him as if he were mad.

'Are you for real, Paul Dargan? You must think I am an idiot. I've been thinking too, and this is not working for me. I'm only beginning to realise this is the Paul Dargan show and I'm a convenient extra, playing a very minor supporting role. I'm just someone to have around when you need someone – someone to feed you, give you a bed

43

and benefits. Well it's over. I'd like you to leave. *Now!*'

'Babe, you don't mean that. You're tired. We're great together. We could get somewhere bigger.' He tried to take her hand, but she backed away.

'We *were* great together, but it's not working any more. It's all about you and your world.'

'I'd do anything for you, you know that,' he pleaded.

'Well, there's the thing. I thought I would feel the same, but today I met someone who really would have done anything for the ones he loved. He was prepared to commit bigamy and go to prison to save his family, and I realised that I didn't have that sort of commitment to, or from, you. Coming in to this,' she said, sweeping her arm around the room, 'this just endorses what I have been thinking for a while.'

'Beatrice, we can work this out. I know I'm a bit of a lad and a lazy lout when I'm at home.'

'That's another thing, Paul. This is not your home. It's mine and I'd like it back, so will you please gather your things and go?'

Still standing, he reached for the zapper and turned the television back on. The roar from the crowd in the stadium filled the room.

'Damn, I missed the end of the fight.'

'Get out, Paul. Now.'

The next day she woke up to the empty flat. She felt a huge sense of relief. How had she not seen through Paul before? He had used and abused her hospitality. It seemed he really did think her flat was his. Recently, he had spent more and more time there and begun using it as a halfway house for his friends too, claiming that was only because it was nearer to the television studios than his own flat.

As she made her breakfast her phone rang. It was one of Paul's colleagues looking for him.

'Hi, Bart. No, he's not here.'

'I can't get him on his phone and he usually has it turned on at this time of the day.'

'Have you tried his flat?'

'But I thought he left there last week?'

'What do you mean?'

'He told me he was moving in with you.'

Livid, Beatrice held her dignity, and replied, 'I think it must have been with another Beatrice, because it's not with this one. In fact, we're not even seeing each other any more.'

'Oh, I didn't know that. I'm sorry. I'll—'

'That's ok. Bye, Bart.' She cut him off.

Beatrice told Irene when she got in to work, and her reaction was a bit of a surprise. 'Oh I am sorry, Bea. What a selfish bastard. I thought he was using you, but didn't know if I should say anything or not.'

'Was it that obvious? How did I not see through him earlier? He had me rightly fooled. I honestly thought he was a keeper.'

'Just as well you found out now.'

'It'll be a long time before I ever let anyone have the key to my door again,' she said vehemently.

'Until the next time,' laughed Irene.

'No, there won't be a next time. I've learned my lesson the hard way.'

CHAPTER 4

It wasn't Damien's busiest time, this period before Easter. The forward strategy meeting was focusing on timetables and his mind was wandering. Funding and fundraising were high on the agenda. Holiday rosters, always guaranteed to cause a row, were living up to their expectations. Many of the medical faculty members had commitments away from their fee-earning ones. There was a good deal of altruism among the professors, with several of them trying to free up blocks of time to go off to developing countries to offer a few weeks of their services in places where medical care was seriously lacking.

Damien watched the batting back and forward, realising he had still not taken his six weeks leave for the past year, and he had this year's to add on to it too. As his work was rarely a nine-to-five commitment, he had also earned a considerable number of days in lieu too.

His sister Rachel kept telling him to take some time off. 'Roll it all in together and take a few months off,' she'd said recently. 'You know what happened in the last place, you just lost the time when you left.'

'I know that only too well, but I've no intention of leaving this job,' he'd argued. 'I've found my niche at the college. HR wasn't really my thing, especially in the IT world. It was all about achievements, goals and targets and I hated firing people. I much prefer the welfare side of student care and the interaction too.'

'You always were the born minder and fixer. I remember Dad saying to Mum one time, "That fella will make some woman a good husband some day. He knows how to care." I'm still waiting to find out if that was true!'

'Do you make that stuff up?' he'd asked.

She'd laughed. 'Anytime I got in a mess, Dad used to say, "Damien will sort that out."'

'And didn't I always?' he'd teased.

'Much as I hate to admit it, you usually did.'

'And didn't your friends all love me?'

'Only because you used to dance with them at the discos in Brittas.'

Damien was lost in thought when someone addressed a question to him. He managed to get out an answer that appeared to satisfy everyone.

Definitely. He'd do something about that leave he was owed. He might even join the volunteers going to India in the summer to help at the project the college funded on an ongoing basis. He'd have to look into that. Damien had been to India before, backpacking during his own college days and later, when working in IT, in five-star luxury. The country had fascinated him and he always said he'd go back.

CHAPTER 5

Beatrice arrived home, laden down with shopping. She was going to blitz the apartment and get rid of Paul completely. It had been a week since she'd thrown him out and she'd had no regrets. It was bliss to come home to peace and quiet – no blaring sportscasts, no beer bottles and cans to be recycled and none of the sweet and sour Szechuan takeaway detritus left behind by his friends.

She put her bags on the counter top and popped *La Bohème* into her CD player. Of all the music she listened to, this had the effect of soothing, elating, calming and transporting her to otherwise unreachable places, far from any troubles or cares. She knew every bar in the score. This was her space, a place she didn't share with anyone. She hummed along with Mimi as she opened her mail. It was just the usual complement of end of the month bills and notices. She made a coffee as she unpacked the groceries and only then noticed the total on her phone bill – €341.78 it screamed. €341.78! She hardly even used the landline, opting instead for the speed dial on her iPhone when she called her mother and her friends. There had to be some mistake. There were calls with a 0061 prefix. She knew 61 was Australia. Obviously a mix up. She hadn't made calls there.

When she called the company from work to notify them of the mistake she was told that there was no error, by a voice that sounded as though it would rather be engaged in anything else other than answering annoying customers. 'The calls were all made to a number in Sydney.'

'Well I never made them. I don't know anyone in Sydney,' she protested.

'Well, it seems someone at your address must because they were made from your landline number.'

It suddenly hit Beatrice – Paul and the commentator he'd met in South Africa – Candy – she was based in Sydney *and* he'd been calling her, from Beatrice's house, on Beatrice's phone.

'Do you wish to make a payment now?' the bored voice enquired.

'Certainly not!' Beatrice shouted into the receiver, causing Irene to look up in surprise from her desk. She slammed the phone down. 'That sneaky bastard, I'm going to kill him. He's run up a whopping bill – calling some floozy in Australia – on my phone!'

When she went to the local for a drink after work with Irene she was still fuming.

'I'm going to text him and ask him to come

around to the flat and I'll confront him,' she said. 'Did he really think he'd get away with it?'

'He probably thought you'd pay by direct debit and wouldn't check your bills and you'd have it paid off before you noticed.'

'I think you're giving him too much credit. And you know, I generally never check my phone bill statements, but this was so large I did a double take when I saw it.'

At that point, when she was in full flight, she noticed Damien arrive with some friends. He came over to say hello to Irene, kissing her on the cheek. He nodded to Beatrice, 'Nice to see you again. I hope I'm not interrupting.'

'No. Nothing serious. I'm just planning a murder,' Beatrice said.

'Well, that sounds pretty serious to me.'

'You're right, it is, and if you'll excuse me, I'm off to execute it.'

'Oh – do you have to go straight away?' he asked.

'Yep. Can't put it off a moment longer.' She gathered her bags and left the two of them staring after her.

An hour and a half later, her bell rang. Beatrice buzzed Paul in and was surprised at almost not being able to see him behind an enormous bouquet of flowers.

'Hi, babe, I knew you'd change your mind,' he said, before she could say anything. 'Put those in water and I'll go back down to the car and get my bags.'

'Don't go anywhere, Paul. I need to talk to you.'

'I know, babe. I've been a bit of a brat, but I'll make it up to you.'

'Well, you can start now, by leaving a cheque for that,' she said, handing over the phone bill, 'and then, when you are leaving, you can take your flowers with you. Maybe Interflora would forward them to Candy in Sydney for you.'

'What do you mean?'

'I mean exactly that. Pay your phone bill. My usual one is around €30 – the balance I believe is yours – all to the same number in Sydney. I called it earlier and guess who answered? Candy! I believe I woke her up. So before you get in any deeper, or try to worm your way out of this one, just write me a cheque and go.'

'I was going to pay it as soon as the bill came in. You wouldn't have known anything about it if you hadn't thrown me out.'

'Is that supposed to make me feel better? You cheating behind my back, on my phone, in my flat, but so long as I didn't know it didn't matter. Is that it? Or is there anything else I should know about? Any other bills that might arrive?'

'No, of course not,' he said indignantly, with the air of being the offended party. He opened his wallet and drew out two fifties and a five. 'That's all I have on me. I'll go to the ATM and get the rest.'

'Post it to me. Don't come back here.' She held the door open for him to leave. 'The flowers,' she said.

'I bought them for you.'

'Thank you, but I don't want them. Please take them away. I don't want any other reminders of you in my life.'

She stood at the door until he had walked back in and picked up the bouquet and left.

'Never again,' she vowed. From her kitchen window she watched him cross to the car park. She saw him take a swipe at a lamppost with the flowers, decapitating several of them. 'Never, ever, again.'

CHAPTER 6

Irene tried to get her to go out a few times, but it seemed as though Beatrice had decided to go into retreat, still angry with herself for being taken in by Paul. She had joined some of their colleagues for drinks on a few Friday nights, but always left early, especially if anyone seemed remotely interested in her.

One day Irene said, 'Damien has persuaded me to take a few tickets for a pub quiz. They're raising money for the charity in India that his faculty is involved with. You will come, won't you?'

'You two are getting very cosy, aren't you?' Beatrice remarked. 'Doesn't Daragh mind?'

'No, we're just good friends, as they say in the best circles. Daragh likes him too. You will come, won't you? You need to get out a bit more. Just because some of those degenerates you went out with have soured your outlook on life doesn't mean you have to live like a recluse.'

'I am not a recluse and I will come. It sounds like a bit of fun. Are the prizes any good?'

'They have to be better than the ones we got at that last quiz!'

They still laughed when they talked about coming second at a quiz and were given two out-of-date boxes of chocolates and three bottles of non-alcoholic wine between the table of five.

'Have we to make up a table or are we joining your Damien and his friends?'

'I'm not sure, but he only gave me two tickets and "my Damien" actually suggested I bring you along,' Irene said pointedly. Beatrice didn't answer.

'There are bound to be lots of his students there, so they'll be strong on sports and music. If we get teamed up with some of them, we might have a hope of not disgracing ourselves,' continued Irene.

'They may be good at sports and music, but students are never hot on arts and literature – medical students never have time to read or go to the theatre or art exhibitions.'

'That's very judgemental and biased, Bea.'

'Yes, and it's true,' Beatrice laughed. 'Maybe they'll put us with a few professors, in which case if they ask any questions about microbiology we should be OK.'

'It's not *Mastermind*!' Irene said.

'I know, but it all depends on who's setting the questions. If I leave here on time this evening, I might even catch the end of *Eggheads*.'

'You know what I hate about that programme? The way that Daphne and CJ nearly have apoplexy when anyone on their team gets a wrong answer and then at the end Daphne always smiles so insincerely as she says sorry to the poor challengers they've just gleefully licked.'

'I like Judith,' said Beatrice. 'She just laughs when she doesn't know something. The others are far too serious, you can almost see them going down through lists in their heads trying to find the right answer.'

'Right, we've got two weeks till our quiz, so I'm off to study the periodic table,' said Irene.

'Right!' said Beatrice, knowing nothing could be further from the truth. 'The only thing I'll be studying tonight is the menu from the local Chinese.'

Two weeks later, Irene and Beatrice arrived at the hotel where the quiz was to take place. They were directed towards the ballroom and spotted Damien at the entrance. He was in the middle of a group and seemed to be busy sorting out teams. They joined the queue to pay and when they reached him he gave them both hugs of welcome.

'I hope you've given us good teammates,' Beatrice said, 'so we can hide behind their intelligent answers.'

'Don't worry. It won't be too taxing. The whole idea is to make people spend as much as they can on the raffle and support the cause.'

'Well, at least we can do that.'

'We've lots of tables and I've put you at number nine, with my sister and Sean, her boyfriend for tonight at any rate. I'll be making up the fifth.'

Irene caught Beatrice's eye and when they had

moved in to the hall, she said, 'I think he fancies you.'

'Don't be such a twit. He's your friend, not mine.'

Rachel and Sean were already seated by the time they had got a drink and found their places. They introduced themselves and sat down.

'In case you're wondering, I'm no good at anything,' said Rachel. 'Sean is brilliant at music and films. I know you're good at trivia Irene, but what about you Beatrice, any particular areas of expertise?'

She replied, 'I was always good at geography and books, but that's not to say I'll know any of the answers, so let's just enjoy ourselves.'

Damien took to the stage before the quiz began, introducing the evening and making an impassioned speech about the new project the monies raised that night would fund – an extension to some medical facility in one of the slums in Mumbai.

When he joined their table Sean was selected to write down the answers. Heads huddled close as they debated who had been the president of France in the millennium year.

'Which UK politician said, "If you want something said, ask a man . . . if you want something done, ask a woman"?'

Groans went up around the hall when the quizmaster asked, 'What was Mickey Mouse's original name in Italy?'

'Okay,' the quizmaster said when the protests had died down. 'I'll give you a clue – it was also the name for the first Fiat 500.'

'As if that will help,' laughed Rachel.

'I'm sure I know this,' said Damien. 'It was Topolino.'

'Are you absolutely sure?'

'Positive.'

'Well done, bro,' said Rachel.

Beatrice looked at Rachel. She didn't look remotely like her brother, she thought.

Then the next question was fired out. 'Who painted *Madame X*?' More good-humoured protests followed.

'Now I know this one,' claimed Beatrice. 'My mother was reading a book about her recently – it was John Singer Sargent.'

'I am impressed,' Damien said to her.

'In which organs in the body would you find nephrons?' They all shook their heads.

'I should know that. It's either the kidneys or the spleen,' said Damien.

'There must be two of them because he said, "in which *organs*",' volunteered Sean.

'In that case I'd go for kidneys,' said Rachel, 'because a nephrologist is a kidney specialist.'

'How did you know that?' asked Sean.

'I went out with one once,' she said. 'Well, that's what he became eventually.'

The next one was a question about rugby, which Beatrice answered.

'I never thought old boyfriends had any uses until now. That's the second one I got right because of Paul,' she said to Irene.

'Who's Paul?' asked Damien.

'Someone I used to go out with.'

'I wish my former girlfriends were as useful as your boyfriends seem to be,' said Damien at an interval when the results for the previous round were being called out.

'A lot of heartache went into acquiring our knowledge, but maybe it hasn't all been in vain,' laughed Irene.

'Well it's certainly paying dividends – we're joint first at the moment,' said Damien.

Rachel asked, 'Will they think it's a set-up if we win, what with you being in the centre of the project?'

'No. I had nothing whatever to do with this event – this was arranged by the fundraising committee, and they used an outsider to set the questions.'

At the halfway stage, he went to the bar and Beatrice went to help carry the drinks back.

'Can I be so bold as to ask if there is a current boyfriend, whose interests might contribute to your general knowledge in the future? Or if your sports knowledge has anything to do with the murder you were planning the last time we met?'

She smiled. 'You've got a good memory. I didn't actually carry that out, but there were some pretty expensive blooms beheaded in the battle. Let's just say that my method of extermination was just as effective even though there was no blood shed. Happily, I haven't seen him since, although he has a habit of popping up in my living room, uninvited.'

'Does that mean you might have lunch with me sometime, or dinner?'

'Does that mean you're asking me to?'

'It might.'

'Then the answer might be yes,' she replied.

'It'll have to wait until I come back from India though, but can we stay in touch, by email?'

'I didn't realise you were going over there. When are you off?'

Rachel arrived at their elbows, making a reply impossible. 'What's keeping you two? The next round is about to begin. Let me carry some of those back.'

They settled down to debate Oscar winners, Jedward's family name, botanical names for daisies, the last countries to be admitted to the EU and a variety of other topics. The competition hotted up, with three teams neck and neck at the beginning of the final round. At the end of it, table nine won and they each received a voucher for dinner for two in the hotel's much-awarded restaurant.

Rachel asked Damien who he'd take and he replied, 'As it happens, sis, I have someone in mind.' He glanced at Beatrice. 'But that's for me to know, not you!'

Just then he was called away to perform some more MC duties. He announced that a staggeringly generous amount of money had been amassed over numerous events in the past year and that he'd happily deliver it in person to the medical centre in Mumbai. 'I'll be staying there for a while to oversee our volunteers as they get the new schoolrooms, canteen and shower block under way, thanks to your generosity and continuing support.'

He rounded off the night with more acknowledgements and left the stage to a round of applause and cheers. He was a popular Dean of Students, and despite being a few years short of his fortieth birthday, he was much respected by his more senior faculty peers too.

CHAPTER 7

The students and graduates had long gone for the summer – some back to their own countries, others to take up internships and further studies and specialities. The administration building was almost deserted, but Damien was still working when one of the porters did his rounds. He always stopped to chat, have a moan about the students, the economy, the price of cigarettes or whatever else was exercising his mind. Tonight, Damien wished he'd just move on. He was trying to clear his desk before starting his extended leave. He felt drained, as he always did at the end of the academic year, but he was really excited about the project. For the past year, some of his colleagues and students had been actively involved in planning this trip to India, and while he'd only recently decided to join them, it had been quickly acknowledged among them all that he'd be their gaffer.

A former dean had been one of those who had initiated and set up the charity some years earlier. Their primary aim had been to raise funds for a medical centre on the outskirts of Mumbai, close to one of the numerous dumping grounds for the city. The facility was intended to help children who otherwise would face the certain destiny of joining the thousands of other rag pickers in their district. However, the scheme had gathered momentum and several volunteers had got involved with the actual construction and staffing of the facility over the years. Now, with his leave, he and a good number of other volunteers were heading out to set the next phase of the programme in operation. Several skilled and unskilled workers would join them later.

The original plan had been to erect two rooms, which could double up as classrooms and recreational spaces. But as the funds grew, so too did the plans. Fortunately, the land was there and the intentions now included erecting a shower block, an additional classroom and a canteen, adjacent to the original medical centre project.

Damien was going to be part of the advance party going ahead to set things in motion before they were joined by another twenty or so volunteers. They had an early-morning flight to Heathrow the following day to catch the Kingfisher flight direct to Mumbai.

He thought the porter would never go. When he eventually did, Damien ran through a final checklist of instructions for his deputy, and scribbled on a few more post-its before closing down his computer. His deputy was someone who didn't enjoy retirement and relished any opportunity to step into his former post at the college. 'Stay as long as you like: it's no problem for me,' he had encouraged when Damien had checked with him before making his plans. Damien still had some packing to finish, but was meeting his sister for a quick drink before he went home.

'I really appreciate the offer of a lift to the airport but, honestly, the Aircoach will be just as handy,' Damien told Rachel as he placed their drinks on the corner of a table, the only space available in the rowdy Friday night melee at the city-centre pub.

'I don't mind. It's the least I can do for my bro when he's going off to save the world.'

He laughed. 'Hardly that, although I'm not sure it will actually be much of a holiday.'

'It doesn't sound like one at all. I watched that video you gave me and the conditions out there are unbelievable. Can what you are doing really make a difference?'

'We have to try. If everyone ignores the problems, they'll never be addressed. Besides, what we are doing isn't unique, there are several other organisations trying to help as well, and if we can get even a handful of kids into education because of it, then we'll have succeeded in a very small way.'

'But it seems like a never-ending spiral. Do any of them ever escape? From what I could see, it seems that generations of families spend their lives sifting through the city's waste, looking for things that might be worth something, and they just accept that as their lot. Do they ever find anything valuable?'

'Not what we would consider valuable. Their treasures,' Damien explained to Rachel, 'are not the kind of good news stories that we read about occasionally in the papers here, where someone has given old clothes away or put them in a recycling skip, forgetting they had hidden their funeral money in the lining, or that they concealed a few thousand pounds in an old pair of holey socks.'

'Did you see that one in the papers recently?' said Rachel. 'A woman had hidden her cache of jewellery at the bottom of the waste paper basket when she was going out and then forgot about it. It all went out in the bin, but once she had alerted everyone, it turned up in the dump.'

'That doesn't happen for these kids unfortunately. They spend all day long literally sorting through the dumps for bits of plastic, scraps and rags, bones and glass, metal – anything – that they then sell on for a couple of rupees.'

'It sounds disgusting.'

'It is, but to them it's a legitimate business and there are often several generations from the same family working together. They are the unofficial recyclers in the city and, you know, they do it with such dignity: it's very humbling. We have to be careful not to go over there being Johnny Do-gooders. That's why it's so important that we work with local labourers and use their skills. With

66

a bit of luck, by the time we leave we'll have left something worthwhile and useful behind.'

'I'm sorry now that I didn't decide to go out there with you,' Rachel said.

'There's always next year. This project is not going to go away. We'll always need fundraisers so you can do your bit while I'm over there, sweltering and slaving away.'

'You better get off then or you'll miss your flight. Are you sure about the lift? '

'Absolutely and thanks.'

'I'll miss you, bro. Make sure you email regularly and Skype me when you arrive, if you can.'

'I promise. Now sis, don't start blubbing on me.' He laughed as they parted company – she was such a softie. He headed home to put the last bits and pieces in his hand luggage. He set the alarm on his iPhone, put his passport and tickets on top of his case and fell into an uneasy sleep, conscious of his early flight and tight connection time in Heathrow.

CHAPTER 8

Iswara thought that she must have met up with all her relations, extended family and school friends since she'd got back nine weeks earlier. Even though she had spent two weeks with her parents in the countryside, she could still sense hostility from her mother. Her father was more conciliatory, suggesting on their walks together that she come to the clinic and give it a try.

'You might be pleasantly surprised and actually like it.'

She knew she wouldn't. Although she hadn't been home for long, she couldn't help but make comparisons everywhere, now that she was cognisant of the freedoms enjoyed by her European friends. Freedoms not only in their personal lives, their beliefs, but in their career choices too. She was also acutely aware of the constraints on her, constraints that she was fighting so hard to break. She knew her father meant well by trying to steer her into his clinic. He was highly regarded as one of the top neurology specialists and, as such, was a senior consultant. Most of those who had graduated with her would thank their gods for such an opportunity. But not Iswara.

When she had been a small child, her grandfather had told her of visiting his patients on a bicycle and of how outbreaks of cholera, typhoid and diphtheria had wiped out whole towns and villages in a matter of weeks, before the 'magic potion' had been discovered. That was what he called penicillin. 'That cure-all was one of medicine's triumphs, and it saved the lives of so many,' he'd told anyone who would listen.

He used to sit his two granddaughters on his knees and tell them, 'When you grow up you must help others. You are lucky children, but you must never be superior to anyone because of your birth. That is just luck and you must share that, because not everyone is blessed as you are. Remember girls, never become complacent. You can and you must leave this world a better place than you found it.'

Iswara knew that being widowed had left a huge void in his life. He always spoke lovingly about her grandmother and she loved to hear how he'd married her – a girl he'd never met before the day of the ceremony. The union had been arranged when she was just three and he was ten. It was, like so many other arranged marriages, a success story. They had enjoyed almost fifty years together before she died of complications after surgery for an ovarian tumour. After that, he'd become involved in several altruistic projects, partly to fill his time but mainly because he'd always been aware that he had been more fortunate than most with his lot in life. Iswara was also aware that he had come from a very wealthy family. His father had been a favoured physician to a *rajah* and *rani* and their household. This had resulted in gifts and jewellery that had been showered on him in gratitude, making their way down through the family, to his late wife and now to his daughter-in-law Daya who wore the pieces with pride, hauteur and flair. He'd lived on his own for a few years before deciding to come and live with his son's family.

Rekna had bored of his stories very easily, but in Iswara he had a willing audience. He'd often have long philosophical discussions with her about his life, where he had been and what he had seen. He'd also discussed his ambitions for her. She knew that if he had still been around, he would have liked to see her working at his hospital, but equally she was confident that if he had been alive today, he would have taken her side against her parents when he heard her plans.

Ironically, it was while studying in Dublin that she had learned of the rag pickers project in Mumbai. Despite being born and raised in the city, her upbringing had sheltered her totally from the other life of the city, where poverty, deprivation and crime existed in tandem with her privileged existence. Chauffeur-driven to school and summers spent in the mountains safely away from the smells and the humidity of the sweltering city had not afforded even a glimpse of it. She had been surprised to discover that such a project existed and that it was being funded not only by an Irish charity, but one originating in her own alma mater. She had immediately felt an affinity with it, especially when she'd learned that it was a medical and dispensary service for those who couldn't afford any treatment at all. Iswara knew only too well that often the magic potion, spoken of so reverently by her grandfather, was not even available to many when they needed it.

'We have a lot to be ashamed of in this great country of ours. Despite its reputation as a leading pharmaceutical nation in the world, many of our own citizens will never be able to avail of the progress being made in medicines here. There is no justice in that, is there?' he had told her.

When her grandfather died, and Iswara still had three years of her degree course to complete, she had decided that she would spend some time trying to honour his conviction that she should help others. Now with her qualifications, her parchment and those treasured letters after her name, she reasoned, where better to start than with those in her city who really needed her help?

Iswara knew it made her mother mad that she was so strong willed and so determined not to listen to her or her father. Daya hadn't spoken to her properly since she'd refused to go for the interview at the clinic.

After another silent breakfast, Iswara took a lift to the city with her father, who knew where she was headed.

'I can't go against your mother, but I do admire what you want to do. Can I come along and see the project some time?'

'Papa, I'd love that, if they'll have me. It would mean so much to me. I just wish Mother would come around.'

'Give her time. She will, I assure you, although she's convinced you won't last three months there.'

Iswara headed to the project, refusing to allow her father's driver take her there. She had dressed simply, choosing to wear a cotton *kameez* over a baggy *shalwar*, instead of a sari – the trousers were more practical. She had plaited her hair and decided against wearing any adornments other than the gold bangles she had worn for years. These had been a gift from her grandfather when she'd left for Ireland. She didn't want to draw attention to herself in any way and knew she would have her task cut out for her if she were to be accepted as someone who genuinely cared about her work, and not just as someone who wanted to feel good because she was helping people.

She had written beforehand and asked to be allowed to visit the centre, and had been told she would be welcomed that day. She took a rickshaw through the pungent, noisy backstreets where everyone seemed to be in a flap. There were vans parked willy-nilly outside the centre and some skinny dogs lying in the shade, and as she went inside she passed a queue of mothers, many with babies in their arms. There were countless toddlers, some too ill to run about or make noise, their large expressionless eyes seeming even larger against their unnatural pallor.

Iswara smiled at one woman as she walked by. She was nursing an infant and had a slightly older child standing beside her, resting his head on her knee. The woman had the saddest eyes Iswara had ever seen and she knew she would have to toughen up to cope with the challenges she'd face here. She couldn't take on everyone's problems.

She went through the doorway. It had a curtain screen made of strings of coloured beads that made hollow sounds as they fell back into place when anyone went through the entrance to the centre. She did a double take when she saw the group of Europeans standing in the small entrance hall, because she recognised four of them.

'Iswara! It can't be you.' It was Damien, her dean from her college in Dublin, with some of his colleagues and Clem, a contemporary of hers from her clinical rotation in Galway.

'Damien, Clem, what on earth are you doing here?' she asked, shaking Damien's hand warmly. 'I feel like I'm dreaming.' She liked Damien. He had always been a favourite with the students, treating them as equals, even when they were mere freshers. Nothing was too much trouble for him to make them feel at home and at ease as they made their way through the course. He was particularly solicitous with his overseas charges.

'We've just arrived. We're helping to get the new extensions started. You're the last person I expected to find. But what are you doing here? Do you work at the centre?'

'Not yet, but I am hoping to, if they'll have me. I'm actually here for an interview.'

Damien laughed, 'If they'll have you? They would be mad to refuse you. Want me to put in a good word for you?'

'I think it might be more polite if we wait until they have met me first,' she smiled at him.

'Here, Iswara, let me introduce you to the rest of the squad. You might as well get used to us before the rest arrive. John and Barry you know, and Clem.'

'Hi,' said Clem, 'I thought you were going to work at your father's clinic. Is this it?'

She laughed. 'No it's not and I'm not. It's a long story. I'll tell you again later.'

'Iswara, as some of you will remember, was one of our star students,' Damien was saying.

The director of the clinic came out at that moment and saved her further embarrassment. He invited her to follow him into a tiny room, passing more patients lined up in the hallway.

'I hadn't realised your reputation preceded you,' the director said. 'Welcome to the nerve centre of the dispensary.' He offered her a seat, took out her letter, glancing through it as though to refresh his memory. 'I knew your grandfather well, and your father too of course. We worked together for several years. What made you decide to apply to us?'

Iswara knew what the next question would be and it was asked before she could answer the first one. 'With your connections would you not have considered joining your father's clinic?'

'Yes I did, but only briefly. I want to work here because of my grandfather. He always told me to help others and that's what I want to do. I've read about what you do here, and I'd like to be part of it. I've worked with children during my training in Galway in Ireland, and feel there is so much to do here. It just feels right for me.'

'Well, you certainly seem passionate. I like that, but this kind of work is unrelenting. We have constant epidemics of cholera, diphtheria and malaria. There is never an easy day. We never have enough time, or enough doctors or nurses to cope with the demand. Sometimes we don't have sufficient medicines either. We can never hope to win all our battles, only make things better for some of the patients coming in. A lot of the problems are caused by malnutrition, ignorance really, so what we are trying to do is teach the mothers how to care for their babies and children more efficiently in the hope that they'll pass this knowledge on to them.'

'I am familiar with the work, in fact I heard about it first in Dublin of all places. I actually know some of the people who have arrived to help with the new building here.'

'Well that could certainly be to our advantage too.' He paused. 'Many of the local workers don't understand English and it would be great to have someone to act as a go-between with the volunteers. Of course, primarily we would welcome your invaluable input from a medical perspective, but would appreciate your help during the building, if that suits you too.'

'I like the sound of that,' she said smiling at him, surer now than she had been since the beginning of the meeting that he may just take her on.

'However, Iswara, before you make your mind up I would like you to spend a morning or afternoon with us, so that you can see what you are getting yourself into. Maybe give instruction to some of the expecting mothers on the importance of looking after themselves. It's a far cry from the standards in the hospitals you've trained in in Ireland and you'll find it very hard to walk away at the end of the day and leave your work behind you. Staying detached is essential if you are to survive here and that is something you will have to learn to do early on if you don't want to go under.'

'I do understand that. I'm not doing anything else today. I could stay – if that suits,' she volunteered, afraid that if she left now he may change his mind.

'You do realise you will earn nothing like the

salary you would get working in a clinic or private practice.'

She nodded.

'Our salaries are paid from the charity and there are no perks from pharmaceutical companies given out here. But if it's job satisfaction you're after – you'll get that in bucket loads,' he said, clasping his hands together.

Before she could say anything he continued, 'I assume your vaccinations are up to date.'

She nodded. Her father had made sure of that before she returned to India.

'Then let me introduce you to Dr Patel, and we'll see if he is agreeable to you aiding him with his workload. We have two other doctors here every day but, as you'll soon see, we could do with twice as many. We have three nurses too, but they are often away on outreach projects.'

Dr Patel welcomed her warmly. He showed her his system of keeping track of his countless cases. 'The nurses look after most of the vaccinations, but no matter how many we administer here we have constant epidemics that could be avoided. We need more staff and we just don't have them. Because most of our patients are so poor, they wait too long before coming in for treatment. They are very proud people and they don't like taking charity. We must always respect their dignity at all costs, but we also need to teach them that we could save many more of their young children if only we saw them in time.'

She was impressed by the unhurried way he treated each new patient. As he went along he explained to Iswara what he expected to find from their symptoms, giving her potted versions and diagnostic hints as he prodded and probed, looked into eyes, ears and throats. His manner was gentle and caring. He didn't baulk at the weeping sores, or the children coughing in his face, but took the little ones' hands and rubbed them between his. He talked soothingly to them and to their mothers or older sisters or brothers, who had been put in charge so that their parents would not miss out on a few hours and a few rupees working in the dumps. He explained why tuberculosis, malaria, typhoid and polio were always of great concern, as an outbreak could rapidly flare into an epidemic in a very short space of time.

'Other regular problems we meet are the many children coming in who are suffering from burns and allergies too. We get our share of dog bites, and of course AIDS and other sexually transmitted diseases are a constant concern.'

Iswara was well aware that many of the older children were driven into prostitution, countless numbers of them slept rough on the streets and were victims of gangs and sexual violence too, and so AIDS was rampant.

'You, of course, understand that these rag pickers are not beggars. Volunteers who come from overseas to help often don't understand that. These people look on their work as their chosen trade and they take pride in it. We must never forget that.'

The day was busy and intense, but the time passed very quickly, the long queue eventually dwinding to a trickle and finally to a handful. Dr Patel was effusive in his report about her to the director, who came in to his room to check how the afternoon had gone.

'I cannot tell you how happy I'd be to have another pair of hands on board.'

'You and I both,' he replied. Then, addressing Iswara, he said, 'If you want to wait, I can give you a lift some of the way home.'

Dr Patel had also offered, but that was before another mother arrived carrying a child of about four. 'I don't know how long I will be – the last patients often seem to take the longest. As you see, we don't exactly work regular hours in here.'

She thanked him and accepted the director's lift. En route he said, 'So do you think you could stand the pace and, more importantly, the nature of the work? You don't have to tell me yet, but have a think about it.'

Without hesitation she replied, 'I already have. I'd certainly love to give it my best.' Not wishing to appear pushy, she had to force herself to add, 'But I would like to ask when could I start?'

His reply surprised her. 'As soon as you are able. Now I have to go to meet the new batch of Irish volunteers you saw this morning. As you already

79

know some of them, would you like to come along and join them for a welcoming drink later on?'

Iswara was exhausted; she couldn't wait to get home to have a soak in a bath and wash her hair, and let the fresh scent of rose water replace the foetid odours that saturated the air and seemed to hang on the fibres of her clothes. But she wanted to hear the latest from Dublin – she missed it more than she ever thought she would. She missed the camaraderie that she'd had with her fellow students, and although they kept in touch by email, she often thought of snatched sandwiches in St Stephen's Green and late-night coffees in Bewley's on Grafton Street. She'd even missed those with whom she'd worked in Galway.

She also knew there would be an interrogation at home about what she had done all day, and that her mother would defrost her cold-shoulder policy long enough to heap more disapproval on her daughter. As though reading her thoughts, the director said, 'I'll be passing your house on my way back into town and could collect you when you've had time to freshen up, if you would like.'

'That would be very kind of you, but I'd hate to impose.'

'It's no imposition. Besides, I could say hello to your father and mother if they're at home.'

'I'm sure they would love to see you too,' she replied.

★　★　★

As Iswara expected, her mother came to the door when she heard her daughter returning, but it was more to ensure decontamination than to welcome her home.

'I'll have your bath run for you immediately. You must get out of those clothes right away. Your father is not yet home, so you'll have time for a good soak before dinner.'

'I'll be going out again, Mama. Some people I know from Ireland have come over for the summer to help on the new extension and I am going to meet them. Several of them have never been to India before.'

She held off saying she was being collected, knowing it would have more sway when mentioned in front of her father.

By the time Raj came home, Iswara had changed into a sari, added some jewellery and blow-dried her hair so that it fell loosely around her shoulders. Raj was curious about how she had got on.

'There's a former colleague of yours in charge. He's going to collect me later to go and welcome the Irish volunteers.' She told him about their chat and added, 'He said he'd love to come in to say hello.'

'Great. Well, she'll be in good hands if he's in charge,' Raj said to his wife, who didn't want to hear this. 'He's meticulous about everything he undertakes. He's a kind man too.'

'He wants me to help with his new development project in a small way, with translations. I even found it difficult today because many of the patients speak dialects that I can't translate, but the nurses are marvellous and between everyone they manage to communicate with each other.'

'If you're helping with translations, does that mean you won't have to deal with those people?'

'Mother, if you mean the rag pickers by "those people", I most certainly will. I'll be working there as a doctor too. That's what I studied for all these years.'

A silence descended around the table. She knew from her conversation in the car that morning with her father that she had almost won him around, but her mother was a different matter. She also knew that her father would not confront his wife while she was there, so saying nothing, she figured, was her best defence.

A manservant came in to announce the director's arrival.

'Daya, Raj, my old friends, I haven't seen you for a long time,' the director said, joining his hands, bowing towards Mrs Singhanid and smiling at her before turning towards Iswara and doing the same.

'I know you are rushing off now,' Daya said, 'but you must come and join us for dinner some evening.'

'Yes, you must,' Raj added, 'and you can tell us all about how things are going at the medical centre.'

'Thank you, I'd enjoy that. I hope you don't

mind me stealing your daughter this evening. I have to make our Irish visitors welcome and she's kindly agreed to help me.'

'She's looking forward to it. She couldn't believe it when she met them this morning. I'm sure they'll be a great help to you', said Raj.

'We are very grateful to them but it says a lot for the way our government looks after its own, doesn't it?' the director said. 'But that's a discussion for another time.'

'I want to know how you got involved in it, and how you manage to juggle your time with your own practice, never mind getting the Irish involved too. We'll arrange a date,' added Raj.

'I'll look forward to it, but I have to warn you, Daya,' the director said to Iswara's mother, 'I tend to get a bit carried away with my subject.'

She laughed, 'I can see that.'

'I'm afraid we must leave, as these visitors will be exhausted after their long flight and we don't want to wear them out before they even begin.'

They drove to the modest hotel where the recently arrived contingent had booked temporary accommodation. Once they got their bearings they intended to rent apartments which they could share more cheaply and which would be more convenient to their work.

Damien was delighted to see Iswara again. 'I'm afraid we've lost John. He had to go to bed,' he said, 'a combination of the travelling and the heat.

He thought it wiser to get an early night to be ready for the real work.'

'You should probably do the same,' she answered.

'Oh I'm a bit of a night owl. It'll take me a few days to adjust to the time difference.'

The director had invited Dr Patel and one of the other doctors from the project along, and after more introductions were made, they all sat down together.

'I won't remember any of those names tomorrow,' Clem said.

'Don't worry. Neither will I,' said the director. 'At least you all didn't arrive at once or we'd never get to know who anyone was. Maybe we should give you all name tags.'

Iswara laughed. 'Don't look so worried, you'll get used to us in a few days,' she assured Clem. 'When I got back, it took me a while to tune in again. I hadn't realised how sing-songy our English is and I'd forgotten how we clip our words too and how people pepper their speech with Hinglish.'

'Hinglish? What on earth is that?'

She explained, 'It's a throwback to English rule. Even people who can hardly read and write use whole sentences in a mix of Hindi and English, and with their regional accents too.'

'If we don't tune in quickly we'll be in real trouble,' Clem laughed.

'What did you do today? Did you get an idea of the place?' she asked Barry, one of the other doctors.

'Yes, we did a tour of the neighbourhood around the hotel and for someone who has never been to India before that was quite a culture shock. I certainly hadn't expected everywhere to be quite so busy and so crowded.'

'Well, there are quite a lot of us,' she said.

'But to be positive, we made great progress today too,' Damien continued. 'We sorted out the bank accounts, met the engineer and some of the crew we'll be helping and we also met the foreman. But here am I rabbiting on about us. How did you get on? Any luck at the medical centre?'

'I got the job, starting immediately, and I'll be on hand if you need a translator or someone to explain our traditions, idiosyncrasies and foibles, and we have lots and lots of those. The director thinks it may be beneficial all around.'

The director interjected, 'I have to admit, I had worried about communication problems before you arrived and then in walked Iswara, an answer to our prayers perhaps. I think having her on board will help you get to know how things are done around here and it will certainly smooth the way when it comes to language barriers. People's accents can be difficult to understand, often *I* can't make out what they are trying to tell me.'

Clem asked, 'How many languages are there in India anyway?'

'No one really knows, but it's in the hundreds if you take dialects into it.'

'I think you're going to be very busy!' said Clem.

'I couldn't believe it when you appeared this morning. I thought I was hallucinating. It's great to see you again.'

'And you too, Clem,' she said. 'I'm dying to hear all the gossip. I know it's only been a few months since I left, but it feels much longer. I really miss Ireland, but on the plus side, it'll be nice to be able to return the favour for the times you all helped me with things over the last number of years, especially you Damien.'

'That was just part of my job.'

'And now I'll just be doing mine too,' she answered.

'You were one of the easy ones Iswara, unlike some I could mention,' Damien said, not looking at anyone in particular. They all laughed.

Clem said, 'Medical students have a certain reputation to live up to.'

'And some of them were relentless in doing so!'

The director explained that they shouldn't be surprised if they found the workers erecting a shrine to Ganesh when they arrived the next day.

'He's one of our gods and is generally regarded as the Remover of Obstacles, though there are those who also believe that he places obstacles in the path of those who need to be checked.'

'Keeping on everyone's good side. He seems like a god with a sense of humour, I like that,' said Damien. 'We had better watch out.'

'He's a non-sectarian deity and Hindus of all denominations invoke him specially at the beginning of any new undertaking, no matter how big or small,' Iswara explained. 'Even if they are just buying a new car or going on a trip. And this new centre is very important for them.'

The director interrupted. 'You'll have plenty of time to learn about such things, so let's call it a day for now. I know you have lots to catch up on, but there's always tomorrow.' He stood up and added, 'Thank you all again for giving up your time to help us.'

It was eleven by the time Iswara got to bed, elated, excited and very pleased with the way the day had progressed. She'd worry about placating her mother tomorrow.

CHAPTER 9

A wall of humid air hit Damien, Clem and John as they walked from the air-conditioned hotel into the bustling street. AA, the foreman on the project, was taking them to the garage where they were going to pick up their transport and then to the builders' suppliers to set up an account. He had already organised some portable loos and a temporary office. These had been placed on-site, although to use the term 'office' was a bit grandiose. It was little more than a large empty metal box with two windows on either side. This had been hired for the duration of the building work and still had to have its power supply connected.

'This heat is going to take some getting used to,' Clem said to Damien. 'Is it too much to expect that these pick-ups have air conditioning in them?'

Damien laughed. 'Sorry we couldn't co-ordinate our holidays with their winter time, it might have put some people out!'

'Never mind the air conditioning, it's the driving I'm worried about,' said John. 'Just look at that mayhem. No one in their right lane, and the horns blaring, it's impossible to know who is being warned or being shouted at. I think I'll opt for site work and leave the driving to the others. It's much too much of a challenge.'

'Welcome to Mumbai,' grinned AA. When they'd met the previous day he'd explained, 'My name is Abdul-Razzaz Mahimakar, but everyone calls me AA.'

'You'll get used to the driving,' said Damien. 'I felt the same way the first time I came over here. Apart from the cars it's those vendors weaving in and out, and the bicycles and the rickshaws that are even more terrifying.'

'There's a simple rule – never give way to anything unless it's bigger than you are,' AA advised.

'That might be funny if it wasn't so true,' John said.

In AA's battered car, they discussed how to divide the new batch of volunteers when they arrived later in the week. Damien had broken them roughly into groups and assigned each a task according to their areas of expertise and willingness they had expressed when they had applied for a place on the programme. AA has been amazed at the diversity of those who were coming over. For the most part they were lecturers, students and graduates of the medical facility, who were providing most of the funding, but they also included builders and other skilled craftspeople, who were willing to turn their hands to anything to get the classrooms, showers and canteen up and running in the four months they'd be here. Some couldn't stay that long, but would be replaced by others when they had to return home, leaving about twenty on-site to complete the work.

Damien was glad to have a few days to get used to the set up and geography of the place before the main contingent arrived. The pick-ups were waiting and as he had anticipated, they had seen better days. Far from having air conditioning, one had a window that wouldn't wind up or down, but it would be fine for ferrying equipment and supplies to the site.

'Mission accomplished,' Damien said when he had safely negotiated the way back to base. Site meetings, strategic planning and the use of the telephone in the medical centre were the starting points. The metal office attracted the heat and even with the meshed, netted windows fully open there was no respite from the cloying humidity. His shirt was already soaked through and he knew there was little point in changing it, because as soon as he'd put on a replacement, it would suffer the same fate. He'd have to organise some fans and water stations or they'd be no use to anyone.

As predicted by the director, when the first of the local labourers arrived on the first morning, there was much discussion about where they should place the shrine to the Ganesh. This done, a picture materialised, representing this deity who had an elephant's head. Some of the workers placed sweets on the little altar shelf they had erected in front of the image. They bowed their heads in silent prayer for a few minutes and only then were they ready to turn the first sod. The honour went to Damien.

Patients who were waiting outside the clinic left their places in the queue to see what was going on. Nut-brown children with gleaming black hair gathered around staring, intrigued as much by the collection of pink-skinned foreigners as by what was actually happening. The nurses and doctors came outside, so too did the director with the rest of the staff. AA led Damien to the digger. He had given him a lesson on how to operate the scoop the previous afternoon. Murmurs echoed through the little crowd as he climbed aboard and sank the digger's bucket into the earth, leaving a gaping scar as he raised it a few feet and falteringly swivelled the machine to deposit the soil in a corner of the cordoned-off site. Cheers and clapping ensued – the project was officially under way.

Inside the office, a hierarchy was soon established. AA, a qualified structural engineer who had spent some time working in Dubai and who was without any dispute the most important member of the team, took possession of the smallest desk and there he spread out his drawings. Most of the furniture and equipment in the glorified office had been well-loved and well-used before they acquired it, and for the moment they would piggyback on the medical centre for computer points and sockets. A proper power supply had been promised for later in the week, but whether it would materialise was debatable.

Damien was treated with great respect and spoken to only by the volunteers and AA. This bothered him. Whenever he tried to talk to the men, they didn't make eye contact with him, but rather seemed to hold him in awe in a reverential way. He was relieved to have Iswara to turn to at such moments and she was always willing to help.

'I feel very uncomfortable with this degree of subservience,' he told her. 'I can't seem to get through to them.'

'It's our way. Our caste system is responsible for a lot of this. These people don't mean to be unfriendly. They are showing respect by looking down. In their world, they would normally never meet or mix with people of your standing and education, never mind hold a conversation with them.' She smiled as she added, 'You must understand that you are also new and a little strange to them. Most of them will never have met a westerner before.'

'Well, we'll have to change that,' said Damien. 'I'm used to my mother calling everyone who ever did any work for her by their first name, and they used her first name too.'

'That would never happen in my home,' said Iswara. 'Our caste system ensures that these gaps never close. My mother is a very good person and gives a lot to poor people, but they come to the back door. Their food is served on special dishes and plates that are kept specifically for them. They even wash them separately from ours. That's how she was brought up by her mother and grandmother too, so she knows no different and she's never going to change now. She's a real traditionalist.'

'How does that work when someone is sick? Are there different wards for the castes in hospitals?'

'Oh no, in hospital everyone is treated the same.'

'How did you get around her to let you study abroad?'

'I think, perhaps, she thought I'd follow in my father's footsteps and join him in his clinic.'

'And why didn't you?'

'I don't agree with such segregation and I'm a rebel. I'm not prepared to do what I am told all the time. I am an independent woman, and being with young people who were allowed think for themselves and make their own decisions has made it even harder to come back here and knuckle down and conform.'

'I can see how that could be difficult,' he said.

'It's even harder than I thought it would be. My mother is sorely disappointed in me working here, with the lower castes. She was afraid I'd come back from Ireland betrothed to a foreigner, but now I think that would have been preferable in her eyes to being an unmarried, at my advanced age!'

He laughed, 'It must be mother-hen instinct. I have a sister your age and she's not married either.

My mother is always dropping hints that I should be more proactive in introducing her to my unattached friends.'

'And what about you? Does she not try matchmaking for her son too?'

'No. She's an Irish Mammy – no one would ever be good enough for me, her first born!' He laughed, and for some reason a thought of Beatrice popped into his mind, as it often did. He'd have to ask her out for lunch again when he got home. He didn't know if she had a partner. She had told him that she had wanted to murder a boyfriend, but she'd also said that he often popped in to her house uninvited. He'd have to ask Irene. Anyway, asking someone to lunch wasn't a statement of serious intent, he rationalised, and he still had the voucher he'd won at the quiz – the perfect excuse for an invite – as they'd all contributed to winning. His reverie was interrupted by Iswara.

'You must come to my home and meet my parents while you're here.'

'I'd really like to do that, but first can you communicate or have the message conveyed to the workers that we'd like everyone to be friends on the site? Maybe explain that's how we do things in Ireland?'

'I will, but it may not make any difference.'

Damien found himself becoming more and more curious about Indian culture, where every little ritual seemed to have been born out of some tribal tradition or another, but he didn't want to appear

94

too nosey at this stage, for fear of being thought rude or, worse, as being superior. He had yet to introduce the volunteers to the infamous dumps or to the vermin and fly-infested, overcrowded ghettos where the workers lived, although he'd given them plenty to read about it before they left Ireland. He'd wait until the last few had arrived to give them that initiation. His first impressions of such poverty and the unbelievable conditions had never left him since his visit to India during his student days. Fascinating, disturbing and unforgettable. Nor had he been able to erase the faces of happy children and the emaciated old men and stooped women doubled over, sifting through the city's waste. Such images had made him promise then that he'd get involved one day. Now his desk in Dublin, overlooking St Stephen's Green, the city-centre park that had originally been a pleasure garden for one man and his family, seemed very far away. What parallel worlds. Yet here he was, and he wondered had serendipity, fate, karma, destiny and providence all conspired to contrive such an opportunity, and if so, why? Such thoughts would come to haunt him, but for now he was certain that whatever had brought him here had been prompted by the affinity he felt with Indian students who came under his remit at the college. He was constantly drawn to their dignity, their reserve, their kindness and their great sense of self.

Outside, the heavens opened. It was monsoon

season, probably not the most sensible time to be here, but it was when they could rely on the biggest number of volunteers to be available. The warm raindrops changed rapidly into continuous noisy streams, slanting into the hardened mud with the force of blades that scored the compacted surface. The noise inside the metal hut sounded like thousands of nails being dropped on the roof. A clap of thunder caused the windows to rattle and the lights to flicker. The rain poured down, making rivulets, then little streams, then gushing torrents, filling holes and drains, creating pools as it coursed along. Within ten minutes everywhere was transformed. The air smelled different, although not clean and fresh, rather humid and sticky. Steam started rising from the ground and as quickly as it had started the rain stopped. Within an hour, much of the surface water had found new levels, leaving a layer of softened mud everywhere. This pattern was to become the norm over the next few weeks, darkening skies heralding yet another downpour. The foreigners took shelter: the natives didn't seem to notice and simply worked on, sploshing through the floods.

The traffic going back to their hotel that day was unbelievable. The frayed canopies on the tuk-tuks and rickshaws leaked torrents of rainwater onto their occupants. Those pulling them ran through the dirty streams of water and car tyres screeched on the slippery road surfaces.

'How long does this go on?' Clem asked.

'Usually for a few months,' Damien answered. 'Jaysus!'

'I never really understood before what we meant at home when we said "soft rain". By God, I know now,' said Barry, as the heavens opened with more spectacular lightning and the vertical downpour began all over again.

CHAPTER 10

Beatrice had reclaimed her life, her flat and her space. She'd moved her furniture around and bought new bed linen one lunchtime with Irene. She'd seen a new soft leather sofa in Arnotts, with huge arms and deep button-back matching armchairs and she fell in love with it. She went to look at the suite several times, sitting on it and visualising it in her living room.

The assistant that'd she'd spoken to on each visit told her, 'If you really like it, buy it.'

'I'm just worried about the size. It seems much bigger than the suite I have.'

'Ok, then here's what you do. I'll give you measurements; you go home and cut the sizes out in newspapers. Then put the pieces on the floor where you want them and see if they fit. If they do, buy; if they don't, then move!'

It was as simple as that. She took the measurements, followed the instructions and found that if she bought the new suite, she'd not be able to open the door to the hallway or keep the square glass coffee table. That was when the seed to buy a bigger place was sown.

Maybe, just maybe, it was time to look around. She'd tell Irene at work tomorrow.

That turned out to be a grey, drizzly summer day in Dublin and Beatrice was surprised, pleasantly so, to find an email from Damien waiting for her when she got in to the office. He had asked if they could keep in touch, but they had never actually got around to exchanging addresses.

Irene was sitting across the desk and, before Beatrice could say a word, she said, 'What about going somewhere for lunch? Cheer us up on this lovely July day? There's something I want to run by you.'

'Sounds intriguing.'

'There's something in your inbox that might work too,' Irene grinned. 'I see Damien is keeping you in the loop. He asked me for your details last time I heard from him. Told you you'd made an impression there.'

'Don't be mad! He's probably keeping everyone in the loop, as you call it, with an eye to the next fundraising event,' said Beatrice.

'Don't be such a cynic!' laughed Irene. 'I'm off to a meeting. See you later.'

Hi all,

I hope you're enjoying a nice cool – real Irish – summer day, because I'm sitting here dreaming about – of all things – rain! Not just any rain but the soft, gentle Irish rain – the kind that just mists your hair and makes it stand on end and gently soaks through your clothes with incredible speed. That is currently my idea of heaven!

I'm sitting here sheltering in our new office – little more than a metal container. Outside the monsoon has arrived with a vengeance. I've never seen anything like it – nor experienced anything like the humidity.

I'll swear I'll never complain about the weather at home again!

It's easing off now.

Back to work – until the next deluge.

Cheers

Damien

Inside the medical centre, Iswara welcomed her next patient. Another pregnant mother, with a babe in arms, and with a toddler at her knee. The mother was suffering from malnutrition. Despite their outreach programmes to educate the women in the vicinity, many still neglected themselves in favour of filling their children's bellies.

'Sajadi, you must eat properly. If you don't, you'll get sick and you won't be any good to your little boys. I'm going to give you some iron and vitamin supplements, but you must promise to take them every morning. Have you anywhere safe to keep them where you live?'

Iswara knew only too well that there were no doors on the majority of the hovels and shanties where her patients lived. The greater part of what they called home was fashioned from cardboard boxes, sheets of corrugated iron and wooden pallets. Nothing was safe there and there was certainly nowhere to hide anything, especially medicine. Before Sajadi answered, Iswara added, 'If not, I can give them to you a two-day supply at a time, but you'd have to come here every second day. It's very important that you take this medicine. You wouldn't have to queue, just come to the nurse on duty and we'll keep them for you here, if you'd prefer to do that. Just come to the back door.'

Her patient nodded gratefully, remembering what had happened to the last medicine she had got for one of the children. She'd been too embarrassed to come back to the clinic and ask for more when it had been stolen and her child's chest infection had progressed to pneumonia. He had had to be hospitalised.

'Before you go, let me check and see if the little ones are due for any vaccinations: there's an awful lot of measles out there at the moment.' Iswara consulted her notes, and satisfied that they had as much protection as was possible, she walked her patient to the door. 'Remember, if you are not feeling well, tell the nurse when you come for your tablets and she'll tell me or one of the other doctors. You won't have to queue.'

Iswara's morning flew by, just like all the others since she'd started working at the clinic. She attended a six-year-old with a large jagged gash on his foot – he had stepped on broken glass in the dump. Another slightly older boy had torn his fingers trying to extricate the tiny filaments from the inside of spent electric light bulbs. She had inoculated numerous other patients, prescribed antibiotics for an assortment of ailments and coughs, and syringed some ears – and suddenly it was lunchtime.

She took off her white coat, washed her hands and went in to the little kitchenette to put on the kettle. The cook at home had packed her a lunch and, as usual, had put extra pieces of fruit and cakes in it. These, she knew, Iswara would share with her patients. Iswara had taken to wandering over to the building office for a chat and to see how work was progressing. She could see the outline of where the new buildings were beginning to grow and, although she could view the progress from her surgery window, she found herself using this visit as an excuse to talk to her friends. She missed the easy camaraderie that she had got so used to in Ireland. Here it was a 'them' and 'us' scenario. Rank was there to be respected. In Ireland, she felt everyone was the same. She could have a chat with the women in the hospital canteen, by name, and ask them how their daughters' wedding plans or pregnancies were progressing, or how a new grandchild was doing. Here, there was no one to gossip with. It would take more than a few weeks to get on that footing with the staff, who, for the most part, treated her warily when they heard where she lived and who her father was.

Damien had taken her out to dinner during the week and the evening had been relaxed and laughter filled. He admitted he had always liked her, but explained to her that because of his strictly kept rule of not fraternising socially with students, he had never had the freedom to date her before.

'Is this a date?' she asked him flirtatiously.

'I suppose it is,' he smiled, 'and the first of many I hope,' he added, suddenly thinking of Beatrice. Would he have a reply from her when he got back to his laptop? He felt a little guilty, sitting here with a beautiful woman and thinking of another. He consciously put thoughts of Beatrice aside and concentrated on Iswara.

'Well, you'll just have to ask me and see, won't you?'

'That I will,' he replied and left it at that.

'You know something, Damien,' Iswara said, feeling a little disappointed that he hadn't suggested a time or venue. 'I really enjoyed myself tonight and I suddenly felt liberated in a way I haven't felt since returning home.'

She was thinking of their conversation again as she approached the office where Damien, Clem and AA were sitting at the open door in the shade, talking cricket.

'I could never get excited about the game. Rugby was my sport,' Clem told AA.

'Cricket is like a religion here, whether you play it or not.'

'I'd better learn a bit about it so,' Damien laughed, spotting Iswara's sari'ed figure coming across the uneven ground. 'So that I can bluff my way through when I'm talking about it.'

'Bluff about what?' she asked.

'Cricket.'

'Ask my father: he's an expert. He knows more about it than any of the coaches or commentators. In fact, he's convinced he could fix any of the teams' problems – if only they'd ask him. Who do you follow Abdul-Razzaq, or should I call you AA too?' she asked the foreman.

'AA, please. I'm a traitor, I support Mumbai, even though I come from Bangalore.' He grinned at her. That was when she really noticed him for the first time. She realised that he had very green eyes. He held her gaze. She felt herself colour and was relieved when he turned to Damien and said, 'Perhaps you'll come to a match with me in Wankhede Stadium while you're here, if the renovations are finished in time. That's Mumbai's home ground, lots of atmosphere and all that, and I can show you what you've been missing.'

'That sounds like a plan,' he agreed.

Clem nodded. 'You can count me in too.'

'Look, the queue is getting long already. I think I'll head back,' Iswara said, nodding in the direction of the straggling line. As she walked, she wondered what had just happened. She was confused. She had felt herself being drawn in by AA, by his gaze – but what really disturbed her was the fact that it had been a pleasurable attraction, even though it could go nowhere. She kept seeing his green eyes, and the crinkled lagher lines around the outer edges, his shining moustache and even teeth. Despite her progressive views there could never be any question of them being friends in the real sense. She and her family belonged to the Brahmins, a high-ranking caste in Hindu society, which generally included scholars, teachers, priests and doctors. AA was Muslim. She shook these thoughts away and tried to concentrate on her afternoon surgery. She started back early, calling in the first woman who had been waiting outside in the sweltering heat.

She needn't have worried about not seeing Damien again socially because her mother had not given up on her matchmaking. She was conscious that every time her husband and daughter discussed her work or the building project, Iswara talked about Damien and someone called AA. She was coming around to thinking that perhaps it would be better to have an Irish son-in-law than an unmarried daughter. As Iswara spoke so frequently about this Damien, perhaps it was time to meet him and check out his potential.

However, she had not yet given up on the prospects of the widower who worked with her husband, Sanjay Ranjan, or on the possibility of getting

Iswara away from what she described to her bridge friends as her 'charity work'. Definitely some networking was needed to break the cycle and open up some new social possibilities. She drew up a guest list for a dinner party and discussed it with Raj when he got in that evening.

Iswara was also consulted and she added Clem, Barry and John to the mix, which already included the director and his wife, Damien, and Sanjay Ranjan from the clinic. Her mother had included her widowed sister and a bridge partner who had lived in London for a while and, of course, her other daughter Rekna and her husband. Her table was perfectly balanced at an even fourteen. She set the date for the following Saturday and started making lists. Before discussing preparations and the menu with her cook, she asked Iswara, 'What do these people eat?'

Iswara hated the way her mother referred to everyone she didn't know well as 'these people' and she had to stop herself shouting 'food' in angry reply. Instead, she said quietly, 'Why not serve a traditional meal, Mama? I'm sure they would really enjoy and appreciate that.'

'Won't it be too spicy for them? After all, their food is so bland . . .'

'It's not bland, it's just more – subtle,' Iswara replied, remembering the spicy Indian takeaways that her student friends used to order – the degree of heat often disguising the fact that they tasted nothing like authentic Indian cooking, apart from the colour and the rice: even that was often way off the mark. 'Anyway, we can serve lots of cucumber and yogurt to tone it down.'

'Will they expect meat?'

'It would be normal for them to have some,' Iswara answered, trying to hold her temper. Her parents often ate meat. She couldn't understand why her mother had to be so confrontational all the time. When she mentioned this to her sister, Rekna said, 'It's because you bring out the worst in her by not doing anything she wants! Papa has her spoiled, as he gives in to her, or he lets her think she's won. I secretly suspect she'd love to have been feisty enough to stand up to her parents and gone to university, but she wasn't.'

'But she's happy with Papa.'

'I know she is, but she sees you standing for things that were impossible when she was growing up and I think she resents it.'

'I hadn't thought of it like that.'

'Go easy on her,' said Rekna.

'I'll try,' laughed Iswara.

As the first weeks went by, Damien was still trying to get his head around the hierarchies and wondered why AA had not been included when Iswara issued the invitations to her home. He concluded that perhaps AA might not be comfortable dining with his director. He was going to ask but decided against it when Iswara told him of her mother's matchmaking plans with some eligible widower who worked with her father – and who had been invited too.

He found Beatrice popping into his mind from time to time and, on impulse, Damien decided to include her in his missives back home. He was not certain if she'd reply, but hoped she would. He'd been delighted when she had.

The flash of a turquoise sari with bands of cerise around the end distracted him as it disappeared around the fence behind the compound. Some curious teenager, no doubt, trying to see what was going on. These kids were daring and they constantly had to be shooed off the premises for fear of injury. They'd be even more of a curiosity when the rest of the volunteers arrived from Dublin the following Monday, because the red-haired Murphy brothers were in that lot, complete with their ample sprinkling of freckles. He hoped they'd pack lots of sunscreen.

Daya fussed over the flowerbeds, the stripes on the lawn, the table settings, the menu. She had checked and rechecked everything numerous times and knew her splendid house was looking just that, splendid. Raj took himself off to his study to read some papers. Iswara was upstairs blow-drying her hair. Everything was under control in the kitchen and the staff was ready. The three hosts were waiting in the hallway to welcome their guests as they arrived. Daya's friend who had lived in England was the first to arrive, followed almost immediately by Rekna and her husband. The Irish were next and were warmly welcomed and ushered onto the terrace for drinks. Citronella candles burned on the tables and on the side of the steps to keep the mosquitoes away.

'You have a magnificent home,' Barry said to Iswara. 'How did you ever swap this for that over-crowded flat in Leeson Street?'

'I never considered that a problem; besides, I loved that flat and have many happy memories of that time, of strange bodies on the floor after the parties and the cramming for exams, although I don't miss that bit of it.'

When Sanjay arrived, Iswara caught Damien's eye knowingly. The suitor, Damien surmised, and smiled back.

Over dinner, talk inevitably came around to the aid programme.

'What if it had not been tackled by our governments?' Sanjay Ranjan asked. 'They are constantly amending and bringing in new aid packages, but nothing seems to improve.'

'I agree, and what is being done is being mismanaged appallingly,' Raj said.

'I read the other day that they found grains, hundreds of tons of them, that had never been distributed. They had just been left rotting in sheds and go-downs – and there was enough to have fed hundreds of thousands,' said Sanjay.

Raj replied, 'There were other foodstuffs too that were never distributed and they've also been found in abandoned warehouses.'

'Forgive me, but wouldn't it be a good idea for the centre to get involved in food distribution?' ventured Damien.

'No, unfortunately not,' said the director. 'In an ideal world, where the problem was much smaller, it could be feasible, but we could never cope with the numbers who would arrive when word got out. It would be a logistical nightmare and impossible to administer, and we'd need storage facilities and guards.'

'There has to be some way around it,' said John.

'There won't be until everyone recognises that we have a serious problem,' said the woman who had spent several years in England. 'There is so much goodwill from a lot of the community, but a huge percentage try to pretend the problem doesn't exist. Look at how the powers that be are trying to massage the figures – they are trying to redefine what poverty is.'

'How can they do that?' asked Damien.

'One of the proposals I read,' said Raj, 'was that they were going to use a new system of evaluation of poverty. If someone has a landline telephone, or they have a house with three or more rooms, no matter how many share them, or whether they are working or not, they will be deemed to be "un-poor", if there is such a word. That will take a huge number out of the system, but will effectively change nothing.'

'It's just a new way of presenting the statistics,' the director said. 'But for some politicians, it will make it look as though they have actually done something to alleviate the awful poverty and to justify their re-election.'

'India is a rapidly developing county but we hide our problems and let people like you come in to help. That, I think, is shameful,' said Raj.

'Dear, this is not talk for the dinner table,' urged his wife. 'It's far too serious.'

'No, Daya, I disagree. It needs to be said, over and over again, until someone listens to it and takes responsibility. In the meantime, we have to be grateful and, believe me we really are, to people like you John, Damien, Barry and Clem for being so unselfish with your time.'

'Trust me, and I think I speak for all of us,' said Damien looking around the table, 'we will get more from this than we will give. Look at tonight. I never thought we'd see such wonderful food and such gracious hospitality. Thank you.'

The others agreed and the conversations moved on to other topics.

Daya was looking at Damien intently, as though suddenly noticing him. She smiled and bowed in acknowledgement when he returned her gaze, but she continued her scrutiny, unnerving him slightly.

When he got back to his room that night, Damien sent an email to Irene and Beatrice.

Ladies, I hope you're well.
I've just enjoyed a wonderful night at a dinner with an Indian family, in their very

111

opulent home in the suburbs, quite close to Juhu Beach, which I am told is where several of the Bollywood stars have their homes. However, this was not a modern flash money sort of house but a traditional colonial one. 'Oozing character and period features' I believe is how The Irish Times would describe it.

There were fourteen of us seated around an enormous table and I'm sure there were at least fourteen different dishes. We were served by what seemed like a small army of servants and the food just kept coming, to be replaced with another dish as soon as we had sampled the previous one. Although I recognised some of the names of the dishes from my limited knowledge of Indian menus in Dublin, nothing tasted even remotely like it does over there. Maybe I should take a few cookery lessons while I'm here and cook something for you both when I get back!

The rest of the gang arrive tomorrow and will be starting work on-site on Monday. I plan to take them on a sightseeing tour of Dharavi (the huge shanty area close to us and the project), where thousands live. I've done it before, but feel it will give us all a better understanding of why we are here in the first place.

Talk about contrasts, but if I were to sum

up my overall impressions of the place this time around – it would have to be intriguing, frustrating, smelly and puzzling!
Cheers
Damien

CHAPTER 11

A week after the dinner party, AA was caught up with several problems. It was eleven o'clock and the cement delivery, promised for first thing that morning, had failed to arrive. He went to phone the supplier only to discover that his mobile was dead and when he plugged it in to charge, the electricity supply had been hit by an outage, one of several every day it seemed. The medical centre had an emergency generator and he decided to go in there to charge his phone. There was no sign of Iswara as he walked by the waiting queue, sitting in the shade of a makeshift lean-to. It only ran half the length of the yard outside the centre, providing some respite for those who had made it that far on the ever-lengthening chain of arrivals that snaked along the muddy road. He left his phone with the receptionist, who was called Bina.

She was an attractive young woman from the neighbourhood, and she had frequently tried to catch his eye as she passed the site. She always wore her hair parted in the middle, and today she was wearing a turquoise sari with bands of cerise along the edge of the fabric. She promised to bring his phone back across to him when it was charged. AA had noticed Bina a few times and had admired the grace and poise with which she moved, but he was a little disappointed that he hadn't met Iswara on his visit. She had stopped frequenting the site hut at lunchtimes and he had to admit to himself that, futile as such thoughts were, he had started to look forward to their little exchanges. He admired Damien, a man of education and standing who seemed to be on an equal footing with everyone. Damien was a Christian, but that didn't stop him being accepted by most people. Somehow, despite his education, being a Muslim in India seemed to be a much bigger transgression. AA often wished things could be different. In discussion with Clem and Damien, he often voiced such opinions, opinions that he couldn't discuss so openly with his compatriots.

'Do you ever wish you had been born somewhere else?' he asked Clem. 'Into a different religion or culture?'

'No, Ireland is grand for me. And as regards religion, it's pretty liberal and easy going these days. My grandparents would have been much more conservative and driven by the rules of the Catholic Church. All that's changed now, thankfully, and despite getting into a right mess over money, the banks and clerical scandals, we have things pretty good back there. If I could change anything else though I'd like a bit more sunshine.'

'I'd change so many things about my life if I could, but I'm enough of a realist to know I can't.'

'You don't have it so bad here, AA.'

'It's just that there are so many social taboos. Falling in love in India should come with a government warning.'

'Surely it's not that bad,' Clem replied.

'It's worse, believe me,' said AA. 'It's a miracle if you get the creed right, never mind the caste. That's why the mothers get so involved. They erect something of a sari security belt around their offspring to make sure they don't stray,' he explained, 'and it stops undesirables getting in too.'

'Are you speaking from experience, or is there a bit of wishful thinking involved?'

'Wishful thinking – always wishful thinking!' he smiled, a broad carefree smile. 'Here we are, a few miles from the centre of Bollywood, and here I am, waiting to be discovered, become a star and then a multimillionaire. Instead, I'm sitting in a rat-infested site, where the arrival of a cement delivery is the highlight of the morning: that and waiting for the power to come back on. Could life be any better than that?'

They laughed.

Beatrice told Irene about her thoughts on moving and Irene, being her usual organised self, grabbed a paper napkin and started making calculations.

'How much can you afford? What will your flat fetch? How much did you pay for it?'

116

'Steady on. I just said I was thinking about it!'

'I know, but it helps to have your facts right there in black and white.'

'Mum bought the flat when I was a kid, when my grandfather died, and she rented it out for years. She let me have it after I graduated and I rent it from her, for a song. She always said she'd keep that rent and put it towards buying a bigger home of my own, but I can manage without that. My grandfather left me a few bob too.'

'Lucky sod. My mortgage costs a fortune.'

Shortly after this conversation Beatrice popped in to see her mother one day.

'I think I've decided to move.'

'I thought you loved your flat.'

'I do, but . . .'

'What brought this on? I hope it's not because of that Paul fellow.'

'No it's not, but in a way he made me look at my life anew.'

'Well, I suppose that's as good a reason as any,' Mary laughed. 'Where are you going to look? And will you go for a flat or a house?'

'I really don't know, but I will when I see it. I'm going to view both. I quite like the idea of having a garden of my own and a big kitchen and some-where for my music.'

'But can't you store all that on a few memory sticks now?'

'I know I can, but I like my CDs and, besides,

they remind me of where and when I got them so I've no intentions of ever getting rid of them.'

'I can understand that. I still have some of your granddad's old vinyl records and all his cassettes.'

'Mum, don't tell me I'm turning into you. You have more possessions than God!'

Beatrice was enjoying a rare occurrence – a lull in her workload. It was too late in the day to start on another case, so she decided to write an email to Damien, including Irene too, as he had done with his.

Hi Damien

Summer is here – it's cold and windy and the sun has decided to ration us to about a twenty-minute blast every morning and afternoon. Some optimistic people have just walked into St Stephen's Green in flip-flops and t-shirts. Do we never learn?

Maybe I need a change of scenery . . .

How are you settling in? Are you making friends over there and how is work progressing?

That meal sounds amazing. Irene and I can't wait to taste your culinary efforts when you get back. Do you cook normally or is this a new interest?

Take care
Beatrice

As she wrote, she realised she knew absolutely nothing about him, apart from the fact that he was a Dean of Students at one of the colleges of medicine and that he was very conscientious about his responsibilities. She found she wanted to know more, but drew the line at quizzing Irene. Much as she loved Irene, she knew her friend would never be able to keep that to herself. She'd be sure to blab it to his sister and probably to him too. And she didn't want either of them to know she'd been asking. Irene's relationship with him was a very laid-back one and she assured Beatrice that there had never been anything romantic between them. Their parents had been good friends and they had all spent summers in their vans in Brittas Bay, went to teenage discos together, had midnight feasts and cider parties in the sand dunes and generally got up to all the adolescent rites of passage, and they had remained very close friends. Beatrice envied her that. Since her debacle with Paul she shied away from meeting new people. Getting to know someone again on an intimate level just seemed too much like hard work.

Yet, next morning she was delighted to find a reply from Mumbai.

Hi Beatrice
   I've abandoned any hope of going to sleep. It's 12.30 and the humidity is un-believable. I've spent the last twenty minutes doing battle with a single pesky

mosquito who refuses to die, despite me dive bombing her several times with neat Deet. (Since coming here I've been told that only the females bite – I'm not sure if that is true!) Her friends have all succumbed, so it's down to a one-to-one shootout, but if I squirt any more of the damned stuff in the room I'll pass out before she does. What an inglorious end that would be!

That sounds full of self-pity, which it's not meant to, but it's hard not to be overwhelmed when you see the scale of the problems over here and there's me moaning about a mosquito with a death sentence over her head!

The rest of the Irish arrived earlier this week and I took them to visit the dumps today. What an experience that was. There are several that surround us on the site, although to me it looks like one continuous area. Even though I had been to some before it still shocks me to see them at close quarters – acres and acres of rotting rubbish, as far as the eye can see, and countless people foraging for whatever might be salvageable or recyclable. Some of the kids look exhausted and underfed, their mothers even more so. You see old men – although I wonder if they are old or if they just appear so from their hard life – struggling under bundles of rags and bags of tin cans and scrap metal. Most are bent over and emaciated. These places are breeding grounds for all sorts of disease and contamination and I'm sure mosquitoes are the least of their worries . . .

I was astonished at the variety of enterprises that seem to flourish in the back streets of the ghettos. We came across tanners, bakeries, barbers, people making everything from pottery to poppadoms and in the midst of all this you have women doing hand embroidery and men, mostly men, selling foodstuffs from little roadside carts.

We were shown the largest outdoor laundry in the world, or so they claim. It's called Dhobi Ghat and it's where most of the linens from the hotels are sent to be washed. It's so vast, it's difficult to describe, but the attached pic should give you an idea of the scale of the operation.

On a cheerier note, I love the sounds and sights of this city. It's so colourful and it was amazing to see the other side of the coin at that dinner party. Apparently, this city has its fair share of millionaires, but then as it's the most densely populated one in India and the financial capital too, that shouldn't surprise me.

And yes, I love cooking, and am truly amazed at the variety of foods here. My beloved sis Rachel, whom you met at the quiz, gave me a cookery course for Christmas some years back and I got hooked on it. As a man for whom no meal is complete without a good serving of meat, I'm surprised at how easily vegetarian dishes are beginning to tempt me.

What about you? What's happening in your life?

Cheers

Damien

Beatrice was pleased that this time the address bar only showed her name and not Irene's as well. She'd wait until tomorrow to reply. She smiled to herself as she rang down for the first case to be sent up to her.

CHAPTER 12

AA hadn't noticed that the receptionist, who had charged his phone for him, was paying a little too much attention to the comings and goings in the site office. Bina always seemed to be about when he arrived and when he finished in the evenings. She had a brother who was one of the labourers working with them and it seemed as though she needed to speak to him an awful lot, necessitating AA's permission to go on site. To do this, she needed to be kitted out in a hard hat and a high visibility jacket, both of which were to be found on a table behind AA's desk.

AA had been unaware of this pattern: it was Clem who mentioned it to him when they were talking one evening. Since then, he had definitely got vibes from this young woman, vibes of a predatory nature. Meanwhile, he found himself looking out for Iswara's arrival and departure with a degree of pleasure. He had been called on to bring her to a house call, or a galvanised hut call. The other doctors were already out on rounds when an emergency was phoned in. A mother had gone into premature labour and was haemorrhaging badly.

AA was in the yard when Iswara rushed out, clutching a wrapped sterile blanket, some towels and her bag in hand and asked if anyone could be spared to help her. She had meant by driving, but it turned out that he was almost a midwife at the birth, which took place shortly after he had lifted the distraught woman into the back of the pick-up. Iswara delivered the baby while AA kept a respectable distance. Then he drove the young woman and her tiny son to the nearest hospital and returned Iswara to the clinic.

'I really needed you there, AA, thank you. I'd never have managed that on my own,' she said, looking at him, and as he returned her gaze he saw she was getting embarrassed.

'Of course you could,' he said. 'Second nature to you. I have to admit it was a bit of a shock for me, though, not exactly the sort of problem I come across every day.'

It was late when they got back. Damien was just leaving the site when Iswara spotted him.

'You're in danger of losing your foreman – he may have a career in medicine,' she called. 'I'm about to make the biggest pot of tea ever. Why don't you both join me?' she asked. Without hesitation they followed her inside. An hour later, they were still talking. Damien explained how he knew Iswara as a fledgling student and she recounted how kind he had been to her, advising her on where she should live and where she should avoid and how he had arranged for her to take some of her exams late when her grandfather died. It seemed to AA they knew each other quite well, and again it hit home to him at just how constrained his countrymen were when it came to social interaction.

The next morning, Bina was hovering again as AA arrived.

'I baked some cakes last night. Would you like some?'

He wanted to say no: it seemed churlish to refuse but he felt that by accepting he was giving the wrong message to her. He wasn't interested in her: she clearly was in him. He smiled and said, 'I'm sure my colleagues in the site office will love these. They are developing quite a taste for your treats and sweets.'

Clem, who had seen this exchange through the window, winked at him as he approached, and muttered: 'I told you so!'

'She's not my type,' AA replied. 'What about you?

'I am happily single and intend to stay that way, thank you very much!' he said. 'And she's not my type either!'

The director came in a while later to see how they were getting on.

'Well, despite the heat, you seem to be progressing very well here. Acclimatising and all that.'

Damien answered, 'I've given up trying to stay cool. Nothing works. I'm losing more sweat than

I can replace with water in a day. My t-shirts are soaking the minute after I put them on, yet you manage to look cool and fresh in a shirt and tie. What's the secret?

'I suppose it's what you're used to. I just came across to say that my wife and I would like to invite you and your compatriots to a small garden party at the weekend. We can arrange transport and as we live beside the coast I can guarantee a little breeze and probably lots of rain too. AA, I do hope you will come along too. You seem to have become an honorary Irishman at this stage,' he joked.

'It would be my great pleasure, thank you,' AA replied.

For the first time in over a week, Iswara came across to the hut at lunchtime.

'Have you recovered from the excitement of yesterday yet?' she asked AA.

'Well, it certainly was different from counting bricks and lengths of piping,' he laughed. 'Any word from the hospital since?'

'Yes, they are both doing really well. Thank you again.'

'Your work is so much more rewarding than what I do.'

'On the contrary,' she said, 'what you are doing is going to make a huge difference to us and to the lives of many. With new classrooms we can teach the children how to read and write, computer skills even. Practically all of their mothers are illiterate and they can never hope to progress out of the poverty they are born into without an education. It is the only way the new generations can hope to achieve anything. You could not have got your job and I could not have got mine if we didn't know how to write our names, yet we take it for granted because it's just something we do automatically. We have to make sure the children coming along become as familiar with it as we were, and only then will it cease to be a huge hurdle.'

AA agreed and told her he was actually studying in the evenings for a degree in IT.

'But you have an engineering degree.'

'Yes, but when I qualified computer studies were only beginning to be taken seriously. I don't think anyone realised how big they would become – I know I didn't. So I've decided to catch up.'

The receptionist passed by them on her way back after lunch. She stopped to enquire if the cakes had been eaten.

'They went down a bomb,' said Clem, emerging from behind the waist-high wall his team was working on.

She looked puzzled. 'Does that mean you liked them?' she asked tentatively.

Iswara laughed. 'That means they were great! Did I miss out? I didn't get any.'

'No,' said Clem, 'they were only for us.'

There was a slight pause. AA thought Iswara was going to say something else, but instead she looked at her watch and said, 'Now I better get back to making some impact on this queue.' Then she added to AA, 'I believe I'll be seeing you on Sunday.'

He nodded and he watched her walk back across to the clinic with Bina.

Hi Beatrice

How are you? Is that boyfriend still popping up uninvited in your life? If so, I can give you a few tips on how to shift him when I get home!

We're getting on really well with work here, despite the obstacles. It's getting easier to follow what everyone is saying to us, and I think they are finding us easier to understand too.

I had dinner with a former student, or should I say graduate, of mine last night. It's kind of strange socialising on a one-to-one basis with her after knowing her for so long. More strange foods and ethnic music. Still getting used to it all!

The director and his wife have invited us en masse to his house for a garden party tomorrow. He's organised a bus so that takes the hassle out of getting there. Not sure if I told you the traffic here defies description, so I avoid driving as much as I can. It's commonplace to see whole families on mopeds – with their shopping too. They look like human club sand-wiches – child, mother, child, father and another child on the handlebars, putt-putting along beside trucks, motorbikes, rickshaws and buses, that and the cows, the dogs, the odd stray goat and the smell of exhaust fumes – it's mental!

I forgot to add that the trains run on tracks through the city, sometimes parallel to this mayhem and mostly with no platforms or anything to protect pedestrians. At rush hour, which seems to be all the time, there are people hanging on at the openings and clinging to anything that gives them purchase. They even clamber on to the roofs of the carriages, which all look as though they have seen better days. It's one way to keep cool, I suppose. I'll have to go on a journey on one of these before I go back – not the roof – the train I mean.

What's the news at home?

Cheers

Damien

CHAPTER 13

There was no letting up. Sunday was another sticky hot day, with menacing clouds threatening rain as AA arrived at the apartments where the volunteers were now staying, but the rain held off. As promised, the bus pulled up on time and they all piled in. The traffic was as mad and chaotic as always and it took about an hour and a half to reach the house.

They were welcomed warmly by the director and his wife. Iswara, her parents, and her sister and husband were already there. A manservant showed them through to the garden where a marquee had been set up, overlooking the sea. Other servants stood around with silver trays holding an assortment of fruit drinks and cordials. Flowers blossomed everywhere in neatly edged borders and some trees, which Damien could not identify, were blowing gently. *A breeze*, he thought. *Thank God, a breeze!* He waved at Iswara and her parents and started off in their direction. He was side-tracked, introducing the latest comers to their host's wife. Clem spotted Iswara and made straight for her, a large pineapple drink in hand.

130

'I never know whether to expect alcohol in houses here,' Clem muttered to Iswara.

'It depends on your hosts. Some people never touch or serve it. Others will offer it to guests and abstain themselves, while there are lots and lots who both drink and serve it.' Then she added, 'I'll be surprised if there is none here today.'

'I can manage without, Iswara,' he laughed. 'I'm not a total alcoholic, you know. Those carousing medical student days are fast becoming distant memories.'

'Well, we all did enough of it back then, and yet I seldom touch it now. It's kind of frightening in a way to be grown up and responsible. When we were doing internships in the hospitals, even though we got to make decisions, there was always someone else higher than us who was ultimately in charge. I miss that cushion.'

'I know what you mean. When I joined the GP practice I was terrified and, I have to admit, I'm terrified about going back because I'll have my own patient list, and not someone else's – that is if anyone comes to me!'

'Stop looking for compliments! You were always swamped with adoring patients wanting the gorgeous Dr Clem to look after them. I suspect you'll probably poach several patients from the others in the practice too.'

'That would be a great way to make enemies.'

Iswara's mother had been watching this exchange from a distance and decided to join in, with her husband in tow. Clem recognised them. 'Hello again, Dr and Mrs Singhanid. Isn't this lovely?'

'Did I hear you say you are going into general practice?' she enquired. 'That's what Iswara's father and I had hoped for her, but our headstrong daughter had other plans.'

Iswara knew that was certainly not what they had hoped. In fact, she distinctly remembered her mother asking her, 'So where exactly do you want to work? In some general practice where you'll sit dispensing prescriptions all day long?'

'We like headstrong women,' Clem answered. 'Men like us need a firm hand to keep us on the straight and narrow. Isn't that right, Damien?'

'Then you'll get on well with my wife as well as my daughter,' Raj said.

Iswara just smiled at Damien and beckoned AA to join them.

'Mama, Papa, this is Abdul-Razzaq Mahimkar, better known to all of us as AA. He's the structural engineer on the new project. And Papa, he's an avid follower of cricket. AA this is my sister, Rekna.'

'Very pleased to met you,' Raj said. 'Iswara tells me work is progressing very well.'

'Yes. AA keeps them all under control, except for Bina,' Iswara said mischievously, looking at Damien.

Damien raised his eyebrows and laughed. 'Yes, except for Bina.'

'And who is this Bina?' asked Rekna.

'She's our receptionist and she has plans for AA, but so far he's managed to frustrate them,' said Damien.

'Romance in the workplace – I think that's never a good idea,' Mrs Singhanid said.

'That's what I feel too,' said AA, 'and don't believe a word of what your daughter is suggesting. There's no truth in it at all.'

The conversation veered to cricket and Mrs Singhanid made off to talk to someone else.

Hi Damien

I too was invited to a garden party, if you could call it that, today. Irene decided to have some friends over, and, as usual in this country, it was all very last minute because with our weather we can never really plan these things with any certainty.

Of course she had an ulterior motive – she's determined to get me hitched up to one of her friends. Says it's time I moved on. They say God loves a trier and if that's true she should get a medal for her efforts. She's even trying to get me to join the golf club and she had wheeled, or should I say rolled, out several of her golfing friends and acquaintances to join the campaign! Now I love sport, but golf leaves me cold. It takes up so much time and I have so many other things to do at weekends. I don't mind playing, but it's when I have to listen to a diatribe about how they all played, what their handicaps are, the difficulty of getting tee times and all that, that's when my eyes glaze over. I get tempted to start talking about something equally as fascinating, like knitting, to see how they'd react if I started by telling them how many stitches I cast on, where I dropped one, forgot to increase before doing a few ktbls and yarn forwards for a twisted cable. See I bet you're dozing already! Anyway, I suppose, from Irene's point of view, this afternoon was a complete disaster, but I enjoyed the food and the wine and we did have a good laugh!

I'm dying to hear how your garden party went. Was it very exotic? Who was there and what did you eat?

And yes, in answer to your question, that former boyfriend of mine is still popping up uninvited from time to time. It's difficult to ban him completely; as you probably don't know, he's one of the sports anchors on national television and unless I impose a blanket ban on watching it, I have to learn to live with his occasional unwelcome and unexpected visits.

Have to sign off now and get sorted for work tomorrow.

Take care

Beatrice

Damien had noticed that AA and Iswara were becoming very friendly. No longer just exchanging pleasantries as they passed each other, they always had time for a chat and a joke. He wasn't exactly jealous, but he'd felt himself getting closer to her as time went by. He loved watching her move with such grace, elegance and poise, her long glossy hair plaited to one side or centred right down her back. On the few occasions they'd met away from work, she'd been wearing it loose. He was taking her to dinner the following Wednesday and was looking forward to some time with her again, away from all the others. He'd ask her about AA then, and if she was interested in him. As a dean, he had always managed to keep the tutor–student distance between them, but now there was no reason why he could not get to know her better. She seemed willing too.

He booked a table in a restaurant Iswara had recommended and arranged to meet her there. The venue was dimly lit with coloured lanterns, and some traditional Indian music was being provided by a trio who smiled at them as they moved to their table. The menu was full of unfamiliar dishes and he suggested that she should choose for him.

'What's it like to be back home again?' Damien asked her, when they had that task out of the way.

'It's great, but I have to admit that I miss some things, especially the friends I made.'

'We're lucky we live in an age of email. It's so much easier to keep in touch.'

'My father still gets longhand letters from some of his college mates who are scattered around the world.'

'That's a dying art. So, tell me, is your mother still trying to marry you off?'

'She'll never stop until I have a wedding ring on my finger,' she laughed. 'She had you in her sights after that night in our house and I noticed she was even eyeing Clem up on Sunday to see if he was suitable material for a son-in-law.'

'And did he measure up?' asked Damien.

'Yes, at this stage he would be very acceptable, but I love him like a brother. We've had great times together as students and I can see him always being my friend, but no more.'

'What about AA? You two seem to have become very matey.'

'Now he's a definite no-no!'

'Why so definite? He's sound.'

'I know that, but culturally it would never be acceptable.'

'Why ever not? He's cultured, educated and great fun.'

'And he's Muslim.'

'Would that matter?'

'Definitely. Marrying outside our faith is just not on the agenda. You've heard of the caste system. Well to marry outside our caste is one thing, to marry a Muslim would mean a woman could never attend her family gatherings, weddings or celebrations ever again – she effectively would be making herself an outcast from her family and friends. It would be social death for her.'

'But surely attitudes are changing?'

'Not in my family.'

'What would happen if you did decide to marry a Muslim?'

'I'd be disinherited and if I had children they'd probably never see their grandparents or cousins. It would be the same for the man. I would never be accepted by a Muslim family and he would be disinherited too, so you'd be virtually isolated from everyone.'

'That sounds rather harsh – and a very high price to pay for love.'

'It is, but we grow up knowing that, so it's easier to avoid such situations. That's partly why Indian families are so close knit – to avoid such disasters.'

'And I thought I knew what bigotry meant.'

'Believe me, Damien,' she said, 'you don't. Some Hindu believers would ostracise me now because I work with the lower castes and the untouchables.'

'But surely doctors have to do that.'

'I know that, and so do the more enlightened people of all beliefs, but old habits and prejudices are difficult to break. Everyone here wants to keep their position or better it, if possible. It goes against our culture to move down the pecking order.'

'It's very difficult for an outsider to understand.'

'I know,' she smiled.

'But do you like AA, in that way, I mean?'

She hesitated for a fraction and he knew he had touched a nerve. 'No! Yes, I don't know. It would be impossible anyway.'

He said nothing for a few seconds and then changed the subject.

They ate their way through several dishes, discussing the food, the project, their co-workers, and Damien was sorry when it was time to part. He really liked Iswara. 'Am I allowed kiss you in public?'

'Better not to.'

'Another social taboo?' he asked.

'Afraid so,' she laughed.

'We'll have to find somewhere more private next time.'

He took her hand and kissed it. He stood looking after her as her father's driver collected her and she waved goodnight from the car.

The next day he saw AA and Iswara, deep in conversation, laughing and looking very comfortable together. He also saw Bina looking on disapprovingly from the little barred window in the medical centre. It wasn't the first time Damien had spotted her watching AA.

CHAPTER 14

Hi Beatrice

I'm glad I won't have to deal with that errant boyfriend for you. And I agree with Irene – it is time you moved on – but golf – that's not my favourite pastime either. I heard two guys talking one day at a conference and one asked the other if he played and his reply was, 'No, I still enjoy sex!' Need I say any more?

I like your knitting idea too. Don't know if I'd get away with it though.

The garden party was exotic. The venue was amazing and everyone, especially the women, always manage to look so serene and composed while we are all melting, sweating and tossed looking all the time. Maybe if I stay here long enough I'll get used to the climate too, but that's not happening yet.

The food at the garden party was terrific. We'd expected to be served some spicy canapés and a few drinks, so we tucked in with gusto as the first plates were passed about. The director and his wife seemed to have a team of servants manning refreshment stations all around their enormous garden. The house itself smacked of colonial charm and serious dosh. I was dying to ask if the servants were all a permanent part of the household, or had just been hired in for the afternoon, but I daren't. They just kept appearing with more and more platters of all kinds of food and we did it justice, I can tell you. No beef or pork, but they certainly know how to make magic with vegetables.

I'm finding it hard to reconcile the poverty and the contrasts, even though I've been before and knew what to expect. The smells are pretty bad and constant and they take some getting used to. We have to pass through a huge area of slum dwellings on the fringe of the dumps coming to and from work, so it's impossible to avoid seeing how the other half really lives. There are emaciated dogs, rats and birds scavenging alongside the little kids, and the filth and stench are unbelievable.

It's all very grounding, especially when you see the contrasts as we are being allowed to. Our hosts had invited several of their friends along on Sunday. These were all well heeled and affluent, and with lifestyles that are so far removed from the people we meet and see every day. We were actually invited to use the tennis courts at one of their friend's houses while we are here!

The director has a string of letters after his name and could command an enormous salary if he worked in the private hospital. I believe he still does some consultancy work elsewhere, but he chose to be the driving force behind the clinic and now of its expansion and I really admire him for that.

Anyway, enough of me rabbiting on.
Cheers
Damien

Hi Damien

You paint a great picture of things over there. I'd love to see inside some of those grand houses with servants and fabulous gardens – they always look so magnificent in films. But like you, I'm both appalled and fascinated, and whilst things are not that bad here, our fat cats managed to have four-wheel drives with the latest registrations sitting outside their primary residences and their holiday homes abroad, not to mention the helicopters to impress their friends when the races were on, while they had no conscience about robbing the country.

I suppose human nature is the same the

world over, and the more people I meet in this job with problems created by overlords and crooked politicians, the more I realise how lucky I am.

The economists are always spouting off about how we all own the banks now; I'd just like to know which one is mine! I won a fiver on the lottery at the weekend. I spent €4 on a quick pick plus, so I'm up a euro. I'm trying to decide where to invest it for the best return.

We're madly busy here – some unfounded report about proposed changes in the legislation regarding non-national parents with children born in this jurisdiction appeared in one of the papers. It made it to radio and has caused a tidal wave of enquiries, and as happens every time there's a whiff of change, even though most never come to anything, we are swamped with applicants and appeals. We'll be working late all week.

I've a student in on work experience too, and he's working out really well. He's actually interested in the clients and their lives, while Irene's one just sits there looking as though she'd rather be anywhere else!

Have the mossies stopped eating you?

Coffee break over now – must fly.

Take care

Beatrice

AA found himself arriving a little early to ensure he was at work before Iswara, in the hope of waylaying her and having a chat. He knew this was going nowhere, but he had never been attracted to any woman as he was to her. The tilt of her head, the way she seemed to glide along in her slippered feet, her smile, the gentle way she talked to the patients who were always waiting no matter how early she arrived – everything about her had him captivated. He'd also seen her pass her lunch box to a patient one day. Since the garden party, he had become even more smitten. She had spent a lot of time talking to him and he felt a real bond with her.

She stopped by the office as she left each evening, lingering and chatting to her former colleagues, arranging to meet them for drinks sometimes and dropping off antihistamines for bites and potions for stomach upsets, which had bothered most of them already, some more than once. AA knew she had gone out with Damien a few times too, and wondered if Damien was seriously interested in her or if it was just friendship because of their shared past and friends.

Bina continued to bring him offerings – sweets made with curds, ghee and jiggery, which was a type of cane sugar. She never addressed any of the others who happened to be in the vicinity when she came in, instead she made straight for AA's desk and it was obvious she'd been watching out to make sure he was there first. He and Clem had devised a plan and if Clem or Damien saw her approaching they began to whistle, at which point AA picked up the hands-free phone and started talking, or he grabbed some papers or plans and walked with intent towards the far end of the site.

Today, he met Bina as she approached the doorway. She greeted him and said, 'I baked some treats for you.'

He replied, 'You seem intent on fattening me up.'

'A good woman must always feed her man.'

This, he decided, had gone far enough and needed to be addressed.

'Bina, we need to talk. Come back into the office.'

She smiled, a gap-toothed smile, and walked over to a chair where she perched herself. He moved some papers aside and sat on the edge of his desk looking down at her.

'Bina, I cannot keep taking gifts from you like this.'

'Why ever not? I like making them – for you.'

'And I like eating them, but it's not right. It's giving the wrong impression and saying things like you just did about a woman feeding her man in front of the others is definitely misleading. I am not, and will never be, your man,' he said slowly and deliberately.

'You could be, if you wanted to be,' she said seductively.

'You are a lovely girl, but I am not interested in you in that way.'

'But you have no wife yet, and I could be the one for you. My brother told me you are free.'

'Well, he was wrong. I mean I am free, but there is someone in my life,' he lied. 'So I must ask you to stop bringing in these gifts.'

Bina's eyes filled up. The tears seemed to hover for a second or two on the lower rims before trickling down her olive cheeks. She bent her head and he felt himself feeling sorry for her. It had taken courage for her to declare herself like that. He leaned forward and took her hand, thinking he had been unnecessarily cruel to her. 'Bina, there are lots of men out there who would give anything to have someone like you in their lives, so don't waste your time on me. Find someone more suitable.'

'I think you are.'

'I'm not, I assure you, and as I said there is someone waiting for me when I move on from here,' he lied again.

After a few minutes, when she had composed herself, he stood up and walked before her to the door and she headed back to work in the clinic.

A few days later, he was checking on the work that had been done that day. He was standing on a makeshift bamboo ladder talking to Damien, who was laying breeze blocks on the level above, when one of the rungs snapped. He grabbed the precarious scaffolding but slipped, catching his arm on one of the bolted fastenings that protruded from the supports. It ripped his flesh and Damien shouted at the workers to go and get one of the doctors.

AA was bleeding profusely and the local workers who hadn't left had closed in to see what had happened. Clem, who had been on the scaffolding farther down the building, jumped the last five feet. 'Jaysus! Don't move him. He may have broken something. We need to stop the bleeding. Get someone from the clinic quick,' he ordered.

Iswara and Dr Patel came as soon as they were alerted, followed by Bina.

'Let's get you inside and clean you up. It looks like it could do with some stitches,' Dr Patel said.

Iswara held a dressing in place over the long cut while Damien and Clem helped AA to his feet and together they walked him slowly across the yard. Bina fussed, trying to follow them into Iswara's room. Iswara told her she wasn't needed.

'I can cope now; besides, AA will need to lie down for a little while after he is treated and we will see that he gets home safely.'

Bina left reluctantly.

Iswara cleaned the wound, gave him a local anaesthetic and Clem assisted as she put fifteen stitches along the injury. Despite his discomfort, AA couldn't take his eyes off Iswara as she worked, coolly, efficiently and professionally.

'How are you feeling now?' Damien asked. He had been hovering, avoiding looking at the procedure. Ironically, blood always made him queasy.

'Not bad at all, considering. I feel a bit of a fool really.'

'It could have happened to anyone. I've never trusted those bamboo ladders and I'll be even more wary after this,' said Damien.

Iswara said, 'You should lie there for a bit. I'm just going to make some tea. You lost a good bit of blood, so don't go thinking you are Superman. You'll feel a bit woozy when you stand up. And I don't want to see you in here tomorrow and when you come back next week it's only to do desk work, until I say otherwise.'

'You're very bossy,' he grinned. 'I'm sorry to be such a nuisance, just at the end of your day. I see I've ruined your white coat and your sari too.'

'That's an occupational hazard and they'll wash. Anyway I always keep a change here. And it's not as though you planned it, is it?' she asked with a smile.

Some time later, Damien, Clem and Iswara saw AA home to the high-rise apartment block.

The next day, Bina was full of enquiries. Could she visit AA? Perhaps he'd need food? Should she go and check on him in her lunch break? She tried to wheedle his address out of Damien and Clem in turn. Both had warned everyone to withhold it from her. She was not very happy and complained to Iswara. When Iswara told her she'd be making a house call to him later on, that made her even madder. Bina banged things on her desk, was rude to patients and sat scowling all morning. When it came to lunchtime she complained of a stomach ache and said she needed to go home. She asked Iswara if she could drop her off after she visited AA, but Iswara knew what she was after. She went to the medicine chest in the storeroom, took a packet of antacids from a shelf, locked up and brought them out to the site where she went in search of Damien.

'Decoy medicine,' she whispered and told him the story.

'The things I do for you,' he laughed.

A few minutes later, he walked into the clinic and, directing his question to the waiting patients and Bina, he asked if any of them knew where the address he had scribbled on a scrap of paper was. Bina said she did and so did Dr Patel, who just emerged from his room. Dr Patel suggested she go in the pick-up with Damien to show him. 'It's right beside your home, Bina, and I believe you were going to be away this afternoon anyway,' Dr Patel said. 'What a happy coincidence.' Bina had been outwitted. Furious, she gathered her things and left with Damien for the short ride home.

Hi Beatrice

I hope your workload is easing up a little. We had a bit of excitement yesterday. Our chief engineer, whom we all call AA, had a bit of an accident. You should see the building sites over here. Bamboo scaffolding, often held together with rope. I passed one the other day where the women in their long skirts were carrying bags of cement – on their heads – up ladders and along these makeshift structures two and three levels up! As for protective clothing!

One of our doctors who was a student of mine in Dublin (I think I mentioned her before) patched AA up. He needed a number of stitches and although there are loads of docs among the volunteers, she was still on duty and had all the necessary supplies on hand when it happened. Our guys just gave advice!

AA's a great guy, but he's being pursued by a young one in the office in the clinic and he spends his time trying to avoid her! We've all taken to whistling 'The Fields of Athenry' whenever she's around to warn him to hide.

Still fighting the mossies – they love us.
How's the love life?
Cheers
Damien

Hi Damien
Well life certainly seems to be anything but dull over there. That lady doc who studied here must be delighted to have you all out there. Did she know many of

the guys who are with you? I hope your friend will be all right after his ordeal.

I ended up having to work on Saturday, but I went on a date that evening. I don't know which was worse. Talk about boring – this guy had the biggest yawn factor effect I have ever come across. The only exciting thing about him was his iPhone cover and that was like a car tyre!

In keeping with that theme, he likes mud plugging of all things (how do I pick them?) and he couldn't understand why I turned down a second date after he said he was going to show me how to do 'scrutineering' at some time trials somewhere. He said it was difficult to find people to do that. I wonder why! I found my time with him trial enough not to want to prolong it. Besides, whilst I don't expect gourmet dining at every date, I do draw the line at wellies and wet gear on a second one. I like a little romance in my life.

Irene thinks I'm far too fussy . . .

The summer is dragging here, mainly because I didn't take a spring break this year because we've a family wedding coming up in Malta and there's a whole gang of us going over for a couple of weeks. Hopefully we'll get some sun, as it's been abysmal here for the last week. However, I'm heading to Galway with a schoolfriend for the long weekend and an extra day and am hugely looking forward to the break.

Take care
Beatrice

CHAPTER 15

Six weeks had already passed. The new centre had its shell erected and they were starting on the roof that day. Deliveries were made as they were needed because, despite the security fences and locks, materials had a habit of going missing if they were left on site overnight. The building was taking shape and you could see where the classrooms would be; one of the larger ones had the capacity of doubling up as a canteen and would be fitted with cooking facilities along one side. This area could be partitioned off to make a smaller room where mothers could learn to cook or have classes when their children were at theirs. It could also be opened into a bigger space to make a small hall for other activities. The shower blocks, one for the boys and another for the girls, were at the opposite ends. The girls' block was almost double in size, because at the director's suggestion, it also had facilities for babies. The intention was that parents could also use the showers when they brought their children to school.

The director had explained to the volunteers how the centre would be run. 'Most of the people using this centre have no running water in their shacks and shelters. They have learned what little they know about hygiene from their own mothers, who were even poorer than they are. If we can teach them all some basic rules and awareness, that will cut down on infection and on infant mortality and other illnesses. The next vital step is to teach the children to read and write, otherwise they have no hope of ever getting out of the mire they were born into. It's such a huge task; it seems impossible, and at times I wonder what difference a small project like this will make, and then I realise that it will make all the difference in the world to those it will touch. As the old English proverb goes: "Large streams from little fountains flow; tall oaks from little acorns grow." So we have to believe we are making something important grow here.'

Damien and his crew would not be around to see the building finished. Twenty of them would be leaving together in two weeks, with just five staying on longer to assist the locals, but they had been there long enough already to see a muddy bit of derelict ground become transformed, albeit into a muddy building site, but one with promise, where before it had none.

Damien knew he'd miss Iswara. The pair had become close and they enjoyed their evenings out together – sometimes with some of the other Irish and colleagues from the clinic, sometimes just the two of them. He liked her, more than a lot, but was realistic enough to know that he had his job to go home to – and there was always Beatrice to get to know better. He smiled at that thought. No one on the horizon for ages and then, like the buses, two come along together.

Iswara checked regularly to ensure that AA didn't overuse his injured arm, now that he was back at work. The day he was due to have his stitches out, she noticed Bina arrive in with more goodies for him. She gave them to him in front of the patients who had made it to the top of the queue and were sitting on the wooden benches along one side of the reception area. Children mooched about, bored with the long wait. One little girl cried, the defeated cry of persistent hunger. Her mother looked embarrassed when she caught AA's eye. He opened the lunch box with Bina's treats and offered the contents to the little one first and then to the others around, most of whom could never afford such food, and didn't have the facilities to bake them even if they could. Their eyes shone as mothers shyly accepted the sweets, breaking them up to fit small mouths before savouring them themselves. They gushed their thanks and AA said, 'Thank that lady there – she's the cook.'

Iswara smiled as she saw Bina witnessing this transaction, who didn't look one bit pleased. She said plaintively as he passed, 'But I made those for you.'

'And I told you not to do that.' He answered firmly but quietly, going in to Iswara's room.

He closed the door firmly and they both laughed, before Iswara set about removing the dressing and then the stitches.

'Look' she said, avoiding looking directly into his green eyes. 'No harm has been done to your beauty at all. That scar will settle down and you'll hardly notice it in time. I promise it won't put the ladies off baking for you.'

'Don't even go there,' he protested. She didn't answer, as she put a light dressing over the wound. The silence was palpable. He was aware of his breathing. He could feel the tension in the room. Everything told him to leave, but he didn't. As she turned back to him, he stood up, reached out and took her hands, forcing Iswara to look at him.

'It's not my imagination, is it?' he asked.

Understanding exactly what he meant she said, 'No, it's not.'

They stood in front of each other, really looking at each other for the first time. He reached for her and hugged her, a deep warm hug that she returned. He pressed his lips to her forehead and they stood like that for what seemed an eternity before he stepped back.

'I'm sorry,' AA said. 'I hope that won't compromise your reputation.'

'No, people around here are used to me hugging my patients.'

They stood there for a few seconds, letting what had just happened sink in.

'What do we do now?' he asked.

'I don't know,' she replied.

'Think about it and we'll talk later, after work maybe.'

She nodded and held the door open for him.

'Don't go climbing yet with that arm. It's still healing, you know,' she said as she showed him out.

He nodded towards the waiting women, who smiled at him as he left, and he ignored Bina, merely gave a wave of his hand in her direction as he passed her desk. Iswara closed the door, went back to her desk and sat down for a few minutes, trying to collect her thoughts. How had this happened? She had been attracted to AA since the first day she'd met him, but now she was in dangerous territory. She had to walk away. Nothing about a friendship with him would be all right, because she knew she didn't want just a friendship. And she told herself, if she were to get involved with AA she would be cut off from her family. Her mother would never forgive her and Rekna and her boys would be told to keep away too.

The rest of the afternoon required much more concentration than usual. She knew what she had to do. Yet, when everyone had gone, she waited to see if AA would come back. He did. They went in to her office and closed the door. Neither of them saw Bina watching from the yard behind.

CHAPTER 16

Clem and Damien arrived at work the following morning to find consternation in the camp. Little knots of workers were grouped around and all seemed to stop talking as they approached. An ashen-faced AA stormed past the pair of them without a greeting. He turned and said, 'I've been dismissed', and kept walking.

Damien ran after him. 'What do you mean "dismissed"? By whom and why?'

But AA put his hand up to stop him, and he said. 'I don't want to talk about it now.' And off he strode into the pungent heat. 'I'll phone you later when I've had time to think.'

When Damien turned around again, he saw Iswara watching from her window. She didn't acknowledge him, but stepped back from view.

'What the hell is going on?' asked Clem. 'Why would he be dismissed?'

'I haven't a clue, but I'm bloody well going to find out.'

They marched off to the director's office only to be met by him coming towards them.

'Damien, Clem, we have a serious problem. Come

into my office please. We can talk there.' By now, whatever had happened had reached the patients' queue and was spreading like Chinese whispers along the line. Everyone looked concerned, even uneasy. The director told them to sit down, but he remained standing.

'It seems our foreman, AA, has made an inappropriate advance, a sexual advance, on one of the clinic's female staff, Bina, and she has made a formal complaint about him. I had no option but to dismiss him, instantly.'

'That doesn't sound like something AA would do,' Damien said, biding time. Clem agreed.

'No, I didn't think so either, but it seems as though she has a witness, who says he has been leading her on for weeks now and last night when everyone had gone, she came back to get something she had forgotten and he attacked her.'

Damien remembered AA heading towards the clinic the previous evening when he and Clem were leaving, but had thought nothing more of it.

'Have you called the police?'

'No. I don't think that will be necessary. If we do, the woman's identity will become common knowledge and she doesn't want that. She is happy with his punishment of instant dismissal.'

'But are you sure he's guilty? Has he given his side of the incident?' Clem asked, realising how lame his questions were. If AA had sexually assaulted someone, there was no excusing it.

'It seems pretty conclusive and, as I said, she has a witness.'

'Have you told the men?'

'Yes, I had to. Not her name of course,' the director replied.

'I'd better go back and see if I can do or say anything to keep morale up. AA was very popular with everyone,' said Damien.

Bina wasn't at her desk as they left, but Damien did catch a glimpse of Iswara. She looked at him, but shook her head slowly and then looked away. Damien backed off. He was shocked and distressed. AA was probably the only other Indian he had really got to know well since coming to Mumbai. He even felt he knew his family because he often mentioned them – his widowed mother in Bangalore and his sisters.

'This just doesn't add up,' Clem said to Damien. 'Bina was stalking *him*.'

'I know. I need to talk to him.' He went back to the hut and tried AA's mobile, but it was powered off.

'If he rings when I'm out on-site, don't let him go,' he instructed.

He wanted to talk to Iswara too, to see if she knew anything, but she had firmly rebuffed him earlier. He knew her well enough to know that she'd come to him when she was ready.

He had to wait for AA's call too. That didn't come until the next day.

'What's the story?' Damien asked him. 'You're not guilty, are you?'

'Do you have to ask?' replied AA. 'Of course I'm not. This whole thing has been a set-up.' He sounded genuinely upset. 'And do you know the worst thing about it? I can't clear my name. Everyone who works there believes her story now and I have had no chance to tell mine – if there was one to tell.'

'Can we meet up for a chat, AA? I can't really talk here. Why don't we go to that little restaurant you brought me to when I arrived?'

They set a time later that day and AA was there early. The first question he asked Damien was about Iswara – had she said anything to him?

'No, she's clearly avoiding me. She looked very upset. Does she know something? Tell me what happened?'

'I can't do that. If Iswara is saying nothing, then I can't tell you anything, except that I am innocent. Iswara knows that, but she can't do anything. As I said on the phone, I've been set up.'

'I'm not sure I understand. If you have, then surely we can prove your innocence,' Damien said rationally, hoping to tease a little more of the chain of events from him, but AA was resolute.

He said sadly, 'I never went near that woman, but I can't clear my name without implicating someone who is innocent, and I won't do that.'

'Dammit man, you've got to. Your reputation is being destroyed here.'

'I know that too, but I can't destroy someone else's to clear mine.'

Over fragmented sentences, stilted conversations about nothing and everything, and a growing uneasiness, they ate a meal that neither of them tasted. AA was to have taken some of them to a cricket match the following weekend, and he apologised that this would not now be possible.

Damien was none the wiser about what had actually happened when he went back to his rooms. He tossed and turned in bed, his mind in overdrive. He wished he could talk this out with Iswara, so that he could begin to make sense of this debacle. He also knew it wasn't his place to ask her, but he resolved to talk to her the following day – to hell with social mores and niceties.

Could she and AA have been together at the time the alleged assault was supposed to have taken place? Was that why AA wouldn't talk?

Dear Beatrice
Less than two weeks left here and I can't wait to go for a walk down Dún Laoghaire pier, feel the wind in my hair and smell the fresh air. I'll never complain again when it howls outside my apartment windows – one of the disadvantages of living on a top-floor flat close to the sea, every breeze seems like a hurricane. Maybe you'll join me one evening and we could have a bite to eat down there?
It's been a hell of a few days. Our foreman

161

has been sacked – for some class of sexual assault. No one except the director seems to know what happened. I can't ask the woman how she's faring because that's not what you do over here. If her honour has been compromised, then to refer to it is taboo or some such. I tried to wheedle it out of the foreman when I met him the other night, but he wouldn't talk either.

There's a horrible atmosphere and it's soured the whole project for us, as we all really liked the guy, and the woman was definitely out to get him, one way or another. Talk about the valley of the squinting windows – it has nothing on the Indian mafia.

I always seem to be complaining when I write to you. It's as though you have become my safety valve. I hope I can return the compliment some time in the future – if you ever need a broad shoulder or two.

Hope you enjoyed Galway. I love that place.

Write soon, I look forward to your mails.

Cheers

Damien

Beatrice and Irene were engrossed in a property supplement at lunchtime, looking for places where the new suite could live, if she could still order it.

'How about a three-bedroomed duplex with spiral staircase in Dublin 6?'

'No, you can't get furniture up those. I know someone who had to have their upstairs window removed and their bedroom furniture lifted up by crane.'

'There's a penthouse here in Killiney, where the annual service charge is seven grand. That's thirty-five grand over five years! You'd get a nice class of bachelor living there.'

'Irene, get real. I haven't won the lottery, nor am I looking for a nice class of bachelor, as you put it.'

'I know, I'm just saying.'

'Here's a ground floor flat with an orchard garden in Ballsbridge, now that sounds nice.'

'It could be very dark or damp. Those old houses can be both,' said Irene.

'You know what, this is all getting to be a bit of a marathon. I think I might just stay where I am. Let's go for a walk around the green.'

Iswara was at home, sitting on the swing seat on the veranda with an open book on her lap.

'I told you working at that clinic would be bad for her,' Daya said to her husband after they had finished eating dinner. 'She has hardly eaten a thing, she doesn't look well and she's been in bad form for days. She never used to be like that. Do you think she's sickening for something?'

163

'Maybe you're right,' Raj agreed. 'She does seem to be off form, but let me talk to her. She'll only get defensive if you try.'

'You are too easy on her. She always had you wrapped around her little finger.'

'She's a grown woman, Daya . . .'

'All right, all right. I'll go away,' she said and left him to go outside.

'How is work going?' Raj enquired, sitting down beside his daughter.

'It's always busy and I lost a patient today – a baby – with measles. I get so angry at how mothers are expected to act as though nothing has happened when they lose a child. It's just accepted as the norm here,' she said tearfully. 'There are other children in the family and I don't know if they'll survive either.'

'I know, and it's even harder when you know that it doesn't have to be like that,' he consoled.

'We are one of the fastest growing nations in the world. We even have a space programme, yet we can't manage to vaccinate our children. Papa, did you know that most of the vaccinations that are used all over the world are made in India? For a pittance – and sold for huge profits everywhere else?'

'I did.'

After a minute, he spoke gently, putting his arm around her shoulders. 'Iswara, may I tell you something? Two of the hardest things you'll ever have to accept are losing a patient, especially a child, and the fact that you can't change the world. You can only hope to make a difference and, believe me, you're doing that.'

'But it's not enough.'

'It's more than most.'

She sat with her head on his shoulder, each absorbed with their thoughts. He felt she was going to say more, but changed her mind. He knew to let her take her time. If it was important, she'd tell him when she was ready.

Dear Damien

I am so sorry to hear about your friend and the assault. That's dreadful. I often wondered what it must be like to know or be related to someone who is accused of offences like that. It must be very hard to stand by them and to be caught in the middle. Difficult not to be judgemental too, I imagine. Have you heard any more since you wrote?

I'd be delighted to walk the pier with you when you get home, that is if I've not been swept off my feet by the latest blind date that Irene has set me up with. She reckons I've been such a poor judge of men that perhaps going on her recommendation might have more enduring results.

He's called Trevor, but goes by Trev! We're going to some stand-up comedy festival on Saturday – not my cup of tea at all – but I can't get out of it as she passed on my email details to him and he's written – practically hourly – to tell me how much he's looking forward to our encounter. God knows what Irene has told him about me, but she's not giving anything away about him. Wants me to form my own first impressions, as if Trev hasn't already done that. I fancy he plays chess and a banjo. I'll let you know.

Please bring a bit of sunshine back with you, we've been starved of it here for weeks.

Take care

Beatrice

Damien had had enough of the secrecy. He still couldn't reconcile AA with a sexual offence, but then you never could tell, could you? After a long and mainly sleepless night, he was determined to confront Iswara. For the past three days, she had avoided him and he hadn't heard a word from AA since their meeting. Damien had avoided the clinic too, and now began to wonder if she had been hoping he might come to her.

Bina was sitting at her desk, and he enquired, 'Is Dr Singhanid free? I need to speak to her urgently.'

'No, but Dr Patel is. Will he do?'

'No, it's Dr Singhanid I need to talk to.'

'She told me not to disturb her. She always does

166

her paperwork first thing. She hasn't started seeing the patients yet, but I suppose you may go in,' she said, opening the surgery door.

'You have a visitor,' Bina announced breezily, before shutting the door after him. He was surprised at how Iswara's appearance had changed in a few days. She looked gaunt, her eyes sunken and sad. She barely stood up to greet him and he went around behind her desk and took her in his arms. They stood there like that for a few minutes until he released her.

'Iswara, what happened?'

'It's all my fault. I should have seen it coming.'

'What do you mean – your fault? Did AA harm you?'

'No, not me, not anyone. But I should have read the signs, God knows there were enough of them.'

'You're being too hard on yourself.' He was totally confused now. Had AA made unwanted advances on Iswara. 'Have you talked to anyone? Can I be of any help, or any of the guys? Clem?'

'No, no one can help. AA is gone and it's my fault that he's been disgraced.'

'Iswara, that's absolute nonsense. If he's guilty he's lucky he's not being prosecuted and put behind bars for what he did.'

'What he did – no, what *we* did – was consensual, but if it hadn't happened, he'd still be here.'

'So why isn't he?' he asked, puzzled.

'Because of that scheming little bitch out there,'

she said indicating to the door. 'Bina caught us together, kissing, in here, and she claimed he attacked her when she conveniently came back to get her purse, which she also claims she had left on her desk. I don't believe that. She screamed at AA about leading her on, then she disarranged her clothes, tossed her hair and ran out in a distressed state to her brother, who just happened to be waiting for her too.'

'But surely you can tell the director that? That AA has been falsely accused.'

'I wanted to, but AA won't hear of it. He said it would compromise me, and my reputation here. I don't know what to do. Instead he has been ruined and I can do nothing to help him.'

'Did she say anything to you?' he asked.

'Oh, yes. She said lots. She told AA that if he continued to see me, she'd go to my parents and the director and tell them what we were at.'

'But that's outrageous. What has she to gain by doing that?'

'I'm telling you the truth, Damien.'

'I don't doubt that for one moment, Iswara. I just don't understand why she would do that.'

'She's been obsessed with AA since he came along and I should have seen the signs – all that going back and forward to the office with messages for her brother, and the lengths to which she went to try to get AA's address when he had his accident.'

He agreed. 'You're right, she was a bit compulsive.'

'Her jealousy took her over. When she caught us she just flipped, but she had to have it planned because her brother was waiting for her. I felt she was always watching me and I was right about that. And he was very quick to say he saw his sister run out from the surgery in a distressed and dishevelled state. I can see how the director had to take their word . . .'

'Have you heard from AA since?

'Yes, but just a few phone calls. He's gone home to Bangalore to visit his mother, and I don't know if I'll ever see him again.'

'What are we going to do about Bina? She can't get away with this.' Damien was incensed. 'She's managed to take AA's character and ruin it. We have to do something.'

'I should have noticed the way she stalked him, the sweets, the baking and the hanging around the site office. Now she knows she has something on me, she's holding it over me because she knows there is nothing I can do to clear his name without damaging mine. The director might turn a blind eye, but my parents would disown me.'

'But the little schemer still has her job, so has her brother. It's only a matter of time before they start blackmailing you for money to keep their silence.'

'I hadn't thought of that,' Iswara said, 'but that would explain a lot and it would give her another motive.'

'We'll think of something,' Damien said. 'Leave

it with me.' He leaned over and kissed her on the forehead. 'We'll sort it out.'

He called, 'Thanks, Bina' when he left , as he normally did, and went in search of Clem.

Beatrice was sitting at her laptop, some classical music playing softly in her apartment. From outside, summer evening sounds wafted through the open windows. She had decided to write to Damien and was surprised at how much she was enjoying getting to know, and like, him through their emails and at how disappointed she was when there wasn't one to be read.

> Hi Damien
>
> Haven't heard from you for a few days so I hope things are settling down again for you.
>
> I met Trevor, sorry Trev, the other night and we went to The Sugar Club and had a drink before the show. First impressions were very good. He seemed perfectly nice, normal, well turned out and had a great smile. All boxes ticked so far.
>
> He didn't try to impress me by talking about his car, his job, skiing holiday, owning a banjo or chess. Still all good.
>
> Then the comedy acts started and as the jokes catapulted from the guests he started laughing. Now what's wrong with that, I can hear you ask. Wasn't it a comedy show

(did I mention that before)? Isn't a GSOH a necessity in a man? Well yes, it is, and I enjoy a good sense of humour too, but his laugh was unreal. The nearest I can come to describing it is to tell you to visualise a braying donkey. It started with a thunderous snort then turned into a high-pitched hee-haw, followed by a whinnying neigh and it lasted so long that the next gag was lost for the audience. Even one of the comics commented on it, asking if he'd join him on tour as his warm-up act. I was mortified!

No more blind dates for me. I'm too traumatised to bother.

Take care
Beatrice

She sat thinking for a while. *I think I'm getting to like this guy.* Then she added a PS.

I might still consent to the walk down Dún Laoghaire pier with you when you get back, if I don't have to wear wellies, pull a caddy car or go mud plugging. And, if you promise not to laugh out loud, I might even buy you a Teddy's ice cream afterwards!

Damien trusted Clem enough to tell him the full sequence of events. Clem was dumbfounded when he heard what had actually happened in the medical building.

'The scheming bitch. Poor Iswara. She doesn't deserve this. She never considers herself, but putting that aside, we can't let them get away with this.'

'How can we stop it, without breaking Iswara and AA's trust?' Damien asked. 'AA was prepared to walk away rather than let the truth about them be known to anyone.'

'Yes, but she's left to pick up the pieces – and it won't end there. That pair see this as an ongoing meal ticket. It'll be demands for payments to keep quiet. Once we're all gone, Iswara will have no one to defend her against them,' Clem argued.

'We have to get AA back and confront Bina and that brother of hers. Threaten them if necessary.'

'Where is AA?' asked Clem.

'In Bangalore. I'm going to get on to the college and extend my leave. I can't abandon Iswara in the middle of all this.'

'You're not her dean any more, Damien,' Clem said. 'Is it wise to get involved?'

'No, but I'm her friend, and that's far more important than being a dean. I'd better change my flights too.'

When he told Iswara, the look of relief on her face was like the lifting of a veil. 'You have no idea how much this means to me. You are the only one I can confide in and it's eating me up. I almost told my father the other night, but why break his heart too?'

'What about your sister? Could you tell her?'

'I thought about it and I'm still not sure if I should. What a mess I've made of things. I never thought I'd say it, but I should have listened to my mother. It doesn't pay to break the mould in this society. Maybe I should just marry Sanjay Ranjan, the widower who works with my father, and take up a placement there too, like they wanted me to.'

'We can't choose who we fall in love with,' Damien tried to placate her.

'No, but we can choose with who not to!' she said sadly.

'We'll sort things out,' he told her, although he hadn't a clue how they would.

Beatrice was marking the days off in her head to when Damien was due back. Irene teased her about it when she let it slip. She just laughed it off and was delighted when she opened her inbox to find he had replied to her.

Hi Beatrice

Sorry for the delay in getting back to you. Whatever about your comedian, I laughed when I read your mail. Are you still in therapy?

Things have kicked off here since the assault episode and it's much more complicated that it first seemed.

I've decided to extend my time by another week or two to see if anything can be done to clear the foreman's name. I think the whole sordid business is a set-up to extort money from someone in return for keeping a secret that has nothing whatever to do with her! Unfortunately and unwittingly, I happen to be caught right in the middle so I can't say any more.

It's the thought of that walk down the pier and the Teddy's ice cream that's keeping me going. If I promise that you won't have to wear wellies, pull a caddy car, go mud plugging or listen to me laugh out loud, can I have a chocolate flake in mine or is that on the taboo list too?

If you were here, I could treat you to a 'gola'. That's a crushed ice treat, smothered with tangy syrup – of your choice – and you slurp the flavour out of it. If you buy it from the street vendors, they mould the crushed ice into a ball with their bare hands! No EU H&S regulations here. My favourite flavour is kala khatta, which comes from black berries called jamun, but there are countless flavours – and all in seriously vibrant colours too. No E number restrictions here either. To top off the gola, they sprinkle a pinch of masala on top. That's a mixture of black salt, pepper and white salt!

Pity I can't bring you one home to try. They're delicious.

Look forward to hearing from you – soon.

Cheers

Damien

CHAPTER 17

Hi Damien

I'm sorry your expedition has become so complicated and I hope you'll have some luck sorting things out. Can't imagine what it must be like to be falsely accused or even to imagine how difficult it would be to clear your name if you were.

I know Irene was planning welcome home drinks for you, but no doubt she's already told you that. She'll be disappointed, as I am, so I'll have to keep the bottle of bubbly I was going to bring in the fridge for a few more weeks.

I'm just rushing out the door. I've starting a Pilates class – with my mother! How sad is that? She has problems with her back and this is supposed to strengthen it and build up muscles. I don't know what to expect, but don't particularly want to build up my muscles. I expect you don't need to either, with all that physical work.

Take care
Beatrice

She read it through and added 'xx' at the bottom.

Damien managed to reach AA, but only after leaving several messages on his mobile.

'Iswara has told me everything. You have to come back if we are to clear your name.'

'Clearing my name is not the problem, keeping Iswara's name out of it is,' AA replied firmly.

'Staying away will solve nothing, because when that scheming pair have us all out of the way, they'll start making demands and who knows where that will lead to. We have to be proactive and stop them in their tracks, and the only way I see of doing that is to confront them. Tell them we know what happened and threaten them with their jobs. We have to turn the tables on them.'

'What about the workers and the volunteers? What do they think happened?'

'Mostly they believe what they were told – the accusation and all that. That's why we have to put them straight. Your damaged reputation is unlikely to follow you to Bangalore, but Iswara has to live here, so whatever you feel about yourself, you owe it to her to come back and try and sort things out.'

'We agreed it would be better if I left and never saw her again, but in light of what you've just said I agree with you. I'll get a flight tomorrow or Sunday.'

'Are you OK for funds?' he asked

'That's not a problem,' said AA, 'but thank you for asking.'

'Great. Ring me when you get the details.'

AA arrived back on Sunday evening and Iswara and Damien met up with him. In his capacity as Dean of Students, Damien was well used to negotiations and dialogues, to stand-offs and interchanges. He was used to dealing with police and irate parents, unwanted pregnancies, even sexual assault on occasion too. He had had to post bail and stand as guarantor for students who got drunk and disorderly, and whose ribald and lewd conduct had caused offence. But this was different and very tricky. Not only were there serious accusations, there was honour and tradition in the mix too, as well as matters of confidentiality. Not to mention the feelings he was experiencing for Iswara, and trying not to let them show through.

'I think we should involve the director,' counselled Damien. 'I think we need to have him on our side.'

AA immediately said, 'Absolutely not.'

But Iswara seemed to hesitate. 'Perhaps it would be a good idea.'

'It would certainly add to our case if Bina and her brother think he agrees with us and is on our side – even if he isn't.'

'What if he tells Iswara's parents? They are old friends, you know,' AA asked.

'We have to make sure he won't, before we tell

him all the facts. Ask to meet him and talk to him in confidence first. What do you think, Iswara? Is it worth the risk?'

'I think it might be,' she answered hesitantly.

The next morning Damien called to Bina as she walked by the site office. She looked uneasy but relaxed visibly when he asked her to fix up an appointment with the director when he came in, as he usually did on Mondays. It was arranged for eleven o'clock. He rang Iswara and AA on their mobiles. Clem was on alert to go in one of the pick-ups to a rendezvous point and wait on the corner with AA. With the pleasantries out of the way Damien asked the director if he could speak in absolute confidence. Once he had been given assurance he told him the facts. He asked permission to bring AA and Iswara in. Bina blanched when she saw AA arrive, followed by Clem and Iswara. They all watched from the director's office as Bina scurried across the yard to find her brother.

'That in itself is pretty conclusive,' the director agreed, before making them all sit down. 'Call them in.'

He made Bina and her brother squirm, confess and then fired them both, making them each sign a piece of paper saying they had lied, that AA was completely blameless and that Bina had fabricated the whole story.

He walked them off the premises, before coming back to his office.

'Well Iswara, breaking the mould again I see,' he

said gently. 'You're an adult and the world is changing and it's up to us older people to accept this, but if you were my daughter I'd like to think I'd be understanding and tolerant, but I fear I probably wouldn't be. What now for both of you?'

'I should move away, out of Iswara's life, but I can't,' AA said candidly. 'Nor can I stay around her and destroy her life.'

'Can you at least stay around until my school-rooms are finished?' the director asked with a smile. 'In return, I'll not see anything I'm not supposed to see in the meantime. How does that sound?'

Iswara couldn't believe what she was hearing. Would her father be as forgiving? Would she have the courage to find out? And what of her mother?

CHAPTER 18

The next evening Iswara visited her sister and told her about AA, and her feelings for him.

'You met him at the director's garden party.'

'He's very handsome. I remember that, but there were so many new faces. I didn't really talk to him.'

Iswara told her about the Bina business, how the director knew. Rekna too turned out to be surprisingly supportive, if justifiably concerned.

'Don't tell Mama before you have to,' she advised. 'If things don't work out, then she needn't know. That way you'll have saved yourself, and everyone else, an awful lot of worry and distress. If things do work out, and you want to go away to be together, then we'll cross that bridge when we must.'

'You're fantastic,' Iswara said, hugging her sister. 'Thank you so much.'

'Can I ask a very personal question?' Rekna said tentatively. 'It's not because of curiosity, it's from concern, I promise you.'

Iswara nodded.

'Does AA have any means? You'll need money if you are going to set up abroad. I have some put by.'

'You're so sweet. I have money too, remember, from Grandfather. But yes, AA is secure. His parents were well off and his mother manages their family businesses. She's a widow and fairly astute from what he's told me about her. She put him and his two sisters, who are older than him, through university after her husband died in a railroad accident. He was an engineer too, a fairly senior one, who had worked for the rail company. His mother did wonders on his pension, and didn't touch the compensation or the profits from the family concerns she inherited. She settled a lot on the two girls when they married. AA told me that once they were married, she began to despair that he would never take a wife, so when he was twenty-five, she transferred his share over to him. So you needn't worry about us.'

'But of course I will,' Rekna said. 'I missed having you around in my life for almost seven years, so I'm not about to let you slip out of it again so easily.'

Hi Beatrice
The problems have been resolved and I now find myself with two weeks unscheduled time in India. I could stay on and work on the project, but I'm looking on these as a gift from fate and I'm going to do a bit

182

of travelling, get to see a bit more of this country – away from dumps, the poverty and the smells. It's really frustrating being so close to the sea and not being able to go into it because of pollution, so I think I might head north, but not to the sea. I'd like to see Jaipur, although Delhi beckons too.

I've always wanted to take a train here. You know the ones you see in films with people hanging off the sides and ends of the carriages, hopping off at stations to buy provisions and then hopping back on again. Not sure if that will get me away from the smells and the poverty, but it would certainly be interesting. I'll keep you posted along the way.

What about you? How was the Pilates class? Is that the regime where you have to curl over those huge space hopper thingies backwards and do all sorts of contortions? Happily with the heat and the work, keeping fit has not been an issue out here, although there'll be a bit of elbow bending this week before the guys head back home.

Look forward to catching up in a few weeks' time.

Cheers

Damien x

Hi Damien

Well lucky you! Off travelling. I always wanted to go trekking on an elephant in India, but I don't know how I'd handle that with the way my back and legs feel after the Pilates. I think I'd probably need a crane to get up on its back, and as to whether I'd be able to get down again, well that could be even more of a challenge!

My mother, who is almost twice my age, hasn't a twinge after the first session and she's supposed to be the one with the dodgy back! And yes, we do use those large exercise balls. All we did was sit on them and balance with our arms in the air, trying to find our 'powerhouse'! That, apparently, is made up of the muscles in the centre of the body – the tummy, lower and upper back, hips, buttocks and inner thighs. The energy is then supposed to flow out into your limbs. I'm not sure if I found mine, or even if my powerhouse is working at all. None of my efforts were helped by the visions of some of the advanced 'yogalates' practitioners at the other end of the studio, who seemed to be some class of a rare species of contortionists. They were able to wrap themselves around the balls backwards and dance at the same time!

Is the new building up yet? I'm always amazed at how quickly these things are built – like Niall Mellon's townships in South Africa, where they seem to build whole streets of new houses in just a month. Will the college keep up its interest and sponsorship of your project once it's finished?

Let me know where you're off to and I can look those exotic places up online and feel envious.

Take care

Beatrice x

Damien took Iswara, Rekna and AA out for a meal before he left Mumbai. It was a bittersweet occasion. The sexual tension was palpable between AA and Iswara. He didn't know how things would work out for them: none of them did, but he hoped they would. And whatever happened, he certainly intended to come back to the centre in the future.

The three of them filled his head with the places he must see and foods he must try as he travelled. He wished them both well and walked Rekna to her car, where she waited for her sister to say her goodnights.

'Your friendship has meant an awful lot to Iswara, and obviously to AA as well,' she told Damien.

'I am extremely fond of your sister,' he answered truthfully. 'And I feel that I really got to know her well since I came out here. I really hope things work out for her, for them.'

'So do I, but it's not that simple. I really like AA too, but I hope for everyone's sake they forget about each other. It would make life much simpler,' she added. 'You'll always be welcome in our home no matter what happens, so that's an open invitation if you ever come back to India.'

'I might well take you up on that,' he laughed.

The next day he made his way to Bandra Terminus to take the train. He had decided against the fast overnighters to Delhi – he wanted to stop wherever the fancy took him along the way.

Hi Beatrice

Just finished the first leg of my adventure and I have to say this country is mesmerising. I took a train going north, and any comparisons between a relaxing City Gold journey to Cork with Iarnród Éireann and other great train journeys of the world went out the window. Everyone seems to travel in clans – the old, middle aged and the young, and, without exception, everyone smells of food, of cooking oil and curry. Most of them have enormous packs and parcels held together with odd bits of string. There are a few goats in the aisles and lots of chickens. They are in makeshift cages at least. It's a fantastic tapestry of life.

I'm a bit of a novelty so everyone stares at me quite openly. The young with their big solemn eyes, the old with unguarded curiosity and toothless grins. Do their teeth just rot and fall out or do they have them pulled out? I keep wondering about that! Funny what occupies your mind when you've nothing to do and all the time in the world to do it.

I'm sitting in a little internet café in a small town where the electricity serves only a fraction of the inhabitants and then only intermittently. I've been warned it may disconnect any second, so this mail could be coming to you in instalments and, indeed, from different locations. The café, by the way, is a shelf at the front of a tailor's shop which isn't any wider than an average landing at home. The owner, who is busily working on a rickety Singer sewing machine next to me, knows a little English and has insisted on serving me some chai in a china cup. The street is full of such enterprises like this one. Next door, there is a sari shop with grotesque-looking mannequins that have seen better days. One is even missing her nose. Outside this there's a young boy wielding a fierce-looking knife. He's denuding coconuts of their hairy coir, then puncturing the top and selling them to the passers-by. They drink the coconut water from the shell. I'm told this is a great thirst quencher, but I haven't tried one yet. I imagine it would be a lot safer than the water though, which at best is of dubious origin and colour.

There are a few skinny cows ambling about too. That's all they seem to do, amble about amid the chaos.

How's life in Dublin? Have you found your powerhouse yet?

Cheers

Damien x

Irene and Beatrice had both got emails from India that morning.

'You look very smug with that grin on your puss,' Irene said to Beatrice. 'Maybe you're hooked on a certain dean?'

'Well I'm not sure about that, but he writes a good email and, let me tell you, having a pen pal is much less demanding than having a real boyfriend.'

'There's no hope for you.'

'Probably not,' she laughed, 'but I feel Damien has taken me to Mumbai, without any intimacy, and without having to do airports or worry about vaccinations and baggage allowances. It's great.'

'Is that all there is between you?'

'Who knows?' she laughed.

'You're a lost cause.'

CHAPTER 19

Iswara knocked on the director's door and went in. 'May I talk to you?' she asked tentatively.

'Of course, come in and sit down. I've been meaning to talk to you too.'

'I had to come in to express my sincere thanks for your understanding,' Iswara said, 'and for having trust in me.' She didn't know how he would react, but she knew she had put him in a very awkward situation and felt she had to address it with him.

'What are you going to do, Iswara? I feel a little responsible for you, you know, especially as your father is an old friend and colleague. But I have to respect that you are a grown-up woman, with a mind of your own, and it's really none of my business how you conduct your life.'

She folded her hands, trying to give the air of being relaxed, not knowing how to answer. She had rehearsed what she would say to him, but she hadn't expected him to say things like that.

He continued, 'I also know you stand to lose a lot financially if you let this relationship develop, and in case you're wondering how I know this,

189

your grandfather asked my advice when he was drawing up his will.'

'He must have been very disappointed that Rekna and I weren't boys. That would have solved a lot of these problems,' Iswara said.

'If he was, he never showed it or mentioned it to me,' the director replied. 'But he did speak of you often. He was very proud and I think he would be even more so because of the choice you made to work here, with the disadvantaged.'

'I think it was probably his influences on my life that led me here.'

'And on mine too. I'm going to tell you something, Iswara, which I want you to keep to yourself. Your grandfather not only founded the private clinic where your father works, but this was another of his projects. He never talked about it, but he was a very successful surgeon as you know, and he used a lot of his private money to provide public medicine here and in some other locations. He was instrumental in me coming here to work. When he was making his will, he made sure your parents were well provided for, and you and your sister too. But it didn't stop there. He left a further legacy for you, as a doctor, for when you reach thirty. He requested that you not be told about it in case it would influence any of your decisions, but he stipulated that it was never to be part of your dowry. However, I feel I have to tell you that if you were to get seriously involved with AA, whom I know is Muslim, then you will be disinherited from this money. It's not an inconsiderable sum either. The other costs you know only too well,' he said quietly.

'I had no idea.'

'That was exactly what he wanted. Your grandfather was very progressive and he had no wish to influence your life. But Iswara, this means you need to think things out carefully. There's more than just a clandestine relationship at stake here and you must decide if you are going to keep on seeing that young man.'

'I don't feel I have any choice. No, that's not true. Of course I have a choice, but having lived overseas and seen the way other races accept inter-marriage, it doesn't seem so terrible to me any more. My feelings for AA are very real and I know his are for me too. Neither of us planned for anything like this to happen, but it has, and neither of us wants to change that.'

'Then we have a problem.'

'So should I give up on my personal happiness to placate others and conform?'

'Only you can answer that. Because of your grandfather's trust in me, and now knowing about this relationship, I am in a seriously awkward position.'

'I know,' she said sadly, 'and for that I am truly sorry.'

AA and Iswara met in a hotel restaurant in a part of the city where she knew she wouldn't be recognised. It was the only way they could spend any time alone together. The intensity of their feelings was deepening, and Iswara was reluctant to bring up the conversation she had had with the director that morning.

As if reading her mind, AA took her hand under the table and said, 'We can't live our lives like this, Iswara. It's not fair on either of us. When the school is finished, I'm going to go away. I have a friend who is behind one of the big projects in Dubai. It's not one that I worked on before, but it's just as prestigious and it's a two-year contract.'

'You can't just go off and leave me,' Iswara said incredulously.

'Have you a better idea?' he asked desperately. 'I've gone around and around in circles trying to see a way forward and I can't. We have no future here. You have your family, your life and your friends and I won't ask you to choose, because that's effectively what you would have to do.'

'What if that's what I want? You're taking the decision away from me. You're making it sound as though it's all one-sided, but you stand to lose too. What would your mother say to you having a non-Muslim girlfriend? I can't imagine I'd be welcomed with open arms by your community either.'

'Iswara, I could get around my mother, and I know she'd love you if she got to know you, but what about your parents? Could they accept me?

And your sister? You don't have to answer – I can see the reply in your expression.'

She squeezed his hand and felt her eyes filling up.

'Rekna says she'll stand by me whatever I decide, but I know she wishes I'd give you up.'

'And how do you know you won't? Is it wise to make that decision just yet? Why not wait a little longer and see what happens?'

'What do you think will happen? That you'll forget me as soon as I'm out of sight? That I'll forget you?'

'We have to be realistic. You may forget me. I'm a bit of a nomad, and can put roots down anywhere. Since I qualified, I've moved around. Everything and everyone you hold dear is here in Mumbai. Don't think I haven't thought of all the possibilities. The only way out of it is to move away, and I couldn't, wouldn't, ask you to come with me. Let's part for a while and see how we feel. I'll get my computer qualifications and, who knows, if we both still feel the same way, maybe we could move else-where, to Canada or America, somewhere where nobody cares who we are or where we came from. Maybe if there is distance between us, we'll find a way. Besides,' he said in an effort to lighten things a little, 'the chances are your mother will probably find a suitable husband for you yet.'

'I doubt that very much. She's exhausted her supply of eligible men. AA, I have some college friends who live in Dubai. Maybe I could come and visit or even get a job out there?'

'That would still mean leaving here and giving up a lot. Think about it, Iswara. There's no other way.'

'Do you ever think that God or the gods must be perverse? They create people and then play with them. It's an accident what religion or what creed we were born into, yet it shapes our whole lives.'

'It also shapes who we are.'

'Yes, but what difference would it make in the grand scheme of things if we defied convention?'

'We'd hurt a lot of people.'

She had to agree.

'When will you go? Will you keep in touch?'

'Of course I'll keep in touch. I love you, Iswara. I'll think of you every minute of every day, but it's for the best and when you think it over you'll see I'm right.'

They sat quietly, oblivious to the other diners in the restaurant. The stringed music being played by a quartet at one end of the room was romantic and haunting. When she became aware of it again she recognised the tune. 'I'll never hear that again without remembering you.'

They listened to it for a few minutes and then she asked AA, 'Why did I ever come home?'

'For that very reason, because it is home.'

'It's also stifling. I feel I'm being smothered. Whenever I mention moving out, my mother has apoplexy. Speaking of my mother, I had better get back. It's getting late and she won't rest until she hears me safely home. How did she ever manage when I was abroad?'

'She had your sister to worry about then.'

They walked through the garden and kissed where they knew no one could see them, beneath the cassia trees, then they took a taxi to a downtown hotel where Iswara had asked her father's driver to collect her.

'It'll work out. Just give it time,' AA whispered.

'Well it seems that I'm going to have plenty of that,' she replied.

CHAPTER 20

Hi Damien

You sound as though you are really enjoying your Indian adventure. I'm madly envious – it makes my upcoming two weeks in Malta sound very mundane. Admittedly, it wouldn't have been my first choice, but as there are quite a few of us going (did I tell you it's my cousin who is getting married over there to a girl who is half-Maltese?) we'll have a great time – and with guaranteed good weather too.

I managed to fall off the exercise ball at the class the other evening, much to the merriment of the others, while my mother is streaking ahead all set to join the pole dancers. She's lovin' it. (Perhaps streaking is the wrong word to use there!) I'm still working on finding my powerhouse, but think the lights must have gone out in it. I do feel about six inches taller at the end of each session though, so maybe something's working in there.

Where are you now and what have you

seen since your last mail? Write and tell me all.

Take care and travel safely.

Look forward to seeing you soon.

Beatrice x

Hi Beatrice

Still enthralled with this fascinating country, where the people are so gracious and welcoming. I was sitting at a little café in a town the other day when a young man walked by. He looked at me, walked back, looked again and as he passed the third time he asked, in English, if I spoke English. He was a teacher in a local school and he asked me if I'd come in and talk to the children as they had never met an Englishman before! I didn't correct him. I went into the classroom full of boys about thirteen and they were fantastic. Once they got over the initial shyness, they asked about the college where I work and were fascinated to hear that we had a lot of Indian students there. They wanted to know if we had computers in our classrooms. When I was asked if I knew Prince Harry or Prince William, I realised that that was my cue to tell them about Ireland. So, with one of those old fashioned maps that you unfurl and drape over an easel, I pointed out our tiny island. The teacher insisted I went home to dine with his family that evening and it was a real privilege to be invited into someone's home just like that.

I am making my way up towards Delhi, but I keep getting sidetracked in the real sense of the word. Definitely train and local buses are the way to travel for authenticity. I just wish I had a few more weeks here, but the beginning of the new academic year is always the busiest time for me too with a new influx of bewildered students. If I ask for another extension they may just tell me to take a permanent one! And I have a mortgage to pay.

When are you off to Malta? That sounds like fun.

Cheers

Damien x

As she was dressing for the clinic, Iswara realised she had been working at the medical centre for three months. Every day had been different.

She still found it hard to come to terms with the living conditions she saw when she went out on calls. She knew she'd never get used to it. While on her rounds she often recalled her grandfather saying that she must never become complacent. There was little chance of that, she thought, as she was constantly shocked by conditions she met every other day. The makeshift shacks clung to the side of more solid buildings. They were stacked one on top of the other and on the periphery of the dumps where the fumes and dust filled the heavy air, making breathing almost impossible for some of her patients. In parts of the ghettos fractured surface pipes leaked raw sewage and this ran in rivulets or lodged in little pools in the gullies outside the doorways. The hems of saris and young children had to be lifted up to avoid further contamination as they went about. Flies hovered, landed, buzzed, mated and contaminated. There was always a makeshift clothesline or two and hangers draped with laundry drying in the foetid air. What little food these slum dwellers had was stored in pots with the lids held in place by a rock or other weight to prevent the rats from getting at it. Many of these tin shacks had no electricity, no cooking facilities and no running water. Hot meals usually only materialised once a day, generally in the evening time, and these were made on an open fire or a small Primus stove, the fumes from the oil adding a top note to the already overpowering cocktail of odours. Overhead, webs of electrical cables hung from poles and junction boxes, in some places so thick they resembled rope rigging on the masts of old ships. Many of these were pirated and the illicit wires led trails to single light bulbs, to rescued television sets, even to a battered fridge or other dumped goods. Others fed little businesses and street stalls. Iswara had been surprised to see a microwave in one shack, before realising that it was used as a cupboard.

It saddened her when she was faced with teenage pregnancies and child mothers, and there were a lot of them. Many of the underage ones were in that situation because they had been inducted into the sex industry, often forced into prostitution by unscrupulous landlords in payment of rent, rent that they had no earthly hope of earning any other way. Other young patients were orphans and many of these, particularly the boys, presented with sexually transmitted diseases and AIDS. Most had no idea at all about how to prevent these things.

When she discussed them with her father, as she often did, he reiterated what he had told her before: 'You can't change the world. Things are getting better, but it's a slow process.'

'Papa, how can you think that? The planners keep coming up with housing solutions – their latest brainchild is to replace the slums with high-rise apartments, for private buyers, now that they have found a way around the four-storey height restriction.'

'Yes, I read that too.'

'It said that they intend to rehouse the slum dwellers whom they will displace in high-rise accommodation – but with units the same size as a single-car garage. But will they also replace all the little enterprises that flourish in the backstreets

200

now? If not, how will these people support themselves? They'll have to move on and set up again
somewhere else.'

'I have to agree with you,' her father said. 'They
don't seem to be making any inroads into solving
these social problems at all.'

Sometimes Iswara despaired. How could anyone
make a difference here? The problems were too
great.

CHAPTER 21

Iswara and AA snatched whatever chance they had to be together, knowing that time was running out on them. On a few occasions, Rekna delivered and collected her from their rendezvous.

Iswara counted the days till AA's departure, uncertain about when his paperwork and sponsorship would be sorted out. When this was in place, he could go back to Dubai to work. Each time she learned of a bureaucratic requirement that had held up the process yet again, she was glad. She didn't know how she'd cope when he was gone, and the pain was even more acute since they had admitted their love for each other. She missed having Damien around to talk to and had been surprised to find such an ally in the director.

'It's not goodbye, Iswara, I promise you,' AA assured Iswara when they spent their last evening together. 'I just need to get away to try and sort things out in my head and I can't do that here when we are surrounded by obstacles.'

In her heart, she knew she didn't really want to leave India again and since she'd found out about her grandfather's connection with the medical centre, she felt even more bound to it. But she also knew she wanted to spend her life with AA, whatever the cost. She had never felt this way about any man before and she felt torn in every direction.

It would be easy to get work in one of the new hospitals in the Emirates, but she found it difficult to contemplate doing that. She even considered going back to Ireland and getting work there. She knew that she'd get sponsorship easily and if they were married, AA could come too. Finding work for him there would be a problem though, as the building boom of the noughties had literally evaporated and there was no development and not much call for engineers. But if he had his computer degree by then that might make a difference, or if they were married . . .

'If we are meant to be together, it will happen,' he said rationally.

'And if we're not?' she asked in trepidation.

'Then something else will be waiting for us.'

'That's what I am afraid of.'

'Don't be. Let's wait and see.'

AA left for Dubai two days later, and he took a part of Iswara with him. She immersed herself in the setting up of the new facility, which was almost completely kitted out by this stage.

Children of all ages were enrolled and they came in in three shifts, when they had finished their mornings or afternoons on the dump, gathering cardboard that was not sodden, rags, aluminium, rubber or whatever they had been sent out to scavenge. This booty was collected and carried in sacks to weighing areas where their meagre stipends were meted out according to how productive their shifts had been. The third wave of visitors to the 'new school', as it was quickly becoming known, were slightly older. This had been intentional, as the workers knew how sensitive this group was about their ignorance of reading and writing. Having adults in the class took the stigma out of that somewhat. Most had had no schooling, and even getting them to sit still and concentrate was an achievement. Iswara found herself staying behind most evenings to help.

This caused even more friction with her mother, who attributed her quietness and weight loss to overwork. Iswara knew differently. The director invited her parents along one evening to see the premises and the work their daughter was doing. Rekna offered to join them.

Daya ranted and raved when the invite had been issued. 'He is insulting me by expecting me to go into those slums.'

'On the contrary, dear,' Raj replied, 'I think he is honouring us by wanting to show us how highly our daughter is regarded by him and his colleagues.'

Daya reluctantly accompanied her husband and eldest daughter for the grand tour and the official opening, and she had to admit she was astonished at how comfortable Iswara seemed to be in this environment.

'She's her grandfather and her father's daughter, you must be so proud of her,' the director said.

Daya smiled grudgingly, but couldn't resist saying, 'I worry about her own health. She's not looking well and I think she's taking on too much.'

'Now, Daya, Iswara is well able to look after herself,' Raj intervened.

'I'll keep an eye on her,' the director promised, looking knowingly at Iswara.

'Thank you,' Daya smiled at him.

Dear Damien

I love getting your mails – I can almost smell the smells and see the sights as you describe them. It makes life here seem very pedestrian. How will you ever settle back to your routine?

When do you expect to travel home? I suppose I'll be off in Malta at my cousin's wedding when you return. Simon, the cousin, is older than most of us and has always been considered to be a bit of a confirmed bachelor, so we are dying to find out who has managed to tame him. We should have good fun as we've never all gone anywhere like this together before. So, as you can imagine, there are phone calls comparing outfits, on whether to wear flats or heels, and deliberations about all sorts of lofty matters that keep the females of the species occupied before such occasions.

Have to fly – more late-night shopping – for and with my mother this time. Apparently, some of the bride's aunts have decided to wear fascinators (when did that word creep into the language for a hat?) or feathers or some such – now everyone feels they have to sport them as well to avert a serious fashion catastrophe. As I'm so near town I've been roped in to help with the rescue mission and we're going for some pasta afterwards. Makes me feel a bit guilty when I think where you've just been!

Anyway, all this nonsense makes a pleasant change from the latest crisis at work. Some failed asylum seekers on a deportation flight to Nigeria and the Congo were refused permission to use Algerian airspace this week, and, of course, since the Libyan unrest they can't fly through theirs any more, so they had to return to Dublin until it's sorted out. Loads of red tape involved, but you have to feel sorry for them, the lengths they go to find a better life, to be rejected and then for this to happen – and here I am exercised with the big question – feathers or not!

Take care
Beatrice xx

Dear Beatrice

You shouldn't feel at all guilty. Life is like that. Unfairly divided. It's also such a lottery where you end up – in a famine-torn country, in one prone to earthquakes or tsunamis or in one at war. All in all I think we got a good deal being born where we were – no snakes, monkeys or starvation. That makes me feel like a sanctimonious prat. You have my permission to thump me if I ever talk like that in person.

I'm assuming you're still going to come out with me when I get back, maybe for that meal we won at the quiz? Is that a big assumption? If not, and you will, you can tell me all about Malta when we do.

Well, the rail voyage continues and continues to fascinate. I'm writing this on a train and will send it whenever I can. I'm still a curiosity on these journeys and am frequently offered slices of mango, pakoras, or naan bread by my fellow passengers, who obviously consider it rude to eat without sharing. As many of them look really poor themselves, I've taken to buying some fruit or sweets so that when they offer I can refuse politely and take mine out of my rucksack and return the compliment.

It's hard to find ways to describe this vast land. When I look at the map and see where I have travelled, it looks as though I've covered no distance at all, yet I have done almost three times the length of Ireland so far.

I do miss the sea though. I'm almost homesick just thinking about it, and I've just realised that most of the people in this carriage, on this train even, will never see the ocean in their lifetime. That's hard to imagine, isn't it? And kind of sad too.

We're fast approaching my station so I'll sign off.

See you soon

Damien xx

CHAPTER 22

AA settled quickly back into life in Dubai. Through contacts he had made from his previous years there, his new assignment was as project manager on one of the futuristic-looking buildings on the coast, just along from the iconic Burj Al Arab. Previously, he had been involved in Sports City, a project whose creators had thought of everything, including designer shops and malls. The buildings, both residential and commercial, that were to front the proposed kilometre-long canal, were to have been the most fashionable addresses in town, but the recession had hit the Emirati dirham-rich countries too and work had stopped abruptly. Many of the elaborate buildings and dreams were never even started. In the centre of town and in the shopping malls, knots of women concealed in their black *abayas* walked about together. The men in their *thawbs*, the pristine white broken only by the black *agals* holding their *ghutras* in place on their heads, sat drinking coffee together.

AA didn't find it strange that hand-holding or other signs of external affection were forbidden and both were punishable by jail sentences. He had the first time he'd worked there, but now he was surprised at how easily he'd slipped back into this sometimes alien culture. Even in privacy couples, non-national or otherwise, could not share apartments if they weren't married, though hotels often turned a blind eye to couples booking rooms and seldom asked questions. If Iswara did manage to come out here, and if they were to spend time together, really together, he'd have to book in somewhere far away from his work colleagues.

This could not be more removed from what I've left behind, AA thought as he closed the door on the small flat he had been given in a less salubrious part of the city. Small was relative. As most of the recent developments had been built to entice over-seas investment and those in the leisure business, a small apartment in Dubai was actually quite spacious by most terms and palatial by Indian standards.

Overhead cranes nodded and bowed imperiously while they raised skylines and hopes – but only those of the rich. Those creating these marvels of architecture, these gravity-defying constructions, were less ambitious. The majority of construction workers came from India, Pakistan, Bangladesh and Nepal, most on contract. Their goals would not be played out on the manicured grass pitches of Sports City. They had no urge to be part of the tallest buildings in the world, or the most expensive and opulent; their goals were to finish their contracts and go home with money in their pockets to give their families a better life. For that, they were willing to forgo many things and to put up with conditions that were pretty awful for the most part.

The lucky ones had fixed contracts and employers with some scruples; the unlucky were shamelessly exploited and the majority of them never got home for years. They worked in the relentless heat and in sandstorms too. By law, they had to be allowed to have a break if the temperature exceeded fifty degrees Celsius – so, officially, it seldom did. They were ferried in and out of work every day, crowded on the back of open trucks. They slept on paillasses on the floors in their work camp accommodation: others in hammocks and bunks. Conditions were bad, but standards had improved somewhat after a few well-placed documentaries on Western television and with the arrival of some foreign developers who brought with them European standards, if not European wages.

AA was welcomed by his compatriots. They were delighted to have a fellow countryman who could understand them, and their ways.

AA also kept in constant contact with Iswara. Even if she did come to Dubai to be with him, he felt it would not be something she would do from free will, and he wasn't sure if that would be too high a price to ask her to pay in the long run. When they had children perhaps?

They talked on Skype.

'I hate the way your voice echoes in that impersonal space.'

'It's not so bad when you get used to it,' he assured her.

'I just want to be there with you to personalise it, put flowers in the vases and buy loads of colourful throws and plump up the cushions.'

'I want all those things too,' he assured her, but when she hinted about coming to visit him, he put her off as gently as he could, blaming a busy work load and lack of holidays for the next few months as a reason.

'You'll be delighted to hear that I've found a way to fill some of the emptiness in the evenings,' he told her.

'Will I? Are you sure?' she flirted.

'I think you will,' he laughed. 'I've joined the India Club and I've managed to get back into college to finish my computer degree, so that will definitely make me more marketable when all this development dries up.'

'What are you doing to fill the hours when you miss me?' he asked. She told him how she occupied her time by staying late and becoming more and more involved in the activities that they were trying to get off the ground in the new centre.

She had devised a nutritional programme that took into account the limited resources of those coming to learn it and, in doing so, had honed some cooking skills of her own. She used to escape into the kitchen at home when she was younger to watch the staff prepare and season the food. Sometimes she was allowed to bake too. Now, in the evenings as she helped the children form letters and write their first words, she often strayed into the kitchen area of the centre to help out.

'I can feel your presence and feel closer to you there. It's a terrific success. The band of volunteers has increased and Rekna has roped in a few of her friends to join a rota, so that most evenings there's some hot food for those who attend the classes.'

Iswara told him how she had broached sex education with the older ones whom she felt were ready for it, or whom she felt were at risk from being ignorant of such matters.

'That was a bit daunting at first, but once I got over the embarrassment, they did too, and Dr Patel talks to the boys so it's all working out well. Whether it will have any effect, we'll probably never know.'

She missed AA and, despite his excuses, she was now determined to go to Dubai and look into job opportunities over there. She had friends scattered around the UAE, several of whom had gone through medical school with her and who would understand her situation. If she succeeded in finding a post, she knew her parents would be mad with her – but, then again, when weren't they, she reasoned.

CHAPTER 23

Hi Damien

You're probably on your way to the airport now, and I'm about to leave. It's great to be free for a couple of weeks, but you'd think we were going for a month with all the planning and discussion. The wedding's not until Tuesday, so we'll have time to do a little exploring beforehand, maybe even get a bit of colour. I'm told the bride's family is typically Maltese and that means they are expecting several hundred guests. They've also arranged dinners and get-togethers all over the place – vying with each other to impress the new Irish in-laws no doubt, and hoping to give us the once over too, so it should be interesting.

No doubt I'll have loads to tell you when we meet – and yes, that dinner date is a definite!

Look forward to it and to hearing all about your adventures.

Lots of love
Beatrice xx

Beatrice went to the airport with her mother and Ray, and they met up with the rest of the Cullen clan at the check-in area. Once everyone was together, they headed for a bon voyage drink before boarding. Beatrice was introduced to the best man, her cousin's long-time friend Jarlath, an accomplice in lots of mischief over the years, as they were to learn over the next two weeks. They met several other friends and relatives in the bar too, and it seemed as though most of the plane would be full with their group. After a boisterous start to the flight, most of them eventually dozed off. They were all staying in the hotels on the tiny island of Gozo, and had a bus arranged to take them there and across on the ferry. The wedding party was billeted in a resort widely known for its Ayurvedic facilities. It even had an Ayurvedic chef and special menus, they discovered on check-in.

When Beatrice heard this she said, 'I wish to announce that under no circumstances is anyone, or anything, going to make me eat healthily, beneficially or holistically on this holiday. I intend to indulge myself in every way possible.'

'And I second that,' said Jarlath, sidling up beside her.

'I have to agree,' her mother said. 'But I've no objection to studying the spa menu,' she said to Ray.

'I might even be tempted myself,' he replied.

'Let the pampering begin,' a cousin chimed in. 'I like this place already.'

A waiter appeared with a tray full of glasses of Prosecco. Someone proposed a toast and those first clinking of glasses and good-humoured banter were to set the tone for the break.

They took their drinks on to a terrace overlooking the swimming pools. The nearer one had an arched bridge straddling it. Jarlath devoted his attentions to Beatrice and later suggested they go for a walk through the grounds. The bride and her family came to the hotel to join them for dinner. The bride's sister, Marie-Terese, was chief bridesmaid and it was obvious to those who knew Simon well that he had talked Jarlath up to her and she was excited about meeting him. Her eyes followed him everywhere and she kept a place by her at the table. He, in turn, bagged two places and indicated that the other one was for Beatrice. Marie-Terese was having none of it.

'This table is for the bridal party only, so that we can all get to know each other,' she said, looking towards her mother for support.

'Would you mind?' the bride's mother asked Beatrice, 'there'll be plenty of other more informal get-togethers?'

'Of course not,' she replied and moved to join some others at the next table. Jarlath muttered, 'Jealous cow!' to Simon as he passed by. Simon laughed and slapped him on the back.

'Told you they'd be fighting over you. Bridesmaids and best men – a volatile combination! You'd better watch out.'

Hi Beatrice

I made it home, back to temperate weather and a sea breeze. Bliss! Just touching base. Jet lagged and somewhat incoherent. Have to get some rest before I go back to work on Monday. Might pop in tomorrow for a catch-up first. Hope you're having a good time.

Take care
Damien xx

Hi Damien,

Having a ball. Lovely to hear from you.

Eating, drinking, dancing. The best man has decided to squire me around the place. He hired a car and we're off to do a tour of the island. No beaches to talk of, but some dramatic rock formations, and the scuba diving is supposed to be fantastic. Might give that a go after the big day.

The hotel is brochure perfect and there's a fight every morning over who is getting what done in the spa. It's far too nice to be indoors so I'm saving that treat until after I've got the tan.

There's Jarlath at the door now. Must fly. Off to explore.

Have a good rest before you go back to work.

Los of love,
Beatrice xx

Rachel invited her brother over the day after he got back.

'You've lost weight, but you look great,' was how she greeted him.

They chatted about all that had happened on both sides of the world and he told her he had been mailing Beatrice. 'You remember you met her at the last quiz?'

'Oh, the bubbly one. I liked her.'

'So did I,' he admitted with a grin.

Jarlath was well chosen as the best man. He steadied Simon's nerves as the day went on, insisting on taking him for a drive and a long walk, but only after he had heard his speech, his vows and his anxieties, checked they had their cufflinks and the rings and that the buttonholes had arrived and were in the fridge in his room.

'Nothing can go wrong at this stage,' he assured Simon, 'and even if it does, you're well able to talk your way out of any situation. You always have.'

The two had been friends forever, had played rugby together, been there when they had lost wheels on their skateboards, had crashed their mountain bikes, had sprained limbs and had broken romances. There had been lots of those.

'What's with my favourite cuz and you?' asked Simon. 'And what happened to Ruth? Last time I asked, you two seemed very – well – very tight!'

'Oh Ruth's all right. I just didn't want to bring

her along, especially when I have to look after you, and the bridesmaid. Apples to an orchard and all that. And by the way, that bridesmaid might be a looker, but she's a bit full-on and possessive for my liking.'

'Well, I did give you a good build-up and when she heard you were coming solo, she put one and one together and saw the possibility of another wedding in the offing! Then you turn up, and glue Bea to your side, so you can't blame her for trying. By the way, if you mess with Bea, you'll have me to deal with.'

'She's fit and I'm not messing with her, so you needn't worry. But we'll have to face an angry bride if I keep you late for her big moment, so let's get a move on.'

'Just go easy with your speech. I don't think there's any need to tell them everything we got up to.'

'Why not? It's the only chance I'll ever get to do that!' he laughed, but seeing the expression on Simon's face, he relented. 'I won't mention your last fiancée and why that didn't work out, or the fact that she slept her way through your friends to get back at you. Oh, and I've left out the bit about the night we got trolleyed in Marbella and spent the night in the clink.'

'Well that's a relief, but it's what you've left in that bothers me.'

'Relax, you needn't worry!'

★　　★　　★

219

The corridors in the hotel echoed with doors opening and closing as the women went in and out of each other's rooms checking on make-up, borrowing hairspray and admiring outfits. There wasn't a puff of breeze as the guests made their way down through the gardens to the gazebo where the ceremony would take place. Although evening time, it was still stifling hot. The beautiful surroundings were enhanced even more by the setting sun, a huge pink orb, taking its leave silently and gracefully behind the silhouetted branches and tree trunks of some gnarled old olive trees.

Beatrice stood beside her mother and Ray. Jarlath winked at her as he passed with Simon to take their places. And Mary squeezed Ray's arm when she saw this. He smiled at her. Tears were shed and discreetly dabbed away as vows and rings were exchanged; then, amid clapping and congratulations, the newlyweds kissed. Cameras flashed and photos were taken, groups arranged and rearranged, everyone captured for posterity – by the water, by the gazebo, under the trees, by the pool and on the bridge.

When Jarlath could disengage from Marie-Terese, he went in search of Beatrice.

'If I have to smile again, I swear I'll do rabbit ears behind whoever is standing next to me.'

Beatrice laughed. 'I'm starving. What time will we be fed?'

'Shortly I believe, but it's not a sit-down meal. That's not how they do weddings over here – it's a running buffet with loads and loads of courses and you just circulate and eat as you go around.'

'I didn't know that.'

'Neither did I, until Marie-Terese told me when I asked her where was the seating plan. I had been hoping to switch a few name cards around, if you know what I mean,' he whispered. 'But I have to say, I'm relieved I don't have to sit through another meal beside her.'

'I thought she was really nice.'

'She is, but I feel I'm being interviewed every time we talk. "What do you do? How many staff do you employ? Could you see yourself living somewhere hot like Malta? Would you like to marry me and have babies together?"'

'She didn't ask you that!'

'No, she didn't, not in so many words, but that's definitely the not-so-veiled subplot. I've met enough women in my time to recognise the signs.'

'What an ego! I bet you're imagining it, or maybe it's just a case of wishful thinking.'

'I'm not, you know. Simon sold me to them as being marriageable, eligible and desperately seeking a wife; now that he is no longer free to go gallivanting with me, he wants everyone to get shackled.'

'You guys never grow up, do you?' she laughed.

'Happily no!'

Jarlath's speech was complimentary, witty and charming and left no need for Simon, or indeed anyone else, to squirm. He presented the bridesmaid with a flower as he thanked her for minding the bride and for looking so lovely. After that, he had the older women wondering where he was when their daughters were looking around for a man.

The dancing started and Jarlath did his duty turns before claiming Beatrice for most of the other ones.

'I can never get you on your own,' he complained as they danced. 'And it looks as though I'm about to lose you again.'

He had spotted Ray approaching to claim her for the next dance. They partied till early morning and Jarlath did his best in chat-up lines to get Beatrice back to his room, but she declined.

Not many of them appeared for breakfast the following day.

Beatrice was going to email Damien and tell him all about the bash, but decided to leave it until later as there was no wi-fi in her room. She was glad he was back in Dublin and was excited at getting to see him again. She thought of him a lot as she spent the afternoon by the pool where a group of them all chipped in at the post-mortem. The style, the food, the venue and the overall experience were rated and all scored highly. It was the following day before she opened her laptop.

Dear Damien
I could get used to this life, lazing about – too lazy to write, so forgive me!

It's taken us a day to recover from the main event, which was great. Everyone has made us so welcome and Simon's new in-laws, all forty thousand of them, are really nice! They know how to party, and with so many of them it was lucky that we had decided to come over en masse, or we'd have been lost in the multitude.

The food was gourmet, unconventional by our wedding traditions, but it was a series of literally dozens of dishes which just kept appearing one after another and all delicious. The local wines went down well too.

Yesterday we headed over the mainland and visited Mdina, an old walled city. This whole place is steeped in history, the Knights Templar, the Crusades and all that. I think it was invaded by everyone at some stage and, although I'm not really into remembering dates and battles, it's intriguing to wander through little alleys and archways that have been intact for centuries. The only traffic noise is from the horses' hooves and that adds to the sense of being back in time. I never get that sense of history wandering around Dublin – maybe visitors do – or maybe I should do it by carriage sometime!

What about you? Are you settling back? Have you done your walk down the pier yet?

We're off to do some diving today.
Hard life!
Take care
Beatrice xx

By the time they met up in the cool foyer of the hotel, Jarlath had made a few phone calls and had made plans. They trooped out and a group of them piled into two jeeps and headed for Xlendi to go diving. The little port was crammed with tourists all waiting to sign their consent forms and have their induction sessions before collecting wetsuits and scuba equipment. The boats at the quayside were filled with enthusiastic passengers and put-putted out into the open sea amid a whiff of diesel and a displacement of gulls. Jarlath's group was divided according to their experience or, in some cases, their lack of experience. Beatrice wanted to see the underwater arches she'd read about, maybe even swim beneath them if that were feasible. One of Simon's friends was determined to see at least one of the many sunken wrecks that litter the seabed around Gozo. Others were both excited and apprehensive at trying a dive for the first time.

'What can we expect to see down there?' asked one.

'Fish, fantastic fauna and amazing rock formations,' their skipper, an Australian marine biologist who was taking a six-month break from his usual waters along the Great Barrier Reef, told them. 'I find people are often amazed by the variety of vegetation and the colours, and of the fish they meet down there. You're likely to see barracuda and octopus.'

'Don't they eat and strangle people?'

'Not around here they don't; anyway, we won't be threatening them. It's amazing what you'll find when you know what to look for. You'll often see amberjacks down there too, near to the wrecks and in the deeper waters off shore. It's ideal around here because of all the caves; it gives them plenty of places to hide.'

Beatrice and Jarlath were on the boat for seasoned divers. It anchored some distance off shore. They made adjustments to their equipment and after a final check by the skipper they launched into the clear waters. Beatrice felt that rush of adrenalin as the sounds of normal life were substituted by those of her rasping breath, her rapid heartbeat echoing in her ears, and the gurgling and bubbling as she expelled air. She was astonished at how bright it was and by the incredible scenery. Jarlath was a few feet in front of her and he pointed to her to look ahead and made signs that he was going in that direction. She nodded and followed him, revelling in the freedom of this other world which was full of activity and beauty and yet one so many people never got to see. Even down here the sunshine made a difference and the sea changed colours from aqua to deep turquoise.

As they approached the narrow tunnel that the rocky arch bridge spanned, it changed to inky blue.

She glided beneath, accompanied by shoals of tiny fish that glistened as they turned suddenly and altered direction as though synchronised. Jarlath was pointing at another sight farther ahead. They swam to the entrance but it was too dark inside to see anything. Beatrice followed Jarlath and some others back through the arch again with her body-guard of minnows whilst larger fish regarded her and her cohorts disdainfully. This was magical. She looked up at the sky above the rocky ravine and it was like an oriel window looking out at infinity.

'That was all over too soon,' she said as they clambered aboard their boat some time later. 'We've got to do it again.'

In fact, the two weeks were going by far too quickly and Jarlath was becoming more attentive by the day. He hinted at moving things on a bit, but Beatrice only had to think of Paul and her resolve of not getting caught up in another relationship web became even stronger. She wasn't jumping into that quagmire again any time soon.

They went diving twice more, some of the group fulfilling their wish of going down to a wreck. They joined a group who dived to one of the two East German minesweepers that had been scuttled in recent years, specifically for that purpose.

'Things seem to be going well with you two,' her mother said to her. They had gone into Victoria to the market and were making a pit stop for coffee in the busy square, Beatrice had already bought shoes and a leather bag. She laughed at her mother.

'Yes. So-ooo?'

'So-ooo, things seem to be going well with the two of you,' she laughed back, knowing her daughter well.

'They are. And I think you should buy that tan bag. It's gorgeous.'

'Maybe I should,' she agreed, then after a pause she added, 'He seems very nice.'

'He is and I'm enjoying his attentions. It's flattering to have the best-looking man around pursue me.'

'But . . .'

'But what?'

'But – this is not reality. It's holidays and I'm not about to forget that. It's way too soon after Paul. Besides, I'm not going to do anything silly.'

'I wasn't worried that you would,' Mary said. 'Just enjoy it and see where it goes – if it goes anywhere at all.'

'Exactly, *if* it goes anywhere at all!' Beatrice said, firmly ending the conversation. 'Now go and buy that bag.'

Dear Beatrice

I take it your silence means you are having a great time and are far too busy to write. You've spoiled me with your daily mails. And now I find I'm missing them!

I'm back a week already and it's hard to believe that I was ever in India at all. Went back into work on Monday and it felt very strange being surrounded by the familiar again. There's a whole new wave of students to shepherd. Thirteen of them come from India and they seemed pleased to hear I'd been there.

It was lovely catching up with the 'old' students, if a bit chastening to think I could go off for eight weeks and not be missed! My deputy even seemed sorry to see me.

Were your ears burning yesterday? You remember Abdul, the Libyan whose papers you helped me with when he had to go home suddenly? Well he did get sorted in the end. His government gave him permission to come back and complete his postgrad studies and he got the place he interviewed for in endocrinology, so he and I are eternally grateful to you, lady.

And yes, I've walked the pier, in fact I've walked it every day. Some people pray or meditate – that is my spiritual sustenance.

I'll give you a call when you get back and we can do it and that meal together.

Best

Damien x

PS A mobile number might help!

Oh Damien

Apologies for neglecting you. I really have no excuse except that of being surrounded by too many people I know, and all of them (and me too!) trying to make the most of this trip. It's a bit like clan gatherings you hear about, when all the Joyces from Galway or the Murphys from Cork get together for a reunion. There's so much to catch up on. You should hear us at meal times, the din is unbelievable. And it's great fun!

We took over a whole restaurant the other night and had a fantastic seafood meal. We all traipsed into the kitchens to pick our choice of fish from the tanks, before they prepared it. There were twenty-five of us initially, all connected through family. Now we've adopted a few more, as well a whole slew of Simon's new in-laws. Several of them have holiday homes here on Gozo, which seems incongruous to us, as Malta, where they all live, is only twenty minutes away by ferry and that's not even twenty miles long and ten across!

It seems like all the villages have their own festivals and everyone joins in. They festoon their balconies with flags and drapes and little food stalls appear everywhere selling things like nougat filled with almond nuts. Delicious! I have to admit I'm addicted. (I'll bring you some home to try.) They also seem to have weekly firework displays here and every so often there's a cannon blast that would waken the dead.

I'm delighted to hear about Abdul. It's nice when cases have a positive outcome and he deserved one. Well done you – for being such a terrier! I promise I'll go easier on you the next time you have a problem with one of your charges.

Flying home on Sunday so we'll talk next week, when I'm back at the grind. Maybe we can do the pier together some evening too.

Till then, take care,

Beatrice xx

She scribbled her mobile number as a PS on the end.

They spent their last evening on Gozo at a farm where the family grew their own grapes and produced their own wine, honey, olives and oil, tomato pastes and all sorts of other things. Although tented to keep the sun off by day, there was an open barbecue area at one end and they stood around drinking wine as their meat sizzled and tempting aromas filled the night air. Jarlath hadn't left Beatrice's side all evening.

'Let's get away from this lot for a while,' he suggested.

'We can't just up and leave,' she protested.

'Why not? No one will even miss us.'

'I wouldn't be so sure about that. Mother-in-law and Marie-Terese have gimlet eyes.'

'Then let's give them something to talk about. Come on, let's go for a walk up the hills.'

He took her hand as they slipped away, not entirely unnoticed. Mary saw them leave. They strolled through the lemon groves, stopping every so often to kiss. Beatrice was happy to do that, but when Jarlath got more amorous and his hand snaked its way under her top as he held her closer, she pulled back. He became more aggressive and she pushed him away.

'No . . .'

'You're giving me mixed messages here,' he said roughly, 'either you do or you don't.'

'Jarlath, I told you. I'm not ready for a relationship.'

'That's not what it seems like to me. Anyway, who said anything about a relationship? I was only thinking sex. What's wrong with that? Don't you want to have any fun?'

'I don't want that sort of fun, and if anything, you seem to be the one who's getting mixed messages. I made it quite clear all along. I like you, Jarlath. You've very attractive and you're great company, but I don't want anything more. Besides, what about your girlfriend back home? Is she not waiting for you, maybe even expecting you to be faithful for two whole weeks?'

'That's none of your business,' he snapped, really angry now.

'It is, if you expect me to help you cheat on her, or maybe you thought I'd be so charmed that I'd fall flat on my back for you, if and when you decided you wanted to have sex with someone. It may work with others but I've no intention of being your holiday bit.'

'That's ridiculous. You don't even know me, and you're jumping to wild conclusions.'

'That's exactly why I wanted to get to know you first, but it looks as though you are conforming beautifully to a stereotype I don't like, and I have to ask myself why am I not surprised?'

'What do you mean?' he shot back at her, his ego dinted at being compared to any other man, never mind a 'type'.

'Suit yourself. You're a frigid bitch,' he shouted at her as he turned and stomped back through the trees, leaving her standing incredulously in the moonlight.

'You bastard. You egotistical bastard,' she called after him. 'And if I'm a frigid bitch what does that make you? A selfish prick who sulks when he doesn't get his own way. Grow up.'

He kept on walking.

She stood for a while, trembling and looking up at the night sky. The moon didn't look as romantic now. In fact, it looked cold and lonely up there in the dark emptiness. *Well, you didn't see that coming, girl, did you? Another disaster to add to your list. You're certainly chalking them up*, she said to herself. She didn't know how long she stayed before following the path back down to the party. He was nowhere to be seen, but Mary had noticed him coming back alone and was on the lookout for her daughter. Once she saw her return, she relaxed.

He kept out of Beatrice's way at the airport the next day and it wasn't difficult to avoid him in the melee in Dublin as they collected their luggage at the carousel and took their leave of the rest of the group, with embraces and promises to keep in touch.

Mary and Ray passed knowing glances at each other, observing the state of play, but neither made any reference to Jarlath as the three of them shared a taxi home, dropping Beatrice off at her flat on the way.

'Back to work tomorrow?' her mother asked.

'No, I'm not in until Tuesday. I need a day to catch up on the laundry and food shopping and all the things I should have done before I went away. I'll give you a ring in the morning,' she called as she took her bags from the taxi man and headed for the security of her flat.

CHAPTER 24

Beatrice did mundane post-holiday things on the Monday, and wondered if she'd get a call from Damien. She didn't and she went back to work on Tuesday a little deflated. It was September, her favourite month, and she could smell autumn in the air.

Irene filled her in on developments. The Nigerian and Congolese deportees who had been refused permission to fly over Algeria had eventually been repatriated, after much negotiation and diplomatic intervention. She was currently preoccupied with a family where a Somalian father had a work permit but hadn't declared that he had a wife and three children when he had got his papers. Now he was trying to bring them to Ireland and the case had landed on Irene's desk.

'Let's go out to lunch,' Irene suggested. 'I want to find out all about the wedding and the holiday.'

They headed to the pub around the corner and ordered soup and sandwiches. Once they had found somewhere to sit Irene said, 'Come on, tell all. Did you meet anyone nicer than yourself?'

'Lots, but not in the way you mean it.'

'No romance?'

'No romance,' Beatrice answered firmly, still too annoyed to tell anyone about Jarlath.

'You're a lost cause.'

'Does that mean you've given up on me and that I won't have to go out on any more of your set-up dates and pretend to be interested in somebody because he comes with an Irene recommendation?'

'You can't stay single for ever.'

'Why not? I'm loving it,' Beatrice laughed. 'So leave my social diary alone, please! Anyway, you're one to talk. When are you going to make an honest man out of Daragh?'

'Never. We enjoy what we've got. We both have our own space and that suits us just fine. As he says, if it ain't broke, don't fix it. And I agree with him.'

'That sounds good to me too.'

'However,' Irene said, pausing for effect, 'I'm going to invite Damien and a few friends around for a barbecue at the weekend before the weather gets too cold, and you have to be there. That's an order.'

'Yes, Ma'am. I think I could manage to behave myself for a few hours!'

The next evening, Beatrice was in a rage, having decided to ignore two calls from Jarlath, who, until now, hadn't tried to make contact since his outburst on Saturday. She put on her music in an effort to retreat from the world, but Mimi's duet was interrupted by the phone.

'Damn and blast,' she muttered. 'How dare he keep annoying me?' But it was a different number that popped up – Damien's.

'It's glorious out here in Dún Laoghaire, and I keep thinking of the ice cream you promised me. Do you fancy a stroll?'

Her first inclination was to think up an excuse, any excuse. She wasn't in the mood for banter or for being social with anyone of the opposite sex. She couldn't think of anything plausible enough to sound convincing, so she reluctantly agreed to meet at the Dart station.

'I can pick you up. It's no bother.'

'No, that's fine. I'll hop on the Dart, it's only a few stops and it means I don't need to worry about parking.'

'There's ample space in my apartment complex if you want to come there.'

'No thanks, I'll take the Dart.' *I won't be going anywhere near your flat,* she thought.

She was unsure how she would feel about meeting Damien again and, on reflection, she felt she had revealed a lot about herself, too much maybe, in her emails to him. But then, she reasoned with herself, so had he. She didn't really know him, yet she felt she did. While she walked to the station, her phone beeped again – a text this time – from Jarlath.

> Sorry, B, can I make it up to you? Give
> me a chance, please.

She deleted it instantly. His girlfriend had probably dumped him, but if he thought Beatrice was going to go running, he had another thing coming.

She had calmed down somewhat by the time she reached the appointed rendezvous spot, where Damien was already waiting. They greeted each other like old friends and hugged, talking for a few minutes before turning towards the east pier, heading past the National Yacht Club and the bustle of activity that always reigned around this hub. They turned down by the slipway that had seen the launch of many lifeboats in its day and headed along the lower level. Couples strolled arm in arm. Parents walked kiddies to tire them out before bedtime. There was a single majestic-looking tall ship docked at the quayside, with its rigging furled and tidy. It was open to the public and manned by a smartly uniformed crew. Beatrice and Damien stopped and read about it on a temporary notice board. It was a training vessel, manned by young people with disabilities, both male and female. The brasses shone, the paintwork gleamed, and the decks were scrubbed spotless.

Beatrice remarked, 'I suppose that's what they mean by "ship shape and Bristol fashion". It's pristine.'

They sauntered on by the moored yachts, some small and manageable, others large and imposing.

Farther out in the harbour, others were heading back after a few hours on the water. A few children ran up and down the bandstand steps. People walked their dogs and a busker played a ukulele. As they reached the end of the pier, the high-speed ferry departed from its dock, leaving an ever-widening gushing, bubbling, foamy crested wake behind it. They watched as it slid between the light-houses at the extremities of the protective arms of the two piers before they climbed the steps to the lookout point. Already the vessel was making swift progress on the open sea. 'If we go for a drink after our walk, that'll probably be reaching Holyhead before we get home,' Damien said.

Beatrice was surprised at how easy it was to talk to him. She didn't feel at all as though they were virtual strangers, or that they were trying to get to know each other. There was a relaxed bond between them and she found she was interested to know what he was thinking. She asked about his project. He told her about it. She told him about work. When he asked about the wedding and Malta, she just said it had been good and changed the subject by remarking on a pair of highly groomed St Bernard dogs being walked by a diminutive woman. She didn't appear to be getting much exercise as everyone kept stopping to admire them.

When they reached the top of the pier they turned left and continued along the esplanade towards Teddy's ice cream kiosk. Ahead, James

Joyce's tower stood out behind the little beach at Sandycove where the last of the swimmers and jet skiers were packing up to go home.

'I do believe you promised me a 99,' Damien said. They crossed the road to stand in the queue.

'Don't tell me you've had one every day since you came back too,' Beatrice said.

'No. I was keeping that pleasure to share.'

She smiled as she handed over her money. They relished the creamy texture, 'yumming' in unison as they sampled the first creamy lick.

'What are we like at all?' he laughed.

'A pair of grown-up kids,' she said and they continued walking.

'You've no idea how I longed for one of these in India.'

'I can't even begin to imagine what it must have been like.'

'You'd have to have been there. It's just so difficult to describe – the scale of the poverty and the wealth, the contrasts and the way everyone accepts their station in life without complaining. I wonder if their belief in karma makes it easier to do that.'

'I'm not sure, but it probably helps if you believe that next time around you'll get a better shake of the bag.'

'Right, enough of that doom and gloom. Let's go and have a drink.'

They headed to a pub in Glasthule and sat in a quiet corner.

'Irene has invited my sister Rachel and myself

to a barbecue at her place on Saturday next. I presume you'll be there too,' Damien said.

'I will. She's already given me my orders and I've warned her no more blind dates.'

'Didn't you meet anyone at the wedding? You seemed to have hit it off well with the best man. What was his name? Jarlath? For some reason I always think Jarlaths should be dentists.'

'I think they should be exterminated,' Beatrice said.

'That's a bit radical, isn't it?' he asked. 'And would that be because they are called Jarlath or because they are dentists?'

'Either is good enough.'

He said nothing and she added, 'Let's talk about something else.'

'Right so,' he agreed and they sat in silence for a few minutes thinking of a subject, before they both started laughing. An hour later, he saw her back to the nearest station after she had refused to allow him drive her home. They were still arguing about this when the train arrived and she hopped on, calling back, 'I'll see you at Irene's on Saturday.'

He stood and watched the lights of the rear carriage disappear into the distance.

On the train, she sent an email to thank him for the walk and the drinks and his reply thanked her for the ice cream. Both said they were looking forward to the barbecue.

★　★　★

Damien sat in St Stephen's Green to eat his lunch the next day. It was a balmy September afternoon. He wondered how Iswara and AA were coping with their separation, and if she had not been attracted to him would Damien have had a chance with her. Even if he had, it probably would have been very complicated with distances and cultural differences. Then he thought of Beatrice and found himself looking forward to their next meeting. She had wormed her way into his consciousness, yet for some reason he felt it wouldn't do to rush things with her.

Saturday was another fine autumn day as Irene set about the preparations for her barbecue. Beatrice had arrived in the morning to give a hand. She'd had five more calls and as many texts from Jarlath in the interim, and had cut each one off the minute the name appeared on caller ID. She was beginning to think he was stalking her and wondered if she would get her message across better if she actually confronted him on the phone. However, she reckoned he was one of those guys who wouldn't take no for an answer. She still couldn't get over the way he had switched from being Mr Nice Guy to Mr Proverbial Prick in an instant.

Irene's idea of a few drinks was to fill the fridge with bubbly and a few buckets with ice and bottles and let everyone help themselves. She had a spacious garden flat, bought with her inheritance when her parents had died and a manageable mortgage. It was in a gated community in Dublin 4 and had a sizeable patio and a garden. Because of her penchant for parties she had quickly learned that the best way to stave off complaints from her neighbours was to invite them along too, so by the time the other guests began to arrive in the early afternoon there were a good few people there, several whom Beatrice had met before.

Damien arrived with his sister and her boyfriend Sean.

'We'll be all right if someone suggests a quiz,' Sean joked. 'We have a whole team here.'

'Make yourself useful and start asking if anyone needs a drink,' Irene said to Damien after he had greeted everyone.

Irene's partner Daragh was the one in charge of the barbecue. Inside, potatoes baked in the oven and desserts joined the growing number of salads as more friends arrived with offerings in hand.

It was a boisterous and lively afternoon. Damien whispered as he passed Beatrice, 'Well, are any of your interesting blind dates here?'

'Yes. Two of them. See if you can spot them. The Laugh and The Golfer are here so far – why do you think I'm hiding back here?' As if on cue, everyone seemed to stop talking and there was a lull, before it was ruptured by a high-pitched hee-haw, followed by a whinny.

Damien caught her eye and said, 'Bingo. I think I got that one. And I actually thought you had been exaggerating!'

'As if I could exaggerate that,' she said, rolling her eyes heavenwards.

As they stood deliberating, a stocky fellow stood out on the grass, lined up an imaginary putt and played an imaginary shot. Satisfied that he had putted the imaginary ball, he repeated the process without pausing the conversation he was having with two guys who were standing beside him.

'I think I found The Golfer.'

'You're good,' she joked.

Beatrice helped Irene bring the food around and then clear up afterwards. 'Does that mean you weren't exaggerating about the Pilates ball either?' Damien asked when they passed each other again.

'Definitely not, and you've just reminded me that classes start again on Tuesday.'

'You don't need them. You look great.'

'Thanks, but I'm really going for the social aspect. When my father died, I was only a tot and my mother's friends were fantastic. I call them my honorary aunties. Ever since, they have done something together every winter. They've gone through all sorts of activities and that's why I'm doing the Pilates class – to meet up with them. Afterwards, we all go out for a drink together.'

'Sounds like a good bit of craic.'

'It is, although I wouldn't necessarily want to do everything they do. Each year someone different chooses the activity. They've done art and pottery, walking even. They once joined a knitting circle and made matinee jackets to send to developing countries. I was doing my Leaving Cert then and it gave me the perfect excuse to get out of that. One of them is a lot older and very religious and she made them all go to a novena every week one winter – to St Jude. That was years ago. My mother met Ray after that and her friend swears it was because of the novenas!'

'Do you believe all that?' Damien asked.

'Do I? Are you mad?' she said incredulously. 'If it were that easy there'd be no poverty, no war, no cancer, no depression.'

'I'm inclined to agree with you there.'

'Stop hogging my best waitress,' Irene said, going back into the kitchen.

'That's us told off,' Beatrice said. 'I'd better pass the desserts around.'

When she went in, Rachel was trying to arrange an evening for them to get together.

'My bro is threatening to cook for us. I hope you'll come too,' she said to Beatrice.

'Thank you. That sounds lovely. I'll let you know,' she said, going back outside with a plate stacked with profiteroles. It was after seven when she called a taxi and got her jacket.

Damien collared her and asked her to have dinner with him the next week. She declined. He looked surprised, but didn't push it. 'Maybe some other time.'

'Yes, maybe some other time,' she said and went out to her taxi, leaving him to wonder what he had done or said to displease her.

CHAPTER 25

Rekna's husband was away on business and Iswara had decided to stay overnight with her, to share some rare time together. Her boys had finally gone to bed and they were enjoying catching up without the interruption of endless questions and demands to play games or read stories.

'So tell me, have you heard from AA and what's happening with you two?' Rekna asked.

'We talk on Skype every other day – for ages – if the connection doesn't go down. I want to go over to visit him because we're at an impasse with such a distance between us, but every time I suggest it he puts me off.'

'Do you think his feelings are cooling?'

'No, I'm sure they're not. I think he's just hoping mine will and I'll go away and we can get on with our lives as they were before we met. But I know I won't ever do that. I can't imagine not having him there in the future, no matter how many obstacles we have to cross to be together.'

'It's not going to be easy, but you don't need

me to tell you that. You know you can depend on us to stand by you no matter what you decide.'

'That means so much to me Rekna, it really does. Thank you.'

'I'm not sure it will be any help when it comes to telling Mama and Papa. They'll be devastated.'

'I know, that will be the hardest part and I don't want to compromise your relationship with them. They won't be too pleased with you for siding with us.'

'They respect my in-laws, and with them on our side – and they will be – that should add weight to your arguments. Besides, they chose this family for me!' Rekna laughed. 'Mama wouldn't have anyone else and isn't her only son-in-law "the head of marketing for half of India"?' the sisters chorused, imitating their mother, who never missed an opportunity to tell this to anyone who would listen.

'But you are happy, aren't you?' Iswara asked.

'I couldn't be happier. I've been very lucky. I have a husband I love, three great and gorgeous kids, and I'm not a bit biased. I might even have a daughter one day that I can call after you! And I have my volunteer work. I just want you to have the same.' Rekna became serious again: 'Attitudes are changing, Iswara, but they won't change overnight and unfortunately religious prejudices seem to have a life of their own.'

'I realise that, and no matter how quickly they change outside, I know that Mama will never accept a Muslim into the family.'

'I'm inclined to agree. So what will you do?'

'I'm prepared to move away and start a new life somewhere more liberal.'

'But surely that's not in Dubai.'

'No, that would be even worse than here. It would have to be somewhere non-Muslim, or more cosmopolitan.'

'You know they'll probably disinherit you,' Rekna said, 'and Mama will probably do everything to stop you getting Grandpapa's money too.'

'I'm not worried about that, although it would make a big difference if I had it and could pass some of it on to the school and medical centre. Perhaps if they give it to you, you could make sure some of it ends up there.'

'Of course. You seem to have it all thought out, Iswara, but these are huge sacrifices. Are you really sure this is what you want? Does AA know about the money?'

'No, and I have no intention of telling him – ever. It would just put more pressure on the decisions we have to make and also give him a reason to walk away. As he thinks he's asking too much of a sacrifice of me already, he certainly wouldn't countenance a marriage if he knew I had given up that legacy too. '

'But how will you live?'

'Happily medicine and engineering degrees are pretty universal, although depending on where we go we'd both probably have to do further studies to get local qualifications. AA's actually doing computer programming in Dubai, to make him more marketable, as he puts it.'

'Well, you seem to be moving things along in the right direction.'

'We are, but he wants to go more slowly, to give us plenty of time to look at all the angles.'

'That sounds very sensible to me. Have you thought about where you'll go?'

'I've thought about Ireland. I have lots of friends there and contacts too, and I would be able to start work as soon as I got sponsorship. Although construction has dried up, there's a huge contingent of Indians working in IT in Dublin, so that's an option for AA too. Or we could look at Canada.'

'I hate to think of you going so far away again. We missed out on so much time together already.'

'You can always come and visit us wherever we end up.'

'That won't be the same.'

'I know, but there doesn't seem to be any other way around things.'

'So what will you do next?'

'I'm going to sound Damien out. He's been a really good friend and I trust his judgement.'

'Will you talk to Papa?'

'I can't. Not yet anyway. He'd feel duty bound to tell Mama and I can't deal with all that until other things are in place.'

'I suppose you're right. They never keep anything from each other.'

'Do you keep secrets from your husband?' Iswara asked.

'Never.'

'Well then, I'll probably end up being the same – if I ever manage to get so far as having a husband to call my own.'

'You will,' Rekna said. 'Of course you will.'

In their affluent home, Daya and Raj Singhanid were discussing their daughters. Daya, still determined to find a suitable husband for Iswara, was planning another attack on those men she considered acceptable suitors. She hadn't given up on the widower in her husband's clinic.

'We'll have them over in the afternoon, that way we can include Sanjay Ranjan's little girls too and they can play with Rekna's boys.'

'Now, Daya, don't tell me you're thinking about wives for them at this stage,' her husband grinned at her.

'Don't be silly, Raj,' she grinned back.

'Try not to be too obvious, dear,' he urged gently. 'Every mother of unmarried eligible daughters has Sanjay on their hit list.'

'As if I would!' she retorted.

'Have you asked her if she likes anybody?' her husband asked rationally. 'She may have a man in Ireland or elsewhere, maybe even that Damien chap who came out to the medical centre. I liked him.'

'So did I, but he's a foreigner.'

'Does that matter so much if she finds happiness?' he urged.

'I know I should say it doesn't, but it does matter to me. What if she marries a European and moves there? We'd never get to see our grandchildren, if she has any.'

'But wouldn't that be better for her, to have a family of her own, even if they weren't close by? Besides, if she did move away they'd probably have her husband's family to indulge the next generation.'

'I suppose so,' she agreed reluctantly, 'but I'd prefer she stayed at home.'

CHAPTER 26

Irene was giving Beatrice the third degree one morning in work the week after the barbecue. She was trying to draw her out on the state of play between her and Damien, but Beatrice wasn't playing the game at all.

Frustrated, Irene asked her right out if she was going out with him again.

'What makes you think he asked me?'

'The way he acted as your bodyguard on Saturday.'

'I hadn't noticed,' she lied.

'Not half,' Irene muttered, then after a pause she said, 'Well, did he ask you or not?'

'He did and I said no.'

'You what?'

'I declined, graciously.'

'You're mad! I give up on you.'

'Well that's a bonus,' she replied.

Beatrice wasn't ready to admit that perhaps she'd made a mistake and had been too hasty in turning Damien down. She had had three more texts from Jarlath and got more annoyed each time another one popped up. She blocked his number. She hadn't contacted Damien since the barbecue and her empty inbox disturbed her. She had got used to seeing his name there in the mornings. She wanted to get in touch, but didn't know how to make that move.

Damien's inbox that morning contained a long email from Iswara, telling him what was happening at the centre and the school, and outlining her dilemma. She asked his advice about getting a permit or sponsorship to work in Ireland.

Damien

I hope you don't mind me asking you these things, but as you know AA too, I feel you understand, and you've been such a good friend to both of us already. I'm planning a visit to Dubai in April. By then we'll have been apart for seven months and we'll know if we still feel the same way. I know I will. If we do decide to get married, we'll do that in India before coming to Ireland.

I've decided to say nothing to my parents until after we've made some decisions. So, depending on how quickly after that they want to have me deported, I'm probably looking for a placement in late summer or early autumn next year.

I really appreciate your help and value your friendship greatly.

Much love

Iswara

Emailing Beatrice had become such second nature to Damien that he now found he wanted to write to her, but he held back. Whatever had happened between them was a mystery to him. He had felt the equilibrium shift when he suggested dinner, but couldn't explain why when they had seemed to be getting on so well. He had been so sure that there was a definite affinity between them. Perhaps there really had been something between her and that best man. Putting that aside for the moment, he began to probe the possibilities of getting a placement and a sponsorship for Iswara.

CHAPTER 27

The autumnal colours had faded in St Stephen's Green as the days closed in. The crisp, fallen leaves, whipped into a frenzy by the sudden November gusts, tumbled and raced along the paths: pedestrians crossing the park tightened their scarves and held on to their hats. Beatrice decided to take a short cut to Grafton Street to do some lunchtime shopping. It had just started to rain and she put up her umbrella, which promptly got caught by another gust and turned inside out. She turned around to let the next one blow it back into shape when she backed into a man hurrying along in the other direction.

'I'm so sorry,' they both said. She was still trying to right the problematic brolly so she didn't really look up at him until she recognised the voice.

'Beatrice!'

'Damien!'

'No harm done. I've just had to bin my one. It was beyond redemption. Shocking day, isn't it?'

'Dreadful. How have you been?' she asked.

'Great. You look as though you're in a rush, but would you like to have a drink some time?'

She found herself saying, 'I'd love to. What about after work today or—?'

'Today's good with me. In the place around the corner from your office?'

'Great, I'll see you there.'

As she hurried to get her errand done she found herself grinning and admitted she was looking forward to catching up with Damien. She had got used to the lack of communication, but she didn't like it. Irene had tried a few times to intervene, contriving meetings and phone calls, but Beatrice had remained resolute. Now she felt she was ready to meet him again.

The smell of damp clothes filled the air as drenched commuters, who had decided to avoid the rush hour, came in to the warm pub to have one for the road. Beatrice had secured a table in the corner when Damien found her. After ordering the drinks he sat down and without preamble he said, 'I've missed your emails.'

She felt herself colour before admitting, 'And I, yours. I wanted to start writing again.'

'So did I, but I didn't know whether you'd feel I was forcing my attentions on you. I had thought we were getting on very well, in fact better than that. Did I say something to offend you?'

'Damien, I'm sorry. That was my fault. Maybe I'll tell you about it sometime, but let's not spoil this. I was in a bad place when I came back from Malta. I didn't want to go out with anyone or get close to anyone again either, and I panicked when you asked me to dinner.'

'Could I expect a different reaction if I were to ask again?' He looked directly at her and she grinned.

'You'll have to ask if you want to find out!'

'Madam, would you do me the honour of accompanying me to dinner one evening – soon?'

'Madam would be delighted to accept.' She remembered he had promised to cook an Indian meal for her when he got back, but she stopped short of reminding him – that was too intimate and too soon.

'Whew! I'm glad we got that out of the way,' he said. 'We've a lot of catching up to do.'

'I have to tell you, though, I'm not in the market for anything serious.' *Might as well get that out in the open from the word go*, she reasoned with herself.

'And why would you think that I want that?' Damien asked with a grin. 'I'm not exactly planning the wedding yet.'

'Good, so long as we understand each other. Now, can I buy you a drink and a bit of pub grub? I skipped my lunch today and I'm starving.'

They chatted until ten o'clock, and after fixing a date, they walked together under her scarred umbrella to the Dart station to take their trains home.

Early the next day, a memo arrived from the head of the faculty. It was addressed to Damien and to several of the deans and administrators.

It's time to schedule a meeting re the recruitment drive and postgraduate programmes in the UAE. Let me know if any of these times suit as we need to get cracking on dates as soon as feasible.

He checked his diary and replied with a few options, then sent a quick note to Beatrice.

So glad we got things sorted. D x

Her reply was even shorter.

So am I! B x

CHAPTER 28

They were under pressure at the medical centre. An outbreak of measles was sweeping through the unvaccinated, both children and adults, and the outreach workers were doing their best to get protection to as many as possible. This was a mammoth task with over 300,000 in the rag pickers' communities in Mumbai. As notices or posters were useless, the most efficient way was to visit the shacks and ghettos with locals and try to tell them of the dangers. They also sent people to the collection points in the dumps close by, where the rag pickers gathered at the end of the day to sell what they had found.

The epidemic didn't warrant any lines in the local newspapers, although the number of the dead had increased, but the doctors and other staff at the centre roped in their friends and families to help, and together they manned the kitchen in the new building, providing a hot meal and drinks to anyone attending the clinic. They were soon inundated with takers and the director sent for some of the street vendors to set up just inside the fence to augment supplies and ensure everyone got some sustenance.

This frenzy of activity had been going on for a week. Everyone was exhausted.

'I insist you go home now,' Iswara said to two nurses who had come straight from their shifts at a local hospital to help out. 'If you get overtired you're only going to be more vulnerable and susceptible to getting sick, so go now and have a good meal before you go to bed.'

'I think it is a question of the doctor taking some of her own medicine, Iswara,' the director said. 'It's time you went home too. Tomorrow is another day.'

She was too tired to argue. She'd been working twelve-hour days, and as well as the army of sick patients and those waiting for their injections, they still had to deal with the usual ailments and illnesses associated with being exposed to filth and decaying detritus, old medicines, punctured spray cans, chemicals and pesticides. Most of these people worked barefoot and barehanded in the dumps, and often in temperatures as high as 45 degrees. The lucky ones found discarded trainers or worn-out shoes to wear.

Her mother was waiting for her when she got home and Iswara anticipated a tirade of re-crimination, but it didn't come. Daya Singhanid didn't chide her for overdoing it. She had been married to a doctor for long enough to know that in times of extreme crisis, the patients came first and although she wouldn't admit it to her daughter, she was very proud of her dedication and zeal.

She said, 'I'll run a bath for you and you can have something to eat then. You must be exhausted.'

The epidemic worked its way out over the next several weeks and Iswara had been so busy she hadn't had time to correspond with AA or fix a time for them to Skype each other. She had just rushed a note one day telling him what was going on and asking him to please be patient.

When they finally got around to a proper call he told her, 'Not hearing from you made me realise what a void there was in my life. I missed hearing your voice. There was no highlight in my days and no purpose to them either. I can't go on like this, Iswara. I love you so much and I want you to be my wife. I want to spend all my time with you. We've got to make this work somehow.'

'Well, I never thought I'd owe my happiness to measles.'

'Allah works in mysterious ways.'

'And my god too, Ganesh, Remover of Obstacles! It could have been his doing too.'

'Let's be doubly thankful then,' AA suggested.

'Does this mean I can actually arrange to come to see you there?' she asked coquettishly.

'Most definitely, yes.'

'Good, because I missed you too, you stubborn man!'

★　★　★

Later that afternoon Iswara received an unexpected phone call from Damien.

'I heard about the epidemic.'

'Who have you been talking to?'

'Ah now, that would be telling,' he said. 'But seriously, well done. That can't have been an easy time. Now, I've been doing a bit of research on your behalf and here's the story.'

He outlined what she'd need to get a posting and papers to work in Ireland and he also told her that he'd be able to find her a willing sponsor if she decided to go down this route.

'It may be somewhat harder for AA, but I believe Microsoft, Dell, Google and some of the other computer giants all have quite a contingent of Indian workers here in Ireland, and with AA's skills he should be an attractive prospect, so I'd suggest that he should contact them directly.'

'You're such a good friend, Damien. I don't know what I'd do without you. Not being able to confide in anyone here but Rekna is difficult and she doesn't know anything about these things.'

'Well, I have another bit of news. The college wants me to head the recruitment drive in the UAE and there's a mission going out to Bahrain and Dubai in late April, so our paths may cross again then if you're over there.'

'But why the UAE?' Iswara asked.

'We've been running our degree and postgraduate courses out there for several years now and one or two of your former classmates are involved in some of the programmes.'

'I'd forgotten that.'

'Well, I was thinking that if your visit coincided with mine, then you might just be able to use that as an excuse for your visit to Dubai, allaying any suspicions your mother might have that anything else might be going on. You could even talk to prospective students for us and tell them what life as a student is like in Dublin.'

'You are devious! Believe it or not, my mother has hinted a few times that she thought you were very nice.'

'Would I be in there with a chance for your hand, what with being devious *and* nice?' Damien laughed.

'Probably not.'

'Well if I can't have you then I want to make sure someone worthy of you can.'

'You flatterer. I'll tell AA. When is your trip?'

'It has to coincide with their graduation ceremonies. I'll check and send you a mail.'

'It's so good to hear from you. I can hardly believe it's all so positive too. I was beginning to feel I was drowning in a sea of indecision and uncertainty.'

'Hang in there. It'll work out in the end and it'll be great to have you back in Ireland eventually, even if you come with your own husband. Give him my best.'

CHAPTER 29

Beatrice and Damien's first real date went off better than either had anticipated. Their conversation was relaxed and easy. They shared the same sense of humour and Damien couldn't help asking her how he scored in comparison with The Laugh and The Golfer and the other blind dates she'd endured.

'On a score of one to ten I'd give your laugh a nine.'

'A nine? Why not a ten?'

'Because I want to hear more of it!' Beatrice said.

'I won't argue with that.'

'For personality, I'd give you nine.'

'Why did I lose the one?'

'Because I don't want to make you big-headed.'

'I see.' He nodded seriously.

'And for entertainment value, I'd give you an eight.'

'This is going downhill.'

'Only because if I give you top marks, you might feel you've passed the tests with flying colours and move on.'

'Fair enough. But don't I get any bonus points for having all my own teeth and a good head of hair?' Damien asked.

'No, because they are the minimum required standards. So, how did I do?'

'Sixes all the way.'

'Sixes!'

'Yes. Sixes all across the board – for everything! You lost all the other marks for making me wait so long for a date, but if you agree to come out with me again, very soon, I reserve the right to revise the scores upwards – so the results are in your control.'

'With pressure like that I'll have to agree, won't I?'

They shared a taxi to her apartment block and she didn't invite him in. She kissed him on the cheek before saying goodnight.

'I'll expect a mail tomorrow.'

'And you'll get one too,' she grinned, and waved him off.

That started a pattern of dates, at first once a week, then twice, then drinks after work, and the occasional bowl of soup at lunchtime.

Beatrice told Mary she was 'walking out' with someone, an expression they had heard in a period drama and thought was quaint. And Mary, as always, held her counsel and didn't ask all the questions she wanted to ask. Instead, she told her daughter she was delighted to hear it.

Irene knew they had begun seeing each other

and would just smile across the desk whenever Damien was on the phone to Beatrice. She always knew it was him calling because Beatrice unconsciously swivelled on her chair, turning towards the window, cutting off the rest of the world while they made arrangements to meet or shared a joke.

After her usual Tuesday evening Pilates with her honorary aunts and her mother, Mary asked her, 'Will you bring this new man to meet us over Christmas?'

'Now Mother, curiosity killed the cat.'

'I know, but there's a glint in your eyes these days and I'd like to see who put it there.'

'Maybe it's just due to this exercise regime.'

'Well, if it is, it's selective. It hasn't had that effect on the rest of us.'

The shops were beginning to go into overdrive for the festive season. It was impossible to avoid the annual music-fest of carols, jingles and nostalgia. They shopped together. Beatrice helped Damien decorate his Christmas tree, which they carried up the four flights of stairs to the apartment because it wouldn't fit in the lift.

'I dream of having a place with a high ceiling like this, so that I can have a tall tree one day,' Beatrice said. 'In fact, I dream of having any space for a tree at all. I love the smell of the pine needles and although my artificial specimen is cute, it's not the real thing.'

They sat in the glow from the dozens of white lights, which cast shadows on the surroundings, magnifying little angels into vampire-like creatures and balls into comets that appeared to be spinning towards them.

It was a seasonally frosty night and you could make out Howth Head across Dublin Bay and the garland of street lamps that fringed the coast road. The sea was an inky black expanse in between, with a silvery wake from the moon's reflection. Every so often, the slow-moving lights of a vessel glided by, heading to or from Dublin port. They ordered a take-away and drank beer. That was the first night she felt tempted to stay over at his apartment, and although it had often been the wee small hours when he'd left hers, she still never asked him to stay. As she thought about it, she decided to go home to her flat and her ornamental tree. If she stayed, there was no going back. He didn't rush her and she appreciated that. She needed more time and he was happy to let her have it. It was after one when he called a taxi for her.

He took her to his faculty Christmas party that week and she felt very much part of a couple. She wasn't sure how she felt about that, but she knew she was happy even though she agonised about being swept along in this relationship, as she had been in others before.

She met his colleagues, and the Libyan doctor whom she had helped. He was almost obsequious in offering his gratitude. She discovered she had mutual friends with a couple at their table, which always seemed to happen in this town. To support the auction for the 'India project', as they all referred to the medical centre and school, she bought a painting she knew she'd never hang.

The bids rose higher and higher as new lots were put up for sale and she whispered to Damien, 'Did no one tell these people that the Celtic Tiger has run away?'

He laughed and whispered back, 'You're forgetting many of these are wealthy consultants and surgeons; besides, there's a bit of showing off and a bit of brinksmanship going on too.'

He pointed to a table to their right. 'See the guy in the purple dickie-bow? He's a top orthopaedic surgeon. And that other guy beside the woman in pink? Well, they used to work together, but Purple Dickie-Bow went out on his own, starting a fancy sports injury clinic in the suburbs. He's doing very well by all accounts and there's great rivalry between the pair, so my bet is that each will try to outbid the other.'

And so they did – swelling the fund by several thousands. When the results were announced Damien was delighted. 'This is fantastic. Much better than we had expected.'

'Will you go out again?' Carla, one of the women in their party, asked him.

He replied, 'I'll probably go back in the summer

and see how they are all getting on. I'd love to do a longer stint, but I'm not sure if they'll give me that much leave of absence again. It was an amazing experience in many ways and we got so much done in such a short time because of the numbers involved.'

'Even though it was so harrowing, I think he misses it,' added Beatrice.

'In a funny way I suppose I do, and I feel I left a little bit of me back there, and I'd love to catch up with Iswara, who's one of our graduates, and the others working there. She's now very involved with the project,' he explained to the others at their table.

Carla said, 'I saw the video on the rag pickers and I watched that movie about the kid who won *Who Wants To Be A Millionaire?* and I found them both very disturbing. How can people live in such conditions?'

'They don't have any choice. Many of them have come to the cities from even worse conditions in the country, others are born into it and don't know anything else. They're also uneducated for the most part. They work collecting rubbish simply because it is just that, work, and it makes them feel worthy to be doing something honourable. Some are third generation. And the language barrier is an issue.'

'What do you mean?' asked Carla.

'At the last count there are in excess of a few hundred languages and dialects spoken in the subcontinent, so not understanding each other forces them to stay together in ghettos. There are a staggering 300,000 slum dwellers in Mumbai and the same in Delhi.'

Damien had a captive audience that seemed enthralled with what he was telling them. Beatrice was captivated too. She hadn't heard Damien speak so passionately about his impressions before this.

'But surely they can't all work in the dumps?'

'They don't, but that's a rough estimate of those living in the slums, and they're not all poor, but for the most part their accommodation would be condemned in this part of the world. They live in appalling shacks, huts and containers as well as in rickety buildings, often dozens crammed in tiny spaces, and most with no running water. In Dharavi, the biggest slum area, there are hundreds of thriving small industries and sweat-shops, supplying local needs. Whenever there is talk of flattening these slums and rehousing the inhabitants, these entrepreneurs become incensed because not only will they lose their sense of community, but their businesses too.' He paused and said, 'I'm sorry. I didn't mean to make a speech.'

'No, go on, Damien,' one of his colleagues urged. 'I had no idea – well – I suppose I never really thought about it before.'

'It's just one of the many contradictions in India. That slum Dharavi that I mentioned is right smack against a thriving corporate block and is on prime land for development. The authorities are offering the people living quarters in high-rise blocks in another district and understandably they don't want to go. They'll lose their businesses and their neighbours and they are not prepared to trade these for running water and a toilet.'

'Humans can get used to anything,' slurred a curmudgeonly ruddy-faced diner, who had said nothing up to now. 'Yes, human beings can get used to anything. I got used to not being allowed smoke cigars inside, anywhere, but I don't think I'd give up my brandy for anyone,' he said, calling a passing waiter. 'The same again, for everyone.'

There were protests from some of the others, pointing out that there was still plenty of wine on the table. 'Well I'll have another of the same,' he said, wagging his glass about.

'I'm sure I'd never get used to no running water,' Carla said. 'If we ever have a water supply cut, I go around filling everything in the house, just in case.'

'It's luxury for most of them,' Damien responded. 'The majority still have to fetch their water from a spigot on the street corner. They have no toilets and use the nearby Mahim Creek as an open public facility. Lack of sanitation is the cause of many of their illnesses.'

'It's difficult to imagine that's what's going on now, while here we are feasting ourselves, decorating

Christmas trees and spending a fortune on drink and useless gee-gaws,' Carla said.

'You can't think like that,' said Beatrice.

'No,' agreed Carla's husband, who had been out at the project a few years previously, when the medical centre was being built. 'For such a wealthy country, there's still no proper refuse management system in place at all, so these people provide a valuable contribution to society in general, albeit one in which they are totally exploited by the authorities who turn a blind eye to it.'

The curmudgeonly one, whose brandies were beginning to slow his speech, said, 'They have a bloody space programme, for God's sake, a bloody space programme, and they expect us to go out there and help them with their poor.'

'If everyone felt like that, no one would give to any good cause,' Beatrice interrupted. 'The same could be said of anywhere where there's poverty or hunger. Why don't governments fix them? The reality is they don't and it's always up to ordinary people with a sense of justice to do what little they can to make a difference.'

'You mean like buying pictures and rounds of golf in Mount Juliet or a weekend at a spa?' the older man said sarcastically.

Damien looked on with pride when Beatrice replied, 'That too.' Then she turned to him and said, 'I'd love to dance.'

'Your every wish, Madam . . .' Damien said, taking her hand and leading her onto the floor.

'Pay no attention to Macker, the old codger. Irritating class of a drunk – the argumentative type. He's great company when he's sober, a brilliant physician, but he has a real bee in his golf cap when it comes to overseas aid and foreigners. I think he's a frustrated traveller. Never went anywhere when he could and now that he can't – he has a bad heart – he resents anyone who can.'

'You better not tell him what I do for a living so,' Beatrice laughed, and he swept her into a twirl as the music quickened. They danced quietly and closely, letting their bodies do the talking.

'Will you come home with me tonight?' he asked, caressing her back.

She looked into his eyes for a few seconds and said, 'Yes!'

He tightened his grip and her pulse raced as she tucked her head into his neck and they continued dancing, oblivious to the crush on the dance floor.

Back in his apartment there was no awkwardness between them as they tentatively explored each other, kissing, caressing, touching, slowly at first then more possessively and passionately, before being swept away on a tide of longing whose vehemence took them both by surprise. They made love on the rug in his lounge, beside the giant Christmas tree, bathed in the silvery aura of the fairy lights. Sated, happy and secure in the afterglow, he led her to his bedroom and they made love again, this time more surely and confidently.

Their friendship had definitely just been ratcheted up several notches and Beatrice realised she didn't mind. She didn't mind at all.

CHAPTER 30

Beatrice spent Christmas Eve at Damien's but went home to her mother for Christmas dinner the next day. He went to spend the day with his sister, Rachel.

'You didn't bring along your mystery man,' Mary said after they had exchanged greetings in the holly-filled hall.

'Not this time,' Beatrice grinned as the doorbell went again. Her mother had set her table with flair and attention. The house was decked out in festive mode, but in a simple, understated way. The smell of the roasting turkey wafted through the house and Ray played host, taking coats and holding presents while the guests divested themselves of layers.

Beatrice went in to put her presents under the tree. Her arrival had been followed by a few of her mother and Ray's friends, who gathered every year to celebrate together. Like their Tuesday outings, they rotated the venue for the festive meal. This had started when Mary had been widowed. She had come to hate Christmas and wanted to be left to spend it alone with her child, away from others who were happy. For her, it was a time of excruciating loneliness and soul-destroying resentment – resentment that, while the carols and the ads all filled her space with messages of joy and good tidings, she had no husband any more for whom to buy socks and other gifts. She always bought those as a joke; after all, no man should be without a new pair of socks on 25 December, they were a mandatory part of Christmas. She felt it acutely that her five-and-a-half-year-old daughter had no Daddy to wish her a Happy Christmas or to share her joy on what used to be a magical morning. She visited his grave on Christmas Eve, not wanting to give Beatrice these memories to be forever associated along with those of hanging up her stocking and leaving carrots out for the reindeer. She hated the Santa part too and remembered so clearly her despair as she fulfilled that duty that first Christmas, thinking that Santa Claus was never meant to be a woman. The pain did ease with time, but it wasn't until she met Ray, and he began to be an important part in her life, that she started to appreciate the sentiments in those familiar tunes again.

She must have done something right back then though, because Beatrice loved Christmas and had no bad associations with it at all. Her memories were of the two of them being fêted and spoiled by relatives and friends, and sleepovers at the various honorary aunts' houses after a surfeit of food that would have fed the whole road, and as many presents. They had always spoiled her. And now, this year, she had someone else in her life to do that and she had just added a few more memories to other happy ones to cherish and remember.

Irene and Daragh invited Beatrice and Damien over on New Year's Eve. It had snowed heavily that day and during the evening, and everywhere looked different. Shapes were softened, noises deadened, the street lamps and gate pillars had white hats. Cars had their new outlines decimated as the snow was scooped off in handfuls to make snowballs for the fights that everyone joined in at midnight. Fireworks added to the enchantment and bells rang out across the city. A new year had begun.

Back inside, Daragh refilled the champagne glasses and Irene said, 'Apart from wishing you all a happy, prosperous, healthy, etcetera new year, I want to propose a toast to Daragh, who has just asked me to marry him – and this time I said, yes!'

'Well, I didn't see that coming,' Beatrice said to Damien, after the congratulations had died down. 'They've been together forever and she never gave a hint of it.'

'Maybe she's getting broody,' he suggested.

'She's only a year older than me!' she protested.

'Well, she could still be getting broody. But what would I know? I'm only a fella,' he laughed.

'Will I need a new hat soon, like this year?' asked one of Daragh's friends.

'That's up to the lady herself. It's taken me six years to get her to say yes, so I hope she doesn't take six more to plan the event.'

'I heard that,' Irene said, coming up behind him. 'And I won't take six years, more like six months. Now that I've decided he can be my man, I want to make sure that no one else will snare him on me, so the sooner we do it the better.'

'My God, what have I let myself in for?' Daragh laughed.

'A life of submission and surprises, my dearest. Think how lucky you are. I could have said no – again!'

CHAPTER 31

The Singhanids were having dinner when Iswara announced that she was thinking of going to Dubai for a holiday.

'I think that's a very good idea. You've been working very hard and a break will do you good,' her father said.

'But why Dubai?' enquired her mother.

'To catch up with several old friends. You know my college has a programme with the UAE? I've been asked to talk to some of the hopefuls about student life in Ireland. It'll also be graduation time for a few people I know who have been doing postgraduate courses and I'd like to be there for that. I might even look into doing one myself, either there or back in Ireland.'

That announcement caused raised eyebrows and a look between her parents, but not as big a reaction as when she added, 'And Damien will be there too, with a delegation from Dublin. He's going there on a recruitment drive to encourage more students to study in Ireland and let them know about the postgraduate opportunities they offer there and in the UAE, so I'll get to see him again too.'

When her parents were in bed her mother said, 'I'm still convinced there's something going on between that Irish man and Iswara. Don't tell me you aren't.'

'Up to now, I would have said no, but now I'm not quite so sure. She could do an awful lot worse, you know.'

'But he's a foreigner. I can only hope that when she sees how well her colleagues are doing that she'll decide to follow their ways and maybe go on to do further studies. That would get her out of that awful clinic. I think working there is holding her back from getting a good Indian husband.'

'Well, I don't agree with you there. And now, Daya, I'm tired, and want to go to sleep. Good night.' He leaned towards her and kissed her. 'Sleep well.'

Christmas used to go unnoticed in Arab countries, but the influx of non-national workers over the past decade had brought about changes that enterprising businesses had been more than willing to pander to. Beneath the towering stained-glass pyramids in the Wafi City Mall, a large crib took centre stage in the display area. Decorations festooned other areas and stores in all the shopping meccas where designer labels are de rigeur and knock-offs frowned upon. At the Mall of the

Emirates, the ski dome was busier than ever as expatriates, many sporting Santa hats, tried to create something of the atmosphere of colder climes to put them in the festive mood, or perhaps to distract them and prevent them from being too homesick.

Santa had been given the glitzy Dubai treatment too and he arrived to the Jumeirah Beach resort by paramotor, doing several flypasts while 'Jingle Bells' was relayed over speakers. Meanwhile, in the rest of the city, it was business as usual.

AA was putting all his energies into his studies, partly because this second degree would give him more opportunities on the global stage, but mostly because it stopped him pining for Iswara. He knew that his destiny was with her, though where they would end up was still unknown. Whatever doubts he had about the future, he knew with an unquestionable certainty that she loved him and he loved her and together they'd make it work, somehow.

Irene wasn't the only one to have a proposal by New Year and when AA asked Iswara if she would be prepared to take this step, she didn't have to hesitate for a moment. She said, 'Yes! I was afraid you'd never ask me.'

AA had been doing his homework. He had found out that she would have to live in the UAE for a few months, on a visitor visa, if they were to marry there and only if, on his work visa, he was granted permission to do so.

'It makes sense for us to marry in India,' AA said. 'That way we'll have none of these problems. I'll need to come back a few days before but I can organise my paperwork from here and you'll have to look after yours. Are you sure you're happy to do this without your parents' knowledge?'

'I'm happy to marry you. I'm not happy to be doing it behind their backs, but as there is no other way we can be together, it's the only way we can do it. And who knows, I may even get the courage to tell them, but my instinct is that they will accept it more easily when it's too late to change things.'

'You're very courageous,' he said. 'I have to decide how to deal with my family too.'

'Are we being foolish?' she asked.

'I've never been more sure about anything.'

'Nor have I.'

'Will Rekna and her husband act as witnesses? I thought we could ask the director too, if they are all still happy to collude in our secret.'

'I'm sure they will,' Iswara said. 'You have it all worked out, but have you thought when we are going to do this?'

'I know you're sitting down because, thanks to the fuzziness of Skype I can see that you are, but I thought, and it's just a thought, what if we married before you come out here and we could make your visit our honeymoon? That way, when we apply for visas or permits to go to Ireland, Canada or wherever, we are doing so as an established married couple. What do you think?'

'It sounds fantastic, but have we time to go through all the formalities so quickly? Can you take leave to come back here?'

'I've already asked about that and it can be done, but I could only come over for a few days and I'd have to come back soon so that I can have time off when you're here too.'

He went on to ask her again if she was sure this was what she wanted.

'I know how important weddings are and you'd be sacrificing all the pomp and ceremony that should go with yours. Are you positive you won't regret this?'

'I'm positive and if it means we can be together when I come over, then that'll make up for everything.'

Before this, AA had looked into the hotel arrangements, choosing ones that were popular with Europeans, where the rules were inclined to be more liberal. Dubai was not an ideal place for romantic trysts, with codes of conduct strictly enforced. They had talked a lot about this after AA had agreed to her visit – would they stay together or in separate rooms – and they had agreed that, apart from wanting to more than anything, it would probably be less complicated to stay together, as husband and wife, if they could find a way to do it. But it was risky as they'd have no papers to prove they were. Now, it seemed, they would.

They spent hours over the next week getting their letters of freedom and other paper-work in train.

Rekna was in on all the plotting. She had a school friend who lived in the country who was married to an Englishman and she understood only too well the complexities of an unconventional union. Her parents had cut her off when she married Malcolm, and had never seen their only grand-child. They were happy to help and invited Rekna and her husband to stay too. That way Daya and Raj had no suspicions, happy that their girls were keeping in touch with old school mates and spending a few days together.

The wedding was set for early April and the trip to Dubai some weeks later.

'I feel very badly about doing all this behind our parents' backs. I really feel I should tell Papa,' Iswara confided to her sister one evening when everything was in place.

'I know and so do I, but you know what will happen then. Papa will feel he has to tell Mama and then if they find out your plans, they'll try to put pressure on you to change your mind. When you confront them after you are married, they will see they can do nothing to alter it. They might even come around about your inheritance. But if they find out beforehand, Mama will make sure you won't get a rupee.'

'I don't care about that, but I hate deceiving them.'

'Is there any other way?' Rekna asked rationally.

There was no hesitation in Iswara's answer. 'No, there isn't and I know that too.'

They shopped together for a wedding sari, and bought one in red-shaded georgette, the traditional colour for good luck and good fortune. It was beautifully adorned with resham meshwork and intricate beading along the border and ends, and had a matching georgette blouse with similar details around the short sleeves and neck. Iswara bought gold slippers to match and Rekna lent her a headpiece, a diamanté-encrusted lotus flower. Everything had some degree of symbolism attached to it – the lotus symbolic of purity of heart and mind.

Their shopping spree saw them buying several other honeymoon outfits, all of which were stashed away in one of Rekna's spare bedrooms.

Iswara still had to ask the director if he would be there in *loco parentis* and she was dreading this too. Knowing that he was a friend of her father's meant she was also implicating him in more duplicity than if she were just asking him as a work colleague or a personal friend.

When she finally asked him, he agreed. He was a man of the world and had been around long enough to know that belonging to a particular culture or creed alone wasn't what made people good, but how they behaved. He told her he admired both her and AA, and felt they deserved to be happy together. So he could agree to go along to their ceremony with a clear conscience, and to take whatever part he was asked to in it.

They were elated.

CHAPTER 32

Damien decided to, finally, cook the meal he had promised Rachel, Irene and Beatrice months before. He forbade Beatrice to come over until it was ready. Sean was away on business that week and Damien had noticed Rachel hadn't been with him so much lately, so it was Daragh and Clem who made up an even six, and he surprised them all with a bill of fare that any restaurateur would have been very happy to offer his clients.

'I hear you're off to Dubai for the faculty,' Clem commented as Damien refreshed their glasses.

'Yes. They've extended the postgraduate courses for next year, with more of an emphasis on medical imaging. We're extending this at home too, so there's a bit of a drive on to encourage more graduates to stream in to this area.'

'That equipment is all so bloody expensive; still, it does promise great job prospects at the end of it,' said Clem.

'I agree, but without the operators and the professionals to read results, it's a catch-22. We're always going to need qualified professionals who are prepared to take that chance.'

'Surely the equipment will become cheaper as it becomes more mainstream,' said Rachel.

'It should, but with the rapid advances in technology it's constantly being upgraded and therefore the costs really only come down marginally, if at all,' said Clem. 'The only advantage in that is the downgraded machines will eventually find themselves in other facilities and demand for their use will increase.'

Clem had recently joined a group of GPs near Rathmines and Rachel asked him how it was going.

'No big consultant fees for me there, I'm afraid. For now I'm the new kid so I have the privilege of covering Saturday mornings and late nights when the others have more exciting things to do,' he told them.

'You're lucky to have got in there,' said Damien. 'They're a good bunch and it's a good catchment area. Marcus Prendeville is due to retire soon so I don't think you'll be the newbie for very long.'

'Will that mean I can push those unsocial shifts onto some other unfortunate then? They're playing havoc with my golf handicap.'

'Remind me never to go there on a Saturday if I need attention. Your mind would be miles away,' said Rachel.

'Actually I'm not that bad. It's just that the old man and I always played a round whenever we could. He's getting on a bit and I feel I'm letting him down when I have to cry off. He also beat me the last few times and that hurt!'

'It's no wonder you're still single. Wounded pride and a golf addiction,' Damien laughed. 'When you're not nursing one you're pandering to the other.'

'Oh, that hurt too!' he replied. 'You could also add that I can't cook like this, so that renders me even more ineligible.'

'Don't let that brother of mine fool you,' said Rachel. 'This is a rarity. He's been promising to feed us since he was in India. He probably took himself off in the meantime to the Cooks Academy to learn how to do this so that he could impress.'

'That's cruel,' Damien said.

'I agree,' said Clem, 'I think you need to show us what you can do Rachel, before we can make comparisons.'

'A challenge! I might just do that some night.'

'And I'm afraid to say anything in case you pick on me next,' said Daragh. 'Before you know it, we'll be into a *Come Dine With Me* scenario and you'll want to rummage through my drawers to see if I have a fetish for leather or wearing women's clothes.'

'If you have, I want to find out about it before the wedding,' said Irene.

'So do I!' he answered.

Beatrice found herself falling in love with Damien, not in a wild, romantic spiral sort of way, but with a slow appreciation of his qualities, his sense of competence, his affability and his kindness. She looked forward to his emails during the day, missed them when he was unavailable or too caught up to make contact. She loved his laugh and the smooth timbre of his voice on the phone and when they were alone and intimate together. She looked forward to their evenings out and in, and to the time they spent in his spacious panoramic apartment. She enjoyed having him over to her compact one too, although increasingly she went to his place in preference.

A few days after that dinner party she introduced him to Mary and Ray when they met for a few drinks in a popular bar on Dawson Street. Later in the evening, Beatrice was waiting for a chance to get her mother alone to find out her verdict.

She needn't have worried – her mother and stepfather had approved of Damien the minute they had met him.

'I couldn't have found you anyone nicer.'

'Mum, you'd say that anyway if you thought he was my choice, whether you liked him or not. I really want to know what you think.'

'God, child, what do I have to say to convince you that I really, really like him. So does Ray. He's lovely, charming, oozes personality and he's very easy on the eye too.'

'So I take it you approve?'

'What's so special this time that you need my approval?' she asked. 'You've never looked for it before. Is there a catch? Is he married? With a hoard of kids, no home and no money to pay alimony?'

'None of the above, I'm happy to say. I just wanted to make sure you like him.'

'Well you can be sure we both do.'

'Please! You can take that look off your face. We've only know each other a wet weekend!' Beatrice laughed.

Within a few months, Damien and Beatrice had already established quite a few things they enjoyed as a couple. They often met after work, stayed in town and went to the theatre or a film. They went to some of the restaurants in Monkstown, which were conveniently located halfway between where they both lived. She discovered that he loved mussels and hated oysters. They shared a mutual appreciation for orchestral music and once they had established that, the Friday Symphonies at the National Concert Hall became part of their regular outings. One evening at her flat, Beatrice made a stack of pancakes for them, filling some with a wild mushroom sauce. She drizzled others with Golden Syrup and a serving of whipped cream and mixed berries. They washed all this down with a bottle of wine Damien had brought over with him. Afterwards, they were cosied up together watching a comedy show, in which a couple with teenage children were on the verge of divorcing.

'Would you like to have children?' Damien asked Beatrice, during an ad break.

'I suppose I would at some stage, although I haven't given it much thought. Not for a while yet I suppose, and not ones who'd be like that,' she said pulling a face and indicating to the family onscreen. 'If I owned that pair I'd have had them put down before they reached puberty. What about you? Would you like a family?'

'I think I would. I think it's part of the continuum thing, isn't it? Man's need to leave something behind him when he's gone.'

'I'm not sure that motivates women as much as men. I think for us it's more a need to have something to nurture and care for.'

'Perhaps.'

They sat comfortably beside each other considering these thoughts. After a while he interrupted their silence. 'We've been spending so much time together, would you consider moving in with me?'

She wanted to say 'yes, yes, yes!' but something stopped her and triggered her panic button. She froze at the suggestion. She moved a little away from him without realising it and didn't answer straight away.

He looked at her intently, a slow realisation emerging from somewhere that he had said the wrong thing.

'Damien,' she began.

'Beatrice, forget I said that. I didn't mean to pressure you and it's obvious you're not ready for anything more than this.'

'You didn't pressure me. It's just that—'

'It's just that the answer is no. Let's leave it at that. Let's not say anything we'll regret later.'

'Damien, I can't. I really like you, you know I do, but—'

'The but's the problem, isn't it?'

'I can't explain, but . . .'

'There's no need to, honestly. I didn't mean to upset you.'

'You didn't upset me.'

'Clearly, I did. I'll leave you for now, give you some space.'

'You don't need to go.'

'I think I do. I'll call you,' he said, standing up and getting his coat from the hallstand. He kissed her on the cheek before he left.

She sat back down on the couch and wondered why she had freaked out at the suggestion. Was it the mention of children that had spooked her? She concluded that that had nothing to do with it. In fact, she realised, if she were ever going to have kids, she could think of no one more suitable to father them than Damien. No, it was definitely the idea of moving in together that triggered her reaction. Damn Paul and damn Jarlath, and damn all the other useless specimens who had floated in and out of her life, she thought. She blamed them all collectively and individually for what had just happened. And even though she was gradually coming around a little bit with Damien, she knew she just couldn't trust enough yet to move on to the next level.

At work the following day, she told Irene what had happened.

'If you're having regrets you should tell him,' her friend advised.

'That's the thing – I'm not, but it really disturbed me. I don't want to move in with him.'

'But you do really like him, don't you?' Irene asked.

'It's more than like. Much more.'

'Well, is there a problem in other areas – like sexually?'

'Absolutely not. That's pretty perfect.'

'Well it's plain to me that something's not working. Would you talk to someone?'

'Someone – like whom?'

'Well, a relationship counsellor?'

'Definitely not,' Beatrice shot that suggestion down instantly. 'I don't need counselling. I just need more time.'

'If you say so,' Irene stepped back. She knew she had reached the end of this thread of conversation and that maybe if she said nothing else, Beatrice would open up more at a later stage. Damien phoned Beatrice later that day and asked how she was. He was his usual cheery self, but he made no reference to the previous evening. She put down her phone with a real sense of loss.

Weeks went by and, although they kept in touch, Damien didn't suggest they meet and neither did she. But she wanted to. He'd be going away again soon and she wasn't sure whether him giving her space was better than not seeing him at all. The more she went over things in her head, the more confused she became.

Damien heard from Iswara and AA and was genuinely delighted that their lives were moving towards a solution, even though his was at a standstill.

He was very happy that his visit to the UAE would coincide with Iswara's and he intended to spend some time with her and AA when he was there.

He was still totally puzzled by Beatrice and her reaction to his suggestion. That was the second time he had misread her and had been pushed away as a result. He wasn't sure if he was prepared to leave himself open for a third rejection, so he busied himself with work and planning for the trip.

It seemed like a fortuitous opportunity presented itself one morning in March when the Dean of the Faculty called him to his office. 'Damien, I'm going to throw something out at you. It's short notice and you don't have to say yes, but I hope you will.'

Damien knew this man's tactics well enough to recognise that, in dean speak, that meant he wasn't going to have much wriggle room.

'No need to go over our expansion plans again,' the dean continued, 'but we've been having a mull over some of them and feel they need a little more supervision from this end. Some of the administrators think it would be a good idea to have some of the faculty members in our Abu Dhabi and Bahrain programmes come over here for three months to familiarise themselves with our practices, exam procedures, postgraduate programmes etc., and I have to agree with them.'

Damien nodded, but still said nothing – he was waiting for the punchline. When it came, he was secretly pleased. 'We hoped you might consider going over there for a few months to provide cover while they're here.'

'I see,' he said.

'You don't need to make your mind up now, but this afternoon would be great.'

'This afternoon!'

'Well, I could push it until tomorrow,' the dean said with a grin. 'But there's a lot of paperwork involved and we'd need to get this in motion asap. I think you'd be perfect for the job. If you could manage it, you'd take the role up directly from the recruitment drive. That would mean you'd be away for about three and a half months altogether.'

'I'd love to,' Damien said without hesitation. 'That stint in India has given me itchy feet and although I've been to Dubai and Bahrain before, Abu Dhabi is new territory for me.'

'I'm told it's the place to go in that part of the world, the real capital in every sense.'

'So I believe.'

'Are you sure about the exchange? We have some fine accommodation over there for visiting professors, and you'll know several of those involved anyway, so it could be quite a pleasant assignment all around. I know I've sprung it on you. I hope it won't impinge too much on your personal life.'

'It sounds good and, on the personal front, the timing's perfect. Who'll deputise for me?'

'Old Kellet again. He's never quite accepted retirement on top of widowhood. He was delighted to be back in harness when you were in India.'

When he got back to his desk, Damien began to wonder if he had been right to agree so quickly. It would put distance between himself and Beatrice, but the more he thought about that the more he realised that he needed to see her face-to-face and talk things over. He couldn't just vanish with nothing resolved. If he was shot down again, he could begin to move on. But if there was some hope, perhaps the distance might just rekindle what they had. He knew that they did have something pretty special. He wished he could talk to someone about this. None of his friends seemed to have had any trouble getting their girl-friends to move in with them. Irene had taken her time accepting Daragh, but Irene was Beatrice's friend and he felt that he couldn't really confide in her. He didn't want to involve his sister either. Strangely, he felt he could have discussed it with Iswara, but emails weren't exactly conducive to such revelations. He'd have to figure out some way to meet Beatrice before he left.

He opened a planner on his computer and began entering all the things he'd need to attend to before his departure. Top of his list was to find Iswara a placement and sponsor.

He decided to send a collective email to all his friends, including Beatrice.

Hi folks

It looks as though my sortie to the Emirates has just been extended and I'm now going to be away for fourteen or fifteen weeks.

There's no need to feel sorry for me. I'll be staying in relative luxury in Abu Dhabi, on an exchange programme. I've just checked out the accommodation and I'll have a few spare rooms so you're all welcome, but not all at once!

The rates will be a bottle of finest Irish whiskey and a few packets of Irish rashers and sausages.

More later.

Cheers

Damien

He didn't get much else done that morning as replies and emails of intent kept coming back to him. Irene wrote wondering if it would be bad luck for her to have her honeymoon a few months before the wedding.

Clem was devastated because, as Johnny-come-lately to the practice, he had his holiday periods assigned to him – in three single weeks. He wondered about smoozing up to the nurse secretary so she would spill her coffee on the diary, pretend she couldn't read the original entries and give him a different schedule.

Rachel just wrote: 'Book me in, anytime. I'll bring two bottles, a friend and some black and white pudding too!' He was a little surprised to find a reply from Beatrice.

I'm delighted for you. That sounds like a great opportunity. Can we meet for a drink sometime before you go? Beatrice

His reply was simple.

Love to. Name the day. D

PART II

PART II

CHAPTER 33

Iswara and AA's wedding ceremony was somewhat truncated. Hindu weddings usually lasted anywhere from one day to a week – a week of feasting and festivities, both before and after the wedding ceremony itself, involving lots of family interaction, numerous changes of elaborate outfits and often a Mehndi ceremony, where the bride, her sisters and friends all gather to have their hands decorated with henna patterns.

Traditionally, the first dress was bought by the bride's parents – the second, usually red and white, by her husband, as a symbolic gesture that she was now his responsibility and he would provide for her from then on. The couples' parents would have played a role in a part of the ceremony, where they accepted these new people into each family. Because of the circumstances, Rekna's friends, who lived about sixty miles outside Mumbai, hosted the wedding at their house. They also gave them their pre-marriage dinner, with the director standing for AA's parents and Rekna's husband for Iswara's.

Their ceremony took place under the stars and the

garden was decorated with flowers and candles. They had erected a four-pole canopy at one side. This *mandap*, under which vows would be taken, had a sacred fire lighting in a brazier. The fire was symbolic of the illumination of the mind, of knowledge and of happiness.

Iswara found a priest friend who was willing to perform a blended wedding ceremony. AA was happy to let this take whatever form it did, saying, 'It's our commitment to each other that counts, not the rituals involved.'

They did take some elements from both their traditions though. The priest read a blessing before they exchanged the rings that AA had bought in the Gold Souk in Dubai before flying home.

'The circle is the symbol of the sun and the earth and the universe. It is a symbol of holiness and of perfection and of peace. In these rings it is the symbol of unity, in which your lives are now joined in one unbroken circle, in which, wherever you go, you will always return to one another and to your togetherness.'

They smiled as they put a *varmala* over each other's heads. Once these long brightly coloured garlands of flowers were sitting properly around the bride's and groom's necks, the priest announced, 'They are now married!'

To confirm their vows, Iswara and AA took their first walk together as a couple, around the fire.

'I ask you all, and Iswara and Abdul-Razzaq, to concentrate upon these thoughts as they take these first seven symbolic steps together on the journey of life,' the priest said. 'May the couple be blessed with an abundance of food. May the couple be strong and complement one another. May the couple be blessed with prosperity. May the couple be eternally happy. May the couple be blessed with children. May the couple live in perfect harmony. May they always be the best of friends.'

AA then gave Iswara a *mangalsutra*, which he fixed around her neck uttering the words, 'May you, the reason of my life, live long, by wearing this sacred necklace.' Iswara's eyes misted as she acquiesced. She would wear this 'sacred thread', as was the custom among Hindu women, until her husband's death.

AA also introduced an element of Islamic wedding tradition when he presented his new wife with a *mahr*, representing his dowry.

After the legalities were completed, the celebrations began. They sat down inside to an impressive meal at a table decorated with calliandras, the red powder-puff flowers that had been a favourite of Iswara's since she was a child. Although the party was small, it didn't detract from the happiness and goodwill that was palpable during the evening.

Mr and Mrs Abdul-Razzaq Mahimkar spent their first night as a married couple in the guest suite at Rekna's friends' house. The bed had been covered with rose petals, and AA brushed these aside as he lifted his bride onto the covers. There began a sensuously slow discovery of each other. They had longed for this unity.

'I want this moment to last forever. If you feel awkward please tell me,' he said as he nuzzled her neck and caressed her.

'I've never been so happy,' she replied. 'I love you so much and I want us to do everything together. I've dreamed about this night since I first saw you walking across the compound.'

'So have I. When Bina tried to spoil everything, I was sure I had no hope of ever being with you.'

'Let's forget about her, karma will catch up with her and her brother one day. We were meant to be together.'

'I feel that too.'

He gently removed the lotus ornament before loosening her hair, and between kisses he began to undress her, marvelling at her softness and the silkiness of her skin, the mystery of her curves, the invitation of her hidden self; she at his hardness and strength. He kissed and stroked her breasts. She arched her back, yielding to him. Soon they were wrapped around each other, flesh to warm flesh. He explored her gently, looking for affirmation again. She encouraged him so when the moment of consummation came their bodies were in complete harmony. Carried on a wave of ecstasy and need, they climaxed joyously together.

They lay back, arms still around each other, and she muttered, 'That was – sublime.'

'Well, I can guarantee plenty more of the same.'

Eventually, they slept the sleep of the just.

They only had two days together before AA had to return to Dubai, and their hosts left them in peace. They revelled in the freedom of being able to sit in the privacy of the garden and hold hands or kiss and not be afraid that anyone might see them.

'I'll miss you so much,' Iswara told AA on their last night.

'It's only for a few weeks. They'll fly by.'

'I'm looking forward to seeing Dubai, and Damien too.'

'I really like him,' AA said. 'He's been a good friend to us.'

'That's Damien for you.'

'He's a very genuine person.'

'And what makes him even more special is that he's like that with everyone,' she said.

As they parted the next day, he whispered to her, 'I plan to give you a honeymoon you'll never forget, Mrs Mahimkar.'

'It can't be any better than the past few days.'

'It can. I promise you, Iswara, it'll be – sublime!'

She slipped her wedding ring off her finger, kissed it and handed it to her husband.

'They belong together until we can be.'

He slipped it onto his little finger.

CHAPTER 34

Irene was full of her low-key wedding arrangements and, as she had asked Beatrice to be her bridesmaid, Beatrice was now somewhat involved in them too. Together they perused back issues of *Irish Brides* for ideas.

Irene hadn't been joking when she had told Daragh that she'd like to get married within six months, but when she asked her friends and family, she discovered that several people she really wanted to be at the ceremony already had holiday plans for the summer, so she pushed it back to September.

One wet lunch break, they were browsing gift registers online. 'Look at this. How desperate would you have to be to include desk and smoking accessories, visitors' books or weather stations on your list?' asked Beatrice. 'There's even a dog's kennel and birdcages here.'

'There's a croquet set on this one – for one thousand and eighty euro – and a set of six coasters for a hundred and fifty,' said Irene. 'For six fecky little coasters! I'd expect them to be monogrammed in gold for that.'

'Look what I found,' said Beatrice 'a pair of salt and pepper mills – *starting* from one hundred and eighty nine euro each.'

'That's it. I don't want a wedding list anywhere. I could just see Daragh's face if I included any of those on it. Besides, with us both having our own places, we probably already have two of everything we could ever need at this stage.'

'I was at a wedding last summer where the couple, they had been living together for a while, opened an account with a travel agency and anyone who wanted to could contribute to this and they put it towards their honeymoon fund. They headed off to the Maldives a few months later, in the midst of our snowy winter.'

'I've heard of that, but does it look very mean?'

'It's no different than accepting cheques, is it?' said Beatrice reasonably, 'and it's infinitely prefer-able to having several sets of saucepans, cabinets full of glasses you'll never use and a decadently expensive croquet set!'

'I'll run it by my lord and master and see what he thinks,' Irene said.

'He's the practical sort, I bet he'll think it's a great idea.'

'Probably. I know he's delighted that I don't want a meringue dress and a load of fuss, just a big party that we can all enjoy, and a gorgeous honeymoon somewhere secluded and sunny.'

'That sounds like my kind of wedding,' said Beatrice.

'Maybe after you see how mine goes you might be tempted to follow.'

'You know I'm not the marrying kind, although for a holiday in the Maldives I could be tempted.'

'Neither was I, and look at me now, submerged in the upcoming merger. Drowning in the sea of what ifs. What if I leave someone off the invitation list? What if I change my mind in the meantime? What if he does, and leaves me standing at the proverbial altar?'

'Don't be so melodramatic!' laughed Beatrice.

'You do know I'll be inviting Damien,' Irene said hesitantly.

'Of course. Why wouldn't you?' she answered, showing no sign of the frisson that still went through her at the mention of his name. She missed him.

'Have you not changed your mind?'

'I don't know. Maybe I was too hasty,' Beatrice mused, almost to herself.

'Maybe it was all just a little too quick,' her friend said.

'Maybe it was,' Beatrice agreed, not mentioning she had suggested meeting for a drink before he left.

Thousands of miles away in Mumbai, Iswara was finding it hard to keep the smile from her face as she went about her work at the clinic. No one there other than the director knew that she was now married. She had taken the gold *mangalsutra* that AA had given her from around her neck and placed it in a tiny purse, which she fastened around her waist. Instantly identifiable as a wedding band, it was too dangerous yet to wear it in the conventional way. That would have to wait until they had told everyone of their changed status, if they ever did.

At home, her parents remarked on how much healthier she looked after her break in the country-side. She'd almost broken down then and confessed to everything.

'And your holiday will do you more good,' her mother said. 'You've been working far too hard at that place, destroying your own health.'

Iswara was too happy to take her mother up on this snide comment, which she would ordinarily have contested. Her father noticed this and smiled benignly. He was very proud of his younger daughter, even though he had to agree with his wife that she had been overdoing things a bit. He had been relieved when she told him they were getting two more doctors at the centre to share the burden. They wouldn't be full time, but extra hands were always welcome. Since the measles epidemic, some of the nurses who had come from local hospitals to help had continued to volunteer and they had made a difference too, particularly with vaccination programmes.

Iswara was going to start dropping hints at home about taking a position back in Ireland, or of the possibility of doing some postgraduate studies, but the moment never seemed opportune. She'd wait until after Dubai.

Until after her honeymoon.

310

CHAPTER 35

Damien looked at the tickets he had in front of him for a corporate operatic evening event at the National Convention Centre. It was on the last day of a pharmaceutical conference and several of his colleagues would be attending. The multinational sponsor had agreed to donate a handsome cheque to the India project and Damien was to collect it on behalf of the charity. He toyed with the idea of bringing his sister along, but Rachel wasn't particularly into this sort of music. After an hour or so, he decided that fate was giving him an opportunity to see Beatrice before he headed off.

'Look, I've been given a pair of tickets for this operatic concert, which I know you'd enjoy. If you could bear to put up with my company for the evening, I'd love to take you along,' he said when he phoned her.

It had taken him all day to decide whether he would just ask her in an email, before he decided a personal call would be better. That way, he figured, he'd be able to read her reaction. Then he smiled a wry smile and thought he hadn't been very good at that in the past, had he?

He was quite relieved when she immediately agreed. 'I'd love to come along with you, Damien. Thank you for thinking of me.'

'I do that a lot,' he said. Without waiting for her to say anything he continued, 'It's black tie and I have to warn you we'll be with a lot of corporate spouses, so don't be concerned if they mistake us for an old married couple.'

'I think I could live with that, for one evening,' she laughed. 'But go easy on the "old" bit.'

He had arranged to collect her by taxi on the night. She was ready when he phoned to say it was pulling up outside. He felt his heartbeat quicken as she crossed the foyer of her building. God, she was beautiful, dressed in slinky crimson with her hair piled up in some fancy new style. She looked adorable. He wanted to take her back inside and make love to her, if she'd have him. Instead, he stepped out of the taxi to hold the door open for her, and kissed her on both cheeks.

Her greeting was genuinely warm and friendly and, once inside, when he'd told her how lovely she looked, she replied, 'This is the pashmina you brought me. And I have to say you look rather dishy yourself tonight.'

He took her hand and she didn't pull away. *Maybe*, he thought. *Maybe . . .*

Still holding hands as the taxi crossed the Samuel

Beckett Bridge over the River Liffey, they got a full frontal view of the venue. The hoops of different coloured lights that outlined the tilted curved glass part of the building defined this imposing conference centre. Taxis stopped outside, dropping off men in tuxedos and women in an array of colours and jewels. Many on impossibly tall, skyscraper heels clung possessively to their partners' arms, as much in fear of tripping in front of everyone as anything else. Beneath the atrium and wall of criss-crossed escalators, the vestibule echoed with chatter and laughter.

'This is the first time I've been in here,' whispered Beatrice.

'It's great, isn't it? One of the better legacies of the Celtic Tiger I think,' he whispered back.

She chuckled. 'Why are we whispering?'

'I don't know.' He smiled at her.

'What's the joke?' interrupted a familiar voice.

'Clem, how good to see you,' Damien said. 'Are you on your own?

Clem nodded.

'In that case can I leave you in charge of my lady while I get us some drinks?' Damien said, and walked towards the bar.

Beatrice and Clem exchanged bits of gossip. He filled her in on his life as the underdog in his practice, she on the latest immigrant scam that had made the front pages and all the news bulletins that morning.

'It's nice to see you two together again,' said Clem.

313

'We're not. This is a one-off. Damien knows I love opera and he kindly invited me along. I'm glad he did,' she replied just as Damien reappeared.

'Is it next week you're off?' Clem asked.

'Yes, Saturday afternoon and I've a shed load of things to get through first, not least spending some time with my neglected mother, who decided to come back from Spain to see me. Her logic is that she won't have the chance over the next few months. The fact that we normally only see each other about twice a year doesn't seem to have filtered through, even though she's been living abroad for almost ten years at this stage. Mothers, eh!'

Beatrice saw someone she knew and turned to say hello.

'I wouldn't mind a break myself,' Clem said. 'India has given me the bug.'

'I have to say I'm delighted it came my way. Just luck really, to be able to tag it on to the end of the recruitment drive. I'll be hooking up with Iswara and AA when I'm there. She's going to give a talk to the students for me – those who are thinking of coming here.'

'Be sure and give them my best. I'm glad they tied the knot, but I'm dying to know how the mother took it. Mothers again, eh?' Clem laughed. 'I thought you might have been in there with a chance. Was there something between you two before AA came along?'

Beatrice was now listening to this exchange with

314

interest, but wanting to find out more she said nothing.

'No, but I have to admit that if she hadn't been one of our students and I'd met her socially here, I would probably have asked her out.'

'Aha, I thought so! And I think the mother had her sights on you for a while,' Clem said.

'She may have had, but Iswara had hers firmly fixed somewhere else. And her mother doesn't know about the marriage yet so keep schtum in front of the others who were out there with us – for the time being!'

'You never told me there was any romance on your trip,' Beatrice said lightly. 'What about you, Clem, did you fall for anyone over there.'

'No such luck. I was so exhausted from the heat and the way this slave driver made us work that I didn't have the energy. I probably wouldn't have been considered good enough anyway. Those Indian mamas seem to have a very close-knit mafia going to protect their daughters from foreigners and from penniless doctors. Collectively they're fearsome.'

Clem said to Damien, 'I'd love to be a fly on the wall when Iswara's mother finds out that her daughter married without her consent or approval.'

The bell rang, telling them it was time to take their seats in the auditorium.

'Well, I certainly wouldn't,' said Damien.

Once seated, the lights dimmed and the music started. They played a melange of well-loved arias, duets, orchestral pieces and some choruses. The first half closed with the 'Humming Chorus' from *Madame Butterfly*. Kimono-clad singers entered from the sides, some carrying little lighted candles in both hands, others lengths of beautifully hued silk which they agitated slowly, keeping time with this hauntingly beautiful music. As it enveloped them, Damien reached for Beatrice's hand, and taking it she squeezed his in response. He held it even tighter and noticed when the piece was over, to huge applause and a truncated encore, that she wiped a tear from her eye.

The lights came up for the intermission and she turned to him and said, 'They always do that – those lighting guys are sadists. They never give you enough time to compose yourself or get rid of the runny mascara!'

'You look perfect,' he said, leading her back into the foyer. They bumped into several of his colleagues and he introduced her to all of them. Everyone seemed to know about his upcoming job swap and he was showered with good wishes. He was called to one end of the foyer where a dais had been erected, and there he was presented with a substantial cheque for which he thanked all concerned.

Damien spoke briefly of the unimaginable conditions at the centre and finished by saying, 'No thanks for such generosity are adequate, and now that I've depressed everybody, I think it's time to go back inside. If you ever wondered why human beings have music and song in their lives, I believe it's to help them escape other realities, and I know I'm ready for more of what we just had.'

They clapped loudly before filing back into the auditorium.

'You were marvellous, I was really proud of you up there,' said Beatrice.

'Thank you.'

'India really got under your skin, didn't it?' she remarked

'I suppose you could say it did,' he replied, just as the orchestra began to tune up again.

This time, she reached for his hand in the darkness.

He was unsure how to read her tonight, not being able to concentrate on anything but the closeness of her. They could have been playing Mascagni, Puccini or Mozart. If he were asked, he wouldn't have been able to answer because his thoughts were doing a form of energetic *Riverdance*. Her familiar scent and her warm hand in his distracted him. Should he suggest taking her back to his place afterwards or going to hers? Would he be in danger of pushing her away again if he did? Wouldn't it be better to wait? Maybe he could suggest meeting next week before he left. Would she say yes? Or should he wait until he came back from his trip, put a little distance between them? Then she might realise that she missed him and wanted him in her life. But that was risky. She'd probably meet someone else in the meantime.

Applause broke out: everyone was on their feet.

'They've done it again, exposed us when we're teary,' Beatrice said, her eyes still glistening with emotion. 'I've heard that at least a hundred times, and I still cry every time Mimi dies. I think it's because Rodolfo only turns his back for a minute and she's gone. That anguished cry as he calls her name at the end gets right to my soul. It's so powerful. I always want an encore, but of course they can't do a reprise of her dying, so I always feel cheated.'

'You're a big softie,' he said.

'I know, but don't tell anyone.'

His recollections of the *La Bohème* plot were that, despite loving each other, this pair had drifted apart and found each other again when it was too late. He didn't want the same thing to happen to Beatrice and himself.

She asked him if he'd like to come in as they drew up outside her apartment block, and he hesitated for a second before refusing. He had decided not to risk breaking this tentative bond, which he felt had been reconnected this evening. He did kiss her, a long lingering kiss which she returned ardently.

He was taken by surprise when she said, 'Can I take you for that farewell drink before you leave?'

'You most certainly can.' He kissed her again after he had walked her to her door.

'I'll give you a call,' he said. 'Night, night.'

He began whistling as he went back to the taxi.

* * *

The following Monday, Beatrice told Irene how the evening had gone.

'Let me get this right. You asked him in and he said no.'

'Right.'

'I don't know what you pair are playing at. It's obvious you still love him and from what you are saying, I'd bet he's still into you, so what I want to know is, why are you playing games with each other?'

'We're not. I'm not. I think maybe he's still hurting from me refusing to move in with him – or maybe it's just a pride thing.'

'Stupidity, more like,' said Irene. 'I told you before, you have commitment issues.'

'And you're a fine one to talk.' Beatrice grinned at her friend. 'Anyway we're going to have a drink together this week.'

'Well, hallelujah for that. Maybe this time one of you will see what's in front of your noses!'

Beatrice's phone rang, cutting off any chance of a response from her.

Beatrice didn't wait for Damien to ring, instead she called him to thank him for a memorable night, and it was as though they had never stopped seeing each other. None of the easy friendship, the sparring and the love even, seemed to have dimmed. They made plans to meet after work on Friday night in town, choosing the local where they had met before.

On Friday night, when they had settled and were comfortable with one another, he asked her straight out, 'What went wrong between us? Was it something I said or did? Did I rush things, put pressure on you?'

'Believe me, Damien, it wasn't you or anything you said or did. It's me. I really do love you, you know. Could we not just leave things as they were?'

'I want more than that. I want you to be a more permanent part of my life, yet here I am scaring you away again. But I can't go away and leave things as they are.'

'You're not scaring me. Really. Look, can we just let things be for now. You'll be away and when you come back maybe we could begin again. I mean really begin again.'

'You could always come out and visit me, you know,' he coaxed.

'I'll think about that.'

'It's only a holiday, not marriage, I'm proposing here.'

'I know, and I promise I will think about it.'

'Meanwhile if you still need space, I'll give it to you, almost four thousand miles of it, but you must promise to write regularly, like before.'

'I will,' she said. 'And thank you for being so understanding.'

'I'm not letting you off the hook, you know. Just giving you a reprieve until I get back, then I'd like you back firmly in my life.'

He leaned over and kissed her.

'That sounds like a plan, a good plan,' she said, touching his face.

That night he did go in when she invited him and only left after several hours, to get home and finish his packing.

What's wrong with me? Beatrice thought when he had gone. *He's everything I ever wanted in a guy so why do I even hesitate?* Then she rationalised that three and a half months is not forever. Maybe she really should talk to someone, as Irene suggested, about her commitment issues. The more she thought about that the more she decided, maybe not!

CHAPTER 36

Rekna drove Iswara to the airport. She had stayed with her the night before her departure and had packed the new clothes she had secreted away in her sister's house.

AA was waiting for her as she came through the arrivals hall. As no public displays of affection are permitted in Arab countries, even though he was meeting her as her husband, she had to make do with his enthusiastic grin, and the adoration shining from his eyes as he saw her approach. Any more would have to wait until they reached their hotel.

They had had much discussion about where they should stay. AA had consulted his friends in the India Club, but when he had told Iswara of his plans, she'd vetoed the extravagance of a stay at the iconic Burj Al Arab hotel.

'But this is our honeymoon,' he'd argued. 'We'll never do this again.'

'I wouldn't sleep at night thinking of what that would cost and of what we could do with such an amount of money at the centre and for setting up wherever you and I go.'

322

'I think you should know that I don't intend to let you do too much sleeping when you're here. If I compromise on the main part of your visit, you must allow me spoil you for a few days, and I mean really spoil you.'

'Just being with you is all the spoiling I'll ever need, but what have you planned?' she'd asked, intrigued.

'You'll have to wait,' he'd told her.

Normally, AA had no need of a car as he lodged close to his work, but he hired one for the duration of her visit. He put his hand on her knee when they were on the open road. She could feel the heat searing through her cotton *shalwar kameez*. She had opted for the more comfortable tunic and pants in preference to a sari for travelling. She put her hand on his briefly before removing it as they came to a junction. She longed for them to be on their own, cursing inwardly as the traffic congestion got thicker as they reached the city; every set of lights seemed determined to delay them even longer.

AA pointed out several landmarks along the way.

'Are you hungry?' he asked.

'Only for you.'

'And I for you.'

They could scarcely believe this day had finally come. They could now be seen together for two whole weeks, as a married couple, with no reprisals from anyone.

When they eventually checked in, they tried to

look decorous as they walked slowly and deliberately to their room, both wanting to run there, to be alone. Once inside, they had to wait for the porter to deliver their luggage and it seemed to take forever before they heard the knock on the door and a uniformed porter carried their cases in. AA gave him a bigger tip than was necessary in a bid to hurry him out of their space.

They laughed when he left. AA turned the lock on the door. He removed Iswara's wedding ring from his little finger and placed it on hers. He carried her over to the bed and they began to undress each other and to discover each other all over again – with a hunger, a passion and a longing that transported them, demanding to be satisfied. It wasn't. They couldn't get enough of each other. Their coupling was both gentle and urgent.

Hours later, Iswara said, 'You know I *am* hungry – no, starving actually. I was too excited on the plane to eat anything.'

They opted for room service and Iswara was in the bath when their meal arrived. Wrapped in fluffy oversized bathrobes, they ate on the balcony overlooking the marina, and beneath a full moon they talked, before making love again. Later, she mentioned Dublin.

He put his finger to her lips and said, 'No serious talking tonight. We have two weeks for that. Tonight, nowhere and no one else exists, there is nothing but us, here and now.'

Cuddling closer to his nakedness, she sighed, 'This is pretty perfect, isn't it?'

He agreed and within minutes she had surrendered to sleep.

They were staying in the Madinat Jumeirah resort, whose heart was a luxurious modern take on a rambling traditional Arabian village, complete with its own souk. They spent their days walking along the beach, strolling through the twisting alleyways and streets, past street performers, through lantern-lit hallways filled with carpet shops and art galleries. Each evening, they took one of the boats along the narrow canal ways that led to the restaurant district. They visited the Mall of the Emirates where, despite AA's good intentions, Iswara refused to allow him buy her anything.

They took the water taxi across the creek. This left them off at the Spice Souk, where their noses were assailed by the most wonderful rich, tangy, tantalising aromas. Just five minutes away, they found themselves in the Aladdin's cave that is the Gold Souk. There in the arcade dozens of individual shops vied with each other for business, their assistants almost disappearing in a cocoon of gold. It was everywhere, floor to ceiling. Thousands of bracelets in all shapes and widths were displayed on poles. Necklaces to suit both eastern and western styles could be bought by the length and their clasps fitted in minutes. The more elaborate costume and hairpieces were displayed individually.

Iswara's protests were overruled this time and AA insisted on buying her some keepsake bangles to remind her of her honeymoon. She chose one of two interwoven strands of gold which twisted around each other like a barley sugar stick and AA slid them over her slim hand on to her wrist, where they joined the ones her grandfather had given her.

The Souk was full of tourists, procrastinating, bartering and haggling. Craftsmen sat in wait to resize or fashion bespoke pieces to suit any indulgent whim. Dazzled by it in all its perplexing yet splendid excesses, Iswara kept saying, 'I'll never forget this – any of this.'

She said the same when she saw the real snow on the indoor ski slopes at the Mall of the Emirates. It was over forty degrees outside. She also said it when she first saw the grandiose Dubai Fountain coming alive in the Burj Khalifa Lake. She made AA take her there three times. He acquiesced immediately, without the need for any persuasion.

'It's one of my favourite things out here,' he told her. 'It's captivating, no matter how often you see it.'

They watched as the water jets waved and swayed to the rhythms, as they arched gracefully or gushed suppliantly skywards, altering their height and direction, making intricate patterns or chasing each other at turbo-charged speed across the lake, to the accompaniment of varying light displays. AA glanced at his wife and saw her wiping a tear away, overcome by the beauty of it all. He wanted to defy convention and take her in his arms, but he knew he couldn't.

When the spectacle ended she told him, 'I always feel disappointed when they stop. It's like being a child at the end of a fireworks display – that sense of wanting more but knowing it's over and that's it. We have to bring Damien to see this.'

'Definitely,' AA agreed.

Damien had arrived in Abu Dhabi that week and was due in Dubai in a few days' time. He had emailed AA for the hotel number and had phoned earlier that day, telling them he was booking an afternoon and evening away from the delegation to spend time with them to celebrate their marriage. Iswara would meet his students the next day.

Damien was sent directly to Iswara and AA's room when he arrived. He was greeted warmly by them both and he offered his sincere congratulations. 'Well Iswara, no one else had a chance once this handsome devil came along.'

She laughed at him and said, 'Nice as you are, and much as I love you dearly, you're right. Once I saw AA, I knew we were meant to be together. I never thought it could happen though.'

'Neither did I,' agreed AA.

'Maybe that obstacle-removing god of yours worked his magic. Perhaps I should give him a go.'

'Have you obstacles to surmount?' she asked.

'Oh yes,' Damien smiled, thinking of Beatrice, 'but haven't we all?'

Damien enquired about the medical centre and the school project, Iswara's parents and sister's family, and the director. He caught up on all the gossip. They left the hotel to walk along the beach and he remarked on how the skyline had changed in the few years since he had been there previously.

'If you think it looks impressive by day, just wait until you see it by night. It's magical,' Iswara said.

They were sitting by the waterfront drinking coffee when Damien brought up the possibility of them coming to Dublin.

'It looks as though it's my best option and one I would be happy to take. I've loved my time there,' Iswara said. 'I have lots of friends around the country. I'm sure they'll welcome us. Do you think it's possible for me to get a placement?'

'There's never been a better time. There's an acute shortage of doctors and although you may have to start at a lower level than you would like, I think we can probably steer you in the right direction there. What about you, AA? Have you looked into the work situation, visas, etc? Iswara did tell me you were honing your computer skills.'

'Well there's not much point in trying to get anything in the engineering line in the present climate, so I'm concentrating on my programming skills. I've already applied to a few of the multinationals in Ireland. They have some government arrangement regarding work permits for qualified Indian IT graduates. And I should be able to get the last bit of paper by mid-July, if I really work at it. That's about the only advantage of being a part-time bachelor. There are no distractions.'

'How do you feel about moving to Ireland?'

'Apprehensive, but if I am to go by all the things Iswara has told me, I think I'll like it too. And working with you guys on the project made me feel I wouldn't be going some place where I knew nobody. Besides, Iswara will be there,' he grinned. 'And I'll be able to take her hand in public or give her a hug when I feel like it!'

'That'll be a bonus all right,' Damien agreed. 'Now, I have a suggestion, and it's just that. How would you feel about having dinner in the Irish Village? That should give you an idea of what you are letting yourselves in for. If you hate the idea, we can go somewhere else.'

'That sounds perfect to me,' AA said, and one look at his wife's face showed it was with her too.

'But,' she said, 'we have to take you somewhere too.' She told Damien about the Dubai Fountain. 'It's really exquisite. We must take our camera and get you to take some photographs of us together. We only have the wedding ones, which are at AA's flat. My copies are hidden at my sister's!'

'Is there no chance that you'll tell your folks before you move?'

'I'm tempted to, but I'd rather do the cowardly thing and tell them when we're far away. That way, they'll have time to get used to the idea, and when we come back in a few years' time, it should be easier all around.'

Damien wasn't sure that this was the right approach, but he knew he didn't understand the cultural and religious differences enough to offer advice.

'Well, you know I'm here for you both.'

Iswara smiled at him. 'You are a really dear friend, and we appreciate your support hugely.'

Later that evening, they headed out to let Damien take a look at the fountains and to give AA an introduction to life in Ireland. This, Damien assured him, would either put him off visiting forever or convert him. Before he left them, Damien reminded them that he would do whatever was necessary to help their transition to the west.

'I'll be back there around the end of July. Meantime AA, if you feel like a break from your studies, I've plenty of space at my pad in Abu Dhabi should you feel like a visit. It's not even two hours away and the roads are very good now.'

'I might well take you up on that,' he replied.

The following morning, Damien rejoined his colleagues at breakfast and they spent the next day meeting and interviewing potential students who had expressed an interest in studying medicine in Ireland. The medical gurus went through the courses and options, while he talked to them about student life over there, reassuring them on many aspects that they queried. Iswara arrived at the appointed time to answer their questions.

She assured them that they could practise their religion freely, find halal food, mix freely with all the students, and wear the *hijab* or *burqa* openly if they so wished. Some wanted to know the ratio of Muslim students and others about postgraduate opportunities. Practically all of them asked which countries would recognise their degrees. By the end of the session, she felt excited about the prospect of going back and her excitement was infectious. AA said he couldn't wait either.

They invited Damien to join them for dinner, but he declined.

'Your time together is limited and precious. I'd like nothing more, but we'll make up for it when you're on my turf.'

As AA walked Damien outside to the taxis, he said, 'I can't thank you enough for everything you did for both of us, but I have one favour to ask. I'm taking Iswara away from everything she holds dear and I need to know she'll have someone apart from me that she can confide in. She trusts you completely.'

'AA, I'll be there for her no matter what. You needn't worry about that.'

'Thanks Damien.' AA shook his hand firmly.

Damien was exhausted, but all of his meetings and interviews had all gone really well. He was tired of talking and was facing another day of the same tomorrow, so back at the hotel he excused himself from his colleagues, headed back upstairs and ordered room service. He opened his laptop to see if there were any interesting emails. He quickly flicked though the dross, deleting some and flagging others for attention later, and kept Beatrice's till last to read.

Hi Damien

How is Dubai? Have you met up with your friends yet? How is the recruitment drive going?

There's not much happening at this end except that I'm thinking of moving, to something bigger. I flirted with the idea last year, but wasn't really serious about it then. Now the decision has been prompted by the fact that I may have a ready buyer for my own, a colleague who is coming to the end of an overseas posting and just wants a bolthole in Dublin. I've been scanning the property pages and looking online and both keep telling me prices are still dropping and dropping. At the rate they're going, I might be able to afford a whole ghost estate somewhere yet! Some property developer in Donegal was offering a 'buy one get one free' in the paper the other day. It said they were unfinished, whatever that means, but I don't intend on going that far away. I don't know what I

332

want really – a house or a bigger flat, new or old. Ideally, I'd love something overlooking the sea or water, but then I think I'd like a garden! Who knows where I'll end up?

Write with all your news.
Love
Beatrice xxx
PS I miss you – lots.

As Damien read this email he wondered if she were telling him something – that a move in with him was definitely not on the horizon? Was this her way of letting him down slowly? He dismissed this as paranoia: she had promised they'd start again when he got home, and there was the matter of her colleague making her a concrete offer for her flat. He could just imagine her poring over the property supplements, or spending hours going through MyHome.ie in search of something that would jump out and make her go look at it. He recalled his own foray into buying and the numerous disappointments before he realised that 'bijou' meant not big enough to keep a budgie and 'compact' vetoed the ownership of a cat. 'Needs work' either meant it hadn't been done up since the sixties, was a probate sale or that it had rising damp, single glazing and you might well be sharing with a colony of mice, or worse.

Dear Beatrice

Everything is going really well. There's a lot more interest in our degree and post-graduate courses than in previous years, and there are a lot more female applicants too.

I miss you too and wish you were out here with me, as I'd love to show you around.

Dubai is as awesome and awful as I remember it. Blingy, ostentatious, over the top, gaudy, yet it still has the ability to mesmerise me. It seems to have spread out an awful lot in five years and there are not as many cranes fringing the skyline as I remember. They seem to have this compulsion to build the biggest, tallest, fattest, widest, brightest and every other kind of 'ests' you can imagine. Someone told me that some of the islands in The World Islands are beginning to sink, but I haven't had the courage to ask anyone about that yet in case I'm never seen again!

Yes, I met my friends the other day. The students loved Iswara's talk and I think her portrayal of student life in Dublin has prob-ably persuaded a lot more of them to give it a go than anything we boring old officials did or said. Anyway, like homing pigeons, we ended up in the Irish Village for dinner. They even have a GAA club over here!

I'm not surprised that the appearance of a buyer would tempt you to move. It's a big decision. I remember looking at loads of places when I was buying, yet the minute I walked into my apartment, I knew it was exactly what I wanted. I'm not sure if it is suitable for a family though, but for a crusty bachelor like me, it's perfect, for now. You'll probably be the same (not a crusty old bachelor), you'll know when you see it.

I must say it's great living by the sea. I love looking out at it in all weathers. Do you know 'On the Sea' by Keats? I think he wrote:"Oh ye! who have your eyeballs vexed and tired, Feast them upon the wideness of the sea" just for people like me. No matter how exhausted I am, just sitting staring out at the water always relaxes me. I'm in danger of getting homesick now, so I'll stop!

I'm dining in my room tonight and my meal has just been delivered – by a uniformed guy.

Uniform designers and manufacturers must be multimillionaires here, as every worker in every hotel has his own and some are quite elaborate. (Not a hair shirt in sight anywhere!)

The food smells delicious, and you know what they say – the way to a man's heart and all that – so I'm signing off now to eat and have a glass or two of wine! Good luck with the house hunting. I love you and miss you, B

Damien xx

CHAPTER 37

On the second Saturday in June Irene went shopping for her wedding dress. She insisted Beatrice came along too. They arrived at a boutique that smelled of expensive scent and discretion. The carpet was plush, the brass door handles and windows were gleaming. The bored assistant wasn't too pleased at being disturbed. Without leaving her seat behind an ostentatious desk, she looked up from her gossipy magazine and asked, 'Do you know what you want?'

'No meringues, corset tops or laced up backs,' Irene announced.

'You're more a Kate Middleton bride, are you? Very popular ever since her wedding, even with stouter brides,' the assistant responded, eyeing Irene up and down.

'No Kate Middleton either,' Irene said emphatically. 'Can I look around for a bit first?'

'Not much point,' was the answer. 'All the gowns are covered. Can't risk them being photographed and copied.'

'I suppose not,' agreed Irene with a glance at Beatrice.

'Do you want lace or satin, georgette or silk?'

'I really don't know. This is my first time out shopping for a wedding dress.'

'We have plenty of magazines, you could look at those and get some idea from them,' the assistant suggested, indicating a low table with an array of fanned out publications.

Beatrice looked at this girl incredulously. They had come in to see the dresses and she was offering them some tatty magazines while they stood surrounded by concealed creations cocooned in opaque plastic cloaks, like ghosts waiting for the light to fade so they could be free to come out and show off. It didn't happen like this in the movies. Brides, their mothers and the bridesmaids too were usually given champagne and treated like, well, like royalty as they deliberated.

'If you could show me a few images you like, we would both know where we are going, that way I would only have to unzip a few dresses and not the whole shop.'

Beatrice exploded, grabbing Irene's arm. 'I'll tell you where we are going. We're leaving your boutique and that'll save you having to unzip any of your precious dresses. Thank you very much.' She ushered Irene out.

'But I never looked at anything,' objected Irene as they walked away.

'You are about to make one of the most expensive, never mind the most important, purchases of your life, and that wagon couldn't be bothered to unzip a few plastic bags. Let's have a coffee and go somewhere else.'

They did, and after being treated properly in the next boutique, Irene found exactly what she hadn't known she wanted. Then they found an outfit for Beatrice. Satisfied with a very productive morning, they went off to have a late lunch in the Unicorn.

'You're lucky to be so sure of your feelings, Irene. I wish I could be.'

'You have to allow yourself to trust and not always be afraid that things might go wrong.'

'That's what my mother tells me.'

'Well, she probably knows you better than anyone. Maybe she has a point.'

'I know you said it before and I shot you down in flames, but do you really think if I talked to someone it would help?'

'From where I'm looking, it can't do any harm.'

'I'll think about it,' Beatrice said.

'What's brought all this on?'

'I've been doing a lot of thinking since Damien left and I feel that what he and I have is special. I've never felt this way before. Yet when he tried to get close, or closer, I pushed him away. Now that we're in constant touch again, I really miss him like hell. I feel this might be a second chance and I don't want to blow it again.'

'Are you going to go over and visit him?'

'No. I think we need the space. I know I certainly do. That would be like a holiday romance and not reality. Besides, doesn't absence make the heart grow fonder?' Beatrice joked.

'And distance makes the faithful wander!'

'Oh you're some cynic!'

'So why the house move?'

'Believe it or not, the two are unrelated. My place was great when I had just started work and had fewer possessions, but I've outgrown it in every way. It's too small and not even a good prospect for resale as I believe the banks have vetoed loans on one-beds. The fact that I have a ready cash buyer who came to me helped me make my mind up too. No matter if I move in with Damien or not when he comes back, I want to buy a bigger place. It would be much easier to let out anyway.'

'I suppose that makes sense. We've decided to hold on to Daragh's house instead of looking elsewhere. It's a fine sturdy house, although his parents didn't do much to it in their last years. It needs rewiring for starters, and he's replacing the bathrooms, the windows and adding a new kitchen. It's all very exciting really.'

'Will you hold on to your apartment?' asked Beatrice.

'We haven't decided yet. Depending on the state of things, we might decide to keep it and rent it out.'

'We're lucky to have the luxury of making choices. So many of my friends are caught in serious negative equity.'

'So when is the house hunting going to begin and what are you looking for?'

'I'm off to see two apartments and one townhouse tomorrow, but like you and the wedding dress, I don't know what I want but I do know what I don't want!'

'I don't envy the poor estate agent.'

'Neither do I!'

CHAPTER 38

Beatrice was definitely coming around to the idea of moving in with Damien. One day she was full sure of it, the next doubts began to take over. She found herself weighing up the pros and cons, and the cons won every time. *Why do I still have lingering doubts?* she wondered.

Between these thoughts, she toyed with the idea of going to a counsellor, and after several more days of anguish, she decided to take Irene's advice and take the plunge. She told no one and headed off after work one Wednesday.

The counsellor's rooms were in a swanky period house in Blackrock, which he shared with others if the numerous brass nameplates on the door were an indication. She only had time to read one, for a hair restoration specialist, before the door opened and she was shown in to a large waiting room by a woman who looked like librarians always did in movies – the grey-hair-held-back-by-two-clips type, who whispered everything.

The room was a mixture of ill-matching chairs, an enormous sideboard and an even more imposing mahogany table with piles of neatly arranged

National Geographic, *Newsweek*, *Reader's Digest*, *VIP* and *Hello!* magazines.

A gaunt-looking young man with seriously thinning hair didn't look up to acknowledge her and she was grateful, while a portly lady immediately put her magazine down and turned towards her. Beatrice knew her type, a neighbourhood gossip who used waiting rooms as reference centres, somewhere to replenish her store of tales of unbelievable tragedy and improbabilities.

Before the woman had finished asking, 'Who are you here to see, dear?' Beatrice got a reprieve as the librarian type called her name.

After the receptionist had shown her up to his rooms, the therapist took the preliminary details and Beatrice took in the surroundings. She was a little disconcerted by Mr Malcolm Daltry's formal and offhanded manner, and by his combover. Even he must realise that twenty-five or twenty-six hairs wouldn't cover his shiny pate, and didn't he realise he was damaging the other consultants' businesses going around looking like that?

He continued to make notes on an A4 pad, and she decided there was no way he was going to fill that with what he'd get out of her. House hunting had increased her awareness of the feel-good factor in a space, or the lack of. This she put in the benign category. No couch. She had expected to be reclining on one: wasn't that what one did when attending one's shrink? Just two comfy easy chairs opposite each other, his with its back to the window. She'd have liked to walk over and look outside. She always liked looking down on gardens. Instead, she concentrated on her surroundings, faded ferny flock wallpaper with velvet drapes in pale green. The carpet was definitely retro – a shaggy type with swirls and abstracts in brown, cream and green, the type that you now only ever see in doctors' waiting rooms. His desk was tidy. He was tidy. She supposed his life was tidy too, all bundled up neatly like the magazines on the table downstairs. Would she be able to relate to this man?

He began with, 'Now tell me about yourself.'

Beatrice almost laughed out loud. That was exactly what she had imagined he would say. 'Where do I begin – now – the present – or when I was young?' she asked.

'Wherever you feel most comfortable. Start anywhere.'

'Well, I'm an only child, I have a good job, my own home, good friends, a great social life . . .'

The fifty minutes passed very quickly as Beatrice found herself talking about her dad and her childhood. She never mentioned Damien. Mr Daltry suggested another appointment for the following week.

'How many sessions will this take?' she enquired.

'That's a difficult question to answer,' he said deliberately. 'Let's see how the next one goes.'

She wondered what he had gleaned from her revelations. A happy home: she wasn't beaten, abused, starved or deprived of education or friends. She had a step-father, but Ray didn't fit into the wicked step-parent category. He loved her and she him. Somehow she, as well as her wallet, felt lighter on the way home.

Over the next few weeks, her therapist was just as aloof and remote, although he did use her first name. He regularly ran his hand over his skull to make sure his hairs were still in place and she wondered if he counted them every morning just to make sure he hadn't lost any.

'How did you feel after our last session?' he enquired one day, as he did at the start of every session. 'Any flashbacks or things you'd like to discuss?'

'No, but I really want to find out if there is something holding me back from having a serious relationship. As I've told you, I haven't exactly been lucky with the men in my life. My relationships all seem to end badly and then I feel I've been used or incredibly stupid – or both. Consequently, when I met someone I really fell for and who wanted to be more serious, I ran a mile and lost him. Now I have a chance to pick this up again. Everything tells me to go for it, yet any time it gets close to even being discussed I shut down. I want to know why am I like that.'

He said nothing. This unnerving silence forced her to continue.

'Everyone else seems to sail through their relationships. Move in together and if it doesn't work out, they just move on. No recriminations and no regrets, or so it seems to me anyway.'

She paused, and instead of just listening to her, as he usually did, this time he surprised her by engaging her in discussion, uttering the odd prompt when she hesitated. He asked her about Ray and her relationship with him.

What age had she been when he had come into her life? Did she resent him? Then? Now? How did she feel about her father? Did she remember him?

'Not a lot. I vividly recall when he died that I was allowed go help Mrs Murphy, a neighbour, with her baking. I can still recall the lovely smell in her kitchen, and that she had more cakes than I had ever seen in my life, cooling on wire trays.' Beatrice smiled at those memories. 'She allowed me to spread jam on some of them and put the tops on the butterfly ones. Then someone called and helped us carry them back to my house. That was the day of his funeral.'

'Anything else?'

'I remember getting money for my money box from an uncle and people telling me I had to mind my mother, as she was on her own now and the two of us had to look out for each other.'

'How did that make you feel?'

'I honestly don't remember. I don't remember feeling sad. My dad had been ill for a while and I was used to him being absent from our lives, although I didn't really understand that then.

I know my mother and I have always been very close. I missed my grandfather much more when he died.'

'I see,' he said, and left one of those loaded silences to linger for a bit.

'I loved him. He used to collect me from school and often I'd go back to his house. He'd take me to Herbert Park. He used to play bowls there. He collected stamps too and he'd let me soak the ones he had torn off envelopes in saucers of water to remove the paper from the back. When they dried we'd mount them with little stickers in his albums. I learned the names of all sorts of exotic places from those.'

'So you've lots of happy memories with him.'

'Tons. He had a beautiful garden and he taught me the names of all the plants he had growing in it. He let me plant bulbs there too. We often went to the Botanic Gardens and we'd always go into the glasshouses. I can still remember the way the humidity would hit you when you went in. It smelled of damp soil. There were gigantic plants with huge glossy leaves in what Granddad called the monkey house and you could go upstairs to look down through the foliage. Of course, there were no monkeys there, but we pretended anyway. There were always people sitting around sketching and painting. He was great.'

'When did he die?'

'When I was ten. Mum and I had been with him earlier that day and he was his usual cheerful self.

347

He just died in his sleep, sitting in his chair looking out at his lovely garden. He loved listening to classical music and the radio was still playing when they found him. I didn't go to his funeral. Mum asked me if I wanted to, but I didn't want to see him being buried so I said no. Sometimes I wish I had, as it was just like he vanished. Like my father did. I hated going to his house after that. So did Mum. She wanted to know if I'd like to live there, but it wasn't the same without Granddad. It felt empty, as if the lights were out and it felt neglected. It had to be cleared out before it was sold and that was awful.'

'Did you resent it when your mother brought a man – brought Ray – into your life?'

'No, I don't think so. I don't even recall meeting him for the first time. He just seems to have been part of our lives forever. I was a flower girl when they married and I thought it was all very romantic, and I wanted them to live happily ever after. Till death do them part and all that. I used to worry that he'd die too and she'd be sad again, the way she had been when my father and her father died.'

She stopped then. After a few minutes she looked up at her therapist suddenly, as though something had come into her mind.

He said, 'Beatrice, I think you've just solved your own problems, your trust issues and your fear of commitment. Listen to what you've just said and tell me if you can see a pattern.'

He was quiet again, with one of those pregnant pauses he did so well.

She wasn't quite sure if they were thinking the same thing.

'I have a feeling that your issues go back to losing your father,' he continued. 'You were too young to understand why he simply stopped being there. Then, five years later, you had the same experience when your grandfather passed away, and suddenly too. That is often very hard for people, and especially for children, to come to terms with. You probably didn't discuss your feelings in case they upset your mother more, and that would have been perfectly normal. Then, when she married Ray, you began to worry that something would happen to him. I perceive that not only have you deep-seated fears of losing another person you loved or could love if you allowed yourself to be in such a vulnerable position, but you added the burden of feeling your mother's happiness is your responsibility too to those issues.'

Beatrice objected. 'I never did!'

'From where I'm sitting you did, and probably quite subconsciously. From what you've told me over the past weeks, you took on board what people told you when your father died – "You must be a big girl now, you must look after your mother, you must be good and make sure you don't do anything to make her sad." Even at five, it filtered through that you were being asked to grow up and be responsible for someone else's well-being. Your

349

mother was your rock and you felt you had to be hers.'

'I think that's unfair.'

'Perhaps it is, but you haven't been coming to me for me to tell you we can wave a proverbial wand and make things better. Life is seldom fair in the way we'd like it to be. You have to face the fact that fate deals our hand, and it's how we turn those cards that shapes us. Unfortunately, when life dishes out the blows, it rarely chooses the most opportune moment to do so. In an ideal world children are supposed to have their parents until they grow up – that's normal. In separation, they can still have contact with them, and no mater how fraught that contact is, the absent parent is still present in their lives. Death deprives children of that. Sudden death is even more brutal. It's hard to explain why someone simply vanishes from their life, especially when we often have difficulty explaining it to ourselves. Young children pick up on the vibes and moods of those around them. Often well-intentioned relatives and friends add to the weight by telling young ones they are the big man or the big sister in the house now and they must help. That can sometimes add to their burden. Some children will end up resenting their siblings because of it, others take their role too seriously, to the detriment of their own friendships and independence.'

'I can see how that would happen, but I never resented my mother.'

'I'm not saying you did, and I can see that you don't, but I think you are afraid to give yourself completely to anyone, to allow yourself be happy with them in case you lose them and have to go through that pain of loss again.'

'I can see the logic in that,' she said.

'I think you should look at that. Mull it over before we meet again and let me know your thoughts next time. You've come a long way today, Beatrice. Well done.'

She didn't need that affirmation to know she had. When she left his consulting rooms and looked at the time, she realised he had given her an extra quarter of an hour, definitely uncharacteristic of her punctual shrink. It reminded her of an article she'd read in the hairdresser's about some street in New York, or was it Boston, where several analysts had their rooms, and the patrons of a diner on the corner referred to it as the Fifty-Minute-Hour Esplanade, because the rush of cabs that came and went five minutes before and after the clocks struck the hour coincided perfectly with the therapy sessions. It didn't matter, apparently, if you were in the middle of confessing to killing your nanny and cooking her, once the sand in the egg timer ran out, so did your meter. Then it was, 'See you next week. Same time, same place. You can pay my secretary on the way out. Now you have a nice day, won't you?'

She was glad her fellow had the decency and humanity to give her the extra time she had obviously needed that evening. He had also given her a lot to think about.

When she got home she was pleased to find an email from Damien.

> Hi Beatrice
>
> How are you? What's happening on the house-hunting front? Any joy with those viewings?
>
> I'd love you to come out for a visit. I'm getting used to the heat and the lifestyle here in Abu Dhabi and I have to admit having the pool at my disposal is a real bonus. I'll miss that when I get back home.
>
> Sorry B, I have to go, a student just dropped by for help with some documentation.
>
> Love you
> D xx

For a second, she wondered was it a female student and could 'help with some documentation' be a euphemism for something else? *God, woman, you really do have trust issues,* she chided herself. *If you married Damien – and who mentioned getting married anyway – female students would be part of his working life and you'd have to get used to that.*

This therapy is certainly making me question myself. I'm glad I have some time to work on my issues before Damien comes back.

She decided to reply before eating, but would ignore his comment on going out to visit him.

Dear Damien

Lucky you, I could get used to having a pool too. Somehow, the idea of joining the other goose-pimpled swimmers at Seapoint or Sandycove after work doesn't have quite the same appeal as a dip in glorious sunshine, especially if it's just to cool down. Outdoor pools never have that awful chlorine smell you get in indoor ones and that's what really puts me off going to them.

House hunting! Don't get me started. How estate agents can get away with the doctoring they do on their photographs I don't know.

One townhouse that caught my eye looked as though you could park a fleet of double-decker buses in the lounge, it was so wide and so high. The reality was that a two-seater couch and a flat screen would have left little space for anything else, and if guests called it would have been a case of standing room only.

The two-bedroomed apartment I saw last Saturday promised sea views – it didn't mention that these were through the top of the bathroom window, which was frosted, so you'd have had to open it out to see the view. You had to open the second one to get the 'views'! And then they were only visible through about a six-inch gap between the houses across the road. The place was grotty too. I then looked at a three-bedroomed one, for around the same price, but this had been given the chip-board treatment by some very enthusi-astic, if totally inept, DIYer. He (I'm assuming it was a he!) had built bookcases all along the hall and over the doorways. It's now so narrow that if you wanted to bring a suitcase in you'd need to turn it sideways. I haven't a clue how you'd get your furni-ture in, or out.

Then I went to see one in the Docklands, great price, but with a 'compact' kitchen. In property parlance, I now know that means it has no room for a cooker, so they had built in a microwave with an oven function and no hob!

I'm thinking of devising a coding system with little symbols to save people from wasting time viewing places that would never suit them. A black cloud would denote that the chimney smokes, or that there's none; a skeleton that you can't cook there; a hat and scarf – the heating doesn't exist or work; an umbrella – something is leaking badly; a sofa with an x through it – no space for furniture, and a set of luggage with an x through it – there's no storage!

This is still a work in progress you understand . . .

Meanwhile, I've decided to start de-cluttering my life – something I've been promising to do for eons. Getting rid of some of my junk will make the move easier too.

Don't work too hard over there and write soon.

Miss you too, so much.

All my love

Beatrice xxx

At the clinic, only the director knew Iswara was planning to leave and had filed her immigration papers. Thanks to Damien's network, she had been offered a place in a medical centre in inner-city Dublin and they were willing to sponsor her. It had a high non-national roll of patients. The hours were unsocial – catering for the after-work consultations and weekend shifts – but she reasoned, if it gave her a bona fide entry visa then she'd work around the clock if she had to. AA's preliminary enquiries to the IT multinationals had also yielded some positive responses and the pair spent a lot of time online planning and missing each other. He had two weeks to go to his exams, the ones he needed to complete his qualifications, and he was quietly confident. There was too much at stake to slack off at this juncture.

'We'll have plenty of time to make it up once we're together,' he assured her.

'I'll never let you out of my sight again,' she vowed.

'You won't have to. I hadn't realised how hard

it would be being separated, once we had been together in the real sense.'

'Nor had I. I can't wait to lie in your arms again.'

'And I in yours. I keep remembering the nights we shared and can't wait for more of the same. I'll never let you go away from me.'

'Is that a promise?' she asked.

'Yes, that's a promise!'

She kept busy, staying later at the centre, helping out with the classes at the new schoolrooms. She discussed basic hygiene, taught new mothers how to bathe their babies and take care of minor ailments. She made many aware of the things they needed to take seriously – fevers, rashes, bites and infected wounds. She used her work as a way to stop her thinking about other things that she preferred not to face – things like deceiving her parents further and the fact that she'd be thousands of miles away from them; that she'd miss Rekna and her husband and she'd miss seeing her little nephews grow up. She and Rekna had become closer than ever since she had come back, and even more so since she'd started volunteering at the centre. They were spending a lot more time together, knowing that it was precious and fast running out for them.

They often took the older boys to walk along Chowpatty Beach, where their own parents had taken them and where they had gone for pony rides and turns on the ferris wheels, and had watched the snake charmers and the yogic contortionists twist themselves into knots. They reminisced at how they used to look forward to the annual festival of Ganesh Chaturthi, which attracted millions to Chowpatty Beach and caused traffic mayhem for days. That was when visitors and locals alike all gathered to watch the parading of giant statues of Ganesh being taken right down to the water's edge before being immersed in the waves.

They laughed together about having their fortunes told there on more than one occasion and wondered if they had them told now would the astrologers have anything of significance to tell them.

'I don't think I want to know my future, I just want to live it, every minute of it, with AA.'

'And you will,' Rekna reassured her. 'And you'll see our parents might surprise us all and accept it once they've had time to reflect on everything. They won't want to lose their daughter forever.'

'I hope not. They'll never forgive you for helping it all happen though.'

'Let me worry about that. I'll get my in-laws working on Mama too, when the time is right. They are much more liberal. Besides, Mama loves my boys unconditionally, and she'll be the same with yours. I can't see her cutting herself off from them, when they come along.'

She smiled and Iswara smiled too, thinking of the family they might have one day.

'I hope you're right.'

'I am, you'll see,' Rekna hugged her sister. 'It's going to be strange not having you around,' she muttered.

Daya had almost completely despaired of Iswara, who she perceived to be her errant daughter. She told her husband on one of the nights that she was working late, 'I really don't see any point in making any more introductions. She has no interest in normal things, like marriage and motherhood. Her career is her husband.'

'If it makes her happy, then maybe that's not a bad thing,' he countered.

'Her work won't give her love, though, will it?'

'No, but it can and does give her fulfilment. Be happy for her. She enjoys helping people and maybe that's where she sees her place in the world. And isn't contentment better than being in a bad marriage? Sometimes, my dear Daya, I think you forget that not everybody is as fortunate as we have been.'

'Thirty years together. Have I really put up with you for that length of time?'

'I think we should take a holiday to celebrate reaching that milestone. What do you think?'

'I'd love that,' she said. 'Let's go back to the mountains.'

'The mountains it shall be, my dear.'

CHAPTER 40

Beatrice and Irene were having their lunch in St Stephen's Green on a glorious June day. There were bodies stretched out on every bit of available grass, sleeves rolled up and faces to the sun, trying to catch the all-too-rare summer rays. A band was tuning up in the bandstand. It struck up some summery tunes and several little boys and girls started marching back and forth. Two diminutive old ladies seated on the next bench clapped genteelly in time. One of the regulars around the park, a down and out who never bothered anyone, stood up by one of the fountains and began waving an imaginary baton, conducting the players.

Relaxed, Beatrice had started telling Irene about her counselling sessions, something she had kept to herself until now.

'Are they helping at all?' Irene asked.

'Much as I hate to admit that you were right, I actually think they are. Evidently, my commitment issues stem back to my childhood, to losing my dad and granddad.'

'That's what the counsellor said? And do you agree with him?'

'I have to. It seems to make sense, now I have to work on shedding those fears, which sounds easier than it really is, but I am happy to give it a try. I realise I want Damien in my life, long term. I really do love him and am not going to risk losing him again.'

'Good for you. Does this mean you'll move in together when he gets back?'

'Not necessarily, but I'm getting there – I think I actually might!'

'That shrink must be good! No, I'll change that – he must be a miracle worker!'

'And I thought you were my friend!' Then she added, 'Please don't mention anything to Damien or his sister. I want to tell him myself when he gets back.'

Beatrice had decided to talk to her mother too. When she told her the following night what the psychologist had said, Mary's eyes had filled up.

'I'm so relieved you went to someone. I've often felt you never grieved properly and I regretted not taking you to bereavement counselling when you were younger.'

'Mum, I don't blame you in any way.'

'I know that, and I should have done that in the beginning, but, you know, the longer it went on the more difficult it became. I was afraid that if I brought it up I'd only upset you all over again, so I left it alone.'

'I can understand that. I suppose you were

grieving too, and having a small child to deal with can't have helped.'

'Believe you me, Beatrice, you were the only thing that got me through. I had to get up every morning and put on a brave smile for you.'

'Well, I think you did a great job on me!' she laughed, just as Ray came in.

'I haven't a clue what you two are talking about, but I think she did a great job on you too!'

Emails flew back and forward between Damien, Iswara and AA, as the newlyweds' plans developed and materialised. AA had agreed to go to Abu Dhabi for a few days to visit and Damien showed him around the campus and the city. AA took photos to show Iswara when they met up again. On the last evening before he drove back to Dubai, he was full of questions about life in Ireland. Would he fit in? Was Iswara giving up too much? Would the price prove to be too high?

'I certainly don't think so,' Damien said. 'Anyway it's not as if there's no way back if you hate it. I know Iswara spent some very happy days there so in a way it'll be easier for her because of that. She'll be able to reconnect with some old friends and that will certainly make the transitions smoother for you both. You are now her life and she is yours and you can be together openly. And I'll be there to keep an eye on you,' he laughed, slapping AA on the back. 'You can count on me.'

'I do know that. You've been a remarkable friend

to the two of us. If you ever find yourself in an intercultural, inter-creed complicated mess make sure you call on me, won't you?'

'I don't even need those complexities. I can manage to find myself in much more convoluted fixes without even adding any of those ingredients!' After a pause Damien continued, 'You're very lucky that you were so positive about your feelings for each other.'

'There was never any doubt. I've decided to go back a few days earlier than expected to break the news to my mother and sisters in Bangalore. I'm hoping to persuade Iswara to come down and meet them.'

'Will that be a problem?'

'Initially, it probably will be. If it is, they'll just have to accept it or they'll lose their son and brother. My first duty now is to my wife, and someday, hopefully, to our own family.'

'Well I wish you the best of luck with all that.'

'I'll need all the luck I can get.'

Back in his solitary apartment in Dubai, AA logged in to Skype and told Iswara what he had discussed with Damien.

'I'd love to meet your mother and your sisters and their families too,' Iswara said

'You have to realise that they may not welcome you immediately, but at least this way you'll be able to visualise them when I talk about them, the way I can when you mention your family. I haven't decided yet whether we should just turn up, or whether I should email them first to give them time to get used to the idea.'

'And I have some news for you. Rekna and her husband came to dinner last night and I told them all about going back to Ireland. They were shocked at first. Of course Rekna pretended it was news to her. Mama cried and said she didn't know where she had gone wrong rearing me. Papa said if it made me happy, then he'd be happy for me.'

'We're getting there, bit by bit,' AA assured her. 'I'll do some net surfing and find out about flights to Bangalore for you. I can't wait to have you to myself again.'

'Neither can I,' she replied, blowing him a kiss.

Two days later, she was examining a rag picker's nasty foot wound. The ugly gash should have been attended to a week earlier. It was very badly infected, smelled of rotting flesh and was oozing puss. As she leaned over to swab it clean, she was overcome with a wave of nausea. She had difficulty stopping herself from retching in front of the young boy. She excused herself, muttering something about going for some dressings, and went outside until she had regained her composure. All morning long, she couldn't expel the rancid odour from her nostrils, no matter how much she washed and disinfected. The director told her she looked tired and she told him what had happened. She also told him about going to Bangalore to AA's family and that she had broken the news to her parents about going abroad.

'It's no wonder you're feeling unwell. That's a lot of stress to be carrying around. You could be run down a little. Take it easy for a few days,' he said, before insisting she went home early that day. She did, and after a long soak in a scented bath she went to bed and slept through till the morning. When she woke, she felt normal again and headed to the clinic as usual.

In just three weeks she would be finished up here. She'd miss the place, despite its shortcomings and lack of facilities. As she sat musing between patients she thought about the clinic; considering the constraints and limitations, they did actually do a really good job here. She knew her grandfather would have approved of the way they were carrying on his ideas and ideals.

At home, Daya had gone into a tailspin trying to organise her daughter's life, while decrying her bad choices. 'I don't know why you have to go so far away. If you were to pursue further studies that would be one thing, but with your papa's clinic there for you . . .'

Raj intervened. He didn't want the women in his life warring again, when they had so little time before Iswara left. His wife picked up on his look and said, 'You'll need warm clothes. I suppose you'll dress in western style.'

'It is more practical, Mama, but I won't stop

being an Indian, so you needn't worry. And you can always come over and check up on me!'

'We might just have to do that, although the thought of that bland European food puts me off.'

'I'll make sure to cook your favourites.'

A few nights later, Iswara was at Rekna's, where she had been secreting many of the personal effects she was taking with her. After the little ones were all in bed they were talking about the centre and Rekna assured her she'd keep up her involvement at it. 'Well it's almost a family business, after all. Grandpapa would never have believed I'd end up helping out there.'

'He'd have been delighted that his legacy proved to be much more than just money. You were always his little princess,' Iswara said.

'And you his raven-haired achiever girl!'

'And we got there in the end!'

'Promise me if you're unhappy, or if things don't work out as planned, that you'll come back. You can always stay with us, and, before you object, I'll handle Mama if that's the case.'

'You're such a great sister, thank you. But I know once we're together, we'll make it work,' Iswara said.

'I'm sure you will. Now you need to get some rest before you meet that man of yours again. You look awfully tired. Cut back on the time you spend at work, won't you?'

★　★　★

The next time Iswara talked to AA she admitted to being nervous about meeting his mother.

'She'll love you, I know it, once she gets over the fact that I did them all out of a wedding feast. We may have more trouble with my sisters – well not with them exactly, but with their in-laws, who may see you as the infidel! But we'll be out of their way after a few days so let's not worry about them. Besides, my sisters think I'm great. They always spoiled me, so they'll probably forgive me anything! They usually do.'

With just three weeks to go, Iswara had several checklists on her computer and was working her way through them. Daya had filled her diary pretty well with farewell gatherings of cousins and friends, any excuse for a party. Iswara had the eighth marked in red and was flying to Bangalore the evening before to stay in the hotel AA had booked. She'd wait there for him.

She had some news to tell him, something no one but she knew about. She was carrying his child and had agonised over whether she should tell him on Skype. She had decided not to. It was far too important and she wanted to read his reaction not from some wavy-lined, often blurry, connection on screen; in reality she wanted to feel his arms around her as he realised they were going to be a real family. It nearly killed her, keeping it to herself. She had had to fight with herself every time she was with Rekna to stop herself from spilling the news. But she knew she couldn't tell anyone before AA. And she was enjoying the privacy of what was happening to her body. Touching her still totally flat stomach when no one was about, imagining the tiny baby taking life inside her. Imagining AA holding it when it was born. Was it a boy or a girl? She didn't want to know, she decided. Then she wondered who it would look like.

Never one to be particularly bothered about her irregular cycle, she marvelled that as a doctor she had missed a few periods and not even noticed missing them. It was only when she had had that attack of nausea when attending that young boy's infected foot – that and the overwhelming tiredness she seemed to be battling with all the time – that she got the message. She was pregnant. Thirteen or fourteen weeks. A honeymoon baby!

Her initial fear was whether she'd be allowed into Ireland on her approved visa when she declared her changed medical status. She had contacted the authorities and, after much discussion, she assured them that neither one of them would be seeking Irish citizenship, nor would their unborn, and they would be prepared to swear an affidavit to that effect if necessary. She was very relieved when they told her the visas would still be approved.

The director insisted on taking her and her colleagues out for a meal before she left. They thought she was going back alone. He told her, 'If things don't work out over there, Iswara, you know there'll always be a place for you at the clinic.'

'I really appreciate you saying that. You know, I can never thank you enough for your support.'

'Just be happy, that's all the thanks I need. And keep in touch.'

She promised she would.

Later that evening she received an email from Damien. It was a brief message to them both, wishing them luck.

> Let me know how things are going. Remember you know where I am if you need me. See you in Dublin!

Iswara smiled when she got this email. What a good friend he was to them both.

CHAPTER 41

Beatrice had found a house, a three-bed semi, one road back from the waterfront at Sandymount, and scarcely a mile from where she lived and from where she had grown up. It did have quite a good sea view too, through the gardens of the big house behind it. It also had a sunroom, a bonus she hadn't even contemplated, and a manageable garden. This had been carefully landscaped with colour-filled beds and compact shrubbery. It had a terracotta brick patio with its own built-in barbecue, an olive tree, three pencil-slim cypresses, all of which lent a Mediterranean feel to it. The owners were an upwardly mobile couple, both lawyers, who had found a bigger house, within the same prestigious postcode.

Beatrice took Ray and Mary to see it and their approval was instantaneous. 'You can literally pack your bags and move in here,' her mother said.

'What about finances?' Ray asked. 'Can you afford it without stretching yourself?'

'Ray, you're a dote! And yes I can. Tony, who is buying my flat, has offered to give me the money

370

as soon as I find somewhere and with my savings it's very affordable.'

Later she wrote to Damien.

Dear Damien

I think I have found my new abode (see link below) and hope you'll approve. I saw it yesterday and went back again today with the folks. It's just two stations away from my present place and it's just perfect. To use that very overworked cliché, it literally does tick all the boxes. Lots of fireplaces, even one in the master bedroom, a super modern kitchen and high ceilings, although not as lofty as your ones. And you know what that means – I'll be able to buy a real Christmas tree this year!

To me it's palatial and I love the idea of a big hallway.

I'm afraid to think it's mine until everything is signed. Can't wait for you to see it.

All my love

Beatrice xx

PS Sorry this mail is all about me, me and ME! I love YOU xxx

Damien felt a tug of disappointment after he had read the email. He clicked on the link and could find no fault with the property. But he wondered how it would affect their relationship if Beatrice spent time and money on this place.

He was surprised at his reaction, but of late he often found himself considering if the time was right to put down roots. He'd never felt like that before meeting her.

Dear Beatrice
     Well it looks as though you have struck it lucky – that's a great buy. Good address, lots of features and add-ons. Can't wait to see it.
     It's manic here today at the college. Some foreign dignitaries are visiting and we're all on our best behaviour. I'll fill you in later.
     Really looking forward to catching up again and to seeing your new home. You'll hardly have the keys before I get back, but maybe if you talk nicely to the estate agent he/she will allow us have a look. Although I've enjoyed my time out here, it will be good to be back among friends and at my familiar desk again too. And I'll be able to help you with your move.
     I love you
     Damien xxx

CHAPTER 42

When her parents suggested seeing her off at the airport, Iswara declined, saying she didn't want any tears and she'd rather say goodbye to them at home. Without actually saying so, she had managed to give them the impression that she was flying directly to Ireland; Bangalore was never mentioned. Instead of going with her father's driver, Rekna insisted on taking her herself, to see her off safely. En route, Iswara got a text from Damien:

> Thinking of you. Have a safe trip and good luck with in-laws. See you both in a few weeks.

As the sisters said an emotional goodbye, Iswara insisted, 'No more tears please, Rekna. Mama cried enough for all of us over the last few days.'

'You know I'm happy for you, but that won't stop me missing you.'

'I'm trying not to think about that. I'll miss you like mad too.'

They hugged one last time and parted. To stop

herself dissolving, Iswara kept her focus on seeing AA the next day. She'd go straight to the hotel and have an early night.

It thrilled her when the receptionist checked the booking AA had made and addressed her as Mrs Mahimkar. She'd have to get used to that. She was so excited about the baby that she'd almost told Rekna in the car. She'd phone her once she had given AA the news. She slept well, eventually, after she decided she'd go to the airport next morning to meet him.

The following morning, she spent a long time getting ready. She fixed her hair several times in different ways and chose one of the saris she had worn when she had been in Dubai.

She took the *mangalsutra* out of the little silk purse that she had worn around her waist, kissed it and put it around her neck, remembering the words he had spoken as he'd fixed it in place at their wedding ceremony. 'May you, the reason of my life, live long, by wearing this sacred necklace.'

Happy with her appearance, she took a taxi to the airport. The charter flight from Dubai was mainly bringing home immigrant construction workers who had been affected by the downturn in the global economy. It had reached the Emirates, not because the Arabs were broke, but many of the overseas property investors were. Some were coming home having made good money during their contracts, which had usually lasted one, two or three years. Others had been less fortunate. Overnight their jobs had ceased to be and they were left with nowhere to live and no means of getting back to India. Governments in some western countries had had to help with the repatriation of their nationals. Others had had to use their hard-earned money or depend on relatives to get back home.

Whatever the circumstances, there was quite a crowd gathered by the picture windows in the new terminal building, all excited and united in a common cause – the return of their cherished ones. Mothers held toddlers up to see their papa's plane arrive. Some of these children would be meeting their fathers for the first time too. Iswara could feel their excitement, and her own. She found herself holding her tummy, cherishing her secret. She checked the time again, and tried to calculate how long it would take AA to emerge through customs and passport control once they'd touched down. She had difficulty keeping a smile off her face as she jostled for a place with a view of the runway. She sent Rekna a text:

Any minute now!

The double-glazing didn't quite block out the noise of the engines as the plane touched down, nor their roar as the pilot put them into reverse thrust to slow it while braking. The tyres screeched as they made contact and left slick marks behind on the already blackened surface of the smooth runway. Cheers and utterances of thanks to various gods reached a crescendo inside the terminal building.

It took only a second or two before the enormity of what was taking place in front of their eyes began to sink in.

The plane moved off its course, its right wheels seeming to lift slightly as the vessel veered to the left, ripping up a fence as it hurtled off the runway and disappeared into the deep gorge, which ran parallel to the landing strip. There was a moment of freakish silence before gasps and screams started emanating from the waiting crowd. Then, as though that shock were not enough, a dull explosive thud sounded before enormous palls of flames and thick black smoke erupted, obscuring the twisted wreck almost completely.

Iswara stood there utterly shocked, disbelieving, then she screamed AA's name and kept screaming and screaming.

She was pushed against the window as those waiting on seats for other flights all ran to see what had happened. She felt herself slump to the floor and remembered little else for a while. When she came to, people whose faces reflected panic, fear and a sense of utter hopelessness surrounded her. She was helped to her feet and escorted to a seat at the end of the empty rows. Distraught families watched as fire engines and ambulances tore down the runway trying to reach the plane. The thick smoke had started to obscure their view and staff members arrived and tried in vain to move them away from the windows. Iswara tried to get back to see. She felt her whole world had just ended. She wished she had been with AA. Then – she fantasised – maybe he'd missed the plane.

'I'm a doctor,' she said to no one in particular. 'Can I help?' She made a run for an open door 'I'm a doctor. I'm a doctor,' she kept saying, only to be restrained by an agitated staff member.

'No one can go out there. The fire and ambulance crews will look after everybody. Please, it's not safe. They have the proper equipment and clothing. Take a seat and we will give you news as soon as we can.'

They were to hear that message so many times over the next few hours that she lost count. A team of officials from the airport heralded those who had been awaiting the arrival of the Dubai flight down a long corridor, into an area with no view of the runway, and they talked to them, first as a group, then individually, offering whatever solace and help they could. They assigned personnel to as many families as they could and made phone calls for them, served teas and coffees, water, and meted out what little consolation was possible. The crowd was predominantly made up of women and children who had been eagerly awaiting the return of their menfolk. Now they sat, huddled together, some crying, others keening, some struck numb with the enormity of what they had just witnessed. Gradually, although Iswara had no idea how much later it was, other relatives and friends began arriving, having heard the news or as the result of anguished phone calls they'd received from those at the airport. The pall of acrid smoke could now easily be seen from many parts of the city and its suburbs.

She had been asked the name and nationality of who she had been waiting for. She gave AA's full name. Would she like them to contact anyone for her? She declined. Her first reaction was to call Rekna, but she held back. She'd wait until she was sure he had missed the plane. She wasn't going to panic. His phone was turned off. Did AA's mother know her son was expected this morning? Iswara knew AA had been talking to her the previous day, but had he kept his plans to himself so they could have time together first? Had he told her about her?

She needed to talk to someone. She thought of Damien, but as she sat there with her phone in her hand, she couldn't remember the name of the college he was working at in Abu Dhabi. She had his and Clem's Dublin numbers in her phone for when she got there, but they were no use. More people kept arriving – extended family and friends who needed to be there at the scene before they could comprehend that this catastrophe had really happened. An official, flanked by sombre-looking staff in company uniforms, all quite clearly shaken, made an announcement.

'No words of comfort will help you at this time, but on behalf of the airline we want to offer our sincere condolences on this tragedy. We believe that this fatal accident has claimed the lives of all but six passengers, who have all been taken to the local hospital. We'll release their names later today, when we've contacted their relatives. In the meantime, if we can be of further service, if there is anything we can do, anyone we can contact, please talk to one of the members of staff.'

She pushed forward again to see if AA was among the six, but she was given the same official line. Hours passed. Police and other civil servants went through the assembly, asking questions about personal effects that might help them identify some of the passengers. Anything – rings, bracelets, birthmarks, scars?

They collated information. Iswara watched as new people continued to arrive – to share their grief with others. Names were called as the officials helped to reunite families. She didn't know what to do. She became aware suddenly of someone uttering AA's name right in front of her. She looked up and saw three women and a tall man gathered around one of the airport staff. The older one looked expectantly at the official who was looking at a clipboard in his hand. She kept repeating 'Abdul-Razzaq Mahimkar' until he nodded, indicating his name was listed there. She turned, clutching one of the younger women, sobbing. 'My son, my only son. No! No! He died alone.'

It was only then Iswara accepted that AA was gone. That he hadn't missed the flight and that he wasn't one of the few to survive. She wanted to run to the older woman and hug her and tell her he was loved more than was imaginable. But as the broken quartet was escorted to some other room, she sat there, so alone, listening to anguished cries of, 'My son, my only son. No! No!'

She thought, *This is all wrong. This was not how I was supposed to meet AA's family.*

The ping that announced a message on her mobile broke through the muddle in her head.

Saw the news. Just checking on you both. Damien

She dialled him straight back, realising she'd had his roaming number all along from the text he'd sent her the previous day. She broke down and he could scarcely make out what she was saying. She kept repeating, 'He's dead and he didn't know. He didn't know.'

'Iswara, listen to me. I'm coming over to be with you. Give me the name of your hotel again. Can someone bring you back there? Do you want me to call Rekna or your parents? What about AA's mother?'

'I can't think. No. Please don't tell my parents. They can't find out now, like this. His mother's here. I didn't talk to her. She's here with his sisters.'

'Iswara, I'll be there as soon as I can get a flight and connections.'

Iswara shut down, too distraught to take anything in, except that Damien was on his way. It was a long time before transport was arranged and she went back to her hotel, to her room – their room.

She phoned Rekna, who was oblivious to what had happened. A busy day with her boys meant she didn't have too much time for news bulletins.

'Oh, sweet God Ganesh, I don't believe it. Come home,' she advised her sister. 'You've got to come home.'

'I can't do that. I can't explain now. I'll be all right. Don't worry about me. Damien's coming here. He'll know what to do.'

'Well, I'm coming too,' Rekna insisted. No amount of persuasion worked and she finished up by saying, 'I'll call you in the morning, Iswara, and let you know my plans. Meanwhile if you need to talk to someone at any time during the night promise me you'll phone me.'

She agreed. She didn't want to relive the horror, but she found she had to. She changed channels, devouring every bulletin.

Surely AA's life and that of his fellow passengers had amounted to and warranted more than the television reports suggested.

A flight from Dubai carrying 187 people crashed into a heavily wooded valley moments after landing at an airport in southern India on Thursday morning, killing almost everyone on board.

The fire-fighters, who were on hand in seconds, carried a young girl out of the smoking wreckage. It is believed that of the six others who survived the crash, one died later on his way to hospital. This flight was popular with migrants from southern India, millions of whom work as labourers in construction sites in the Persian Gulf.

'Everything was good until we landed, then it felt as though the tyres burst,' one heavily bandaged survivor told a local television crew from his hospital bed. 'Within seconds there was an explosion of fire and everywhere filled with smoke. I jumped out through a wide break in the side of the fuselage and I was dragged away by a fireman. I have some broken bones and cuts, but thanks to the will of Allah, I'm alive.'

Iswara listened as officials and flight investigators speculated. Some said the plane had missed the landing threshold, a critical portion of the runaway at airports, on top of particularly difficult landing conditions. Others debated whether the miscalculation was due to an instrument malfunction or to human error and promised that all that would be established at the enquiry.

Later reports carried more. The wing had fallen off as the aircraft plunged into the valley.

The little rescued girl had escaped without a mark, but had lost her siblings and parents.

Aviation officials said that the runway was dry, the weather was clear, with over five kilometres of visibility.

Others pronounced that the pilot was very senior and very experienced, with both the runway where the crash had happened and with the type of plane involved and that he had landed there frequently in the past.

And that was it. The next item was about the grandiose wedding of two popular Bollywood stars. *Tomorrow*, she thought, *they won't even mention it and it will all be forgotten about.* But not by her. She'd never forget the way the plane disappeared from sight, to be replaced by the smoke from the burning fuel. She'd never forget the panic she'd felt, or the way her soul curled up and died inside her. Her mind went around and around like a carousel that she couldn't stop to get off. She took her *mangalsutra* from around her neck and held it tightly in her hand as she lay down. It was wet from her tears when she eventually fell into an exhausted asleep.

Damien had had the television on, tuned, as he usually left it, to Al Jazeera English, when he heard the news of an air crash in India. Somehow he knew, with some primeval instinct, that this would touch his life. He immediately thought of AA. Wasn't he due to fly in to that very airport that morning? Had Iswara gone to the airport to meet him? He dithered about whether he should call, decided he was being alarmist, and then he punched her name into contacts before he could change his mind. She responded to his text instantly. She sounded distraught and bewildered, confused about what was happening – and he knew then that he would have moved mountains to get to her side.

His work was almost finished. The new curriculum and study modules for the postgraduate programmes had all been set out and he was really here for these last few weeks in a caretaking capacity until it was time for the permanent Dean of Students to return. He had made several calls to Ireland, clearing the way for his imminent departure; then he'd gone online to find the quickest way, forgetting that Bangalore airport would be closed for a time.

Glad of his familiarity with the complicated rail system in India, he'd managed to book two connecting flights and a short train journey. He was nearing Bangalore when he called Iswara again. 'I'll be with you in less than half an hour.'

He felt in some small way responsible for what had happened. He'd colluded in their deceit: he'd encouraged their relationship, helped her get a job, and prompted AA to move to another continent. He was devastated. He hadn't a clue what he'd say to Iswara when he met her, but he knew he had to go to be with her.

CHAPTER 43

The sun was shining gloriously that Thursday when Beatrice signed for her new home and the papers were handed over. A lucky omen, the solicitor assured her, as he showed her out of his office. She'd taken the day off and was going to head into town after she'd finished with all the formalities. On the landing, she found herself standing beside Jarlath. She'd forgotten all about him and what a creep he was. She'd forgotten that he was a solicitor too, and that he worked at this partnership.

'What has brought you here? Come looking for me?' he asked with a cocky smile.

'Don't flatter yourself. If I'd known you worked here, I'd have gone somewhere else for my conveyancing.'

'Don't be like that,' he made to touch her arm and she recoiled. 'Can I call you?'

'Most definitely not.'

The lift came and he stood back to let her in. But she stepped aside and said, 'I've changed my mind. I'll take the stairs.' He was waiting when she'd got to the bottom of the two flights.

He began to pester her again and she told him where to go.

Despite the summery weather and the euphoria of making her first house purchase, that unwelcome encounter put a dampener on her day. She told her mother about it that night when she met her and Ray for a few celebratory drinks and Mary advised her to forget him. Then her mother handed over a sizeable cheque that she had saved from her daughter's 'rent' over the years.

'I can't take that,' Beatrice objected. 'After all, you bought the flat for me in the first place and I have the profits from that sale. That's yours. Go wild on it.'

'You have to take it. That's why I banked that rent all those years – for this very day.' Ray nodded in agreement. 'She did too, so take it and enjoy it. Buy what you need or put it off your mortgage. Now let's have some champagne to celebrate.'

It was late when she got home but she sat down to fill Damien in about her day before going to bed.

Dear Damien

Just a brief note to tell you the deed is done. I am now the proud owner of a des res in D4. I won't get the keys for three weeks though, as the former owners need that time to have their new place redecorated.

I'm so excited I feel like a kid again and

387

I can't wait to move, and put my bits and pieces into it.

Met that awful Jarlath – remember my cousin's best man at that wedding in Malta last year – well, it was a case of 'of all the solicitors' offices in all of the world I had to walk into his'! He actually had the gall to ask if I'd tracked him down deliberately! I told him if he attempts to contact me at the new address I'll report him to the Law Society for using confidential information!

Can't wait to show you around.

Hurry home

All my love

Beatrice xx

There was no reply the next day, or the following one. Then she got a one liner on the Saturday.

Sorry Beatrice.

Caught up in something big – not able to write.

My love

Damien xx

He was close to the end of his tour of duty, so she figured he was probably trying to get through his workload before he had to return home. Maybe he was off campus, in the desert somewhere, with no coverage.

She heard nothing more from him over the

weekend and by Monday she was really missing hearing from him. She headed off to her counselling session, confident that it would be her last. She had mulled over all the points they had discussed in this now very familiar room and she had come to some pretty big conclusions. She loved Damien. She loved him enough to trust him with her happiness. She now knew herself well enough to know that if things didn't work out, life would give her other opportunities, and the ones she was being offered now were important enough to take the leap forward.

She knew what she was going to do. She was going to ask Damien to move in with her.

CHAPTER 44

Iswara was inconsolable when Damien got to her hotel. He had managed to get a room there too and had literally dumped his hastily packed bags in it before phoning her to let her know he'd arrived. Rekna had got there earlier and opened the door to him. Iswara was sitting on a couch looking lost and pale. An untouched meal sat in front of her on a low table. He took her in his arms and let her cry until she had no more tears left. Bit by bit, he realised with horror that she had witnessed the accident and he wondered if it would be possible for her ever to forget such a thing.

Over the next few hours, together he and Rekna forced Iswara to agree to eat some food and that was when she told them both about the baby. She told them about seeing AA's mother and the two women with her that she assumed were his sisters; the man was probably one of her sons-in-law.

'Once they had found AA's name on the list, his mother broke down and they were shepherded away by some officials, for counselling or formalities. I knew I couldn't just go up to them and tell them who I was. They were distraught.'

'Do you want them to know about you and the baby?' Damien asked, not sure if this was the right time to press her on anything.

'I've done nothing but think about it since . . . since the accident, and I still don't know. What would you do?'

'I can't give you advice on that. It has to be your decision,' Damien said, and Rekna agreed.

'I'm not even sure if AA told her he was bringing me to meet them. If he did then I feel I have to face them. I owe them that no matter what it costs me. If he didn't, then I think it would be best if I don't. They don't need to know about me now.'

'Or the baby?' said Rekna, more as a question than a statement.

'Or the baby.'

'Would it help if I went to see her?' offered Damien.

'How would you explain being in Bangalore?' asked Rekna.

'I'll tell her that when I heard, I was visiting some former students of the college, who came back here after they qualified. That's plausible because we've had several from here over the years. Besides, I knew AA in Mumbai and he's sure to have told them he visited me in Abu Dhabi recently.'

'What if she asks about me?' said Iswara.

'If she does, I'll tell her I know you, both as a student and a colleague at the clinic, and I'll ask if she'd like to meet you. If she doesn't, I promise I won't mention you at all.'

'You won't mention the baby.'

'I won't mention the baby.'

They persuaded her to try and get some sleep. Damien went back to his room and managed to track down AA's family from the information Iswara had given him.

He phoned and spoke to a man who told him his mother-in-law was unavailable. He left his details and really didn't know whether to expect a return call.

Drained from the raw emotion of the past few hours with Iswara, he lay down on his bed and went to sleep. He didn't know where he was when the phone started ringing on the bedside locker.

An unfamiliar voice identified itself as AA's brother-in-law. AA's mother would welcome a visit from him the following day and he gave Damien directions. Damien glanced at the time. He'd wait until the morning to tell Iswara. When he did, she insisted that she had changed her mind and wanted to accompany him. All night, she kept seeing his mother's face, pale with grief, and his sisters, all united in their loss.

When she went with Damien to their house, she had decided to go as a colleague with whom AA had worked in Mumbai, nothing more. His family were very hospitable and welcoming. They were served Arabic coffee, with fruits, nuts and dates. His mother told them, 'We appreciate you coming to see us. We are a very tight family. He told us about you, Mr Doyle, and you, Dr Singhanid.'

Iswara sat up in her chair waiting for whatever revelation would follow. Perhaps she did know . . . But she continued, 'You both stood by him when he was wrongfully accused in that unfortunate incident last year. He told us when he came home at that time.'

'There was never any doubt in our minds,' said Iswara. 'AA, Abdul-Razzaq, was an honourable man and the accuser was deranged.'

Damien explained to Mrs Mahimkar, 'We foreigners could never get our tongues around some of the Indian pronunciations, so we all called him AA.' She smiled, anxious for any snippets she could glean about his life in Mumbai and Dubai. She told them, 'He always had wanderlust, that one, and I was happy to lose him to his travels and work, but not to lose him like this. I looked forward to him having a family and maybe living close to us with a wife and children of his own. An air crash, who would ever have thought it? And to think I was worried because he had announced he was going so far away, to Ireland, and changing his career too.'

They let her talk. She needed to say these things to people who had known her only son.

Damien said, 'He was really looking forward to the challenges ahead.'

They both knew from the way she talked that Mrs Mahimkar had known nothing of AA's relationship with Iswara. They both held their breath when she said, 'He told me he needed to see me before he left. He wanted to discuss something important with me. He also said he had a surprise for me. Now I'll never know what that was. That's the awful part. Not being able to ask him. Never being able to talk to him again.'

Iswara sat there, trying to keep herself together. Sitting in the home her husband had grown up in, taking in the surroundings that he'd never see again, listening to his mother's quiet voice tremble, wanting to tell her that she was that something important and that she was carrying his child, the child he had died knowing nothing about: her grandchild. But she said nothing. Now was not the time to add to their grief – to let them know AA had gone against their Islamic traditions and married secretly, or that his child would be kept a secret from its other grandparents too.

Rekna was waiting anxiously for their return and was not surprised when Iswara just shook her head and said, 'She didn't know.'

Damien announced that he had booked a table in the restaurant in the hotel for lunch for the two of them. When they protested he said, 'There's to be no argument about it. I insist. You sisters have things to say to each other and you don't need me interfering.'

'I'm not hungry,' protested Iswara.

Damien caught Rekna's eye and held her gaze for a second before she said, 'Well, I am.'

He smiled at her and excused himself. 'I've work to do in my room so I'll catch up with you later.'

He found several emails from Beatrice, wondering if he was all right, had he been kidnapped, got locked in a harem, stolen by the slave traders? Write, write, write, was the common theme. He did.

Dear Beatrice
    A series of unexpected events has kept me busy since I last wrote. Sincere apologies for the total breakdown in communications. I'm actually en route home, a little early, so I hope you'll be pleased, but I've had to stop off in India, in Bangalore. No time for sight-seeing this trip though.
    I should be back sometime on Tuesday.
    Hope all is well with you.
    Love you
    Damien x

Rekna wanted Iswara to come back home. 'We can handle this together. There is no way our parents are going to turn you and your baby out onto the side of the road. Of course, they'll be mad as hell and disappointed – and no one does disappointed quite as well as Mama – but she'll get over it. You can stay with me.'

'I can't come back now. Maybe sometime in the future, when I feel strong enough to face up to having deceived everybody. You know that although

we're all supposed to be protected by the consti-
tution and cannot legally be discriminated against
on the grounds of creed, colour or caste, in reality
life isn't like that. Every one of us all knows stories
where someone married outside the system and
they were banished from attending family gatherings, weddings, funerals, even of their own parents.
I couldn't ask you to do that.'

'You're not asking. I'm offering.'

'You can't compromise your relationships and
those of your in-laws like that.'

'I'd do anything for you.'

'Don't you think I know that, Rekna? Do you
think the accident is due to bad karma?'

'Of course not!' she said, taking her sister's hand.
'Listen to me. Would any god have brought down
a whole planeload of people because two people
whom He made attractive to each other in the
first place followed their nature? Don't ever think
like that.'

'I can't help it. I'm looking for an explanation.'

'I know, but so are all the other people who've
been affected. It was a terrible accident, that's all.'

The director of the medical centre phoned her
after Damien had contacted him. He offered her
his condolences and told her that her position
would always be open for her if she felt like going
back.

'That means an awful lot to me, but I'm expected
in Dublin next week and I'll be there to take up
my new job. Damien has managed to get on the

same flight, so it won't be as hard as going on my own.'

Damien refused to allow Iswara to go back to the airport to see off her sister.

'But I'll be flying out from there in a few days,' she argued, though she was relieved that she didn't have to stand about reliving Thursday.

'Yes and I'll be with you.'

She said goodbye to her sister at the hotel. Another tearful farewell, only this time instead of her future being filled with expectation and hope, there was a void – which she wondered if it would ever be possible to fill. She was going miles away, pregnant, widowed and heartbroken. Damien took Rekna to the airport in his hired car. He indicated to the glove compartments, where she found an envelope.

'These are photographs I took of the two of them when I met up with them in Dubai, on their honeymoon. I was going to get them framed when I got back home to give them as a sort of welcoming present. She hasn't seen them yet, but I thought you'd like to have them. I can get more printed when I get back.'

Rekna opened them and she choked up when she saw the ones he had taken in front of the Dubai Fountain. 'They look radiant in that.'

'They were.'

'They didn't even have a month together.'

'Doesn't it make you realise how precious every moment is?' he said.

'I know I can't wait to get home to my family, to hug them all and tell them what they mean to me. They think I'm visiting a good friend who's just had a baby. How ironic is that.'

'In a way, I feel somehow responsible. Romantic that I am, I always believed that love could conquer most things. Now I think they would have been better off if I had disapproved of their relationship too and tried to prevent them being together. I was so sure they'd get around their families in time and that they'd be accepted as a couple.'

'You couldn't have prevented any of this happening. They knew what they were doing and they were so happy, if only for a minute in time.'

'I'll take care of her, I promise, and I'll keep you posted. You have my details so feel free to contact me any time you want to.'

They arrived at the terminal building and he got out of the car and took Rekna's bag.

'I know you will,' she replied, and not caring who saw her or who she offended, she reached up and hugged him, and said, 'Thank you for every-thing, Damien.'

She was fed up of the conventions and the mores that had put her sister in this awful situation.

Over those few days, Iswara was to gather all the information she could, scouring the web and tearing out newspaper articles, trying tenuously to keep AA alive in her mind for a while longer. She had so many questions to ask. Had be died instantly? Had he been badly injured? Had he suffocated? She hoped he had, before the flames reached him. Had he known she was there waiting for him? She'd only decided the night before to surprise him. Now her biggest regret was that she hadn't told him he was going to be a father.

When Damien got back, he told Iswara that he needed to talk to her.

'That sounds ominous,' she replied.

'It's not, I assure you, but things have changed somewhat and we need to have a game plan for you.'

He suggested they get out of the hotel for some fresh air and a change of scenery, and he was surprised when she agreed. He took her to Someshwar Beach, about nine miles south of the city, a place the concierge had recommended. It was, he had assured Damien, famous for its sunsets. And there in the magnificent splendour of a beach bathed in the soft evening light of gold and pink, they talked about her future and made plans that would cause further ripples.

CHAPTER 45

The weeks were running away from Irene. Her invitations had gone out. The renovations to Daragh's family home had been accelerated. The builder needed money to buy materials to start another job and, as Daragh refused to give it to him until the work was completed, he had no choice but to finish it, ahead of time.

'We might be able to move in straight from our honeymoon,' she told Beatrice.

'That would be fantastic. And I'll be in mine too, all going well. I might even have a housemate by then,' she grinned. 'One with benefits.'

'I don't believe it! Have you asked him yet?'

'No, I'm waiting until I show him around. I don't know how I'll feel about having someone with me all the time, but I'm prepared to give it a shot, and I know he's the one for me.'

'You could always do what Daragh and I did, spend four or five nights a week together and let the rest be me-on-my-own-doing-the-laundry-having-the-girls-around time. That way he was able to have his rugby and golf days off without feeling he was neglecting me! It worked for us and neither of us ever felt we were smothering in our relationship. You know, thinking about it, maybe we should have drawn up a pre-nup, keeping the status quo!'

'I'm not sure it would work in a marriage, but for Damien and me it's certainly worth a try,' Beatrice said. 'Have you two drawn up the dreaded seating plan?'

'We have. Daragh, ever the pacifist, decided that we should do one for the top table only. It's a free-for-all for everyone else. That way neither of us can be accused of favouritism or of trying to encourage war or peace between the in-laws, the out-laws and the factions that don't fit into either camp. And you can't blame me for keeping you two apart!'

'It sounds like you've thought it all out.'

'I hope so. I don't want to have to think about anything on the day, only about enjoying ourselves, so the less that can go wrong the better.'

'Amen to that.'

While waiting for the keys to her house to come through, Beatrice packed her belongings, culling her wardrobe, her books and music collection. She made numerous trips to the nearest charity shop and brought boxes home from the supermarket to pack other bits and pieces. Tony, who was buying her place, had decided that he'd take some of her furniture. It made good sense to let him have it.

His time in Ireland was limited. He only wanted a bolthole and didn't really want to have to buy any big pieces of furniture whilst he was here. She selected what she wanted to keep, took pictures of what she was happy to leave behind and sent them to him. She wanted to make the new place her own, surrounding herself with things she had chosen for it and not make-dos. She felt she was finally putting down roots.

By the time Damien was home, she'd be ready for her move.

She had scarcely heard from him over the past couple of days, but that didn't stop her from emailing him.

He hadn't mentioned whether he was flying home direct or through London, so she couldn't go to meet him. She'd just have to wait until he got in touch. She was sure that he'd have sorted out whatever had caused his change of plans and couldn't wait to tell him about her counselling and the outcome. With half her life already stacked away in boxes, she planned to take him out for a romantic meal the night after he got back. That would give him a chance to unpack and rest up a bit. Then she'd ask him about moving in together.

By lunchtime on Wednesday she had still heard nothing.

'He must have gone straight to bed when he got home,' she told Irene, as they crossed the road to have their lunches in Stephen's Green. The band was playing, the benches were full, the flowerbeds filled with colour. It was one of those glorious days that you long for in the dark days of winter.

They found a spot on the grass that had just been vacated by a group of noisy Spanish students and settled themselves, when Beatrice thought that she saw Damien walk down from the little bridge on the other side of the park into the area where the fountains are. She felt like a teenager with a crush, imagining seeing the object of her adoration in every bus queue, walking down every street, drinking coffee at every coffee shop. But it wasn't Damien. This man had darker skin and had much shorter, fairer hair. Her gaze moved to the striking woman walking beside him. She was elegant, poised and beautifully dressed in a turquoise sari. Her black hair glistened in the sunshine. Beatrice looked back at the man at exactly the same moment he noticed her. He stopped, took his companion's arm, said something to her before they changed direction and came towards them.

'There's Damien,' said Irene, only just noticing him, 'with one of his students.'

Beatrice couldn't believe it. He was back. Her heart did a flip and she jumped up to greet him.

'You're the last person I expected to see in here today,' she said. 'You look different. The sun obviously agrees with you. Look at that tan and your bleached hair. You look fantastic.'

He smiled as she made to kiss him. Instead he turned his head and hugged her awkwardly, before hugging Irene too.

'When did you get back?' she asked.

'Tuesday.'

'Tuesday?' asked Beatrice. 'But it's Thursday now.'

He looked embarrassed as he drew the beautiful woman into the conversation and avoided Beatrice's eyes. 'This is Iswara Singhanid from Mumbai and we're engaged to be married.'

'Married? You're engaged?' said Irene.

Beatrice thought she had misheard and said nothing.

'Yes, we just got engaged this week. I was going to ring you later and tell you,' he said.

'It's very nice to meet you,' Irene said, putting out her hand, 'and congratulations to you both. That's great news.'

Iswara's smile made her look even more beautiful, if that were possible.

'We're on our way to an appointment and have to rush now,' Damien said, looking at his watch.

'And we've to get back to the office in a few minutes,' Beatrice lied.

'I'll call you later,' he said.

When they had walked off together Beatrice said to Irene, 'Why didn't I tell him to go to hell? So that's the "series of unexpected events" that caused his "breakdown in communications". I feel as though as I've been punched very hard in the stomach and am winded. A fiancée – and he was going to tell me over the phone? So much for his declarations of undying love. It seems I was taken in again by another louse, doesn't it?'

Irene didn't have to answer. Each time she went to speak, Beatrice launched into another tirade. But Irene was puzzled. She had only been talking to his sister the night before and Rachel never mentioned anything about an engagement or a fiancée either when they talked about Damien's return.

Beatrice didn't know how she got through her work that afternoon, and she had to deal with a particularly slick operator, a Nigerian, who had been granted Irish citizenship and had worked as a taxi driver around Limerick for seven years. He was now trying to apply retrospectively to bring the rest of his family over to Ireland. Ordinarily, it shouldn't have been too much of a problem if handled the right way and if they fulfilled the necessary criteria – but this family didn't. The problem was that his 'family' consisted of three wives and nine children. He'd been home earlier that year and two of the wives were now pregnant again too.

'That's why I want to have them with me,' he explained.

I'm sure you do, Beatrice thought. She had to stop herself asking him if he'd never heard of contraception and how he thought he'd be able to feed fourteen extra people on his taxi takings or did he expect the state to pay them all allowances. By the end of the afternoon, she was exhausted. That man had turned nasty, promising to write to the minister and threatening to have her fired for being obtuse. She knew she hadn't crossed the line, but by 5.30 she really couldn't have cared less if she had been fired. Irene insisted on taking her for a drink and she turned her phone off.

'Could he have thought you'd finished with him?' Irene asked.

'Absolutely not! He knows I love him. I just needed space and he was happy to let me have it. We were going to begin again when he got back. He kept telling me he loved me too, right up to last week.'

'She's very beautiful.'

'Is that supposed to make me feel better?'

'Do you think he'll want to bring her to my wedding? I mean he and Rachel have been my friends all my life. I can't imagine my wedding without them being there.'

'Oh, God, I didn't think of that. What a mess. I blew it again, didn't I? Procrastinating.'

'No, Beatrice, you didn't. He obviously wasn't meant for you. Anyway, at least now you know you're ready to have a relationship when the right opportunity comes along.'

She didn't agree, but wasn't in any mood to argue the point. 'I know I've said it before. I'm never, ever, ever getting involved with anyone again.'

When she got back to her apartment the light was flashing on her answering machine, several times, but she wiped the messages without listening to any of them. She didn't want to hear excuses. She had a life to get on with and a house move in the offing. It was time to forget about Damien.

In the morning her positivity had vanished. Despite her intentions, she felt mad as hell: let down, disappointed and more than a little incredulous at how fickle he had turned out to be. Just like Paul and Jarlath.

On Saturday, her doorbell rang. She wasn't expecting anyone and when she flicked on the intercom screen she saw it was Damien. 'I have nothing to say to you. You strung me along for long enough, now please leave and don't try to contact me again.'

'Please, Beatrice. Let me talk to you.'

'No, you've done all the talking you'll ever do to me.' She disconnected the intercom and thought, *So much for all the counselling sessions. What a waste of bloody money. I could have had a winter sun holiday for what they cost me. Come to think of it, Dr Combover is probably having one at my expense.*

She got through the weekend, calling on her mother, who immediately knew something had happened. Mary tried to tell her daughter that if he had been right for her it would have worked out. Beatrice didn't agree with such logic.

'Maybe if I'd meant something to him at all it might have worked out. And as if that wasn't bad enough, they'll probably be at Irene's wedding.'

'Well you can't get out of that,' Mary said. 'You'll just have to put on a brave face. It's her day.'

'Don't I know it!' Beatrice replied.

Irene never mentioned the wedding for the rest of that week, and although she had been emphatic about not wanting a hen night, as her bridesmaid, Beatrice felt duty-bound to arrange something for her girlfriends. Her heart wasn't in it, but she felt mean spirited and had to have a serious talk with herself. *It's Irene's dream, join in and share it with her. It's not about you, no matter how much it hurts.*

'Now, about your hen night? I know you don't want a stripper and L plates, but we have to do something.'

'Do you know what I want? A really nice meal, with just my six closest friends. Honestly – no frills and no surprises.'

'That seems so ordinary.'

'It's not, because this time you'll all be paying for me and I want lots of champagne, the real stuff, none of your Prosecco that night!'

Rachel was one of the six friends, and not realising the state of play between her brother and Beatrice, she started talking about the surprise he had landed on them all – his fiancée.

'She's drop-dead gorgeous. Wait until you meet her. She has amazing eyes and perfect skin. She was one of his students here.'

Irene interrupted, 'We already have met her, in

Stephen's Green and, yes, she is rather lovely. Does your mum approve?'

'You know Mum. She's in Spain, of course, and as you know, no one is good enough for her son. She just wants to know what's wrong with me. Still single and a brother working with all those eligible doctors! And now a sister-in-law-to-be who's a doctor too – talk about heaping on the pressure.'

They all laughed and Irene called for more champagne.

Beatrice told her about the house and her plans to move the following weekend.

'Not on a Saturday, I hope,' said Irene. '"Saturday's flitting is a short sitting" and all that.'

'No, on Sunday, and then the following week it's your big day. Talk about busy times.'

CHAPTER 46

Initially some of the gloss of the move was tarnished by the new chain of events. Beatrice had visualised Damien moving their furniture about and sitting by the fire next to her; reading their papers in the sunroom and barbecues on the terrace on summer evenings with friends over. She'd even seen them pushing a trolley around IKEA together, accessorising the place.

Instead, Ray organised Beatrice's move. Some contact of his had a van and as she was leaving the big pieces behind it fitted the job perfectly. She was in the new house when Mary arrived with a new vase, an armful of flowers, an apple tart, cheese, crusty bread and a bottle of wine.

Then Irene and Daragh came, with more food and a new set of wine glasses. Their arrival was followed by two of the honorary aunties with yet more gifts and supplies. She placed the cards on the mantelpiece and put the flowers in the vase, stood back and said, 'See, it's home already.'

They retrieved plates and glasses from the packing cases, took the kitchen table into the garden and had an impromptu housewarming.

'I hear you're moving when you get married,' Mary said to Irene.

'Yep, this is all ahead of me. Years of clutter to sort through. If I wasn't going to let the place out, I wouldn't mind so much but it has to be cleared out completely so it can be redecorated.'

'That's a lot of work before the wedding.'

'Tell me about it. We were hoping to have it all ready for the decorators beforehand but that's not going to happen now. Luckily we're not in any hurry.'

CHAPTER 47

September acted in character, mellow, warm, sunny and blue skied. Irene spent the night before her wedding with Beatrice, who had managed to put together a guest room with odd bits and pieces. She was taking the following week off to shop for her new house, delighted to have a project to keep her mind off Damien and his behaviour.

Everything was planned with precision. The wedding ceremony would take place in City Hall. When that was over they would head to St Stephen's Green to have photos taken before making their way for the celebratory meal in a nearby hotel.

Irene radiated happiness as she and Daragh said their vows. The setting was stunning, marbled colonnades framed the Rotunda. Above, the circular windows around the dome captured the sun and the border of stained glass in the ceiling reflected coloured lozenges on the tiled floor. Everywhere was bathed in a honey-coloured light, perfectly complementing the bride's choice of champagne for her dress.

Even though they were from Dublin, many of

the guests had never been there before and as a venue it got top ratings and set high standards for the rest of the plans.

Beatrice knew she faced challenges that day. Irene had told her that Damien would indeed be coming, with his Plus One. And whilst she didn't exactly ask her to behave herself and be civil towards them, Beatrice knew that was the unspoken message.

She reassured her, 'You need have no worries. I'll be a lady.'

'I know you will, and thanks. I also know it's going to be difficult.'

You don't know the half of it, Beatrice thought, but she was determined to perform her bridesmaid-ly duties with care and with a smile. She spotted Iswara and Damien looking up at one of the frescos, he appeared to be pointing out some detail to her. She was dressed exquisitely. Her hair flowed down her back and was tucked behind one ear and held off her face by some flowers on the other side. Damien, she noticed, was sporting a tie that matched her dress.

He made no effort to talk to Beatrice at all: not while the photos were being taken on the marble staircase on the steps outside, in St Stephen's Green or back at the hotel. She wasn't sure if this upset her more than if he had. Just before the meal, as everyone found somewhere to sit, he passed by her chair and said, 'You look stunning today, Beatrice.'

She could feel his breath on her shoulder. It sent a tingle through her, but she was saved from replying by the announcement that the new Mr and Mrs Daragh Mulvey were about to enter the room. Everyone stood up and applauded.

They enjoyed the food and the speeches were short enough to prevent any wins among Daragh's friends, who'd all placed bets on how long they'd last.

Later, when the dancing had started, Beatrice was a popular partner. Then Damien asked her to dance. She remembered her promise to be a lady and accepted graciously. She'd already danced with two of the disastrous blind dates that Irene had set her up with, before . . . well before Damien. Life now seemed to fall into two categories – before and after Damien. Now she *was* confused. When he took her in his arms she felt as though they had never parted. She felt at home, safe and protected, and wanted to snuggle closer to him, breathe in his tangy aftershave. When he looked at her, she felt he still cared. But he couldn't. She was being fanciful again, so she made small talk.

'Did you see that The Laugh and The Golfer are here?'

'I saw you dancing with one of them. I couldn't remember which one it was though.'

'Isn't this a lovely day?'

'Perfect.'

As soon as she'd said, 'So you'll probably be next to tie the knot,' she realised that it was she

414

who had brought up the one topic she didn't want to discuss.

'Well, we've no date set yet. What about your house? Irene told me you'd moved in.'

'It's great, I love it.'

There was an awkward silence and again she spoke without thinking and regretted it the minute she had spoken. 'When did you two meet?'

'Beatrice, I have to talk to you. It's not that simple.'

'We *are* talking. Have you known each other for long?'

'I mean really talk.'

'That's what I'm doing. Was she one of your students?'

'Yes, as a matter of fact she was, but I need to explain something.'

The music stopped and she said with a smile, 'There's no need, really. Thank you for the dance, Damien.'

She made her way back to her table with as much dignity as she could muster. She saw them leave a while later, before anyone else, and she felt let down all over again.

Despite that major upset, the day was going well until Beatrice found herself standing beside Rachel at the bar and couldn't help but overhear the conversation she was having with two women.

'No, Iswara was exhausted,' Rachel said. 'She needs her rest.'

'I remember that stage of my pregnancies, I could

never keep my eyes open either. Fortunately, the tiredness usually passed as the months went by. Aren't saris an elegant way of hiding a bump? I never even noticed.'

Pregnant. She was pregnant!

Well, he certainly hadn't wasted much time. He'd told her he'd like a family, but she hadn't realised that he was trying to put an order in for one right then and there. Normally, she would have gone straight to Irene to discuss this snippet of information, but she felt she couldn't. Not today. She couldn't help but wonder when it had happened. In Dubai or in Abu Dhabi?

CHAPTER 48

Life quickly fell into a pattern for Iswara and Damien, once she had started her new job. The practice was a very busy one, with long hours and late-night openings. As it was right in the city centre, there was a real divide in the nature of their patients. During the day it was office workers with sore throats, minor ailments and mothers with sick children. At night it was often drug addicts, drunks who had fallen and cut themselves, women who had been pushed around by frustrated partners and lonely people who just needed to talk, and she was a good listener. The surrounding area was one of high unemployment, several ethnic groups, many with little or no English. No two days were the same.

Damien loved Iswara, not in the way he loved Beatrice, but he'd made a commitment. He had promised AA he'd look after Iswara and he intended on honouring it. He showed his fiancée off with pride and introduced her to all his family, friends and colleagues. His mother had yet to meet her, and he was contemplating taking a long weekend to Spain to introduce them. He helped

Iswara find contact details for her former college mates who were now mostly married, many with kids, and were dotted around the country in general practices or specialising in the various hospitals. He admired her strength of character; the stoic way she accepted what had happened to AA, and her determination to start a new life with his child, but without him.

He kept his distance, respecting that she needed time to grieve and to grow to love him too. They had always liked each other, so the basis for their relationship was a friendship that had grown deeply during his time in India. He remembered telling her if AA hadn't come along, he'd have made a play for her and he'd meant it. She'd laughed and said if AA hadn't come along, she might have been tempted.

In those dark days after the crash, it broke his heart to see her empty, distraught and lost. He wasn't sure if she had been right in deciding to follow the plans she and AA had made together. He came from such a liberal background that it had been difficult for him to understand how entrenched and enslaved the Indian caste and creed system was. The time he spent at the clinic had opened his eyes to just how deep-rooted and inflexible the social rules and religious traditions were. Meeting Iswara's mother had only endorsed these realisations further.

Damien treated his fiancée like a delicate exotic flower that needed to be nurtured and tended, until it was ready to bloom. He had to be patient, but he understood because he had cared for AA and his death had left a void in Damien's life too. He knew taking care of Iswara would be no burden to him and it would be a privilege to be part of AA's child's life.

He had made his mind up the day he had taken Rekna to the airport. He would marry Iswara. Give her the respectability she deserved, and a good life too. She would be among friends and he knew her parents would not object too strenuously to him. They would naturally have preferred an Indian son-in-law, but he would come a long way ahead of a Muslim.

When he had returned from the airport that day, he had parked his hired car and asked the concierge about the best place to view the sunset and he had recommended Someshwar Beach.

He'd known what he wanted to say to Iswara, a proposal in the real sense. He was about to propose that he become a husband and a father in one action. He'd realised that if he were to give himself marks out of ten for timing, he'd have got zero. But then, time meant nothing any more. They had been moving like androids in a world that had been brutally smashed, and right in front of Iswara's eyes too. It had been as final as it could be, yet she had been denied closure. There had been no body to bury, no funeral to attend, no family to share the grief. Where possible, DNA matching of the charred remains could take months and there was no one to tell her when, if ever, a burial might happen.

Iswara had reluctantly agreed to the drive when he told her they needed to get out for some fresh air. They had strolled along the shore, and she had slipped her feet out of her sandals and walked barefoot. He had done the same.

'You were right, Damien. I feel better for coming out here, but what is this game plan you said we had to discuss?'

'I know this is going to sound wrong, no matter how I phrase it, so please hear me out, and then all I want you to do is think about it.'

Then, he had outlined his proposal, and had finished by saying, 'Don't say anything. Just promise me you'll think about it. Look on it as an arranged marriage, except you already know me, and we wouldn't get married until you felt ready. Now let's talk about something else.'

The sun had begun to lower towards the horizon and they had sat down to watch it. The powdery sand had been patterned with footprints, some perfect, others unclear and damaged – all that remained of those who had walked or run here earlier in the day. *Just like life*, thought Damien. *We all leave a footprint and some are more defined than others.*

'Is he out there somewhere, do you think?' Iswara had asked, breaking his reverie, looking towards a horizon that was totally devoid of any distraction, only the shimmering reflection of the setting sun, which gave the impression of having laid a pathway from it across the ocean right to the water's edge.

'I don't know,' he'd answered honestly.

'Let's hope he is.'

They had sat in silence, each absorbed in their own reflections as they watched the tranquil sky take on a golden tone, before bathing the sea and the sand with a pinkish hue. The water had lapped in a long, slow soporific rhythm, supplying a peaceful lullaby for a turbulent day. An apology, perhaps for turning her world off its axis.

'Thank you for bringing me here,' she'd said. 'I can never forget him or this. I feel as though I've just said goodbye to him, and he's telling me he's at rest.'

'Perhaps he is.'

CHAPTER 49

By the time they had arrived in Dublin, Iswara had agreed to marry Damien. It made sense on so many levels. She loved him dearly and he demanded no more of her. He had known AA and was happy to give his child his name and to bring it up as his own. Her parents would be disappointed when they learned she was pregnant, without being married, but as she wasn't around, flaunting this situation in front of her mother's bridge-playing friends, she would be forgiven once the baby was born. Iswara was sure of that.

They had liked Damien when they had met him and when they got over the shock of him taking advantage of their daughter, they'd forgive him, and her. Rekna, dear, dependable Rekna, would be delighted to know that Damien would be there for her sister and that she wouldn't be a single mother coping alone in a foreign country. The only downside Rekna could see was that in marrying Damien, Iswara wouldn't be coming back to live in Mumbai.

He had promised he'd put no pressure on Iswara

to set a date. It was important that she had this time to adjust to losing her husband.

Life settled into a pattern and Iswara got to know her colleagues a little better. She made contact with some of her former student friends and tried to keep positive. One day as she and Damien were walking along the seafront she said, 'It can't be doing your reputation any good to be living with a former student, and a pregnant one too.'

'It didn't take long for that news to spread,' he laughed. 'But I have broad shoulders and it's your reputation I'm thinking of. Take whatever time you need. There's absolutely no pressure.'

'Can we wait until after the baby is born?'

'Of course we can.'

'Maybe Rekna would come over.'

'Maybe your parents would too.'

'If I ever have the nerve to tell them.'

'You will. We will, when the time is right, and you haven't met *my* mother yet!'

His sister was thrilled about the baby and scolded him for telling her on the morning of Irene's wedding. 'Have you any more surprises that you're keeping from us,' she asked, 'any revelations to make at Irene's housewarming?'

'None whatsoever,' he answered, realising he'd forgotten to reply to Irene's invitation.

That autumn saw Beatrice's mother and the honorary aunties decide on their activity for the coming winter. A book club was the verdict.

423

'I'm just surprised you've waited so long to come up with that idea,' Beatrice said.

'We only waited until you had a place big enough to accommodate us all,' one of them replied.

'Right then,' said Beatrice, 'the first one will be at my place, if my suite has arrived by then. If not, it'll be at Mum's and I'll do the following one.

'Tea and coffee only?' suggested another.

'No way!' said Mary. 'It's a night out. Prosecco and grub, at the very least.'

'At the very least,' said Beatrice. 'This beats Pilates any day and it'll make me get my skates on and finish unpacking the last of the boxes. I still have a few in one of the bedrooms.'

'What'll we read?'

After much deliberation they settled on Anita Brookner's *Hotel du Lac*, which most of them had read years before.

Beatrice tried very hard not to let the disappointment of Damien's engagement and impending fatherhood get her down. She kept busy. She also knew their paths would cross along the way, because of their mutual friends, and possibly through work too.

Irene and Daragh's housewarming was just one of those occasions. It was on a Saturday night. Beatrice got her hair done, bought a new dress and spent more time getting ready than she would ordinarily. She was delighted to see Rachel again but was surprised to see her with Clem. *I'm really out of the loop*, she thought.

Iswara arrived, not as Beatrice expected, in a traditional sari, but in a softly draped crepe dress, flattering her now gently obvious bump. She looked wonderful and Beatrice told her so when they came face to face. Damien came up behind her and said, 'May I offer you the same compliment? I love your new hairstyle. It really suits you.'

'Thank you,' she replied and could think of nothing else to say.

After a clumsy pause, Irene materialised and said, 'No drinks? Where is that husband of mine? He's supposed to be looking after everyone.'

The house was beautiful. The renovations were finished, the curtains had only gone up the day before, and it was filled with touches of Irene's quirkiness and even had a home cinema, which Daragh told them was his den.

'We might show a chick flick once a month, but that's a privilege that'll have to be earned,' he said casting a meaningful glance at his wife.

'That's grounds for a divorce,' someone said.

When she was trying to sleep later, Beatrice kept going over and over things again trying to find the moment she lost Damien. *Was it the first time he'd asked her to move in? Was it when she told him she'd think about it while he was away? Or was it nothing to do with her? Had that woman been in the background all the time? Had he had a fling, or more, with this former student while she was in college? Had she been the reason he got so involved in all that fundraising stuff for the rag pickers charity? Was that why he'd gone to Mumbai? Was she the graduate he'd mentioned in his emails? Had she missed something there?*

No matter how often she went over this litany, she still found no answers. All she knew was that she was filled with regrets. She was lonely. She missed him and was still very much in love with him.

One day the following week, Irene's phone rang persistently while she was out of the office. She'd had a tummy bug for a few days and had decided to go out to the chemist to get something to settle it. After the third call, Beatrice picked it up to take a message and was taken aback when she heard Damien's voice.

'Damien, it's not Irene. It's me, Beatrice.'

'Oh, hi. I thought I recognised that voice. How are you?'

'I'm fine. How are you and – Iswara? Is she keeping well?'

'Yes. Yes we're both well, thank you.'

There was a pause before he said, 'What are we like, talking like strangers?'

'Now that's not exactly my fault, is it?'

'I deserved that. Beatrice, I'm so sorry things worked out as they did.'

'So am I,' she said. 'I'll get Irene to ring you when she's back.'

'That's great. Thank you.'

Later, when Irene returned with antacid tablets, the one-sided conversation Beatrice heard was, 'No, we haven't got a renter yet.'

'Well it's been completely redecorated and even though I'm saying it, it looks great.'

'Yes. Defying conventions and all that, I can just imagine. Yes consternation all around.' A laugh.

'No, the weekend would be perfect.'

'Why not drop around after her shift and pick the keys up?'

'Absolutely not! You could have a bite with us and I can explain the vagaries of the heating system.'

'Yea, perfect solution for everyone. Great, see you both later. Bye.'

Beatrice pretended to be absorbed in some paperwork, but Irene knew she had heard everything.

'That was Damien. Iswara is going to be my new tenant for a while. Seems they want to be seen to be living a more 'conventional' lifestyle until the baby arrives.

'It's a bit late for that surely.'

'Apparently there are some very conservative people in the faculty and Damien is trying to keep his head below the radar. He's out of favour after terminating his stint early in Abu Dhabi, upsetting locums and holiday leave for others.'

'Am I supposed to feel sorry for them?'

'That's not why I'm telling you. I feel trapped

in the middle of the pair of you. Damien and Rachel have been my friends since we were kids. You're my best buddy. I can't fix whatever happened between the two of you, and, for what it's worth, I was shocked and upset for you when he arrived back with Iswara, but I have to be happy for him, as he would be for me. What should I have said? No, Damien, you can't have my flat for your fiancée: it might upset Beatrice.'

'I'd never ask you to do anything like that.' She started to cry, frustration and hurt overwhelming her. One of their colleagues had noticed something was going on in their corner of the room and was all ears. Irene threw her eyes in her direction and said, 'Come into the kitchen. We can't talk here.'

Beatrice composed herself and followed Irene, carrying their empty cups from earlier.

'I know it's hard for you, but you have to understand where I'm coming from.'

'Honestly, I do.'

'I don't want to stop being friends with either of you. I want you both at the table when I have dinner parties and, as she'll be Damien's wife, I'll want to have Iswara there too, and at girls' nights. I don't want to have to go pussyfooting around any of you.'

'I'm sorry you feel that you have to. I hadn't realised I had become a problem for you. I think it would be easier all around if you just leave me off the guest list, until I meet my next disaster. And that might be quite a while because I still love that bastard!' Beatrice stormed out of the kitchen and went back to her desk. Neither she nor Irene spoke another word to each other that afternoon.

There was an atmosphere at work the next day. They both greeted each other civilly, but there the communication stopped. Instead of a shared lunchtime, they both did their own thing and simply nodded recognition to each other when they came back. The chilly atmosphere was still there the following Monday.

Around ten o'clock, Beatrice got an email from Irene, who sat opposite studying a file.

How can I ask you to be godmother to my child if we're not talking?

Beatrice stared at the screen for a few seconds before jumping up and going around to hug Irene, who put her finger to her lips, warning her to say nothing. One of the guys at the next pod said, 'Hey everyone, the row's over!' Some of the others clapped.

'Can't we even have a fight in private in this place?' Irene asked, laughing.

She sent another email.

Remember that tummy bug – well it turned out to be morning, or in my case, all-day sickness. No one else knows yet so say

429

nothing until I give you the nod. I assume you will be its godmother! And sorry!

Definitely – I'd be honoured. Let's have a drink after work.

Make mine an orange juice. How my life is about to change – forever!

PART III

CHAPTER 50

Iswara was two weeks overdue and they had walked Dún Laoghaire seafront so many times they had lost count, trying to make things start. When it did, the labour was long and the staff attentive. Damien and Rachel took turns at her bedside. Iswara and he had discussed whether or not she wanted him to be there for the actual delivery. She had been emphatic.

'You're the dearest person to me in the world, Damien, apart from my family. Of course I want you there, unless you'll feel uncomfortable about it. Besides, I don't want to be on my own. It's going to be hard enough knowing the baby will never know its father and how wonderful he was.'

'We'll make sure he or she does,' he'd said, endeavouring to comfort her, yet knowing it would be heart-wrenching for her when the moment actually came and her baby was a reality.

He still felt as protective of her as he did in those awful days after the plane crash. When she looked at him with those big sad eyes, often moist with unshed tears which she tried to hide, he was help-less. And that helplessness was always followed by

433

thoughts of Beatrice and how he had hurt her. Those thoughts he pushed aside. He had to, but they left him with a deep sense of guilt. He knew she'd understand, or he felt she would if she knew why, yet he knew he couldn't confide in her, or anyone. This was Iswara's story, Iswara's secret, and not his to tell. And he had given his word, willingly.

On St Valentine's Day, Iswara was safely delivered of a little girl. She was dark skinned like her parents, with a mop of black hair and dark eyes of indeterminate colour. Damien was still in shock and in awe. He couldn't have been more excited if the baby had been his own flesh. He couldn't quite believe that this miniature creature had been packed away, living safely in her mother throughout all the trauma of the past months. He stood looking on in disbelief as they cut the cord and a nurse wrapped her in a pink blanket. She mewled like a new kitten.

'She's a long one. She'll be tall and lean like her daddy,' she smiled at Damien as she handed Iswara her baby, settling her in the crook of her arm. He just nodded at the nurse. He could see the love flowing from Iswara as she embraced her tiny daughter for the first time. Then she started to cry, quiet, heartbroken sobs.

One of the nurses whispered to him, 'Hormones. They all react differently. She's a long way from home too. Missing her family, most like.'

He agreed, and sat down beside Iswara and took

her hand. He didn't have the necessary words. In fact, he knew there were none. Even Hallmark hadn't managed to come up with a card for such an emotional occasion, although they probably had one for Valentine's Day birthdays, he thought irrationally.

Visitors streamed in and her room was soon filled with flowers. Several of her former college mates with whom she kept in touch all sent presents and good wishes. So did one of the doctors from the practice where she had been working and would return to when her maternity leave was over – she brought a large hamper of baby goodies and a card signed by everyone. Irene appeared behind a fistful of pink helium balloons and wanted all the details of the labour and what she could expect. Beatrice sent a minute pair of denim dungarees with a red-striped top and matching socks. Rachel couldn't get enough of her new niece and Clem arrived with an enormous teddy bear.

'Has this beauty got a name yet?' he enquired.

'Not yet. We want to get used to her and see what suits her,' Iswara replied, glancing up at Damien, who nodded in agreement. She had scarcely taken her eyes off the Perspex crib beside her bed, willing the baby to wake so she could cradle and feed her again.

Damien collected Iswara and her daughter from the hospital and brought them back to his apartment. He had assembled the cot and prepared everything for the new arrival. Even though they had bought the nursery items in advance, Iswara hadn't allowed him take anything out of their boxes – just in case . . .

She could move back to the flat when she was ready, if she wanted to. Until then, she was welcome to stay with him. She took to motherhood with ease, but with a sadness she didn't talk about. He watched her looking at her little girl and he could see how tortured she was. He took a few days leave to be there in case she needed anything, even though he had shopped for a siege. He hated the thought of going back to work and leaving her alone.

Iswara was in constant contact with her sister, and that helped. He knew they missed each other but he couldn't fix that either.

After about a week, Iswara said, 'I've decided on a name for her and I hope you'll like it. I'm going to call her Anita. It means full of grace. What do you think?'

'I love it,' he said.

'It also begins and ends in an *a*, for AA.'

'Will you tell her that when she's old enough to understand?'

'I'm not sure. Probably. I will tell Rekna though. She's been pestering me to pick something out, but I knew once I found the right one, it would jump out at me and Anita did.

'It's a great name and it's used here as well, so you're straddling the continental divide with it.'

'That makes it even more special.'

He broached telling her parents about the baby, but she told him she wasn't ready.

He thought Iswara seemed happier since Anita had arrived, although sometimes when he came home he knew she had been crying.

His mother, strangely enough, provided a catalyst when she arrived from Spain unexpectedly, with a trunkful of tiny frilly dresses and a complete flamenco costume with matching black patent shoes for her 'to grow into'.

'I'm only here for a fleeting visit,' she announced as soon as she arrived, 'to meet my future daughter-in-law and my granddaughter.'

But once she had met Iswara he couldn't stop them talking, and within hours she told them she was going to change her flight and would stay another week – 'to be around'.

Iswara was thrilled; she knew she would miss Damien's mother when she went back. She couldn't get over the fact that Damien's mother didn't seem the slightest bit bothered about them having a child out of wedlock. In fact, it was never even hinted at by anyone.

One evening after three-week-old Anita had been fed, she fell asleep with Iswara and Damien gazing at her admiringly, and to the sound of the two of them talking. Way out at sea, a ferry's lights punctuated the inky blackness as it made its way from Dublin port. Overhead, a plane had put on its landing lights, making its approach to the airport.

'Is it too soon to discuss the wedding?' he asked, his arm behind her along the back of the sofa.

'I've been thinking a lot about that lately too.'

'I don't want to be insensitive . . .'

'Damien, darling, you're not. You're the most sensitive man I've ever met. Would I hurt you if I said I'd like to wait until AA's anniversary has passed?'

'Of course you wouldn't. I understand perfectly and I promise I'll not mention it until then.'

Several weeks later, an end-of-exam party got out of hand and Damien was called in the small hours to go to Store Street Garda Station, where three of his foreign students were under arrest for unsocial behaviour. There had been a fight with a group of youths and a knife had been pulled. At that stage, he wasn't sure who had had the weapon, but the upshot was they had all been refused bail and would go to court in the morning.

If they were found guilty, it could negate their visas and he knew he'd have a fight on his hands to extricate them from such a mess. He got a solicitor to represent them and was in court the next day.

The judge decided that they had been victims of a brutal and unprovoked racist attack and let them go, charging one of the attackers with carrying and threatening to use an offensive weapon.

The students' relief was marred when two of them realised their passports had been stolen. As usual, Damien rang their embassies to organise the documents for their replacement and got in touch with his contact in foreign affairs regarding their visa status. He was put through to Beatrice's phone.

'Well hello. I was just thinking about you last night. I mean, I just finished reading *A Passage to India*, our book club choice. Have you read it?'

'No, I saw the film though. Great. David Lean directed it. Look, Beatrice, I have a problem.'

He proceeded to explain his students' dilemma. She answered his query efficiently and to his satisfaction. She was totally unsettled when he hung up. She wondered again how long it would take to get him out of her system. Just hearing his voice was enough to remind her of how much she missed him.

'You must be exhausted,' Iswara said when he came home that night. 'You hardly got any sleep last night. Did things work out?'

He filled her in on his day. Even holding little Anita didn't quite lift him from under the cloud he felt hovering. Normally, her big green eyes and perfect velvety skin made him feel so protective and necessary. Tonight his mind was on other things. All the way home, he had thought of the things he could have said to Beatrice. It was always the same whenever they met or spoke. Since the phone call he had kept remembering bits of the film she'd mentioned and wanted to ring her and discuss it – talk about Judy Davis, Victor Banerjee or about anything.

Iswara sat down beside him and let out a deep sigh. 'Are you too tired to talk?'

He repositioned himself on the couch and said, 'No, not at all.'

'I've had lots of time to think over the past few weeks and I've decided I'm going to write to my father, a good old-fashioned pen-on-paper letter, and tell him about the baby and our engagement. I'm going to ask him how I should approach Mama, and the best way to go about it. What do you think?'

'I'm delighted. I think that's a good plan. After all, your father knows your mother better than anyone, so he'll know how to handle this. They might even approve and decide to come over for the wedding.'

'They might, but I wouldn't like to take bets on that just yet!'

'Send him a picture. He won't be able to resist. In fact, I'll take one of the two of you together to send him.'

He had hesitated for a nanosecond, but she had noticed, and it wasn't the first time he had done that.

She smiled at him, 'Damien you can call her "your daughter" or "our daughter". You've earned that right and one day she'll be as proud of you as I am.'

He leaned over and kissed her.

'Thank you for saying that. I didn't want you to think I was taking AA out of her life.'

'You'd never do that.'

'Let's have some friends around to wet the baby's head, as we say in this part of the world. We'll have a naming ceremony for her.'

'That's a lovely idea. Thank you.'

They picked a Sunday morning, the first in April, the anniversary of her wedding to AA. It dawned bright and windy. The sea was choppy but sparkled in the spring sunlight. Already, little yachts from the various clubs were braving the breakers and heading from the protection of the harbour out to the open sea.

Iswara had insisted on making many of the Indian delicacies they would serve later. Rachel arrived with a tray load of goodies, as did Irene. Anita was dressed in a beautifully embroidered garment sent by her Auntie Rekna just for the occasion. It was a soft celadon colour and almost matched the one her mother was wearing.

Damien was surprised when Beatrice arrived. He hadn't invited her and saw Iswara go to greet her warmly. Curious, Damien excused himself and crossed the room to say hello.

Iswara said, 'I forgot to tell you I met Beatrice at Irene's the last time I was there and I asked her to join us. I'm delighted she could come.'

Damien didn't know how to greet her and instead of a hug, which most of the guests received on arrival, he extended his hand awkwardly and shook hers. 'You're very welcome, Beatrice. Let me introduce you to our daughter.' He led her across the room where she was presiding over the occasion from her bouncy chair on top of a table. 'Meet Anita Rekna.'

'Well, isn't she a stunner? Look at those big eyes and those long lashes. She's totally gorgeous.'

Damien looked at her with pride. 'She is, isn't she?

'Makes me broody just looking at her.'

'Your time will come,' he said.

'I don't know about that,' she replied.

It felt peculiar to be back here in Damien's flat, yet to feel she was an outsider and not a part of it or his life any more. She recognised quite a few of the guests, Rachel and Clem, Daragh with an obviously pregnant Irene, who gave her a thumbs up and a grin, and some of his colleagues. She had really wanted to find an excuse not to turn up today, but she couldn't find a plausible one. She reasoned she would have to meet them socially over the years to come, so for her own sake and that of their mutual friends, the onus was on her to be nice and as normal as possible; after all, none of this was Iswara's fault, was it?

After Damien and Iswara had officially named their daughter, and the toasts and speeches were over, everyone crowded out onto the balcony where they lit paper sky lanterns and watched them float away, with wishes of love, luck and longevity for the three of them to enjoy together. Damien saw Iswara wipe a tear away with a corner of Anita's blanket and knew she was thinking of AA and their wedding just one year ago. He wanted so much to make her happy. He reached over and drew them closer to him.

Back inside, out of the April wind, Rachel asked Beatrice about her house.

'Well, I finally got my dining table delivered,' said Beatrice, 'after twenty weeks! It was supposed to take eight and I was beginning to wonder if I'd ever see it, or if the company would have gone into liquidation with my money before it was finished.'

Daragh joined them and said, 'Now that the table's arrived, we'll expect the dinner invite any day now.'

'Well, I'm right out of excuses now, so let's make a date.' She found herself inviting them over, with Damien and Iswara and Anita too, of course.

She whispered to Rachel, 'I'm not sure if you and Clem are *à deux* and if I should invite him too.'

Rachel laughed. 'You're sweet to ask. No, not yet! We're just great friends and we're still on the fundraising committee for the India project. I might even go over there myself next year. He's great company, so by all means ask him along.'

That was how Beatrice started socialising with her ex and his fiancée. In her rational moments, which were few where thoughts of him were concerned, she had to admit that Damien had, in fact, done nothing wrong. He hadn't promised to be faithful, nor had he demanded that of her. All he had done was fall in love with someone else. And made her pregnant.

She looked back at the baby again and thought, *She could have been mine.*

CHAPTER 51

Iswara checked the postbox every day waiting and willing a reply from her father, but it didn't come by post. Instead, he phoned her one morning.

'I have to say I am very disappointed in you.'

'Papa—'

'Iswara, please hear me out. I have a few things I need to say. Firstly, I thought we had a good relationship and I feel very let down that you felt you could not confide in me about you and Damien and about the baby. When I met that young man, he impressed me, but I would have preferred if he had come to me and talked to me, before taking you away from us.'

'Papa, I asked him not to. As I told you in my letter, I didn't know how to tell Mama. And I felt if I told you it would put you in an impossible position.'

'You've done that now anyway. This is the first time in thirty years that I have gone to bed keeping a secret from my wife. I'm not happy about that.'

'I'm sorry, Papa. I didn't know what to do.'

'Now that I've said that, how are you and the

baby? Are you happy and is she feeding and sleeping for you?'

'Papa, I love you. Only you could lecture me and love me at the same time. I miss you all so much and, yes, she's wonderful, beautiful and good.'

'So tell me, can I phone this Damien and talk to him man to man? Does he intend to marry you and is that what you want?'

'He's a good and kind man, the sort Mama would have chosen herself had he been Indian and Hindu, not Irish and Christian.'

'It might surprise you to know that your mama hinted that you might have had something going on between the two of you when he was here, and I said definitely not!'

'I didn't know that.'

'No, because the two of you were too busy being at loggerheads with each other all the time. It's very quiet without you.'

'So how do I tell her?' asked Iswara

'I haven't decided yet. Her blood pressure has been a bit high and they are fiddling around with her medicines to contain it, so I'm inclined to wait until that's sorted out first. See, you've got me caught up in your web now.'

'I never intended things to happen like this.'

She was considering telling him the whole story when he asked, 'Does Damien know about your inheritance? I'm sorry if it offends you that I ask this, but it does matter to me.'

'No, he hasn't a clue. It's never come up and even if he had, I don't think he'd want it. He's not like that. If you prefer, you can give it to the medical centre, as I already have what was left to me by Grandpapa. I don't need that and they do.'

'We'll see about that,' Raj muttered noncommittally.

'Papa, there is something else I have to tell you and please don't be mad. Rekna knows about the baby and about Damien.'

'When did you tell her?'

'When I found out. Please don't blame her. It's my fault. I asked her not to tell.'

'Quite the expert in deception, aren't you? And to think I never thought of you in that light before.'

Iswara could tell he was even more hurt by that revelation, but Anita spared her. She had woken up and had decided it was time for some more food.

'She sounds healthy, my little granddaughter. Look after her and give her a kiss from me.'

'I love you, Papa.'

'I know you do, and I love you. I'll get back on to you when I decide how to handle your mother.'

She shed a few tears after that, as her baby nuzzled her contentedly.

CHAPTER 52

The table was set, the flowers arranged, the starters chilling, the meat marinating, and the bubbly and wine were in the fridge. Beatrice still had cream to whip for the dessert, but she was very happy with the way everything looked. This was the first time she'd cooked a sit-down meal for ten. She'd included her cousin Simon and his wife. She'd also asked Tony, her colleague who was back in Dublin and living in her old flat.

The fires were lit in the dining and sitting rooms, and the dividing doors were open. When she'd changed, she lit the candles she had placed earlier all around the window shelves in the conservatory. She dimmed the lights a little and stood back to admire her handiwork.

She had bought wisely. She loved this house. It was developing its own personality, and reflected her taste. She wouldn't allow herself to think about what was missing, even though Damien seeing it with his partner and child was not how she had imagined his first visit was going to be. Just before the first ring on the door, she switched on the lights and the water feature in the back garden. The scene was set.

Everything went as though choreographed. The mix of guests was great, because adding the unknowns to the blend stopped it being a cosy group and presented plenty of opportunity for debate. Irene knew that Beatrice had gone out with Tony a few times since he'd bought her apartment, so when she announced that she and Daragh were hosting a table at a fundraiser she invited him to come along.

'Now, Irene,' Beatrice said to her in the kitchen, 'I recognise that matchmaking glint in your eye. Just to put the record straight, I've only gone out with the guy a handful of times and I am not remotely interested in him romantically, so you needn't order the confetti yet! Besides, he's abroad most of the time.'

Irene laughed. 'Touchy, aren't you?'

'I am not touchy. I just don't understand why everyone is so intent on getting me up the aisle. I'll only come to that charity do of yours if you promise I can sit where I want and that you won't make any of your pointed remarks. If you do, I'll get an instant migraine and go home.'

'OK. I promise!'

Back at the table, Irene targeted Damien and Iswara.

'I hope you'll be having your wedding in Dublin, so we can all come along.'

Iswara answered, 'We've not decided on that yet.'

'Indian weddings are so colourful and spectacular,' said Beatrice. 'Saris are so flattering and elegant. I believe there's quite an art in putting one on.'

'Well there's a lot of material in them, anything from three and a half to eight and a half metres, so you have to put it on right or it'll come asunder during the day.'

'I've seen weddings in Bollywood movies,' said Simon's wife, 'but I always wondered if they were exaggerated.'

'They're not,' laughed Iswara. 'We go a little over the top by western standards.'

'Will you stick to all the rituals and the ceremonies?' she asked.

'No. It will be a very pared-down affair. Back home, it's not unusual to have hundreds of guests and the celebrations go on for days.'

'It's the same in Malta.'

'Will your folks be mad at missing out?' Irene asked.

'If they had their way, I'd have to go through the whole thing again back in India. Why do you think I ran away to Ireland?' They all laughed at that.

'Well, why did you?' asked Tony, who didn't know she had studied in Dublin.

'To follow my man,' Iswara said simply.

Damien, Iswara and baby Anita were the first to leave. Beatrice saw them to the door and this time he kissed her on the cheek.

'Fabulous evening, fabulous food, fabulous

hostess. What more could you want? Thanks for inviting us.'

She avoided looking at him, focusing her attention on Iswara and the sleeping infant in her little seat.

'It was a wonderful night. Lovely company too. I hope you'll be very happy here in your new home,' said Iswara.

'We're off too,' said Irene. 'This mother-to-be needs her beauty sleep.'

The others left shortly afterwards. Beatrice kicked off her heels and flopped in an armchair, but not before pouring herself another glass of wine and settling down by the dying fire to brood.

CHAPTER 53

The weeks in the run-up to graduation time at the college always meant a lot of extra work for Damien, as well as others in the faculty. He was expected to attend lunches and dinners, some hosted by the drugs companies, although tighter regulations and codes of practice had seen that pattern decrease somewhat in the past few years. Nonetheless, he was expected to make his presence felt.

It was a bittersweet time too. Friendships that had been forged over five, six and seven academic years, longer in some cases, meant farewells as the qualified graduates took their skills to other parts of the country as well as to some of the dozens of nations they hailed from.

Damien had watched many of these students progress from those early encounters when they had first shown up, successful HPAT candidates with the required number of points and with attitudes ranging from brash and cocky to shy and absolutely terrified. Studying medicine had taken the corners off most of them. Many didn't stay the course, but he knew he had made a difference to some, persuading them to hang in there. Whenever they thanked him, he used to joke that he'd expect free consultations for life in return. He recognised that no matter what branch they chose to study, it was a gruelling road which required much dedication. So it was always with a certain degree of pride that when they had made it, he could admit that he had played a small supporting role.

It was great coming home to Iswara too, as she had seen the whole process from the student perspective and understood the challenges of his work.

After one particular dinner, which had included too many long-winded speeches, he hailed a taxi to go home. It had been a long day, and he was tired. He opened the apartment door very quietly so as not to waken either of the women in his life, and was surprised to find Iswara was still up.

'I thought you'd be in bed,' he said, walking over to give her a kiss. Anita was in her arms, sleeping happily.

'Has her ladyship been acting up?'

'No, she's been an angel, but I wanted to talk to you,' Iswara said.

'I know I've been neglecting you a bit these past few weeks, but I'll make it up to you.'

'That's not what I want to talk about.'

'Why do I get the feeling I'm not going to like what you're going to say?'

Iswara chose not to answer that and he recognised someone who was on a mission, someone who had rehearsed what needed to be said and wasn't going to be distracted.

'I've been doing a lot of thinking since I spoke to my father. Before that I was too fragile to face up to everything and you were there to shelter me.'

'And I'll always be here for you, you know that.'

'I do know that. But now that I've had time to put things in perspective, I've made some decisions. Some big decisions that will affect you too.' Anita chose that moment to wake. He waited, wondering what was coming next, while Iswara settled her again. Before she dozed off she deigned to throw a few glances in Damien's direction.

'I'll put her down in a few minutes,' Iswara said.

'She's going to be a heartbreaker. She only has to flutter those eyelashes and I'm hooked and she knows it too. I think she's getting more like AA.'

'So do I and, in a way, it's because of that that I've made some decisions. You know this wedding we are planning – well, I can't go through with it.'

He hadn't expected this.

'What? Has your father forbidden it?'

'No. Let me finish. I have to get this all out. The wedding won't happen, because I'm going home. But first I'm going to Bangalore to see AA's mother. She lost her son, and I began to realise that she didn't deserve to be deprived of her grand-daughter. So I wrote to her. I didn't tell you because I wasn't even sure that she'd reply. I felt she at least deserved to have the choice as to whether she wanted to meet us or not. I was wrong to try and manipulate other people's lives.'

'It's called survival and you did that for the best reasons.'

'Yes, I know, and you were . . . are . . . wonderful, the way you stepped in to protect my good name and to make my life bearable again. But I've played with too many people. I deceived too many of them and I'm not very proud of myself.'

'Don't start blaming yourself,' Damien said. 'You did what you thought was right, for yourself and for your family. For AA's family too.'

'I know, but now that I'm able to look at it from the outside, I realise it's a very different point of view. I panicked. Not only did I lie, I involved you all in my subterfuge. So I wrote and told Mrs Mahimkar the whole truth.'

'You . . .'

'I told her about marrying AA and that when I discovered I was pregnant I wanted to tell him about the baby in person. I told her that I watched his plane land and then crash, and that I was there when she and her daughters came to the airport. I explained that AA had mentioned he was going to tell her about us before we left India and that I had gone with you to her house to see if she already knew. I told her how I almost broke down when she told us that AA had said he had something important to tell her and I realised he hadn't had a chance to. I also told her how much I loved her son.'

'That took a lot of courage, Iswara, but I don't understand why our marriage has got to be called off,' he said. 'I love you and this little bundle. I also know I'm not AA and can never take his place in your heart.'

'I know that too, Damien, and I had prepared myself for rejection from her. If it had come I would have gone ahead and married you and I now see that would have been wrong too. I would have been continuing the pattern of deceit. I knew when I wrote to her that what I was saying was going to be a shock, but despite the obstacles that faced us both, I was proud to be married to her son and I am proud to have his child.'

'I wonder how she took that news. She'd need no more proof that he's AA's if she saw those green eyes of hers. That is, if she gives you a chance to introduce her.'

'She has, Damien. I sent a photo to her and she wants to meet us. Here, read her letter.'

Damien didn't know what to think as he took the paper from Iswara.

My dear
Thank you for writing to me. I cannot tell you how much this letter has meant.
Since we lost Abdul-Razzaq, my life has seemed so empty and pointless. He was too young to die.
I have constantly wondered about what it was he wanted to tell me. And now to

find out that he has a child, a beautiful, little girl, who does look so like him as a baby, I feel he has been given back to me, to us all in the family, in some small way.

Life has taught me many lessons, and if I had been given the choice between having my son marry someone who made him happy or marry someone of his own creed who didn't, I know which one I would choose in a heartbeat. I'd give anything to be able to make those choices again.

I am sorry you had so little time together and that he never met Anita.

Forgive me raising a delicate matter, but are you coping financially? If not, I'd like to help.

You will always be welcome to come and visit or stay with us.

I just wish you were not so far away and that I could have the chance to hold my son's child, and to get to know you.

Kindest regards and sincere thanks
Fatima Mahimkar

'That's some letter,' Damien said.

'I have to go and visit her. I owe her and AA that. You must understand, there is so much I need to say. I need to let her know that I'm not looking for financial support. I'd hate her to think that. I want to tell her that I kept the marriage and the baby a secret from my parents too, and how you stepped in to give us respectability and your name.'

'I thought I was offering more than that.'

'What you offered, Damien, can never be quantified – you know that.'

'Well, then, this letter shouldn't stop us getting married.'

'It does. I can't live with the lies any more. While I worked at the medical centre, choosing the rag pickers over my father's clinic and his private patients, everyone kept telling me how proud my grandfather would have been of me. He wouldn't. Because I'm not proud of myself. When my father said I had become "quite the expert in deception", it hurt. It hurt badly because it was the truth that I had been running away from. I just needed someone to tell me.'

'I think you're being very hard on yourself. Confessing won't change the attitudes you wanted to leave behind.'

'No, but having my family's love and support is more important and if Mama comes around as AA's mother did . . .'

'There are a lot of ifs in this story.'

She smiled. 'I know. It's like building a house of cards. If the bottom ones stay standing, I can proceed to the next level. If they collapse, I'll have to start again. All I know is that if I don't do these things now I'll regret them later on. If anything happened to either of my parents and I hadn't seen them for years or if they died without ever meeting Anita, I'd never forgive myself. She also deserves to grow up knowing her cousins and her Auntie Rekna and learn about her Indian heritage.'

'Where does that leave us?' he asked, agreeing on one level with her logic while rejecting it on another. 'You know AA said to me jokingly one time, "If you ever find yourself in an intercultural inter-creed complicated mess make sure you call on me", and now I wish I could.'

'What did you tell him?'

'Something about not needing those complexities to find myself in a mess. It seems I was right.'

'I don't mean to hurt you, but I have no choice. Can you be patient a little longer and let's see what happens?'

'It seems I don't have too much choice here either, doesn't it?' he said quietly, standing up. 'I'm off to bed.'

Things came to a head quicker than either of them had expected. A few days after their conversation, Damien was still no clearer about his feelings and was still getting used to the idea that Iswara might soon go back to India. She hadn't suggested that it would be a temporary thing, nor had he asked.

That evening Iswara got a call from her sister.

'Iswara, Mama's been taken to hospital. They think she's had a heart attack. I thought I should tell you.'

'What happened? Is she going to be all right?'

'Yes. She's in the cardiac unit and they have her

wired up to all sorts of machines. She was getting ready for bed when she got bad chest pains.'

'Should I come home?' Iswara asked.

'Wait until you talk to Papa before you make any decisions. He'll be able to tell you. I'll ring you if there's any change. Does it matter what time I call at?'

'No, Rekna, call anytime, just keep me updated.'

Although she knew she may not be needed, Iswara started to put some things together, just in case. She was folding clothes into neat piles when Damien got home. She told him what had happened.

'You can't arrive back with the baby if your mother is that ill,' he said. 'She won't need any other shocks like that. I can look after Anita. I've loads of leave left and she can go into the college crèche for a few hours if necessary. If it's anything long term, I can fly over with her.'

'It seems like your role in life is to be my rescuer, Damien.'

'Always happy to oblige, Ma'am.' He bowed, sensing they had just reached a truce of sorts. 'Now get some rest, you may have a long day ahead of you tomorrow. I'll check on flight availability, just in case.'

She wasn't quite asleep when her father called with news that in fact her mother hadn't had a heart attack, but a severe angina attack.

'I was going to come home,' she told him.

'There's no need, not because of this anyway.' She sensed his disapproval of her still.

'Papa, will you tell Mama about the baby as soon as she's up to it? Because I need to come home and tell you the full story.'

'There's more?'

'Yes, I'm afraid there is, but if you can forgive me, both of you, I'll be coming back to Mumbai again to live.'

'I'll be the one having a heart attack if you spring much more on me, Iswara. As your mother loves to say, "Where did we go wrong with that one?"'

She smiled. 'Please give her my love, won't you?'

Relieved that there was no crisis to necessitate a mad dash halfway around the world, Iswara waited to hear from her father again. But when the Indian prefixes announced a call, she was surprised to hear her mother's voice at the other end of the line.

'Mama, how are you? Should you be ringing me? Are you well enough?'

'You know your father, fussing over me as though I were made of porcelain. I'll be around for a long time yet.'

'I'm glad to hear that. I miss you so much.'

'And I miss you. Now what is this I hear about you? What sort of a mother do you think I am that I would ostracise you for becoming pregnant and moving thousands of miles away to hide it from me? I could have been there for your labour and to help you when the baby came along.'

Oh dear, Ganesh, help me, Iswara thought. *If that were all I had to tell her it would have been easy.*

'Well?' probed her mother.

'A typical protective Indian one, Mama!' said Iswara. 'That's what I thought and I also thought I'd be an embarrassment to you in front of your friends.'

Her mother laughed. 'You've always been that, Iswara, as well as being headstrong and self willed, you stubborn young woman. And if I were that typical do you think your father would have married me? So when am I going to meet my little granddaughter?'

'As soon as you're up to it.'

'I knew your papa had been hiding something from me; I even began to wonder if he had taken a lover, he was acting so secretively. Anyway, when he told me I wanted to fly over straight away, but he vetoed a long-haul flight for the moment. So you'll have to bring her here.'

Iswara couldn't believe what she was hearing. Her conservative socialite mother was going to openly defy convention. 'Will Damien come with you?' Daya asked. 'I want you to know I do like him.'

'So do I,' she laughed, 'but I'm not sure if he can get away right now.'

'You could get married over here.'

Stymied, Iswara played for time. 'We'll have to see. I'm sure there are all sorts of legalities and he'd probably have to be resident there for three months or something first.'

462

CHAPTER 54

Damien sat in his office staring blankly at his computer screen. He kept thinking about the bombshell Iswara had dropped a few days earlier. He had willingly and voluntarily asked her to be his wife, and since then if he had any doubts they usually centred on thoughts he chose to push aside. Thoughts relating to Beatrice. He had almost willingly and voluntarily asked her to be his wife too, and would certainly have done so if she had not rejected him so resolutely, twice. Yet when he had gone to the UAE everything had been good again between them, and from the tone of her emails he felt he was definitely in with a chance, even though she never actually said so. Who would have thought a plane crash in India would have had such an impact on his life? He wondered if he would have done things differently could he have, but he knew without any doubts that he would have made the same decisions again.

He had done the right thing by AA and Iswara. He had always admired her and when they had gone out on those few occasions when he'd been in Mumbai he'd really enjoyed her company, probably a little more than that if he were honest with himself.

That was when Beatrice and he had begun to correspond. He thought back to the first emails she had sent him and how he had learned so much about her from them, about her humour, her observations and her hopes and dreams. He knew he'd fallen a little in love before he came home and when they did start dating it had been wonderful. A natural progression from there had seemed inevitable. He remembered the first night she'd agreed to stay over and they made love in the light of the Christmas tree and she'd—

His desk phone ringing brought him back to reality. It was an excited Iswara, who normally never called him at work. 'Your mother? Is—'

'Mama knows. She knows and she wants me to come home. Straight away. I had to tell you. She rang me. Isn't that wonderful?'

'I suppose it is,' Damien replied. 'Yes, of course it is. How is she feeling?'

'She said Papa was just fussing. I can't believe it. I've so much to tell you and so much to do.'

He replaced the phone and had a 'what if?' moment. What if Beatrice knew the whole story? Would she come running back to rescue him? Well? *Right! Dream on, mate!* He pushed his chair back and grabbed his jacket. He'd go home to Iswara and be happy for her. He was the one who had willingly sacrificed all possibilities with

Beatrice. Yet on the train, it was Beatrice who kept coming in to his mind. Usually, he dealt with these thoughts by being more attentive to Iswara and her baby.

He had given a commitment to them, one he had intended to keep with every fibre of his body. He had been in control. Though now it seemed that his life was going to change, or be changed, and there was no course of action that he could take to stop it. The realisation that he really didn't mind as much as he should was beginning to unsettle him, bit by bit.

Things had been at an impasse over the past few days, so he made a real effort. Iswara had done nothing wrong. She had every right to be delighted. Things were panning out better than she had ever anticipated and no matter what challenges lay ahead of her she'd have her family and maybe even AA's behind her now.

'Damien, please don't think I've taken advantage of you.'

'I could never think that, Iswara, because I know you didn't.' He put his arm around her shoulder and drew her towards him. 'We could have had a good life together,' he said.

'We could, but it wouldn't have been right, or honest, and maybe we'd have ended up resenting each other.'

'I was willing to take that risk. I'll miss you, both of you, so you'll have to email me tons of photos and tell her about her Irish uncle.'

'She'll be sick listening to things about you. Maybe some day she'll end up back here, studying like me, following in the family tradition and finding a sympathetic dean like you.'

'That's jumping a little ahead, isn't it? First we have to face your parents together and tell them about AA.'

'*We?* You'd do that for me? Come back over, I mean. I was wondering how I'd handle that. They still think we're engaged. Mama even suggested getting married over there.'

'Then I'll just misbehave, leer at the servants, pick my teeth at the table and slurp my food. That way she'll think me so unsuitable that she'll be relieved when I leave you.' They laughed at the thought and he realised they hadn't done too much of that lately.

'Rekna told me Mama's already planning a nursery for Anita. She said she approved of her name too, so that's another plus.'

Emails and phone calls flew back and forth. She contacted the practice where she was expected when she finished on maternity leave. Damien made all the arrangements and booked their flights. They were heading to Bangalore first, where Mrs Mahimkar was expecting them. Then they were going home to her own family.

Iswara went into overdrive. 'When will you tell your friends? What about the flat? I'll have to clear that out before I go. Are you sure you don't mind shipping it all back for me? And I thought I'd offer

Irene the cot and all the baby bits and pieces, if she'd like them. Would she be insulted? Is it OK to tell her everything?'

'I'm quite OK with her knowing, but tell her to keep it to herself. Otherwise, you'll be pestered with an inquisition from everyone. I was going to tell Clem and Rachel tonight, and I'll deal with the rest when I get back.'

'Tell Rachel to come over tomorrow. I can't leave without seeing her.'

Beatrice and Irene were having a coffee break when Iswara rang.

'Tonight's fine,' said Irene speaking into her phone. 'Never mind short notice. My social diary's not exactly crammed since I swapped wine for orange juice and began retiring at ten o'clock. OK, I'll pop in on my way home from work. See you later and thanks.'

'You probably gathered that was Iswara.' Irene told Beatrice. 'She asked me to call over. Says she has something she wants to ask me. Probably to babysit and get a bit of practice!'

'It'll be weird not having you across the desk from me.'

'You won't even notice I'm not there after the first week.'

Damien met his sister first and they headed to a pub off Grafton Street. Clem joined them later, straight from surgery.'

'Clem,' Damien started, 'I've something to tell you.'

When Damien had finished, Clem reacted first. 'Jaysus, man, you sure know how to complicate things!'

Irene was speechless. She couldn't believe what she was hearing. And, yes, of course she'd be delighted with all the baby paraphernalia.

'You wouldn't believe that if you read it in a novel. You'd say it was too far-fetched.' Then she kept saying, 'You poor thing. You're lucky to have Anita.'

'I was lucky to have Damien. He's one in a million. He's been fantastic.'

They promised to keep in touch.

Their cases were packed and everything was ready for their early-morning flight. Iswara stood looking out across from Dún Laoghaire to Howth Head. 'I love that view and when I'm sweltering in the humidity back home I'll think of this.'

Damien joined her at the window. The sky was criss-crossed with the remains of the fading jet streams and one plane descended gracefully towards the airport. Whether it was that or something else that jogged her memory he didn't know, but he suspected she didn't need many prompts to remind her of how much she missed AA. As though reading his mind, she turned towards him and kissed him gently on the cheek.

'AA was my soul-mate in every sense. I love you, Damien and I know you love me, but we're not in love. I don't know if I am capable of ever being so again.'

'You know I would have tried to make you happy.'

'You have, and you would, but it's your turn now. Go after Beatrice.'

'What?'

'You heard me, Damien, I said go after Beatrice.'

'Who's been talking to you?'

'No one, but there's nothing wrong with either my vision or my instincts! And as a doctor I've learned to read body language. I've seen the way the two of you skirt around each other, trying so hard not to have to talk to each other, never looking each other in the eye, yet following each other's movements around a room when you think no one else is looking. The connection between you is like an electric current, fizzling and sparking.'

He didn't know what to say.

'You urged me to follow my dream, and even though it only lasted a blink of time, I wouldn't give up one precious second of what I had, the dreams, the hopes and the being together. Go for it, Damien. Knowing that you have will make me happy too.'

Iswara put her arms around him and hugged him so that he could hide from her the tears that glistened in his eyes. She didn't tell him of her last deception. After that she had resolved that she was never, ever, going to lie or deceive anyone again. Her last deception had been to meet Beatrice and tell her everything.

At Dublin Airport, Damien decided to call Beatrice, to ask her if she'd meet him when he got back from India. He wanted to ask her if she'd let him explain properly what had happened, why he'd got engaged to Iswara, that Anita wasn't his child and how his feelings had never changed for her. He rang her mobile. She recognised his number and cut the call. Dejectedly, he turned his phone to airplane mode and went back to join Iswara and her sleeping baby at the boarding gate.

CHAPTER 55

A few days later, Beatrice was at her desk, wondering what time it was in Mumbai. She was still shell shocked by Iswara's revelations. *Would Damien try to contact her again? Did he still have feelings for her? Should she have taken his call? Did he deserve to be listened to?* She wondered what would Dr Combover make of this situation.

Irene looked across at her and said, 'I've just had a mail from Damien.'

'Really?' Beatrice replied, trying to sound casual.

'Yes, really!' She said nothing more and Beatrice realised that there was something being left unsaid. She looked at her friend intently and said, 'You know!'

'I was told to keep quiet,' said Irene, 'and I've tried, but it's hard sitting across the desk from you with that long face, looking as though you've lost everyone in the world belonging to you.'

'Sometimes it feels like that. So, what does he have to say?'

'I'll forward it to you.'

Hi, All good here. Should I contact B yet
or is it too soon? D

'I'm off to make herbal tea for me, and a strong
coffee for you, because you look as though you
need one.'

Beatrice sat in her neon-bright office, with
phones ringing all around her, the hum of conversations and the clicking of computer keys. Yet she
was oblivious to any of it. Outside, the queue of
non-nationals was snaking along the path, full of
hopefuls wanting to be allowed to work in Ireland.
It was going to be a busy day.

She tapped back to Damien.

'*No!*' And then added, '*It's not too soon. Come
home.*'

A few seconds later, her message had travelled
halfway around the world and had been replied
to.

I'm on my way!
I'll explain everything when I see you.
I love you. I always have.
Damien xxx

I know and you better!
I love you too.
Beatrice xxx